# THE FORBIDDEN BOOK

A NOVEL

Joscelyn Godwin and Guido Mina di Sospiro

Published by:
Disinformation Books
An imprint of Red Wheel/Weiser, LLC
With offices at
665 Third Street, Suite 400
San Francisco, CA 94107
*www.redwheelweiser.com*

 Previously published as *The Forbidden Book* by Joscelyn Godiwn and Guida Mina di Sospiro. eISBN: 978-9-34708-83-5.

ISBN: 978-1-938875-01-4

Library of Congress Cataloging-in-Publication data available upon request

Cover design by Jim Warner
Cover image © Greg Stadnyk
Interior by StanInfo
Typeset in Adobe Caslon Pro

Printed in the United States of America
MAL

10 9 8 7 6 5 4 3 2 1

*To Stenie and Janet, our beloved wives.*
*–G.M.d.S. and J.G.*

# Contents

*The Forbidden Book* is based on facts. While the characters are imaginary and bear no relation to any living persons, the allusions to contemporary life are representative of early twenty-first century reality. Likewise, all mention of historical events and attributed quotations are authentic, translated when necessary by the authors. The Afterword at the end of the book explains some items that may be of interest to readers, preferably after they have finished the novel.

# ONE

"Look up, Leo. This is *it*," said *Professore* Salvi.

They were inside the immense Basilica of San Petronio, in the heart of Bologna. Leo did as he was told, and rested his eyes on the fresco; as he was taking in the disturbing scene depicted, the *professore* spouted:

"His guts were hanging out between his legs;
His heart gaped forth and that disgusting sack
Which turns to shit whate'er one gobbles down.
While I was all absorbed in seeing him,
He stared at me and with both hands he wrenched
His chest apart. 'Look how I rip myself!
Look at how mangled is Mohammed here!
In front of me Ali treks weeping on,
His face slashed from his forelock to his chin.

"And that's exactly what the fresco describes. Does this sound familiar?"

Leo was embarrassed. His Italian colleague had recited the lines theatrically before a large congregation right before the beginning of Mass.

"Well?" Salvi insisted.

"Of course it's familiar; it's Dante," Leo heard himself answer, in a hushed tone, "a scene from the *Inferno*."

"A-ha!" commented Salvi, "and what about it?"

"I can't believe this guy!" thought Leo as he replied, "It's the 28th Canto. Dante and Virgil are in the ninth chasm of the eighth circle in hell; it's the one of the Sowers of Discord, and the punishment there is to be mutilated. Mohammed shows his guts to the poets while on the left stands his son-in-law, Ali, his head split open."

"Precisely," said Salvi, smirking, "both were sowers of scandal and schism, and as such Dante punished them, and they're burning in hell."

"Shush!" said an elderly woman from a pew nearby, scowling at them.

"That's our cue," said Salvi, still loudly, "let's get out of here."

As they began to walk toward the exit, Leo said, in a whisper, "If you don't mind, I was planning to attend Mass."

“Really? What for?”

Leo didn’t reply.

After an awkward pause, Salvi resumed, “Well, suit yourself. But before it starts, let’s go have a quick espresso.”

Walking briskly, they crossed the *piazza maggiore*, and entered a busy café by the Fountain of Neptune.

“Two espressos,” barked Salvi, “and quickly; my colleague here has an appointment with God!”

The barista only imperceptibly raised his eyebrows and then busied himself behind the coffee machine. He dealt out saucers and spoons, adding their clatter to the babel of voices and the gory lines of Dante still echoing in Leo’s mind.

As Leo lifted his cup, a tremendous blast shook the café. The customers froze, met each other’s eyes and saw fear.

After a few very long seconds, the two professors rushed out to the square, where smoke, dust, flying trash, and an acrid smell assailed them. Wailing voices came from the direction of the Basilica. Leo groped forward through the swirling air.

“Stop,” cried Salvi, grabbing at his American colleague, “don’t go there!” Leo shook himself free of the restraining hand. He reached the steps of the Basilica, but there was no portal: a cavern-like entrance gaped. The screams for help were clearer, and louder.

“You can’t do anything for them! Let’s go!”

But Leo went on. He slowly climbed the steps and peered into the church. Beams of sunlight burst through a newly rendered hole in the roof and made a bright column of the settling dust. All around were bodies, half smothered in fallen stone. Some were twitching feebly, like squashed insects. Others were struggling to their feet with groans, screams of pain, choking coughs. In the ray of sunlight, the same elderly woman knelt as in supplication, waving her arms. There were no hands on them, and beside her was a man with no head.

Leo was in a daze, his head spinning, his heart racing, his mind unwilling to grasp the enormity of what had happened. He must *do* something, but what?

He searched his pockets frantically for his rented cell phone and automatically punched 911. No reply. What in hell was the emergency number here?

To his left, only a few feet away, he saw an old man sprawled on the floor, blood gushing from his mouth. He knelt by him, holding his head with his hand. The man briefly looked at his rescuer, then his eyes closed. As Leo tried to revive him, a huge section of the roof caved in with a deafening crash, crushing yet more people beneath. Two fires were raging at the far end of the church.

Seconds passed, or minutes, Leo didn't know, and finally police sirens began to wail and the first ambulances swerved into the piazza. The louder screeching of fire engines reached his ears. He remained on his knees, trying to comfort the dying man.

# TWO

Two days later, the train to Verona was almost a phantom train, with hardly any passengers. After the massacre at the Basilica, Italians were staying home. Leo himself was haunted by what he had seen. If he had gone straight to Mass, instead of to the café with Professor Salvi, he might have been . . .

When he got off the train, the few people he saw had a vacant stare in their eyes. He made for the exit, blinking in the late spring sunshine. A man in a dark suit approached him. "*Professore* Kavenaugh? *Professore*?" he said in a heavy accent. This must be the Romanian butler Orsina had said would collect him. The man bowed: "Welcome to Verona; follow me, please."

The butler hefted Leo's bags and led him to a large car that looked entirely different from anything in America—a Lancia. Doubling as chauffeur, he ushered Leo into the back seat, then took the wheel. Soon they were out of the suburbs and in the countryside, with vistas over vineyards to right and left. After thirty minutes of raising clouds of dust as it raced along worryingly narrow roads, the car swept onto a graveled drive between high gateposts.

This was no mere villa, thought Leo as they ground to a halt before a columned portico, but a minor palace. Painted in the faded yellow color of polenta, grand and genteel, it gave a feeling of ease. Once he met with Orsina and solved her problem, he was definitely going to enjoy his stay in such an idyllic place.

A bag in each hand, the butler led the way through airy frescoed halls, up a marble stairway, down a broad corridor, into a high-ceilinged corner bedroom. The view from the three large windows: a romantic garden to the left, with mature trees inviting walks beneath them; in front, rolling hills and vineyards, and the gravel road they had traveled on snaking through them. No other buildings in sight.

But where was Orsina? The butler had disappeared, so Leo ambled downstairs looking for someone, while taking in the frescoes of gods, giants, and heroes, the worn Persian rugs, the antique walnut furniture, and great Chinese vases filled with flowers.

Turning a corner, he almost bumped into a white-haired housekeeper who smelled, oddly, of vinegar.

"*Buongiorno*," he said, and inquired about Orsina.

"*La g'hè no la Baronessina*," she answered in what was presumably the local dialect. So, he was learning, Orsina was addressed as "Baroness." More urgently, she was not there. Where was she? he asked. When was she expected? Marianna, the aged housekeeper, mumbled a few more sentences in her dialect, but Leo couldn't understand them. Born Leonard Kavenaugh, of an Irish-American father and an Italian mother, he had learned Italian from the cradle, but never any dialect. He nodded intelligently to Marianna and walked out into the garden. The Romanian butler found him there. "Would the *Professore* like some refreshments?" Leo nodded and took the glass. "The Baron expects you before dinner for an aperitif at half past seven. Formal attire is requested."

Leo gave in to the charm of a delicious pre-summer breeze in the shade of a walnut tree and, sitting on a teak bench, sipped his iced tea with peaches. The bombing in Bologna seemed light years away, and his mind turned to Orsina. Hired by Leo himself, she had been at Georgetown University a few years before, teaching Italian language and working on her own thesis. He had heard nothing from her since she left Washington. Then out of the blue had come a letter inviting him to spend some time with her in one of the family's ancestral homes. Her uncle, she wrote, had given her an ancient book, supposedly of great importance but exceedingly hard to interpret. Would he help her to study and understand it?

Leo had accepted the invitation on impulse, and added a few days of research in Rome and Bologna. During the train journey he had tried to collect his memories of Orsina while wondering at his own decision. The trip had begun with catastrophe—or salvation. What else was he letting himself in for?

He went up to his room, to change and get ready to meet her uncle. The butler had unpacked his suitcase and left out what was evidently judged his best outfit. Leo had a distinct feeling of stepping back in time: a feeling both warm and disorienting, as if he had arrived in a novel set in Edwardian England.

When he came down, he found all the windows of the salone open to the cooling breeze. Baron Emanuele Riviera della Motta was sitting in an armchair, dressed in a mohair-and-silk suit of midnight blue that made Leo's readymade wool blazer look inadequate, and too warm for the season. The Baron stood up. He was not tall but compact, and his sixty or so years had added no superfluous flesh to his frame. His white hair was swept back from a high, bronzed forehead. But what struck one most was the nose: a perfect Roman beak, crooked as an eagle's.

"Professor Kavenaugh, I presume?" he asked. "How do you do?" and shook hands both firmly and formally. "Will you have a drink? I'm having bitter Campari. Would that suit?"

Leo had tasted it once and carefully avoided it since, yet he found himself saying "Perfectly, thank you." When he sipped, it reminded him all over again of cough syrup on the rocks.

"My niece spoke highly of you," the Baron said, staring at him appraisingly. For a moment, Leo felt as if he might add, "I wonder why?"

As the Baron occupied himself with his drink, Leo tried to make small talk. He mentioned the antique spinet in the corner, but the Baron cut him short, dismissing it with an English pun as "an instrument for spinsters."

"And I have to sit through dinner with just him . . . " Leo said to himself.

"You've heard the news, I take it?" asked the Baron.

"The bombing in Bologna? I was in the Basilica minutes before the blast."

"Really? Then you should be happy you're alive! Dumitru, give the professor another Campari."

"Oh no," Leo thought as he smiled gratefully at the butler.

"A great tragedy," added the Baron, "they're now counting corpses. A difficult task, with some blown to smithereens, others charred beyond recognition, and some still under the rubble. The terrorists timed the explosion well, right during the High Mass of Corpus Christi Day. You yourself have seen the huge congregation. All told, I wouldn't be surprised if they counted hundreds and hundreds of dead."

"My God, it's so horrible!" exclaimed Leo. "But why? Who did it? Are there any suspects?"

"Who did it?" The Baron looked away from him, and concentrated on the frescoes on the ceiling. "You've heard of Giovanni da Modena, I take it?"

He had, from an Italian colleague of his, just two days before.

"That means you hadn't heard of him before that? And you are the chair of the Italian Department at Georgetown University?"

Leo opted for another sip of Campari.

"I suppose he is not one of your major painters," the Baron continued with exquisite condescendence, "but his frescoes in the Bolognini Chapel were brilliant. You see, Giovanni da Modena surpassed himself in the fresco of Mohammed and his son-in-law in hell. So, some Muslim guests of our country decided that this was an intolerable affront, and that the fresco was to be covered. Or, better yet, removed. Imagine that," he said, raising his voice: "it's as if you came to my home and told me that I must either cover or remove one of my frescoes!" The Baron was visibly angry. He continued, composing himself: "Some time ago, two Moroccans were overheard planning to bomb the fresco in the Basilica; they were arrested, then released, of course, though they had ties with Al Qaeda. Now it seems that Muslim terrorists have not only removed the fresco, but the entire Basilica with it, and the people inside it."

"Is this conjecture on your part?" Leo finally asked.

"Yes, and no. To me it's as obvious as a fact. Of course, it'll take the *carabinieri* some time to reach this conclusion, and even more to prove it. Unless, of course, Al Qaeda or whatever group of Islamic terrorists speaks up and claims responsibility for the bombing. One way or the other, the ecumenical western world will soon have to come to grips with this reality."

"But how can you be so sure they did it?" asked Leo, still in disbelief.

"Let's say that I have a hunch, and that B inevitably follows from A. Anyway, I expect that it's just a matter of time before everybody knows from official sources what I suspect."

"Uncle," said a voice entering the hall then, "don't tell me you're haranguing our guest!"

The same delicious breeze that Leo had enjoyed earlier in the garden had wafted her perfume in before her voice. Still troubled by the Baron's assumptions, he got up to greet her.

"Professor, meet my niece, Donna Angela."

"It's a pleasure to meet you," said Leo as he leaned forward to kiss, or rather graze her hand with his lips. It was Orsina herself who had taught him, years before, this old-fashioned greeting, and the great hall itself seemed to invite it.

"The pleasure's mine," Angela said, looking as if she meant it. "Sister never mentioned you were so cute!"

The word was more appropriate to Angela herself, with her shock of blond hair and risqué minidress. "You are Orsina's sister? Why, she never mentioned *you*, and that's a far graver omission." Angela seemed flattered by his remark, and the Baron surprised. The American could be gallant?

"Shall we go to dinner?" Angela asked. "I had a table set outdoors, under the cherry tree."

"Is Orsina not coming?"

"Not tonight, Professor. But I hope I don't disappoint?"

"Of course not, but—"

"I'll tell you all about her at dinner, I promise," Angela cut him short.

Candles flickered in the evening breeze. Dumitru had been trained well in the dying art of waiting at table, and his wife Afina, Angela explained, had become an excellent cook.

"I didn't doubt it," said Leo. Suddenly he was thriving on polite remarks. But no, there was something else. The way Angela looked at him.

Leo had inherited his father's blue eyes and tall stature; his mother's black hair and fine facial features. The amalgam had been a success, and young women had taken notice. Now in his early forties, he had kept slim, and was reasonably groomed, if not as fastidiously as the Baron.

"So, Orsina really never told you she had a sister?" Angela asked, turning so that her dress revealed just enough of a perfectly sculptured breast.

"No, she didn't. Perhaps you were very young?" Leo was enjoying his present company, but Angela had promised that she would tell him about Orsina, and he was impatient to know. Eventually, he asked.

The Baron himself replied: "They phoned an hour before you arrived Her husband thought that, given the circumstances, they should delay their coming to Italy for a few days. I thought you knew. Anyway, I could bet that there won't be any more bombings for a while, so they will reach us soon."

"Her husband?" wondered Leo in his mind.

"Why, Leo," said Angela, leaning into him, her flaxen hair fluffy in the breeze, caressing his face, "do you miss her?"

"Well, I haven't seen her in years, but I do have fond memories of her when she was at Georgetown."

“So, you do miss her,” she insisted.

“Yes, of course.” After the unspeakable tragedy he had lived through, Angela had managed to make him blush. How did she do it?

Dinner continued without too many more awkward moments.

When he got back to his bedroom, he found a “sweet dreams” message on his pillow, a chocolate, and some rose petals. It was signed by Angela. He smiled at her flirtatiousness and began his evening prayers.

# THREE

The next morning, Orsina called early to speak to Leo. She would be arriving that evening. "The Bologna attack is on everyone's lips, even here in London, but Alitalia seems to be flying on schedule, if that's not an oxymoron."

"I can't wait to see you."

"Me too." She paused and then added, "my . . . husband doesn't think we have anything to fear in the countryside, so we're still coming. See you soon."

At breakfast, Leo made the conscious decision of not looking at the newspapers. There was a selection of them on the table, from the national *Il Corriere della Sera* and *La Repubblica* to the local *L'Arena*; still, he knew he couldn't stomach the gruesome photos. As he was saying a silent prayer for the victims, Angela swept into the breakfast room, dressed to kill in tennis shorts and high-platform espadrilles. She ate a hearty breakfast as she leafed through the papers and said, "This is too bad." Setting them aside, she went on cheerfully: "I'm going villa-hopping. You can come along if you like." Seeing his puzzled expression, she explained: "There's a whole bunch of us that have known each other for years. As soon as school's over they all come back to their villas for the summer."

"I've caught a glimpse of a library crammed with ancient books, and I think that'll be more up my street," Leo said, adding, "do you think your uncle will mind if I browse through the collection?"

"Not at all," said Angela, with an ambiguous expression that made it impossible to understand whether she was disappointed or relieved, "you're free to roam. By the way, Uncle will be working all day in his studio. We'll all meet for dinner."

Leo made straight for the library. The room was flooded with light that came from the four east windows, striking across the inlaid patterns of the floor and reflecting off the tall, glass-fronted book presses. In the center of the room was a marble table holding a vase of white lilies, and four antique, backbreaking chairs. Leo's first impression was of a typical villa library of its period. There were the Latin and Greek classics, the Italian poets, histories ancient and modern, a large topographical section concerning the Veneto region, and a mishmash of theological, medical, and legal tomes bound in vellum or old calf.

He explored it until Dumitru announced that a light lunch had been prepared for him. Leo thanked him, adding how thoughtful it was of his wife. As he exited the library, in came, almost on cue, a chambermaid wielding a feather-duster. "Excuse me, Professor," she said, "if you're leaving, I'll dust the books; I dust them every day, Baron's orders."

It was a matter-of-fact piece of information, yet her delivery had been coquettish. He put it down to her being young and conscious of her good looks. "I didn't realize I was holding you back," said Leo. Samanta, the maid, beamed at him and went about her business.

The Baron, too, was going about his business. He was painting a picture. His studio was a converted hunting lodge some two kilometers south of the villa, on the other side of a knoll. It contained a large, square room with a tall ceiling, lit by a clerestory and, opening off it, several cubicles. One was a bathroom, another held a double bed, and the others served as miniature kitchen and laundry. The walls were painted in Renaissance style with fantastic plants, animals, satyrs, cherubs, weapons, and musical instruments. But Emanuele did not paint grotesques like these. He painted from life, in oils, on large canvases. At this moment, his model was Angela.

She reclined on a small sofa with one high end. Her right arm was raised, the hand beneath her head. One leg, too, was crooked, with its foot on the sofa, while the other dangled. Her mop of golden hair hung loose, and her face was turned to the ceiling in an uncomfortable pose of ecstatic abandon. Apart from the espadrilles, she was naked.

Emanuele had no pretensions as a painter. He never showed or gave away his canvases, and certainly never thought of selling them. In fact, he scissored and burned them as soon as they were finished.

He had been working on this painting for half a year now, putting in an hour most days. He worked very slowly, and when he lacked the model, he worked more slowly still, for it took extra effort to visualize the image. He used painting to attain a certain state of mind that required concentrated attention; and he found it easier to achieve when contemplating such a sight as he now had before him. Like the turning of a prayer wheel, he moved in a regular cycle: eyes to the model, eyes to the palette, brush to the paint, brush to the canvas, and so on.

Neither of them said a word, though Angela took regular breaks to stretch her limbs and take a sip of water. The process seemed to put her, too, into a strange state of mind, for at the end of the hour she rose like a sleepwalker and padded to one of the cubicles, the one with the bed. Emanuele half undressed himself in the bathroom, then joined her.

Nobody knew that he made love to her, nor could she have explained to anyone why she allowed him to. Assuming that it was love. There was something clinical about it, and perhaps ritualistic. It certainly was all very deliberate. This uncle was violating all the taboos. Angela was no rebel against society's norms. She had boyfriends, and sometimes let them make love to her. But there was a quality to Emanuele's lovemaking, always preceded by a session of painting, that was completely different from theirs.

Afterwards she felt as though she had only just entered the studio, as though it had all been a dream that took two seconds of waking time. She was not even certain that it had happened.

After lunch, Leo returned to the library. The sun had moved away, and no longer blinded him to the three narrow bookshelves in between the windows. On moving across to these, he was surprised to find them devoted entirely to works of alchemy and the so-called "occult sciences." These books, too, had been in the family for two centuries and more. Nearly every volume carried the same Della Riviera bookplate, and was annotated in the same spidery eighteenth-century hand.

Eventually Leo felt that he had been cooped up too long, and decided to take a stroll through the garden. The mature trees all around made him regret his botanical ignorance: each seemed to be of a different species, and most of them unfamiliar to him. All were massive, undoubtedly centuries-old, yet he marveled at their crowns being as green, thick and luxuriant as those of younger trees that still have much to grow. Perhaps a combination of fertile soil and favorable climate? He could only guess.

There was no one beneath the trees, but a disconcerting presence in the form of many statues. Half hidden by the foliage and overgrown by lichens, they seemed to leer at him—or worse, as in the case of a Priapus who thrust his oversize phallus at him as he rounded a corner.

Many of the statues were of semi-human satyrs, fauns, and Pans. In a clearing, however, some more classical figures were grouped around an altar holding a large stone vase. They were deeply eroded, but evidently represented the seven planets: Mars, easily recognizable with his helmet and the stub of a broken sword; Saturn, with what might once have been a scythe; Jupiter with a wingless eagle; a still shapely Venus, and so on. Leo could just make out the inscriptions on their plinths. *Pater eius est sol, mater luna*, he read: "Its father is the sun, its mother the moon." They seemed to date from the early 18th century, the rococo period, and Leo wondered whether the ancestor who had annotated the alchemical books was responsible for them.

The path twisted and turned, occasionally breaking out of cover to offer a glimpse of distant hills, until Leo feared he had gone too far. Then to his surprise it led him back to a terrace on the opposite side of the villa. Before getting ready for dinner, Leo lingered here, looking forward to enjoying the twilight. What had happened just days before in Bologna was appalling; he had no words to describe it. But for all its uncanniness, this place, he realized, worked as a balm: how easy it was to leave behind all worries and, above all, the real world.

At dinner, he was annoyed to find that Angela had not returned. He would have to make conversation with Emanuele again. The library would be a good topic, though, and as soon as the first course arrived, Leo said: "I gather from Orsina that you know a lot about this mysterious book she's been given," he ventured. Was this too much, too soon? he wondered as Emanuele knitted his eyebrows.

"Did she mention it to you? I'm surprised," he replied coldly. "It is something particular to our family."

"Really? That reminds me of the Borgias, and the secret poisons they passed on from generation to generation, or something of the sort."

The Baron stiffened. This was evidently the wrong thing to have said. Leo tried to patch things up: "Orsina said that she couldn't make head or tail of it, but I assure you that I haven't set eyes on the thing myself."

"She could very well have asked me," came the response. Another uncomfortable silence amplified the very faint noise of their forks. Emanuele sipped some wine, and something seemed to thaw in him. He looked Leo straight in the eye, and said with a smile, "Well, since you brought it up, I can tell you that the book is in the public domain. A good friend of our family brought it back into print in the Thirties, and you can look for a modern edition at any good bookshop—of which there are as many as three in our country, no, four."

The Baron kept a straight face, so Leo replied, as seriously as he could: "I'll make a note of that."

Emanuele ignored his reply and continued. "It is a centuries-old tradition that the eldest son of the family receives a copy of this ancestral work on the occasion of his marriage. After about 1900, it was given to the daughters, too—a mistake, in my opinion, but now a tradition. It is presented on the wedding eve in a peculiar ceremony. But as a scholar, you would be more interested in the unexpurgated version, which did not need to obtain the Imprimatur of the Church." He stopped abruptly. Changing tone, he resumed: "Unfortunately there is no chance of reading this edition. Simply because one is not a member, that's all. You must forgive these aristocratic restrictions. They must seem incomprehensible to an American."

It sounded to Leo like a big fuss about some book that was probably just an Italian *Kama Sutra*. But there must be more to it, since Emanuele, still looking indignant, rose from the table and excused himself.

As Leo himself left the dining room, he turned to go back to the library. Emanuele's words had piqued him, and he felt sure that this family fetish was somewhere there. But he was interrupted by a scurry of servants, and before he had left the hall, Orsina entered.

Was this Orsina? The beauty was all there, in its full impact. Her long, wavy hair of the red hue Titian favored in his paintings, and her sunny green eyes. Her deportment, her elegance too. But there was something more stately about her now. Would the Orsina of Washington have found this stateliness a bit pompous? wondered Leo, overcome with feelings as he looked at her. Or was it dignity? He thought he caught a strained expression in her face, but attributed it to their long day on the move. She smiled broadly, and kissed him on both cheeks.

Her husband came forward, his hand outstretched. "Nigel MacPherson," he said in confident tones.

"Leo Kavenaugh," said Leo, disengaging from the other's hand. "I'm very pleased to meet you."

"Likewise," said Nigel. He was tall, well-built, and heavily jowled; twenty years ago he must have been handsome. Orsina was talking to Dumitru. She turned to the men, speaking English: "Since it's late, and I for one have no appetite, shall we just have a drink, perhaps in the library?" At that moment Emanuele materialized and greeted the MacPhersons with what looked like a genuine show of affection. For Nigel, too, thought Leo in surprise, as he followed the family cortège. Emanuele produced a decanter and four glasses from a hidden cupboard.

"This is rum from Guatemala, thirty years old. I presume you've never tried it." Leo shook his head. "Oh, I have, and I love that stuff," said Nigel. "I must say, Orsina, I'm so glad to be here. The last couple of days have been sheer hell."

"Were you stuck at airports?" enquired Leo.

"Stuck like glue, for hours and hours, then marched out of the bloody plane and marched back on again. Courtesy of the terrorists, and of Alitalia. I could have driven here in half the time if we'd known. From now on, we're using private jets only, didn't I say, Orsina?"

"You did, dear," she replied, "but it would have been even worse in Bologna."

"It would have," said Nigel, accepting a second glass from Emanuele, who then said goodnight and left.

Nigel broke the uncomfortable silence. "Orsina tells me you're a brilliant professor," he said. "I don't know about literature, but you certainly taught her English."

"She spoke excellent English before I even met her," said Leo, "and I didn't actually teach her anything. I just hired her and let her loose."

"Let me loose?" said Orsina, opening her eyes in mock amazement. "I was totally uptight from beginning to end, afraid that I'd commit some literary solipsism!"

"So-le-cism," said Nigel.

"Yes, dear, that was a joke."

"Sorry to be pedantic. It must be the effect of all these *books*!" Nigel rose from his uncomfortable chair and walked over to the shelves. "I suppose this is a goldmine for you scholars, but Italy for me is sun, cypresses, and glorious wine. Also motor cars. Do you know cars?"

"I've driven in the past, but in Washington I get along without one. Do you have an Italian car?" said Leo, half-heartedly trying to bridge the gulf between their worlds. Nigel drew a long breath, but before he could reply, Orsina broke in.

"Let's save this till tomorrow. There'll be plenty of time then, and we're exhausted."

"Quite right, dear." Nigel held out his hands, inviting Orsina to rise from her chair, put an arm around her shoulder, and staggered toward the door.

Orsina turned to Leo as they left. "Goodnight. Sleep well."

Perhaps he was just imagining it, but he had the feeling that she wanted to linger in the library with him. Not wishing to leave the light on, he looked for the switch, which was a tricky search, as it was not by the entrance door. Finally, he found it and, not a foot away, lying in full view on a small table, the "forbidden book": *The Magical World of the Heroes*. Leo was about to grab it when he started at Orsina's voice:

"Leo? Are you still there? I don't know if Samanta or anybody asked you yesterday, but would you like some mineral water for the night, in your room? Fizzy or plain?"

Leo said she didn't have to bother, but she insisted. "Follow me to the kitchen; there should be some in the fridge."

A few minutes later Leo found himself alone in his room, with a bottle of mineral water. The presence of the forbidden book had taken his mind off even Orsina. She couldn't have known how untimely her thoughtfulness had been. But now he was in a bind. After what Emanuele had said, he could hardly read that book, yet that was the reason Orsina had invited him in the first place. He was tempted to go downstairs immediately and take a good long look at it. Emanuele would never know.

By the time he had put on his pajamas, the temptation was unbearable. He would go back to the library. But not sneakily: he would turn on the lights as he went, and leave them on too. If someone surprised him, he had a perfect excuse: he couldn't sleep, so he was reading.

He made straight for the forbidden fruit. The green morocco binding was stiff, like a new book. *Il mondo magico de gli heroi*, he read on the title page, *Stampato a Venezia a spese della famiglia nobile Della Riviera, MDCCLVII.* Printed in Venice in 1757 for the noble Riviera family—very beautifully printed, too—and scarcely opened, it seemed, till today. In fact, he made another discovery: the folded sheets were still uncut. Who would have thought it? This way, the book would be unreadable until someone had separated them with a paper knife.

Now that he had the rarity in his hands, he could not open it without making it known that he had read it, or at any rate that *someone* had read it. There was nothing else for it: he replaced it on the table exactly where it had been and went upstairs to his room, pacing along the corridors as he turned off the lights. As far as he could tell, no one had seen him.

# FOUR

"What's wrong, Uncle?" It was their first breakfast together in a long time, yet the Baron hardly spoke. Orsina donned her best smile, the one that rarely failed her. Her uncle still said nothing and looked the other way.

"Is it something I've done?" she insisted.

"Yes." The Baron had finally broken the silence. "I'm surprised you wouldn't realize it."

"What is it? I still don't know what I've—"

"Enough, don't add insult to injury. But listen very carefully. You should never have mentioned the family edition of the book to anyone, least of all to that hapless American. And asking him to help you do the work you should be doing on your own, that is blasphemy. Just don't show it to him."

"But Uncle, I'm no expert in archaic Italian and Latin, and he is."

"Nonsense: do your homework yourself, and you will reap the fruits. No one is to see our edition, absolutely no one. Is that clear? You're warned now. That is enough. Learn from your mistake, and don't make it again." Anger and resentment seemed to fade instantly as he added, in a considerate tone: "Drink your tea, dear. It's your favorite blend, grandmother's."

Lunch was a more communal affair, this time indoors, in the frescoed dining room Leo had admired in his walks through the villa. Angela was finally in attendance, her bubbly self as usual. Nigel and Orsina walked in, holding hands. She looked quite different from the lively young woman who had smitten Leo ever since that interview in Rome. She was still beautiful but seemed strained, worried.

"Hello, all," said Nigel as they sat at the table. "Sorry to keep you waiting but it couldn't be helped," glancing over to Orsina. She turned a deep shade of red, and was thankful that his cell phone interrupted what she feared would be an embarrassing conversation about her. "I really must take this call," he said, and moved to the adjoining room.

It was a cold lunch, so the Baron ordered Dumitru to start serving, and commented: "Nigel should not bring his phone to the table."

"Oh, Uncle, you know how Nigel is about making billions, who can blame him?" Angela said before Orsina was able to apologize for him.

"I wish you wouldn't say that, Angela; we've been brought up differently and know better than to discuss money at table."

Nigel returned, pocketing his phone. "I *am* so sorry, Baron. Terribly rude of me." He still addressed Emanuele by his title, which seemed to please him, since the Baron held up his hand in a gesture of forgiveness. He turned to Leo.

"Professor," he said, "we're yet to hear your voice. Are you all right?" Leo blushed slightly, and replied, "I'm fine, thank you, and enjoying the company."

The Baron insisted: "Don't tell me you are still thinking about the terrorist attack?"

"I am. I just can't get it off my mind."

"I don't blame you, but don't give in to survivor's guilt; that'd be criminal. This is an oasis, and none of that should concern you here."

"Yes, it's a privilege to be here, and I really appreciate your hospitality."

"Don't mention it. Dumitru, pour some more Custoza for the professor." Angela raised her glass. "Let's toast to life."

"To Life!" they all echoed.

After congratulating the Baron on his choice of the sparkling wine, Nigel announced his plans for the day. "That last phone call was from Maranello. It's all set. Gianni, one of the mechanics, will pick me up in fifteen minutes." They would drive down to Maranello, see the Ferrari Gallery, and then test-drive a few cars. "I've been courting a Ferrari from 1967, and might just add it to my collection."

"May I come with you? Please?" asked Angela, with an irresistible smile.

"What do you think, Orsina? Would you mind?" asked Nigel.

"No, I don't mind," she said. "Go and have fun. Just try to drive safely, promise me."

Angela gave her sister a hug. "Thank you, Orsina. And you, Nigel. We *will* have fun."

"Speaking of driving, Baron," Nigel added, "I have a little something for you." He handed over a small package. The Baron opened it and smiled at its content. "Driving gloves," he said more warmly, "thank you, Nigel."

"Glad you like them. *Peccary* driving gloves, the supplest. For a while, I had cornered the world market of peccary leather, fancy that. I think I still own a warehouse or two in Lima packed with it. Have you ever been to Lima, Peru? It looks as if the city's been bombed, yet it hasn't."

As they were sipping coffee in the drawing room, a mousy-looking man turned up, apologized for intruding on them, and approached the Baron. He whispered something in his ear. The Baron snapped: "Your lack of manners never ceases to amaze me, Giorgio. Whispering in one's ear! You must forgive my secretary," he continued, addressing his guests, "a loyal man, but still in need of some polishing. You may go now, Giorgio. I'll join you shortly." As the secretary left, the Baron commented: "His manners still don't seem to stir from hibernation."

"What could he possibly mean now?" wondered Leo in his mind, but simply asked, "Did you say 'hibernation'?"

"Yes. His grandmother was the chambermaid of a Marquis from an ancient Veronese dynasty, good friends of ours. That he would get her pregnant was a minor scandal, if at all. What surprises me is that, two generations since, the one fourth of nobility in Giorgio's blood has not yet revolted against the larger but weaker three fourths of plebeian blood in his veins. That's what I mean by 'hibernation.' The noble blood is still asleep. But I don't despair: sooner or later, it will awake."

Leo did not know whether he should be blown away by what he had just heard, or whether the Baron was joking. It was impossible to tell because he seemed always to keep a straight face. The Baron resumed: "Anyway, Giorgio was just telling me that my . . . how shall I call them? . . . sympathizers? are already arriving." The puzzled look on the guests' faces prompted him to elaborate. "I've been doing this on and off for about a year now. I've accumulated so much knowledge down the years, it was time to share some of it with young enthusiasts. Perhaps it's just an old man's excuse to feel important."

"That would be in character," thought Leo; he had never met such a self-important man.

"Why don't you two join us?" Emanuele asked. "I've been working on a lecture you might find to your liking."

Orsina and Leo felt obliged to attend.

About a hundred sympathizers were waiting for the Baron, all male and all more or less formally dressed. "So the ballroom still has a function," thought Leo as he entered it, following Orsina. "But definitely not for dancing," he added to himself, seeing that the walls were thickly hung with ancient weaponry: enough halberds, sabers, and crossbows for a small battalion. Chairs had been placed in front of a podium with a lectern in its middle. The two of them sat in the back row. Giorgio stepped up to the podium, checked the microphone, and said:

"Baron Emanuele Riviera della Motta needs no introduction to most of you. To those who are new, I say welcome. You will count this seventeenth of June as the first day of your new life. You have the good fortune to be admitted to the presence of one who, more than any other living man, embodies the perennial wisdom. To listen to him is to hear more than words: it is to experience an initiation."

Giorgio stood aside and bowed to Emanuele, who with the most cursory acknowledgment took his stand. As the audience clapped, he put on his reading glasses. His theme, Orsina and Leo learned, was transcendence.

"There are three ways to attain transcendence," said Emanuele, "and each is appropriate to a different caste, as Hindu tradition calls them: the Brahmins, who are priests and scholars, the Kshatriyas, who are princes and warriors, and the Vaishyas, who are merchants.

"The Brahmin is an intellectual. He achieves transcendent states without any external aids, through meditation alone. Do not confuse it with prayer. It is the hardest of the three ways, and those who follow it are convinced that it leads to the highest state of all.

"The warrior is a man of action, and he has two ways to achieve transcendence. One of them occurs in war. If he can rise beyond the point of caring whether he lives or dies, in the heat of conflict he may enter a transcendent state of sidereal coldness. At this point it really does not matter whether he kills or is killed.

"The warrior's other way is through the use of woman. Women are *not* equal here, any more than they would be on a battlefield. The warrior—and we are talking of an elite here, not just of the average military rapist—uses sex for his own purposes."

"Wouldn't you know it?" thought Leo, amused, "the *use* of woman? Sex?" He had an inkling that this elaborate production was merely a pretext for the Baron to gab about his obsession before impressionable young minds—and bodies. The Baron had paused to drink some water.

His timing was theatrical, though to Leo that made it look all the more farcical. Yet the young men listened with rapt admiration.

He resumed. "The woman the warrior is using may have no idea that he is doing so. The relationship can still be perfectly satisfactory from her viewpoint. For him, it is a matter of what he does with his mind during the sexual act. It is like meditation in some ways, but the atmosphere of sexual union provides an energy that can carry him faster and further than most meditators.

"The man of the third caste lives by buying and selling. He has no business on this path, but if he insists on it, he needs particularly powerful assistance. He doesn't have the mind control of the other castes, so he takes drugs. They give him a glimpse of transcendence, but of an artificial kind, and his reward is often to get addicted.

"As for the fourth caste, the Shudras, they should be satisfied with their work and their family life, and loyal to their masters. But I am speaking of a traditional situation. The castes are all mixed up today, and have lost the sense of their own nature. It is foolish even to speak of these things to modern people: it's casting pearls before swine."

"Well, I'm *so* glad you've thrown me a few!" thought Leo, who was fed up. "How can these young men take him seriously? Look at them: they're as alive as zombies! Ah, kids!" But irony and irritation vanished instantly as Orsina took his hand into hers. What was this, now? he wondered. He didn't look at her, but kept his eyes on her uncle, still lecturing, though he was happy to notice that he no longer heard his words. Then they stood up and quietly left the ballroom.

# FIVE

Orsina and Leo crossed the terrace and took the woodland path. She passed the statues of the gods without comment, and continued until the first break in the trees. It opened onto a wide meadow, rich with wild flowers. "Let's sit here, on the grass," she said.

Leo should have told her of his strange incident with *The Magical World of the Heroes* the night before. But he found that he had no intention of bringing the book up. It was so much better just to be there, beside her. She brought it up. "Uncle was very angry at me, this morning."

"Was he?"

"Yes," she answered, and explained why. Then she added, "It's obvious that he doesn't expect a woman to have a clue."

"Really? How fitting. But forgive me if I ask: what business does he have in telling you how to lead your life, with permissions and prohibitions?"

Orsina looked him in the eye and said: "Before the accident, I suppose I wouldn't have cared."

"What accident?"

"My parents. They were killed in a car accident."

"I'm so sorry, Orsina, I didn't know, you—"

"I'm twenty-eight and married; I can cope with it. It's Angela I'm concerned for. You must have noticed we're quite unlike each other?"

"Yes and no; you're both very beautiful."

Orsina looked up at him, incredulous. "*Now* you tell me!" she finally said.

Blushing, he added: "I'm just stating an obvious truth. But yes, your sister does seem a bit frivolous."

"Frivolous? That's an understatement. I don't think I'd choose her as a friend, but as her elder sister I still worry very much about her, and try to care for her.

"After my parents died I offered to become her legal guardian. That would have been customary, but instead she chose Uncle over me. I tried to insist, but that only made matters uncomfortable. I don't know if he's really cut out for the role."

Leo couldn't agree more, but said nothing about it. He asked: "Isn't she eighteen yet?"

"She will be in a few months. I can't wait. She's already been accepted by the University of Bristol. Of course Uncle hates the idea: you can imagine how he feels about anything non–Italian. But I think she needs to get away from here—as I did, but sooner. The sort of people she hangs around with are not a good influence. I'll go to Bristol this summer and help her find a place to live."

"How does that work? I thought Italian high school lasted five years."

"She's done the International Baccalaureate at the English School in Padua. But then again, perhaps I shouldn't have worried: our parents have been dead for almost two years, and she seems fine. You've seen her yourself; she's in perfect health and acts so cheerful."

That was true, thought Leo.

"Anyway," she resumed, "I try to be particularly obliging to Uncle while Angela is in his care."

"Of course, that makes sense."

"So, I won't show you the book, after all." Leo said nothing. He was actually thankful. "You don't seem to mind, do you?"

"About having come all the way for nothing? That's not how I see it at all. True, I won't get to read that odd book, but I'm here in your company, and this alone is worth the trip." Once more, he was inadvertently playing the gallant; it was not like him, and Orsina was now a married woman. He added: "Besides, the setting here is infinitely preferable to anything we knew in Georgetown."

"Even the Chinese restaurant that you swore served dog meat?"

"Yes, and the movie theater where the projector blew a fuse halfway through *Jules et Jim*."

At the memories, her face relaxed in a smile that allowed her, for the first time in Leo's presence, to relinquish that strained expression. Soon, however, she was rummaging in her purse. "Still," she said, her hand emerging from the search, "here are a few samples for you."

"Are these excerpts from the book?"

"Yes, I'm sure Uncle won't mind. Well, I'm not so sure, but he doesn't need to know. Promise me you won't tell him."

"I promise."

"I've been puzzling over these passages, and working on these codes. Perhaps you can shed some light? It may be all the help I need. I've been making some progress on my own, and I think the secret of the book may lie in them."

"All right, let me take a look."

All along Leo had been skeptical about any great secret being hidden in that book. Still, he was eager to help Orsina in any way he could. They moved to a stone table in the garden, and she put a sheaf of papers on it. Birds were atwitter in the dense foliage of the surrounding trees. It was an Arcadian moment, but he must not be distracted. Here was the matter at hand. Each sheet had a Latin phrase at the top, he noticed, and a series of letters derived from it, which Orsina was trying to make into words. He read: "*Lux naturae.*"

"I'm sure that means the moon," said Orsina.

"Why, and how?"

"Look: you take the first two letters of each word, like this: *LUx NAturae*, and they spell LUNA. The moon is the light of nature. Here's a harder one: '*Mensura structurae verae magiae.*'"

"That means 'the measure of the structure of true magic.'"

"Right, and I think the word is MENSTRUUM."

"That's right," said Leo, who was catching on quickly, despite his reservations, "Of course: U and V are interchangeable in Latin. Could it be something about women's mysteries?" he asked, trying to be delicate.

She was not embarrassed. "I think it may be. Look at this one: '*Vulva tumens radiis.*'"

"That seems pretty explicit," said Leo: "the 'vulva swelling with rays.' But it doesn't make any sense."

"Yes it does. You see, the word here is VULTURA, vulture."

"And why on earth do vultures come into it?"

"The text says that the vulture is the purest of birds, because it doesn't kill anything to eat, not even plants."

"Well, that's new light on vultures; they feed on carrion, for God's sake! What's so pure about that? But does it get you anywhere?"

"I only wish I knew," said Orsina. "Here's one I can't figure out: *Pulsa cineres, elige lacunam.*"

"Pound the ashes, choose an orifice," translated Leo in a puzzled voice. He thought for a while, then said: "These Latin phrases, I'd venture, all seem to have to do with reproduction. You know, I think this might be a sort of Renaissance manual for newlyweds, that tells them things like how to conceive male children, and how to avoid conception. All this stuff about moons and menstruation.

"And look at this one," he went on, warming to the subject: '*A caelo totum*,' meaning 'Everything from heaven.' From it you get, let's see . . . ACETUM, vinegar. The diphthong 'ae' in *caelo* is rendered with an 'e,' of course. Perhaps the ashes and vinegar come from some folk-medicine knowledge about the role of acidity in conception; and the things from heaven may well be babies. They couldn't write these things openly then, because official medicine didn't even pretend to know them. But one hardly needs a book like this to regulate one's married life today."

"Maybe you're right," said Orsina. "That may be one meaning of it. But I think there are other meanings."

"If there are, they escape me. But I've only seen a few fragments."

"Why would Uncle be so opposed to my showing the book to anyone?"

"I don't know, it may be one of his idiosyncrasies. He told me that the book is passed on at the wedding day of the eldest son—or in your case, daughter. It's the latter's duty to study it, and put its suggestions in practice. All obsolete by now, but it's a family tradition, and he lives in the past."

"There may be more to it. I think the book's meaning is not so much literal as symbolic."

"Very well, then," said Leo, who, from what he could judge, was relieved to find the book quite harmless, based on these excerpts at least. "Maybe reading it is a kind of do-it-yourself psychoanalysis."

"You're trying to put my fears to rest, aren't you?" she asked as she returned the pages to her purse.

"No. I simply don't think there's much to it. I mean it."

"Leo," she was staring at him with a sudden intensity that was hard to bear, "do you remember that letter I left on your desk, at the university, years ago?"

"Yes," he answered straightforwardly, no sense in pretending he didn't.

"Why didn't you answer?" He kept silent.

"Why didn't you? It's as if I had never written it to you."

"I never opened it."

"What? Why didn't you, you fool?"

He did not answer. She continued: "I had poured my soul into that letter, Leo!" She was very close to him; indeed, she had grabbed the lapels of his jacket to pull him closer.

"I'm sorry, Orsina. The last thing I'd ever want to do is hurt you."

"Right, and you threw away my letter, maybe unopened—did you?"

"I . . . I gave it to my secretary with other papers she was to shred."

"You shredded my letter without reading it?" Orsina's eyes were wide with amazement. "But why? Didn't you like me in the least? Were you not attracted to me?"

"Oh yes," he conceded at last. "I found you very attractive, from the first time I set eyes on you in Rome."

"Then why didn't you act on it? Why, for Heaven's sake? Out of some ridiculously bourgeois code of behavior? Did you think having a relationship with your intern would be, what? Improper? Inappropriate? Unseemly? Please! You're wiser than that. Nothing so silly could hold you back if you really wanted me."

There were tears in her eyes. Tears, spent over him? He could no longer refrain from telling her the truth. He hated to see her so miserable. "Orsina, please don't be angry. *Please.*" She composed herself, but he sensed that it would not last unless he came clean.

"People wonder about me," he said, trying to look for the right words to make his confession to the point. "Some think I must be a closet homosexual, living alone with two cats. But when I was younger I was not like I am now. I was cocky and vain, and didn't pay any attention to people's feelings. Girls thought I was 'good-looking,' and that was enough for them to fall into my arms.

"Then, in graduate school, a girl became pregnant with my child. She wanted to get married, or failing that to bring it up as a single mother. But I persuaded her to have an abortion, and in a weak moment, she agreed. There were complications. As a result, she became sterile. And that wasn't all. She had a nervous breakdown, and began to take antidepressants. I'm still in touch with her. I've tried to help her, but she's hardly a functioning human being anymore.

"I felt only disgust for myself. Not knowing what to do, I took refuge in my Catholic upbringing. I joined a Third Order, in which one doesn't become a monk or a priest but takes a vow of celibacy. And I tried to become a decent human being. That's all. I'm very sorry, Orsina, if I've caused you pain. I only wish to help."

She said nothing, but kissed him on the lips, lightly. That was an unexpected reaction.

"You must have been wondering about my choice for a husband?" she asked, having gotten a hold of herself.

"I try not to judge anymore. And I'm sure he is a man of many qualities."

"None of which he has shown you yet."

"*I* didn't say that."

"Enough of this. He's fine. And he offered me a chance to get away from all *this*." Leo was puzzled by her last words. "Oh, there are things you don't know, and they'd be hard to explain anyway. But getting away from here, from Italy, from my family was good. Am I in love with him? No. But I am faithful, and nice to him. Is he faithful to me? I don't ask. It's a very friendly arrangement. It works. So," once more she changed tone and expression, and he braced for another emotional outbreak, "tell me: if I kissed you now, what would that make you, Professor? Unethical? Worse? A breaker of your own solemn vow? An adulterer?"

He had no time to respond as she was kissing him passionately and he was kissing her back, tasting the saltiness of her tears mixed with the sweetness of her saliva. She pulled away from his embrace, and brought a hand to her mouth, then both hands up, to cover her face. She was weeping, then laughing, and then in his arms again, kissing him with a passion he had forgotten, or perhaps never known. Leo was holding her tightly, basking in her scent, living a moment he had dreamed about, and did not want to let her go.

"I could have been yours, you fool! I don't care about money. You could have taken me away from all this ballast. We could have gone to Australia, Argentina, whatever; we could have started from scratch."

"I'm sorry, I didn't realize. If I had—"

"Don't speak, don't speak." She kissed him again, as if this long kiss could breathe life into each other. Then, suddenly, she hastened back to the villa, leaving him in the garden, overwhelmed.

# SIX

Leo had told Dumitru that he would not be having dinner, and then stumbled back to his bedroom. He felt sick. And stupid, immensely stupid for having thrown away, he now knew, his happiness, and maybe Orsina's too. He spent the night awake, his bed light on, staring at the ceiling while resisting the impulse to run to Orsina's room to make love to her.

At breakfast came the moment he had been dreading: being alone with Orsina again. And there she was, sitting at the table, leafing through a paper, her head bathed in the slanted sunlight streaming through the window. She looked up at him, and said: "Good morning, Leo." She seemed agitated. "The news is horrible: 531 dead and many more wounded in San Petronio. The whole world is in shock."

"It's a terrible tragedy," he commented. It was too, but was Orsina defusing tension by referring to it? As he sat down, she asked, gently:

"Will you be doing some research for your book, Leo?"

Those few words, that sisterly smile, spoke volumes. Aristocratic reserve must have taken over and there would be no more show of soul. The time for regrets was over. Still, he couldn't help noticing how beautiful she was.

"I was expecting to, Orsina. But I got a phone call this morning, from a colleague at the university, back in D.C. He wants to collaborate with me on a project we've been putting on hold repeatedly. So I'll be leaving tomorrow."

"Tomorrow? Already?"

Is there something else you need to tell me? Leo wondered in his mind as he sat silently. No, he concluded; she's just being polite.

"Well," she continued, "everybody will miss you. I hope this has been the first of many visits, here or at our place in France, Leo. It'll always be a pleasure to host you."

So that was how she wanted to play it, mused Leo later, alone in his room, as he was packing. She wants to know that I'm willing to come back to visit.

Of course, Leo had invented the phone call from his colleague. And of course, Orsina had guessed so, but had not insisted.

Leo left the villa after lunch. Nigel took him to the railway station with his roaring Ferrari. The Baron had bidden him a very formal *arrivederci* the night before, and both sisters had kissed him on both cheeks, Angela hugging him more tightly.

Immediately before his departure, Leo had given a tip to Dumitru and his wife, and to Samanta. He had then looked for Marianna. She too was given a tip, and a sealed letter. In Italian, he had told her: "This letter is for Orsina. Make sure you give it to her personally." "*Comandi*!" It was understood. Then, on the spur of the moment, Leo had hugged the vinegar-smelling aged woman. Somehow, he felt that of all the people in the villa *she* loved Orsina the most.

Leo arrived in Rome's railway station, and immediately noticed that security had been increased through checkpoints and a heavy deployment of *carabinieri*. The taxi he took had to go through a few roadblocks set up by the army itself; near the Vatican, they became more numerous. One of the four bookshops the Baron had recommended was there. Leo arrived just before closing time.

A large, bearded man behind the counter was lighting a cigarette.

"Yes, *signore*?"

"Do you have a copy of *The Magical World of the Heroes*?"

The owner narrowed his eyes. "Where have you heard of it?"

Taken aback, Leo replied with the unadorned truth: "*Barone* Riviera della Motta recommended it; he said that I might find it here."

"The *Barone*? Why didn't you say so?"

The man busied himself in the search, leaving a smoke-trail behind him as he moved between the piles of dusty volumes. Leo browsed through the books on display on different tables. Some bore alarming titles, *Our Mussolini* and the like, but for the most part they were about alchemy, the occult—in short, esoterica. The owner returned with a dusty book and a smile. "Here it is," he said, "the last copy."

That evening, in a nondescript airport hotel, Leo leafed through the book, reading here and there at random: mentions of alchemy, Cabala; planets and satellites; riddles and codes; a wild potpourri of quotations from Trithemius, Iamblichus, Rabbi Achados, Geber, Empedocles, Proclus. . . . It was puzzling and, try as he might to make some sense out of it, he grew frustrated. This was the regular edition, anyway. According to the Baron, only the special edition for the Riviera dynasty contained the "secrets."

He put down the book and revisited in his mind the days he had spent in Italy. In his letter to Orsina, he had kept a very amicable tone. She would realize from the beginning that he was not proposing anything illicit. He simply stated that she could count on him for anything, anywhere, and at anytime.

Back in D.C., Leo woke at five in the morning in his apartment, and recognized the symptoms of jet-lag: in Italy it was already eleven. After unpacking and tidying up the place, it was still too early to bring back his cats Galileo and Garibaldi from the cattery or go to the office. He turned almost instinctively to the book he had bought in Rome, and read the title page:

Cesare della Riviera

*The Magical World of the Heroes*

*Which deals with uncommon clarity with what the true Natural Magic is, and how the true Philosophers' Stone can be fabricated,*

*by narrating, one by one, the prodigious and ineffable effects that a perfect Hero is enabled to attain through the said means.*

He read here and there for an hour or so, wondering all the while how the author could boast of "uncommon clarity." He was reaching the end of Book II, *The Powers of the Tree of Life*, when his eyes fell on the reassuring name of Saint Thomas Aquinas. What was the great theologian doing in this company? He read:

> Thus the glorious Thomas of Aquinas, in his book *On Being and Essence,* writes that one can obtain within an hour from a watermelon seed the leaves, the flowers and the fruit. "I saw, as we began to eat, that a watermelon was sown in a certain prepared soil, sprinkled with some concocted water—and unrestrained leaves, flowers and then fruits came forth from it, so that, before we left the table, we could eat of them."

Was Cesare della Riviera misquoting, or even inventing something entirely? Leo remembered reading the very treatise, but could not recall any mention of magic watermelons: it would positively have stood out. Still, he read on.

> Although the natural *magus* produces marvelous effects in all three kingdoms through said nature, nevertheless the God Priapus works his miracles in an easier and faster way in the vegetable kingdom.
>
> Thus the Hero can create gardens in which, despite winter, it is possible to enjoy a perpetual and most sweet springtime—for both in the extreme cold and in the excessive summer heat, there are fresh herbs, green and tender, and aromatic flowers; but likewise there is also a constant mild autumn, offering at all times and with abundance delicious and delicate fruits.

Priapus? Had he not just seen a statue of that god on the woodland path of Villa Riviera? He reread the whole chapter, this time avidly. Then began to wonder. He had only been at Villa Riviera for a few days during late spring, but had noticed some oddities in the garden. He was no expert, far from it, but the trees in it had looked both centuries-old and youthful at the same time; and what of that ever-present breeze that made the climate just perfect? Even the grapes in the vineyards, he had been told by the Baron himself, benefited from such an ideal climate.

Was the Baron, as the book's "wise hero," realizing marvels in his own backyard?

"Nonsense!" Leo said aloud, "what am I thinking? Besides, that part of north-east Italy is renowned for its mild climate." He closed the book and turned to the serious business of the day.

"I think I know how to make the most of being here," Nigel said enthusiastically as he and Orsina were having coffee after lunch at Villa Riviera. The Baron, ever busier with his sympathizers, had not turned up; and Angela, as usual, had gone villa-hopping on her Vespa. As Orsina looked quizzically at him, Nigel elaborated. "I intend to find the perfect Amarone. Somewhere in this region it's waiting for me. What we have here," draining his glass, "is close, but I believe we can do better. And I like driving around vineyards."

"What a noble pursuit!" said Orsina. They both laughed. She would not accompany him because his driving style didn't mix well with many wine-tasting stops. She spoke from past experiences in France.

"All right, I'll see you later," he said.

Orsina walked to the garden, and sat on a chaise longue beneath a majestic tulip tree. The family's secret book was in her hands. She had placed Leo's letter, still unopened, at the very beginning of the first part, *The Conquest of the Tree of Life*. In the company of the massive tree, towering to almost 150 feet, she expected to be inspired to approach the book in a new light. Uncle Emanuele had once more told her that she must take the book very seriously and study it every day. Now, perfectly relaxed in the deep shade of the thick foliage, she turned to the first chapter and read:

> The most exalted and liberal Maker deliberated to give form to man; whose model or idea he did not take from supercelestial forms, but only (O infinite goodness!) from Himself, making it in His own image and likeness.

It *was* a promising beginning. She must make a clean sweep of what she had read of it before, casually dipping in here and there, and make a fresh start. And so it was time to make a fresh start of her relationship with Leo. It was curious how she hadn't read his letter yet. Marianna had dutifully handed it to her over a week before, the very day of Leo's departure. Orsina had thanked her, and put the envelope on her dressing table, where it had waited for a few hours before finding its way to a drawer. Nigel might have noticed it.

Giuseppe was clipping a boxwood hedge nearby. She called the old gardener a few times till he heard. By the time he reached her, she had ripped the unopened letter into many pieces.

"Here, Giuseppe: put this on the compost heap."

# Seven

Two days later, Leo was in the Library of Congress, ready to begin his summer research project. As he waited for the books that he had ordered, he wondered if the library's 23 million volumes might include the "secret edition" of Cesare della Riviera's treatise. Several different editions of *The Magical World of the Heroes* appeared in response to his search, and he ordered them all. By now, he had read the book from cover to cover. It seemed to him very bombastic, but he was intrigued. After lunch, when the books arrived, he set aside his literary studies to examine them.

Most were the same as the modern version that he had bought in Rome; some had the same content but with the original, archaic spelling; lastly, there were a few translations, in Spanish and French. Leo was disappointed. He had the uneasy feeling that the Baron had been playing a scholar's prank on him, and what is more on Orsina too, leading them on to believe in something that had never existed. Even the uncut copy he had fleetingly held in his hands could have been part of the elaborate plot. But why? Perhaps there was no accounting for the vagaries of an eccentric egotist with a lot of time on his hands.

Still, Leo's curiosity was far from appeased. He felt that the only way to keep a dialogue open with Orsina was through *The Magical World of the Heroes*. And because he could not get her off his mind, his curiosity about the book had grown exponentially since he had returned to the States. What was he to do?

He mentioned his failed search to Hanna Schmidt, an under-librarian who had often helped him. "Do you know of any books that exist in a secret or private version, different from the published one? And how one would track them down?"

Hanna was a Germanic blonde, almost as tall as Leo himself, with infectious good spirits that often broke the silence of the library with a laugh. Leo sensed her liking for him, but felt reluctant to mention *The Magical World of the Heroes*. She had been known to break librarian's etiquette by passing comments about the books that people borrowed. "I can't tell you offhand," she replied, "but I can send out my bloodhounds."

Leo spent the rest of the day working his way through a stack of antebellum literary journals, searching page by page for references to Italian literature. Once he had enjoyed this kind of scholarly spadework, but now his heart was not in it. At any excuse he left his place: to visit the cafeteria, the men's room, the exhibition hall, or to exchange a whispered word with a colleague whom he spied across the pillared reading room. The next morning, as he arrived at his favorite seat, Hanna waved a sheaf of papers at him. "Professor Kavenaugh!"

"Hi, Hanna; how are you this morning? Did your bloodhounds sniff out anything?"

"And how!" She read from a printout of several pages: "A Secret Gospel of Mark, different from the one in the Bible. Military manuals from World Wars I and II, published with deliberate mistakes in case they fell into enemy hands; the correct editions only issued to commanding officers. A Japanese handbook of martial arts; for centuries, the Yagyu family alone possessed the complete version. Aubrey Beardsley's obscene novel *Venus and Tannhaüser*, well known in its bowdlerized version as *Under the Hill*. Paschal Beverly Randolph's *The Grand Secret*, 1860, with the passages on hashish that were eliminated for general publication the following year. . . . The list of secret editions goes on and on. Which one would you like?" she asked with a sly smile. "They're all in the public domain now."

Leo felt that he'd gotten into deeper waters than he had bargained for. He returned her smile. "Thanks very much. This is quite a feast!" He ran his eyes over the list. "I certainly don't want to read most of them. I was more interested in the principle of secret editions, and only for the sake of a footnote. It looks as though it'll be a long one!"

"Be sure to mention the hashish, then!" said Hanna, and left him with the satisfied look of a good dog that has pleased her master.

On reflection, Leo decided that Munenori Yagyu's *Book of Family Traditions on the Art of the Sword* was worth a look, as being most similar to Della Riviera's—and even contemporary with him.

When an English edition arrived, he learned that this samurai family had allowed a text to circulate that was full of bombastic promises of what their warriors could do: make themselves invisible, move faster than lightning, kill instantly, even with a wooden sword. Yet, there was not the slightest practical advice on how to *achieve* such wonders. The book made them seem like boastful charlatans trying to look important. But this, the editor explained, was a stratagem. The Far Eastern art of war advises those who are strong to appear feeble. Potential enemies take no account of them, but if they are ever attacked, they have the advantage of complete surprise. The secret edition of the Yagyu's treatise, on the other hand, contained the real secrets of the killing moves and the mental processes that went with them. It showed how to deliver on the promises.

Leo thought back to *The Magical World*. Here was a dynasty involved in analogous power struggles: those of early modern Italy. Like any literature professor, he knew something of its canonical authors. As he refreshed his memory from an encyclopedia, it came home to him how universal the belief in magic was in Italy during, before, and even after the Renaissance.

Marsilio Ficino drew down the influences of the planets by singing to the lyre, and landed a job as the house philosopher of the Medici family. Giordano Bruno trudged around Europe trying to sell his magical politics to Queen Elizabeth, Emperor Rudolf II, and anyone else who would listen, but ended up a burned-offering to the Holy Inquisition. On the other hand, Tommaso Campanella, author of the utopian *City of the Sun*, had the last laugh.

Convicted of insurrection and heresy in 1603 (the year of *The Magical World*!), Campanella languished in prison for a quarter of a century. Finally, in 1628, Pope Urban VIII ordered his release and summoned him to the Vatican as his personal magician. Pope and magus were frequently closeted together, and this, Leo read with astonishment, is what they did:

> First they sealed the room against the outside air, sprinkled it with rose-vinegar and other aromatic substances, and burnt laurel, myrtle, rosemary and cypress. They hung the room with white silken cloths and decorated it with branches. Then two candles and five torches were lit, representing the seven planets. There was Jovial and Venereal music, which was to disperse the pernicious qualities of the eclipse-infected air. For the same purpose they used stones, plants, colors and odors, belonging to the good planets Jupiter and Venus. They drank astrologically distilled liquors.

And it was a *Pope* doing this! Not only that, but the former jailbird was called to the court of France to make a magical diagnosis of the newborn heir to the throne. After examining the child, he pronounced that "This boy will reign for a long time, sternly but happily. He lacks mercy, and in the end there will be great confusion in religion, and in the realm." And that was a spot-on prophecy, for the child would become Louis XIV, the Sun King.

Leo was not a specialist, but he knew that in Cesare's century the lines dividing religion, magic, and science were fuzzy. If popes and monarchs believed that they could increase their power through magic, noble dynasties must have tried it too. But anyone reading Cesare's book would have had the same serious objection. All Leo had to do was read the index from the edition he had bought in Italy: it promised the "magical hero" the gift of twelve "fruits" from the "tree of life," down to something close to a divine or immortal state. Yet, not a word was spent on *how* exactly one would obtain such fruits. Was Cesare completely incompetent? He promised so much while delivering so little. As with that Japanese book, readers would have dismissed him as a learned waffler, and the book as a vanity publication.

And what if it were true? Baron Emanuele was arrogant and unlikable, mused Leo, but there was no denying that he was powerful. He had made his world conform exactly to his will, complete with that band of impressionable "sympathizers."

Late that night, Leo browsed through the book with new respect. In its beginning, it made much of how the Hero creates his own magical heaven and earth, and the mythological beings he encounters there. Where could this possibly happen, if not in the imagination? As he said the words over to himself, he thought about the similarity between "magic" and "imagine." According to the dictionary, they came from different Latin roots, but the intuition seemed a fruitful one, as Leo knew something about the power of the imagination.

After becoming a member of the Third Order, he had joined a group that practiced the Spiritual Exercises of St. Ignatius Loyola. They consisted of controlled meditations, imagining scenes from the life of Christ, especially the Passion. One was supposed to visualize them in every detail, noting what the background was like, what the people were wearing, what their expressions and emotions were. Most of the group's members had difficulty in keeping their minds concentrated and making the inner images precise and realistic. Leo found the process not only easy and natural, but frightening. As soon as he tried the guided meditations, the scenes leapt before his inner eye with the clarity of a movie, and left him emotionally exhausted. Already laden with guilt enough, that familiar feeling, he had decided then and there that this was not his path.

Perhaps the practice of the "hero" was something like this. He just might try a meditation on some theme of the book, and see if his old gift returned.

The next evening, as Leo was feeding his cats, regrets came flooding back while he revisited in his mind his conduct during Orsina's year in Georgetown. His celibacy and self-sufficiency had saved him from the risks of further involvement with women: the risks of giving one's heart to someone else, who might hurt it. It was so much less complicated to give it to books, to cats, and, as he had imagined, to God.

Instead, chance had offered him a pearl, and he had thrown it away. He should have followed his first impulse, the one that had made him hire Orsina without a second thought. He should have told Orsina about his past, his vows, and, yes, his feelings for her. Leo saw his reflection in the window, and took a good look at himself. Regret for what he had done to Sylvia, the woman to whom fate had yoked him all those years, had been tempered by time; but regret over what he had *not* done, that seemed inconsolable.

But Leo did not wallow in his regret, not that night. Once more, as he thought about Orsina, he felt drawn to the *The Magical World of the Heroes*. His apartment was overflowing with books, but that small one he had brought back from Rome was monopolizing his attention lately. He had begun to reread it, this time little by little and carefully. He had tried a meditation on the theme of the hero, but no images had appeared before his inner eye; his old gift had not returned yet. But what did the author mean exactly by "hero"? Chapter III was entitled "The Magus and the Hero." Leo read:

> It is generally understood that he who operates virtuously, and through glorious and memorable actions makes himself conspicuous and noteworthy in everybody's eyes, should be

numbered among heroes. But it is a most evident thing that nobody shall ever accomplish those outstanding deeds, which can readily and naturally be accomplished by the Magus thanks to natural Magic, so that only he is entitled to be called a hero.

# Eight

Nigel was on his search for the perfect Amarone. He had been traversing soft undulating hills, hurtling along dusty back roads and confirming that Gianni, the mechanic from Maranello, was right: the 365 GT *was* in perfect driving condition. He had not yet tasted the ideal Amarone, but was definitely enjoying himself. On the crest of a hill, he came to a curve. The dirt road was peppered with potholes, and he had to slow down considerably. Past the curve, a new vista opened before him, with much of the same, give or take a cypress here, a farm there, and an ocean of vineyards. But there was also a scooter parked on the edge of the track, its rider standing beside it.

"A turquoise Vespa?" he wondered. "Could that be . . . " The rider waved at him, and he stopped.

"Angela? Are you all right? What happened?"

"What does it look like? I'm sunbathing in the middle of nowhere."

"Well, you've certainly picked a secluded spot for that, but doesn't one usually take off one's clothes?"

Angela laughed. "Come on, help me. Do you think you can fix it?"

"Your Vespa? No, I'm a useless mechanic."

"Great. So now what?"

"You might just be in luck. This must be the only vintage Ferrari with a decent boot." With her help, he lifted the small Vespa and placed it in the trunk. It just fit, though the top wouldn't close. "Now, will you join me?"

"Of course, my rescuer." She got in, giggled, and off they went.

Around the middle of July, the Baron was addressing a much more select group of sympathizers. The theme of the lecture was "spiritual warfare."

Giorgio had barred all doors after they had entered the ballroom. Sitting on the podium, the Baron was quoting St. Bernard's homily to the newly founded Knights Templar:

> "Go forth confidently then, you knights, and repel the foes of the cross of Christ with a stalwart heart! The knight of Christ, I say, may strike with confidence and die yet more confidently, for he serves Christ when he strikes, and serves himself when he falls. If he kills an evildoer, he is not a mankiller, but, if I may so put it, a killer of evil."

The Baron looked at his meek flock. He repeated: "'If he kills an *evildoer*, he is not a mankiller, but a *killer of evil*.'

"Consider the man who said this, Saint Bernard. He prophesied, worked miracles, cast out demons, wrote many books, destroyed heresy, healed a schism, glorified the Virgin Mary, established the Knights Templar, launched a Crusade, guided councils, ended a pogrom, advised popes, accomplished every mission assigned to him, yet took no pride in his successes and ever longed to return to his cell in the monastery.

"How did he do it all, you may well ask? And how did those crusader knights succeed in liberating Jerusalem?

"They believed that God was on their side. But we are beyond such fairytales: there was no god sitting up there on his throne, doling out power to his favorites. Those men *were* gods."

A murmur of surprise, or assent, ran through the audience, and the Baron's voice became more confidential: "You may recall one of my favorite sayings: *Est deus in nobis*, 'there is a god within us.' It is for us to make it come true."

The listeners were visibly impressed as his lecture continued. Toward the end, the Baron paused to drink some water, then resumed.

"Unfortunately, there is a converse to this process of becoming a god. Last week I described the technique of separating the soul from the physical body, but forbade you to practice it. There was good reason for that. You should know that in that state, one may encounter entities. They may have no objective reality at all, but that does not make the slightest difference to you. They will be as real as the man sitting next to you. And they are much more dangerous than any human being.

"If you encounter one of these entities, your job is to command it. But that takes an extraordinary degree of self-collectedness, because the entity will use every ruse to command you. Don't expect to meet fire-breathing dragons or demons drooling with blood. For you, the entity is much more likely to take the shape of a human being whom you revere. It will approach you in a friendly fashion and you will find yourself tempted to welcome it and take its advice. *Do not on any account do this*! Regard it with the utmost distrust, and command it, no matter how outrageous this may seem.

"There is a well-known expression in the Zen tradition: 'If you meet the Buddha on the path, kill him.' Yes, you heard me: *kill your Buddha*, desecrate your own temples. This is not the only meaning of that precept, but it is one of them."

For a moment, he glanced at Giorgio, who was gazing at him with adoration. And so were his disciples.

"If you can pass this test successfully," the Baron continued, "then the entity will vanish, and you will feel a profound relief. Then you may pass to the next stage of transcendence. If you fail, be warned: the entity will take you over. You will seem to fall into a blissful sleep, but your body will awaken. With your soul dormant, your body is then at the disposal of the entity, and it can do whatever it likes with it. Can you imagine the horrors that could ensue? These entities crave a physical body, and their one goal is to obtain the temporary use of one.

"Yes, it is only temporary. You will wake up sooner or later, but you may be unpleasantly surprised at where you find yourself, and at what your body has been doing during your absence.

"If you are not prepared to face this trial, go no further on this particular path of initiation."

Emanuele closed his notes and stepped down from the podium. There was no applause. This was not an entertainment, but a warning of the most solemn kind. The listeners seemed not only convinced, but moved by the Baron's words. Giorgio unbolted the main doors, and they filed silently out of the ballroom. As the last of them left, the Baron spoke quietly to Giorgio:

"You see what an effect it has when the truth strikes the heart. But remember that you, with your one fourth of noble blood, have an advantage over these young men. They are well-intentioned, but they cannot hear the call of the blood. Only when that is present can one hope for the higher initiations."

"Yes, Baron. I hope for them more than I can say."

One young man was hanging back from the departing crowd, and he now turned to the Baron. Like many of the others', his head was shaved and he was dressed in black. There was something ascetic, almost monastic, about his drawn features and eyes, burning as though riveted to some distant and fascinating sight.

"*Barone*," he said in a distinctly Spanish accent, "may I speak personally to you?"

"There is nothing personal about the doctrines for which I act as mouthpiece," Emanuele replied. "But go on, tell me your concern."

"I feel like a bomb about to explode." The Baron frowned. "Forgive me, that's *not* an appropriate thing to say these days. But it's not enough just to listen to you. I must *act*, I must *do* something to validate what I'm learning from you." The Baron stared at him penetratingly, and said nothing.

The young man elaborated. "I feel ready to tread this path, and I have no fear of any entity I may encounter. I feel strong enough to master it. But I can't just do it for my own sake."

"Why not? For whom else would you do it?"

"For the world!"

Emanuele was silent but appraising. The zeal of the Spaniard, almost palpable, was the only reason he had not dismissed him yet. "Like many of the group," the young man went on, "I'm a traditional Catholic, and see no conflict between my faith and the esoteric tradition that you represent. St. Bernard's fathering of the Templars only strengthens my conviction. But I haven't found my *mission*, and I know that I have one, maybe of the greatest importance."

"That could be a dangerous illusion," said the Baron, finally passing judgment.

"I don't say it lightly. But I submit myself to a higher power. I'm going to Santiago de Compostela. I will pray for guidance where so many pilgrims have prayed before."

"That might be the right course of action. I have a profound respect for the sacred sites of Europe, and for the influences that may still be effective there. As a believer, you may find better guidance there than I can give you. Go with my blessing."

"Thank you, *Barone*."

The Baron, his face unusually flushed with a solemn exultation, made his way slowly down the horse chestnut path to the car park, got into his Lancia and headed for the hunting lodge, where Angela was awaiting him, as arranged.

The easel now stood empty and the palette caked with dried oil paint; the Baron had discarded his painterly preludes in favor of a more powerful ritual, and sacrament, of sexual alchemy.

His former practice had been a kind of slow-motion archery. The hour of preparation was like a gradual bending of the bow to the point of maximum tension, until the release of orgasm carried his will to the target which he had held, the whole time, in his imagination. Today, and conveniently for his purposes, Angela was menstruating. If she felt any discomfort in the procedure, which was more than usually clinical, then she did not show it. Her deportment was as detached as a sleepwalker's.

Emanuele entered her and, in time, ejaculated; this was merely the initial phase of the ritual. His next action required contortions that were awkward, and which Angela in her normal state would have found grotesquely comical. But now she lent herself to them with the grace of a priestess, as he gradually sucked in to the last drop the mixture of "solar" and "lunar" fluids to be found around her labia, inside her vagina and wherever they might trickle. Finally, Angela wrapped herself in a duvet and went to sleep.

After adjusting his ritualistic garb, Emanuele seated himself in a straight armchair. He assumed the pose of an Egyptian statue, his hands resting on his knees, his eyes open but his vision turned inward. He visualized his stomach as an alchemical alembic containing *rubedo* and *albedo*, or more precisely, two dragons, red and white. Below it, in the region of the bowels, he imagined a fire. As the vessel heated, the dragons twisted and squirmed, clawing and biting each other, and their mingled blood, red and white, seethed and foamed. It reached a critical state that threatened to shatter the vessel, and, in earlier stages of his practice, had often done so, causing a fit of uncontrollable vomiting. Then the chaos subsided, leaving nothing but a vague silvery cloud, shot with gold.

Having now digested the potentized substances, Emanuele passed in review each of his inner circle of disciples. They would have been surprised to know how clearly he could visualize each one, and even more surprised to know that he was now, in his imagination, sodomizing them one by one.

Emanuele had no homosexual tendencies, but the ritual required him to implant a subtle seed in them, which would grow like a fetus, or rather a parasite, and subject their will to his.

With this, the sacrament was concluded. It had taken a few hours. Angela had awakened, cleaned up with incongruous cloistral modesty, and already left on her Vespa. Emanuele, drained but triumphant, looked forward to a restful night of sleep.

# Nine

Leo learned about what had happened in Spain when he glanced at his newsfeed during a break from research. Apparently a bomb had gone off inside the Cathedral of Santiago de Compostela, near the statue of Santiago Matamoros, Saint James the Moor-Slayer. Leo and the world held their breath. Was this another San Petronio? Was the world going mad? What next?

A few hours later, a more detailed version of the facts was broadcast. The attack had not been as devastating as the one in Bologna. The cathedral was largely undamaged, but a baroque statue of Saint James on horseback, slashing with a sword into a group of Moors, had been blown to smithereens. The human cost was still unclear. Many had been wounded directly by the explosion; many more, though the exact number was not yet known, had been injured and outright killed in the resulting stampede.

The worldwide repercussions of this new act of terror were enormous, and in Europe the reactions were severe. The four hundred Islamic places of worship in Spain, ranging from mosques to garages, felt under threat, and with good reason. In Santiago itself, a mob stormed into the park where a mosque was under construction, and set fire to the building site, damaging the bulldozers and cranes before the police half-heartedly dispersed them. The question of who was responsible for the bombing was scarcely considered by the authorities, or anyone else. The days around the July 25 Festival—the Apostle St. James's Day, the Patron Saint of Spain—had been as frenzied as ever, with tens of thousands of pilgrims, tourists young and old, students and loiterers crowding the narrow streets of the small medieval city. It was assumed that the perpetrator had secreted the bomb by the statue, and got away unobserved in the confusion.

Work on the Santiago mosque was suspended indefinitely, as on others throughout Europe. The official explanation for such a drastic measure for once did not evade the issue: they were breeding grounds for terrorists. And that was not all: the plans to admit Turkey as a member of the European Community, already advanced in spite of massive public opposition, were also suspended. The nationalist parties of every country redoubled their challenge: "Assimilate or leave!"

Every summer, towards the end of July, Baron Emanuele was in the habit of giving a dinner party. This year he had asked Orsina to organize it, and had invited most of the neighbors. His niece had done things in style, and within a week twenty guests were having dinner with them under the cherry tree on a grand mahogany table purposely moved from the dining room under the cherry tree. More staff had been hired for the occasion, and hundreds of candles had been lit. They struggled with the breeze, but it was never strong enough to blow them out. The full moon contributed to the illumination with its benign rays. Nigel had provided dozens of bottles of the Amarone that, so far, he had picked as his favorite.

The Baron sat at the head of the table, Orsina to his right, Angela to his left. His cycle of lectures had finished a couple of days before, and he seemed drained of his energies. His mind, however, was far from inactive. He observed each of his guests, and passed judgment on them all. "Noble rot," he said to himself, a sip of wine lingering on his palate.

The Amarone is made by harvesting ripe grapes and drying them on straw mats, which concentrates the remaining sugars and flavors. Depending on the weather, the wine is influenced by "noble rot," the benevolent form of a gray fungus. But from the Baron's perspective there was nothing benevolent in his guests. They were all struggling, he knew, to keep their villas or palaces, all competing in the bourgeois world by working in ordinary offices and striving to make ends meet with petulant wives and insolent sons and daughters. Would their ancestors have been proud of them? Of course not. He considered them a putrefying subspecies. "Noble rot" was the perfect epitaph. His nieces, fortunately, represented an exception: Angela, whom he knew intimately, and Orsina, who was clearly the more gifted of the two.

The dinner party was a success; Orsina had organized it brilliantly. The Baron, however, excused himself before the dessert, and withdrew to the library. Might the *Corriere della Sera* have something more interesting to offer than his guests?

Emanuele took off his reading glasses. He had just read an op-ed article by the last surviving Colonel of the Fascist era, reflecting on the church bombings and the violent popular reaction to them. The old warrior (he must be 100 by now!) deplored the violence on both sides, of course, but predicted a new European solidity as the "unexpected fruit of tragedy." Every such incident, he wrote, would simply bring Europe closer to its moment of awakening. We should look forward to it.

Yes, Europe was fast asleep, and the house was full of burglars, thought the Baron. He looked out of the window over his moonlit box hedges, rococo statues, venerable trees. He thought of his other ancestral home, the Palazzo Riviera on the Grand Canal, and of the generations that had won the right to live as such men were supposed to live. His mind went back to the eve of his wedding, when his father had initiated him, as the eldest son, into the mysteries of the family:

"The Riviera is one of the most ancient families in Europe. We are descended from the Gens Rivalis, ancient settlers on the banks of the River Adige. From them came a clan of heroes, whose exploits are glorious in the annals of war and peace." Various examples had followed.

"But our heritage is more than blood alone. We are the hereditary guardians of ancient secrets. We know the means by which heroes are made, and by which, after a triumphal death, man makes himself immortal.

"On our heraldic shield appears the Tree of Life. We know the secret of this tree, and the Paradise from which man was never expelled but through his own weakness. We know how to nourish the tree, and how to make the River of Life flow from its roots. Through this knowledge, the Gens Rivalis has always flourished, and always brought forth heroes. These heroes are still with us. From their Olympian splendor, they watch over us, waiting to welcome those who prove worthy to join them."

Then his father had presented the book, *The Magical World of the Heroes*. "Take this book, written by our ancestor Cesare della Riviera. Cherish it; study it; master it. It is a cryptic work, impenetrable to the common man, but if you can learn to read it, you will tread the secret paths that other Riviera have trodden before you. I repeat: Cherish it; study it; master it, and you will find the hidden stone." The last words had been in Latin: *invenies occultum lapidem*.

Had he not obeyed them? Had any Riviera applied himself more assiduously to the study of the ancestral book? The Baron thought not. He had found the secret paths, had performed the rites that ensured the continuation of the clan. Or had he? To his great sorrow, he had not performed the simple rite of propagation on the physical plane. "A congenital sterility of the seminal fluid," the specialist had said, after a ten-year marriage had failed to produce offspring.

Who would keep the Gens alive after him? As with many great dynasties, the family line had contracted to almost zero, and ended now with only two young women: Orsina and Angela.

Emanuele's gloomy thoughts turned back to Europe. It needed a spiritual impetus to awaken the continent, even one at the level of popular religion. For better or worse, Christianity had become the religion of Europe, after shedding much of its Middle Eastern peasantlike baggage. It had been the spiritual mainspring of the Holy Roman Empire, of the Knights Templar and other orders of chivalry, of the Courts of Love in which European art, literature, and music came of age. It had toughened the warrior caste through the Crusades.

Yes: it was time for another Crusade, thought the Baron, and the Infidels were not across the Mediterranean now: they were right here, battering on the door. How could anyone stay asleep at such a time?

On second thought, Emanuele concluded, what Europe needed was a new *Reconquista*, and maybe it was already starting in Spain—again. St. Ignatius Loyola, the Spanish founder of the Society of Jesus, had been a warrior. As there were no more crusades, and the Moors had recently been expelled, his ambition was the conversion of Muslims to Christianity.

"Good," the Baron mused, with a dry smile. "We might recruit the Jesuits too for the Reconquest. It wouldn't be the first time they oppose the Pope." That American of Jesuitical leanings he had recently hosted—that friend of Orsina's—came to mind: Professor Kavenaugh. And the mere thought made the Baron break into laughter: he, a warrior? He laughed again, heartily.

In the early afternoon of the next day, Giorgio announced that a young man had come to the villa and was requesting a private interview.

"Do we know him?"

"Yes, Baron, he has attended some of your lectures."

"Which ones, can you recall? The ones held behind closed doors?"

"Yes, some of those too."

"I see. Very well, show him to the library. I'll meet him there."

Felipe stood in front of him, anxious, shortish, and skinny. The young Spaniard, the Baron learned, had felt compelled to resume the pilgrimage to Santiago de Compostela that he had interrupted halfway through to attend the lectures. He had gone by the traditional route, on foot, but returned by train immediately after the bombing. At this point, Emanuele expected the worst kind of emotionalism, and called Giorgio. He was ready to have the young man escorted out. But as Giorgio was answering his call, Felipe surprised him. The library became charged with an electrical intensity as the Spaniard told his story.

"It was when I entered the Moroccan suburbs," Felipe was saying, "that my mission became clear to me. Think, Baron, an Islamic encampment on the very fringes of the sacred city!" By the time Giorgio turned up, the Baron sent him away with a single imperious glance.

"There was a park there," Felipe added, "and right in the center they were building a mosque. I learned that the local politicians had given away the space to buy the immigrant vote.

"It looked like a white mushroom, and I realized that the goal of my mission was to destroy it.

"I have to confess that as a student I was a convinced Marxist, and I and my comrades made plans to attack various bourgeois targets." The Baron frowned, but allowed him to continue. "We stole the ingredients to make bombs, and were almost ready for action when the engineer in the group got cold feet, and nothing came of it. But I can never forget the training we put ourselves through, the sense of purpose. And now I knew what it had all been for.

"But working alone, I couldn't begin to make a bomb large enough to destroy the mosque. After long meditation and the offering of my own life, if need be, I received an answer.

"Do you recall, Baron, the phrase that you used: 'If you meet the Buddha on the path, kill him'? I felt that Saint James himself was saying this to me. I was to kill his image, only his image, and he would do the rest. I made my plans so that the fewest possible people would be hurt, and trusted the Saint to ensure that no lives were lost. His statue would be destroyed, but it was only a statue. We would wake up the people, the Saint and I, and they would take over my mission.

"But you know what happened: there was a stampede, and twelve innocent Christians died. True, the mission has been launched, and grows stronger every day; but I feel guilty of deaths and injuries that I never intended to cause. I can't take this guilt anymore; I must turn myself in."

Felipe had looked at the Baron then, half fearful, half defiant, expecting him to pick up the phone and call the police. The young man was ready for martyrdom.

"What I have just heard," said the older man, with Olympian calm, "is as though it were whispered to the reeds. In fact, I have never heard it. Clearly, you acted on an impulse not of your own; you were beside yourself, possessed, temporarily incapacitated. Therefore, you shouldn't be held accountable. Now listen carefully, and take my advice: return to Spain, and do nothing unusual. Keep a low profile, make yourself inconspicuous. Is that clear? Take no initiatives and keep your impulses in check. In other words: keep your mouth shut, and do absolutely nothing."

Felipe was taken aback. This was not what he had expected. At the same time, his instinct of self-preservation came to the fore, and he was grateful. And there was more: he also realized belatedly what a disgrace he had been to the chivalrous ideal. The Baron had been magnanimous; he resolved to do exactly as he had been told. He bowed his farewell and left with a spring in his step.

Alone in his studio some time later, Emanuele was revisiting Felipe's words in his mind, and gloating. "Is it my own magical activity that has caused such a catalytic event?" It seemed that no conscious effort could have come close to this. It could be a perfect illustration of chaos theory: the drop of rain that fell on a butterfly's wing, and started a deluge. But the Baron, of course, did not believe in chaos theory.

# TEN

Nigel stepped from the water-taxi to the dock of Palazzo Riviera. "I hardly got a look at this place when we were married," he said to Orsina. "It's even bigger than I remembered. It must get terribly damp in winter."

"It does," said Orsina. "That's why I prefer Provence."

The servants appeared and were quick to take their suitcases. Orsina greeted them: "Hello Bhaskar, hello Soma. How are your children back in Delhi? Are you going to be able to bring them over soon?"

Bhaskar was short and earnest, in an off-white Nehru jacket and narrow trousers. Soma, dressed in a blue-green sari, was an attractive woman in her thirties, plump and bustling in response to Bhaskar's muttered orders in their own language. "Oh, Madam, thank you for asking, but it is very difficult." Orsina listened attentively to his halting but formal English. "The air fares and maintenance for five children are so expensive, but we hope to bring them over in twelve months' time."

Nigel was looking around the androne, the hall at canal level that stretched from one end of the palace to the other. "Do you still use these gondolas?"

"No, they're decrepit, and I'm sure they leak like sieves," said Orsina. The servants had vanished up the broad ceremonial staircase, and Nigel followed.

"These are funny," he said as he passed the statues of winged infants on the banisters. "Especially this one . . ."

"He's pretending to be Priapus," said Orsina. "Do you recall . . ."

"Oh, right, the big fellow in your uncle's garden."

The staircase swept magnificently to the ballroom. Nigel craned his neck and swiveled round to look at the somber painted vault. "This I do remember." He looked down at the intricate geometry of the parquet floor and grunted. "So much labor, but to what end? At the moment I'm more interested in lunch."

"So am I," she said. "You can see the rest of the house afterwards." They crossed to the dining room overlooking the Grand Canal, where Bhaskar and Soma had set out their lunch. Orsina had reassured them that, as a Londoner, Nigel was fond of Indian cuisine. As they ate, he sweated profusely, while she explained the logistics of modern palazzo life. "We mostly live in these four rooms. Uncle has a suite at the top, where no one dares to go. We barely use the third floor, except for our stingier friends and relations who'd rather share the one bathroom than stay in a hotel."

Nigel had enjoyed the luxuries of Villa Riviera, with Dumitru and Afina, Samanta, even the aged Marianna all attentive to his needs. He was not sure, now, about spending August in this cheerless palace, with a smelly canal on one side and swarming tourists on the other. But he had come with a purpose: to learn Orsina's language properly.

He kept at it every weekday from nine until four. Then, his head spinning with Italian phrases, he would buy the *Financial Times* and the *International Herald Tribune* and read them in a café, making calls on his cell phone. A pleasant evening with Orsina followed, with dinner in a restaurant, or the odd party in nearby villas on the Brenta River.

It was early morning in Leo's apartment and the phone was ringing. He let it ring till it stopped. But then it rang again. "Not her, not again!" he thought as he stood at arm's length from the receiver. "I'm going to have to get a phone with caller ID. . . ." Lately, he had spent much time consoling Sylvia. He had even accompanied her to her first appointment with a new psychiatrist. As they sat in the waiting room, he couldn't help noticing how fat and ugly she had become, like an old spayed cat. The analogy was cruel, he knew it, but had come of its own accord. And to think that, in her twenties, she had been so beautiful. The phone rang again; Leo finally picked up.

"Hello? Leo? Is that you?"

"Yes!" Relief and surprise left him at a loss for words.

"Leo? Are you still there?"

"Yes, I'm here. It's wonderful to hear your voice, Orsina; how are you?"

"I'm well, thanks." After a few more awkward moments, a conversation got under way. "She must have read my letter, and now she wants to keep in touch," thought Leo, taking the phone to a comfortable chair, while she thought, "He must have expected me to be passionate after reading his letter; but my tone has thrown water on the fire." Leo said:

"Glad to hear you're fine. It's been a pretty grim week and I could do with some light relief."

"You mean the news? Yes, that Santiago business has sent my uncle into a tizzy. He's behaving even more eccentrically than usual. Anyway, Nigel and I are staying at the palazzo in Venice for a while. In case you wanted to get in touch, now you know where to find me."

"I certainly don't want to lose touch." One more awkward pause. He resumed.

"How's Nigel? Did he buy the Ferrari?"

"Of course, and he's driven it a lot. He said he had to make the most of it before being condemned to a city without roads."

"Who condemned him?"

"He's sworn to do a month's intensive Italian course, and I've found him a language school nearby."

"A language school? Those are for college students. Why doesn't he take private lessons?"

"He says he misses the rough and tumble of school life."

"And what will you do while he's learning his irregular verbs?"

"I'll catch up with all my school and college friends who live here, and I want to check out a restoration project that I've helped with." Orsina hesitated. "And I'm going to study that book, Leo. I really am, this time. I refuse to let Uncle think that the female brain is incapable of it."

"Talk about living in the past! I'm studying it too. I bought the modern edition on my way through Rome, and I've read it already. I actually liked the chapter about the plant world. It made me wonder if Emanuele is working magic to get those huge trees looking so young?" He said this in jest, and was surprised by her reply.

"Do you believe in magic, then?"

"Well . . ."

"Well?"

"Let's say I've had a few experiences, a very few, that incline me that way. Actually, the Jesuits used to have a great respect for natural magic, the sort that's done through understanding how nature really works, but without intervention by spirits. But the kind of tricks they used to regard as natural magic are so far outdone by things like the telephone, the movies, the computer, that there's not much room for it these days."

"I've had experiences, too." Orsina hesitated again, then swerved back onto firmer ground. "Leo, do you think we could study *The Magical World* together? After all, that's what made me contact you in the first place, and yet we never got around to it. Together we could really get somewhere."

An excuse for regular communication with Orsina? Leo's heart leapt, but he forced it down like a pesky dog. "I'd love that," he said.

"Great! Now, we have different versions, and I still have to respect the family's taboo, but see if your edition talks about the Cave of Mercury. It's near the beginning, just after the quote from Orpheus."

"The book's right here," said Leo, crossing the room to his crowded desk. "Let me see. . . . Yes, I have that in Chapter Four, and we can start with it."

"Let's give it a few days. I'm so glad we can do this together! I hope it won't interfere with your research."

"Such fine acting," he thought, "God bless her." She knew perfectly well that he would postpone any research for her. So, things were to be on a sort of professional basis. But heaven forbid that she should suggest collaborating by e-mail. "Don't worry, my other collaborator is doing most of the work this summer. But I hope we can do ours by phone. It's so much subtler than e-mail," he said.

"I hate e-mail," said Orsina, "and I was hoping that you wouldn't suggest it." So it was settled: Orsina was back in his life! And she needed him. Leo had not felt this excited in years. Yes, he reminded himself that she was married now, but still, just hearing her voice made life seem so much more promising. He should thank *The Magical World* for this unexpected joy. He propped the book up in front of his dinner, and began at the beginning.

An hour later, he realized that he had eaten his dinner without giving it a thought. He made himself a pot of coffee, then settled with his feet up on a sofa, beneath a single reading lamp. One particular cryptogram had drawn his attention. It had to do with "Tartar." This, said Cesare, was not the common tartar that crystallizes in old wine barrels, nor Tartarus as another name for Hell, but the magical Tartarus that "resides in the dark center of our virgin Earth, in which there burns the continuous and occult fire of Nature." Its true meaning, the exasperating alchemist went on, is revealed cabalistically by the phrase *Terrae ARdor TArdans RVtilantia Sidera*. Leo translated this as "the heat of the earth impeding the glittering stars." What exactly did it mean? Perhaps he should simply concentrate on this image.

And how rich it was! The five Latin words opened suddenly a world of significance and awe-inspiring imagery. The earth is hottest, of course, at its center, reputedly occupied by a mass of white-hot iron. Leo brooded on the paradox of something brilliantly white from which no light can escape. He saw in his mind's eye the graduated colors of the earth's layers, going from white to yellow, orange, dull red, then the brownish-black of the planet's crust. Yet through all of this there radiates a heat as from the heart of a living body. Yes, he said to himself, the earth is a living being, edible, drinkable, breathable, and that is why beings can live on it. But the soul, which Leo had from childhood thought of as something white and deep inside him, is as invisible as the earth's core. The stars, on the contrary, radiate whiteness from their surfaces. Are they then visible souls? What does it mean for their light to reach us; and what about its being impeded by the earth's warmth?

Like a hunter chasing a white deer through a forest, Leo's mind followed these associations. Soon it ceased to verbalize them, and he was led on by images alone, then by colors of inexpressible significance. Truths beyond words seemed on the verge of revelation, when a tremendous shudder ran up his spine and he opened his eyes. He had distinctly heard the bedroom door behind him open. It's just one of the cats, said his rational mind. He got up. Even the dim lamplight dazzled him as he crossed the living room to greet the cat. Angela stood before him, stark naked.

Leo stopped, stunned, gaping, his heart rushing. There was something oddly glacial about Angela, far removed from the bubbly blonde presence that charmed all about her. Her face was without expression, but she beckoned him to follow her through the door.

As he stepped in, it was not into his own familiar bedroom with its single bed, its antique quilt, its crucifix and childhood teddy bear. He found himself floating amid interstellar space, with Angela's perfect female body floating beside him. She shone with the reflected light of a myriad stars, which turned her pubic hair to silver fur and purged all color from her breasts. She was beautiful beyond words, and he felt himself sexually aroused; but he feared, no, he knew that to touch her would chill him to the bone. She was of moon-stuff, a virgin Diana, huntress of stags and men.

They were moving fast, in a timeless rush through airless space. She looked him in the eye for what seemed to him an eternity. Then she spoke. "You don't like me, do you?" Indignation welled up as Leo protested to the contrary, but she cut him short. "Look out for my sister," she said in the same toneless voice, and another wave of emotion surged up, at once warm and desperate, like a crimson, enveloping sheath that excluded all other senses. As the wave passed, the starlight returned, but Angela was no longer there.

She had led him to the brink of a gaping abyss. Leo could not resist looking into it, but the starlight could not reach its depths, and it might well be bottomless. He felt himself being drawn into it, not as a climber loses his hold and tumbles into a crevasse, but as a weighted diver sinks towards the seabed. Or else the seabed rises to meet him, as the bottomless abyss seemed to be rising towards Leo. The stars faded and went out, and there was only night, silence, and a feeling of warmth that gradually localized itself at the region of Leo's stomach. For the first time in what seemed an eon, he made a voluntary movement, and with that returned to consciousness of where he was.

He was lying face upward on his bed, his feet dangling to the floor. He raised one arm and felt a cat—no, both cats—lying on his stomach. The rest of him was getting cold, and it was pitch dark. That was strange, since he hadn't turned off the reading lamp when he got up from the sofa. He felt along the bed to the bedside table lamp, and turned the switch. Nothing happened. He stood up and groped his way to the light switch beside the door; again with no result. "It must be a power outage," he thought, trying to keep cool, "and a serious one, because there is no city light coming through the window."

The whole of Washington was in total darkness: that was a sobering thought. "Perhaps there's been some terrorist attack," thought Leo. But surely there would be the wailing of ambulances, police cars, fire engines. No, there was nothing for it: he'd have to wait till dawn, and since he was so cold, he got under the bedcovers. As he settled, hoping for sleep, he heard the familiar early morning noises outside the window. He got up again and slowly made his way to it, opening the curtains by feel. The world was wide awake, but Leo, whether awake or dreaming, was in utter darkness. Overwhelmed by the terror of the unknown, he fell to the floor by the window, shivering with cold, and saying to himself: "It will pass, it will pass . . . "

# Eleven

The sacristan awoke early every morning, looking forward to his stroll down to the Cathedral with the ancient iron keys chained to his belt, and to unlocking its doors. A pious old man who had been born in Chartres and dedicated his life to the great church, he never ceased to marvel at its beauty and spiritual power. On this day in August, however, he was *running*, and *away* from the Cathedral, straight to the police station.

It must have been fifty years since he had run like this. Unable to catch his breath, he could not tell the gendarmes what he had to say. He could only point to the Cathedral, and look terribly distressed. The policemen recognized him, and two of them left for it at once.

A large crowd had already gathered, pilgrims, tourists, and townspeople. "Let us through, let us through!" the gendarmes shouted. They made their way to the central portal. On its great doors, still locked, there was a large graffitied slogan in scarlet spray-paint. It read:

*Seize them and put them to death wherever you find them, kill them wherever you find them, seek out the enemies of Islam relentlessly.*

One gendarme copied the sentence into a notebook; then the pair headed straight back to the station.

The Mayor of Chartres had a rude awakening, as the chief of police told him the news. He was not only offended by the sacrilege, but alarmed. After the bombings of San Petronio and Santiago, he knew that this was no trifling incident. He told the chief to evacuate the area around the Cathedral, and to keep its doors locked until further notice. Immediately after he hung up, the mayor awoke his secretary, and told her to get him in touch with the President himself, in Paris.

"*Monsieur le Président*?" the secretary had wondered. Had she heard correctly? She had.

Soon after the President of France, the media heard the news; shortly after that, France and the world knew that the doors of the great cathedral had been soiled with a passage straight out of the Koran.

The Chartres incident, however, was only a beginning.

In the weeks that followed, scarcely a day went by without a report of some desecration of a beloved Christian site. Like the fanatical Taliban who destroyed the Buddhist rock carvings in Afghanistan, the perpetrators delighted in knocking off the heads of statues and damaging altar paintings beyond repair. Not since the Revolution had France seen such vandalism as now occurred, first in Chartres, then in the Sainte- Chapelle of Paris, where priceless stained-glass windows were smashed; the glorious pilgrimage church of Vezelay, where the solemn figure of Christ in majesty was covered in oozing dung; and, perhaps worst of all, the smiling angel of Reims Cathedral, whose head was never found again. In Italy, Spain, Austria, and Catholic Germany it was the same tale of desecration.

The Vatican made every effort to hush up the incidents; besides, no one had been physically injured. The clergy in the places affected were forbidden to talk to the media, and discreet calls were placed to TV, radio, and newspaper editors. But the attempt was futile. It was just what the media needed: the scenes of vandalism and the distress of the witnesses made good copy, and the op-ed writers competed in hand-wringing. There was intense pressure on the Muslim communities to stop protecting those responsible, and angry denials of any involvement only made matters worse for them.

"Professor, I have news for you."

Leo was anxious to know it, after his eyes had gone through a battery of tests.

"Let's see: the pupillary reactivity is normal; there is no corneal opacity; no lenticular cataractous changes; no opacification of the vitreous cavity; the optical nerve looks discreet and normal in coloration, and the visual field is within normal parameters. In short: everything seems to be fine." The ophthalmologist, a plump man in his sixties wearing thick glasses, spoke in a particularly persuasive tone.

"Thank God! And thank *you*, Doctor." After a short pause, he added,"But if everything is fine, how do you explain what happened?"

Sitting helplessly on his living room's floor, unable to see anything, Leo had waited and waited. Eventually he had groped his way to the phone and dialed, by feel, 911. The ambulance had arrived, and the paramedics had taken him directly to Georgetown's Hospital. As he was waiting to meet the ophthalmologist, his vision had begun to come back to him, slowly and tentatively at first. By the time the ophthalmologist had started to examine his eyes, his vision seemed restored. The doctor's words stirred him.

"Well, Professor, we need to find out more. Temporary blindness is a rare phenomenon. It may be a symptom of something else. But before we get into that, there are more tests you need to take."

"More tests?" wondered Leo in his mind. Two CAT scans and an MRI with "galadinium enhancement," he was told.

The tests took hours.

Late in the evening, the ophthalmologist saw Leo in his office. With his file spread open on the desk, he said: "I can't find anything wrong with your eyes, Professor." He almost seemed frustrated, as he added, "I'm going to refer you to a colleague of mine."

"What for? I trust your judgment, Doctor."

"A second opinion can't do any harm. I'll call him, and let him look at your file. He is one of the country's best neuroophthalmologists."

The MacPhersons' routine was interrupted at the end of the second week, when Orsina picked up the phone and heard Emanuele's voice. "I'm coming to the palazzo on Sunday. It's against all my principles to set foot in Venice at the height of the tourist season, but I have urgent business. I won't be bothering you and Nigel, but I want you, Orsina, to spare me an hour of your time for some family matters."

Nigel thought it best to steer clear of him—"After a while, he gets on my nerves," he admitted—and to drive for the day to the villa.

Orsina was uneasy as she waited for her uncle. The atmosphere of the palazzo was oppressive and aloof. It seemed to embody both the hopeless parenting that she had received, and Emanuele's obsession with aristocracy and family tradition. Her year in America had been like coming up for air, and ever since, she had embraced another way of life less haunted by the past.

To distract herself, she turned her mind to the redecoration of Nigel's flat in Kensington, and leafed through the brochures and samples that the interior decorator had sent them. She jumped when the bell rang to announce her uncle's arrival in the androne. She hurried down and greeted him with the conventional kiss, but sensed that he was preoccupied.

At the appointed hour, Emanuele and Orsina sat on two facing sofas in the salone. He spoke, as usual, in formal tones. "You have heard some of my lectures, my dear Orsina, and maybe through long association you have an inkling of my philosophical life."

Orsina nodded deferentially, which seemed to be the right response. Emanuele resumed. "There are many dimensions to this philosophical life of mine, and as a woman, you could not possibly share them all. But you do carry the Riviera blood, and with it, an *obligation*. You are twenty-eight, and if you died tomorrow there would be nothing of you worth remembering. It is time you faced your responsibilities."

His arrogant and paternalistic manner annoyed her, but Orsina felt relieved as she thought: if he's going to urge me and Nigel to hurry up and have children, I'll tell him that it's none of his business. But this was not the Baron's theme.

"You and your sister are now the only heirs of the Gens Riviera in its unadulterated form. My own physical incapacity is to blame, otherwise I would be saying this to my eldest son." Emanuele paused, and for a moment Orsina thought that he was going to break down in tears or, worse, in a fit of anger. "But that is Fate," he continued. "Now, you know that I have urged you to pay close attention to that book, *The Magical World of the Heroes*, which was presented to you before your marriage, as it is to every eldest and legitimate Riviera. Yet so far your sister, who is *not* supposed to read it under any circumstance, has shown more interest in it than you!" He had raised his voice, and then gave her such a wintry stare, a shiver went down her spine.

"Yes," he added, "I caught Angela leafing through my own hallowed copy of it, in my studio. She knew that it is absolutely forbidden, and still she dared. What can I say? *She should have known better.*"

Orsina was taken aback. Now her uncle sounded menacing, even vindictive.

"But you," he continued, "you who have the privilege, how could you not be dying to learn its secrets?" She had never seen her uncle so livid, nor had she expected to be terrified. She very much wished for Nigel to be there with her.

"You must wonder what the book's significance is," the uncle continued, after having calmed down with an effort of will. "Like any profound treatise on magic, it works on several levels. First there is natural magic, of which the noblest form is the Royal Art of alchemy. I don't expect you to set up an alchemical laboratory, as I myself did in my youth, but that is one possible application. This book gives practical instructions under the veil of allegories and symbols.

"Alchemy has another meaning, but it applies specifically to the male. The female anatomy and mentality are not adapted to the practice of sexual alchemy, so I pass over that. Perhaps to your relief?" he said, with a half smile. Orsina, now listening intently, felt apprehensive. This was the first time that her uncle had spoken to her of his esoteric interests. "Sexual alchemy," coming from him, was certainly an alarming concept. But to feed his penchant for lecturing might soothe him. "No, please don't pass over it. I want to understand it all," she said.

"There is no way to understand it all, my dear child," he said, turning his profile to her as though addressing an audience outside the window. He continued, quoting from memory from *The Magical World*:

> 'He who knows the use of the female vessel kindles the secret fire, which flies like an arrow whithersoever he will. Thereby he achieves results that few would believe possible.'

"That's why I will not describe them to you." He warmed to his theme. "Another form of magic is celestial.

> 'But the adept who uses celestial magic commands the invisible forces that rain down from the planets, and bends them to his purposes. He applies them to the kingdom of plants, to that of animals, and to those humans who are little better than either.'

"This is the magic that sustained the great, lasting civilizations of the past. Never mind what idiot historians write in their preposterous books. But in our time, the masses have become so degraded that it's a total waste of effort to try to better them. It's enough to use this magic for the benefit of the few families that deserve it. I will leave you with that hint.

"Yet there is a higher magic still, which operates in the world of immaterial intelligences," he added, looking up and hooding his eyes, as if in an afterthought.

> 'It is there that the Hero attains his goal, beyond earthly time and space. He destroys all that is human in him, and becomes of the same substance as the Sun, yea, no less than a god. For such a man, death is an incidental event of no significance to his true nature.'

He stopped and looked Orsina in the eye. "But this is all I will tell you, because these things have to be discovered for oneself. For centuries, the eldest Riviera has been entrusted with a book that is the key to their discovery. Others may read this book, in its watered-down and incomplete version, but they will not know the lock into which the key fits. That is our possession alone."

The tirade seemed to be over, but Orsina was not going to take it all with feminine passivity. She returned his stare, mastering the anger that was welling up in her. Her voice trembled as she said, "Thank you for telling me this, Uncle. I have heard all I need to hear." She got up from the sofa and started for the door. Then she swung around and broke out: "But what use is a key, if one can't find the damned lock?"

There was a longer silence. Then the Baron assumed a more friendly tone. "Don't go yet, my dear. You know the Mercury Room?"

"Yes," said Orsina, "the storage room with no windows. I never knew why it was called that."

"The room is decorated with a frieze showing Mercury stealing Apollo's cattle and hiding them in a cave. *That* is the lock," said Emanuele, "and the book is the *clavis magna*, the grand key."

He paused, giving her time to absorb his words, and came over to her. She shrank back, dreading another embrace. "Anyway," he continued, reaching into his inner pocket, "you should also have this." He placed an envelope in her hands. "You ought to know what our most illustrious ancestors accomplished after having metabolized *The Magical World of the Heroes*. It's a sketchy outline, but it will have to do for now. Immediately after you have read it, *destroy* it. Is that understood?"

Orsina nodded, turned, and left the room.

# TWELVE

Squeezing past the tourists, Orsina reached the area at the back of the vaporetto. The rush of water under the propellers and the breeze were a relief from the sticky heat. When the boat stopped at San Marco, most of the tourists got off and she was able to sit down. The route continued around the island to the Fondamenta Nuove, where Orsina disembarked and bought an ice-cream. She saw a larger steamer about to leave, and on impulse ran to the gangway. "Just a moment, please, Madam: I need to check your purse," said the armed guard.

Once on board, Orsina stood in the bow, leaning over the rail and enjoying the wind in her hair as the boat picked up speed on its way to the outer islands. It stopped at San Michele; at Murano, where again most of the tourists left for the glass workshops; Burano with its garish houses; and finally Torcello.

Orsina took the gravel path that led to the cathedral of Torcello, the oldest settlement of the Venetian lagoon. She entered the venerable building, so cool and different in atmosphere from Palazzo Riviera. After sitting for a while, she decided to climb the tower.

She arrived at the top, out of breath from the steps but exhilarated by the stronger breezes and the view of the little island beneath. Here, of all places, no ghosts of her heroic ancestors were hovering around. She could bear to open her uncle's letter at last.

The envelope produced a single sheet of paper, neatly typed on both sides. It read:

> A very brief sketch on how some of the Riviera employed the magical powers obtained from a lifetime study of *Il mondo magico de gli heroi*.
>
> The first one known to us was the author of the book, Cesare della Riviera. But for you to realize the enormity of his audacity I must remind you of the climate in Europe at the time of the book's publication, in 1603. Despite Giordano Bruno's burning at the stake in 1600 and Campanella's imprisonment by the Inquisition, Cesare della Riviera influenced the Holy Office to

approve the publication of the abridged edition (nobody outside the family ever heard of the dynastic edition) at a time when certain Cardinals of the Church were planning to have him arrested and tried for heresy. The official imprimatur took the wind completely out of their sails. But he had another motive: to show the other noble families dabbling in magic that he was just a pretentious ass, and therefore harmless. Why, his book promised everything and delivered nothing! It was very convenient that they should think him a charlatan and leave him in peace.

Later in the seventeenth century, there was Anastasio della Riviera, the builder of the villa. He applied his power to the acquisition of property, and to persuading moneylenders and builders to act in his interests, rather than their own. Many of the properties we still own were bequeathed to the family by him.

Then there was our military hero, General Giuliano della Riviera, who fought with Prince Eugene of Savoy. He was a master of men, and incidentally of horses, and could do exactly the same: persuade them to act in his interests by hazarding their own lives. His regiment was known for its fearlessness.

Paolo, his twin brother, studied the art too, but he went by a different route. He lost his wife and first child when they were still young, and decided to renounce family life and become a missionary. He went to Mexico, at first with a party of Jesuits but later on his own he founded a community of natives whom he had converted. I would classify this as another example of persuading people to act against their own best interests. They built a virtual city in the midst of impenetrable jungle, which he ruled like an uncrowned king; but Paolo's success at converting the Mexicans caused jealousy among his superiors. He was recalled to Italy, and on the voyage home he died, supposedly of a fever. His city and all its inhabitants faded back into the jungle.

More recently, my grandfather was an adept. You know that he was a politician. But you didn't know how he had such a long and unblemished career. He sat in parliament, and oversaw the passing of several bills under King Umberto. All such bills had been initially opposed, some vehemently; still, he succeeded in having them ratified. It was the same power: he knew how to influence the thoughts of men.

As for myself, it is not yet time for you to know how I have employed and am employing the power. But what you must know is that your time has come to possess yourself of the book's magic. Start studying it today—and burn this sheet of paper at once.

As if on cue, the hour struck. The bell was only feet away from Orsina, and the shock and noise were extreme. When the sound had died away, Orsina took out a book of matches from her purse and after a few attempts managed to set the letter on fire. Holding it into the wind, when the flames neared her fingers, she let go, and it fluttered away to nothingness. She slowly descended the tower, overtaken by mixed emotions: awe, fear, and—why not admit it?—morbid curiosity. *The Magical World of the Heroes* was no empty pretense, of that she was becoming convinced. She would no longer put off studying it. But where should she begin, or rather, how? She rejoined the steamer, stopped off for dinner on Burano, and let herself into the palace around midnight.

The next day, Orsina was still asleep when Nigel returned from the villa. "I met Emanuele on the way out," he said. "His smile was as cold as it gets. I left the Ferrari in Mestre, with the wine in the boot, but Bhaskar's going to go and fetch it by motor launch."

"Did you see Angela?"

"Yes, she was in a good mood and says hello. Now I must get to class. I've missed an hour already."

Alone in the palace, Orsina began to feel the sense of oppression returning. She wondered why she had heard nothing from Leo: it was two weeks since he had suggested that they study *The Magical World* together. Could he have said so in the heat of the moment, only to cool off and find his other research more absorbing? That was impossible, or was it? She was about to call a girlfriend and suggest lunch together, when the phone rang.

"Leo? Is it you? What time is it there?"

"Four in the morning, but I couldn't sleep."

"How are you?"

"I'm all right, thank you. How's Angela?"

"Angela? She's fine, probably villa-hopping, as usual. And I thought you missed *me*!"

There was an awkward silence. If Angela was all right, then there was no need to worry Orsina by telling her about his vision. "I'm sorry," he said. "It's the professor in me. I remembered that you're helping Angela settle in at Bristol. That's all. Tell me: how are *you*?"

"I'm fine, but I'm really bored with being alone in this place, with Nigel out all day. I've even been reduced to reading *The Magical World*!"

"I have, too; in fact I've been reading it intensively," said Leo cautiously.

Orsina could not resist pushing her luck, now that the subject had been broached. "So, Leo, have you been reading about the Cave of Mercury?" That was the lock, her uncle had told her, and the book was the key.

"Yes," replied Leo, "in fact I've read the chapter many times. After the thing I've told you about, I had the idea that this Cave could be oneself, one's inner consciousness. Cesare makes it seem as though 'Mercury' means everything, which I found very unhelpful earlier on. But it may signify that the whole of experience can be recreated in the imagination."

"Yes, and in my edition he adds something: he says that Mercury is *the vehicle that brings the soul down from heaven into the body*. That links up with his idea that the whole universe is present in us, the macrocosm in the microcosm. Do you know, Uncle has started talking to me about these things, too. He's given me some clues about the book, and how it concerns the Riviera family. I can't say any more."

"I'd hope it was more universal than that. Is there any hope of a humble Kavenaugh learning about it, too?"

"Ah, Leo: there's also an aristocracy of the spirit. But anyway, you know Uncle and his family chauvinism. No one is supposed to be as good as we are. But for once, he gave me a concrete hint. There's a room in the palace that's actually called the Cave of Mercury. I'm going to explore it."

"Oh yes, you do that. And watch out for—what does the book say?—Pygmies, Gnomes, Vulcans, and Salamanders lurking in the dark."

"I will!"

That afternoon, Orsina equipped herself with a large flashlight and entered the storage room. She laughed at herself as the beam fell on an electric wall sconce. Of course, the whole *palazzo* had been wired, and they'd hardly leave out the one room without a window. She turned on the light, which revealed stacks of chairs, trestle tables, and a wheeled stepladder that she had seen used for changing the light bulbs. There was space enough to circle the room, but the black-painted walls were smooth and featureless. No other door led in or out.

There was, however, a broad cornice, then a painted frieze, well above head height. As in other rooms, it was half painted and half modeled in plaster, so that some of the figures protruded from the surface. The frieze was darkened with age and smoke, and hard to make out. By aiming her flashlight, Orsina could see some details, and memories of well-loved Greek myths came back to her. Of course: they were the stories of Hermes, Mercury to the Romans. There was a herd of cows that an infant was driving into a cave; they must be the cattle that Hermes stole from Apollo. The nativity scene must be, in fact, not Mary giving birth to Jesus, but Mercury's mother Maia giving birth to him in the cave of Mount Cyllene. On the third wall, Mercury had grown up and was exchanging his lyre for Apollo's golden staff. And on the east wall, opposite the door, were two scenes Orsina did not recall: Mercury locking the door of his cave, and the same nude figure, now almost separate from the wall, flying up to join Jupiter, enthroned on the ceiling.

"There must be a clue here," thought Orsina, "if only I could read the myths more closely." Perhaps she should ask Leo; he knew Greco-Roman mythology inside out. But that could wait; she was in the cave, why not use the ladder? It was not difficult to push it into position. She climbed to the platform, some six feet above the floor, which brought her face level with the frieze, and worked systematically around the room.

When she came to the east wall, the shock made her stagger and almost lose her footing. Mercury's cave, which had looked black and featureless from below, contained a distinct, square outline in relief. Moreover, it had a keyhole.

"The book is the key," Emanuele had said. Orsina climbed carefully down the ladder and returned to the salone, where she had been discussing the book with Leo. How was one to find an actual key in an allegorical book? Unable to keep her discovery to herself, she picked up the phone again and dialed Leo's number.

It was busy.

She redialed, and again, for ten minutes in a row.

When he finally answered, she had to control herself from scolding him for having been on the phone with someone else—who and what could be more important to him?

Leo listened with awe to her account of the black room. When she asked him the same question she had asked herself, he thought for a moment.

"Didn't the book mention a key? I'm almost sure it did. Let me go look at it again. I'll call back in a little while."

Fifteen minutes later, Leo said: "Yes, here it is, in the chapter before the 'Cave of Mercury': Jupiter gave Mercury a lot of treasure for the benefit of mankind, but Mercury locked it up in his cave, and flew back to heaven, carrying the key with him. Orsina, I think you should take a closer look at the flying Mercury. Will you?"

"If I do it right now, will you stay on the line with me, Leo? I'll take the phone with me." A minute later she had returned to the Cave and was already up the ladder.

"Here I am," she chronicled on the phone. "But the flying Mercury is above my head. Let me shine the flashlight on him. . . . Oh my God, he's got a key in his hand! It's three, four feet away at the most, but I'm already at the top of the ladder. I'll have to get something else to stand on."

"Don't be crazy, Orsina, please! You'll fall off. Go and get a broom, or something with a hook on it. Orsina? Are you there? Orsina!"

# THIRTEEN

Leo heard a crash, and the telephone in his hand went dead. Desperately, he redialed Orsina's number, but a metallic voice told him that she was "not available at the moment." In overreaching, Orsina had teetered, dropped the cell phone, and fallen sideways onto the mountain of folding chairs, from which she had slid to the ground. She was not badly hurt, but was shaken, as much by her uncle's revelations and her own discovery as by the accident. She limped to the bathroom and examined her scrapes and bruises, then poured herself a stiff drink and sat down to think.

She was about to call Leo from the house phone when her husband returned. Something, what exactly she could not say, made her reluctant to tell him about the Cave of Mercury. For the first time in their married life, she lied to him, saying that she had slipped while reaching into a high cupboard for some old childhood photographs. Nigel comforted her, and offered to get them down for her. "No thanks, at last I got them down," she said, and had some in a dresser drawer that she quickly produced. Why was she doing this? Lying to Nigel, and then going out of her way to corroborate her lie?

Her husband kept her company for the whole evening, so no opportunity occurred for a private call to reassure Leo. Only after Nigel had gone to sleep did Orsina creep to the house phone to call him.

Leo had suffered agonies of the imagination, compounded by his own impotence to save her. When he heard her voice, it was as though she were his savior. She told him what had happened, "But I'm not trying again until I'm really prepared for it. By the way, Nigel knows nothing about this."

"You really shouldn't try it alone," he said, then regretted having invited himself, by implication, to the Palazzo Riviera.

Orsina did not hesitate: "I could wait until you come and visit us in Venice," she said. "By then we may understand the book better, and be ready for whatever is through that door." They said good-night to each other, but then lingered on the phone for another half an hour, speaking of this and that.

Over the following days, they talked several times about the progress they were making with *The Magical World of the Heroes*. Or rather, the lack of progress. Leo knew all about Greco-Roman mythology, as well as the writings of the major saints. These had an important role in the book. He understood the language perfectly, down to its baroque nuances. Yet many passages baffled him. The author, he concluded, simply belonged to another world, not only historically, but culturally and philosophically. So to penetrate the book, perhaps he should try to penetrate Cesare's mind, which meant first of all to learn about alchemy.

But alchemy is not taught at universities. Rather than invite ridicule from his colleagues by speaking about his new preoccupation, Leo decided to go back to the Library of Congress.

Hanna was wearing not her glasses but contact lenses, and wondered if the professor would notice. He did not. A little disappointed, she heard his request. It surprised her that he would be interested in esoteric books. She eyed him appraisingly, and said: "Maybe you should start with C.G. Jung? I've read a few of his books. He became very involved in alchemy, of all things. But he had an orthodox scientific background, so his take is supposed to be well-balanced."

"Well-balanced?" That adjective stuck in Leo's throat as he plowed through Jung's *Psychology and Alchemy, Alchemical Studies and Mysterium Conjunctionis*. To his lucid Jesuitical mind, there was nothing well-balanced about alchemy, even as explained by Jung. For days he perused the thick books, diving into a universe of weird metaphors and outlandish symbols. Salt, Mercury and Sulfur; *Nigredo, Albedo*, and *Rubedo*; Coagulation, Sublimation, and Condensation; Chemical Weddings and Mystical Unions; the Alembic; Hermes, Aphrodite and the Hermaphrodite; Signatures, Signs, and Seals of the oddest sorts; the Philosophical Egg and the Matrix; Kings and Queens, Suns and Moons and so on and on. "Was there a method to the madness?" he asked himself when he finished reading. Or were the alchemists, with Cesare della Riviera and even Jung among them, deluded or outright mad?

On skimming through a biography, Leo learned that Jung himself had had visions and come close to losing his mind. After his own vision and the blindness that had followed it, Leo could well believe that the whole thing was a byproduct of mental illness. And what was more, Jung readily admitted that many of his notions stemmed from patients who were schizoid or borderline psychotic.

The books Leo had read were illustrated with drawings both by the alchemists themselves as well as by mental patients. The images exuded that alien and icy atmosphere that he had encountered in his vision. Maybe it was better to leave *The Magical World of the Heroes* undisturbed, even in its incomplete version. But by now he had an obligation to Orsina to take the plunge—dangerous, perhaps, for him, but even more for her. He must prevent her from getting into trouble. Having become familiar with the images and symbols employed by alchemists, he went home and reread *The Magical World*, penciling in notes around the margins.

"I've been trying to make out what these philosophic substances are," said Leo in one of his clandestine phone calls to Orsina. Again, they were attempting to decipher the book, and comparing notes. "Take Vinum, for instance," he elaborated. "It's apparently another name for the magical Egg. I wish everything weren't the same as something else; talk about misleading! Anyway, it appears in the perfect colors of red and white wine. It's extracted from the magical Grape, and takes the same time to make as common wine, and like that it foams, boils, and digests, thanks to the internal and invisible fire. You can tell that it's perfect when its colors become gold and silver. Then it says that its name comes from *Vis*, Latin for force or energy, because all the magical energy is contained in it."

"And the rest of its name comes from one of those cabbalistic phrases, *VIs NUMerorum*, the energy of numbers, because this magic depends on number," added Orsina. She had come to the same conclusion. "I think it must be describing an inner process of some kind, done with two opposing forces."

"Gold and silver are equivalent to the sun and moon. Solar and lunar energy. Could they be like thought and feeling? One has to blend them to create a new kind of magical energy. How does that strike you?"

"Sure, why not? As though solar thought were directed and masculine, but it takes the feminine component of emotion to arouse it."

"Maybe . . ." Changing tone: "Don't you get the feeling we are off course, Orsina? Jung's writings have been growing on me, but I fear that's a dead end. It may be one aspect of alchemy, I mean as a kind of pre-psychoanalysis. But isn't this supposed to be the real thing—magic?"

"Wasn't Jung a bit of a magician?"

"So one biographer tries to make out, but—"

Orsina had hung up. Perhaps Nigel had come home. This was getting ridiculous, Leo thought as he made a note of what he was about say, and saved it for the next time.

"The next substance is vinegar, *acetum*," Leo told Orsina the next day. "I remember that was one of the first things we talked about, when I suggested the book was a manual for newly weds."

"I've grown out of that idea."

"Yes, well, so have I. Cesare della Riviera says that this *acetum* is made from the wine through 'mechanical Magic,' by getting rid of its spirits. Then he gives the clue: *acetum* comes from *A CAElo TotUM*, 'everything from heaven.' In other words, it still contains spirits infused in it from the heavens, and he calls its power 'great and incomparable.' That's high praise. I wonder if it's a more intense inner state."

Orsina was riveted; Leo could tell, and was glad to intrigue her so. "This is beautiful, what he says next," he continued, "the vinegar causes the separation of the magic gold and silver, turning the latter into a water colored like finest azure or emerald, and the gold into tiny golden scales. This makes the magical solution that is the principal basis and key of the heroic Magistery."

Orsina made no reply, so he said: "If you were to meditate intensely in these terms, I wonder if that's what you'd see with your inner eye."

"I don't think we'll ever know unless we actually try it," said Orsina. "And something about it scares me."

"Is there something you're not telling me, Orsina?" he asked, adding in his mind, "Am I not the ideal confidant?"

"Of course, Leo!" Which question was she replying to? Was she reading his mind? "You realize," she elaborated, "that you don't have the book's secret edition."

"Ah, that," he said, again in his mind. "Yes, I do;" and aloud: "Why? Is the forbidden book so different?"

"I can't answer that. Uncle has told me things about our ancestors that anyone would have a hard time believing. I myself wouldn't have, only a few years ago. Or maybe not: now and then, when I was much younger, I had. . . . Oh, never mind. Anyway," Leo recognized an impending mood swing, one of the traits he enjoyed so much about her in spite of himself, "keep doing your homework, now. Be a good boy. Good-night, my dearest."

Leo hung up, repeating the last two words over to himself, trying to get their exact intonation.

With electrodes attached to his head, Leo had taken the VEP, or visual evoked potential test. Dr. Elander had explained that the VEP's objective was to test the optic nerve's ability to send information to the brain. He was checking the results before Leo's eyes. The neuroophthalmologist had a long record of research work conducted in hospitals and, especially, in psychiatric wards.

"I see nothing remarkable here, Professor," Dr. Elander commented at last.

"Good." Leo breathed with relief and added, "Could you take the electrodes off my head?"

"Not yet. Let's try something else."

The next test, Leo was told, was called ERG, or, electroretinogram. "It tests the rods and cones, a group of receptor cells around the macula."

Leo realized that he was sweating and that his heartbeat was rushed as Dr. Elander and his assistant, an equally thin and serious young man, busied themselves behind a complex-looking machine. They both acted in a very methodical way, which exasperated Leo. Maybe he did not want to find out what had caused his blindness anymore; maybe he should be content with the fact that it had not happened again, and stop looking into it. Had he *imagined* being unable to see? What was he thinking? He remembered vividly his vision with Angela, naked and inviting; then the abyss; then the impenetrable darkness that had lifted from his eyes only hours later, at the hospital.

"Good enough," said Dr. Elander, and asked his assistant to remove the electrodes.

Without another word, the doctor concentrated on the results. Some interminable minutes later, he said: "Professor, nothing remarkable transpires from this test either." Then, he gave him a piercing glance. Leo dreaded and yet expected the logical question: "Are you sure you went blind? Or did you only imagine it? Or invent it? And if so, why?"

Leo didn't know what to think anymore. The doctor waited for a while, and since no answer came, he eventually told him to go to the waiting room and collect his thoughts there.

Sitting alone in the waiting room, Leo was no longer sure he wanted to know anything. Also, he was beginning to doubt his own version of the facts. Maybe he had fallen in the dark, hit his head, and remained unconscious for a long time. A contusion in the back of the head, he had been told, could account for temporary blindness. But no trace of contusion had been found. Again, he was sweating. He was now also beginning to feel embarrassed. What if the doctor thought he was hallucinating? Or lying? Or—

"Professor, could you step inside?" the assistant asked. "Dr. Elander is ready to see you."

The doctor's face gave nothing away. Leo was invited to have a seat. They were now in his studio, with no machines in sight, but rather framed diplomas and shelves crammed with books. The doctor seemed still to be expecting an answer, but Leo kept quiet.

"Here's what I can tell you," Dr. Elander said at last. "I confirm that there is no organic basis for your episode, and no residual damage to your eyes or in their components. Now," he added in a different tone, "would you mind describing exactly what you remember doing *before* the episode?"

"I told you already, nothing special."

"Are you sure, Professor?"

"Well, all right: I was doing a sort of meditation," Leo confessed at last, "but something completely harmless, like daydreaming, or—"

"What sort of meditation? Transcendental? Or something religious, like the Spiritual Exercises? I've been around Georgetown enough to know that those exercises can cause strange reactions."

"No. I was meditating on the earth and its relation to the stars."

"Yes? Go on, there's no reason to feel embarrassed."

"I was thinking about heat and light, and the ideas became very strongly visual. Then I seemed to go into a world of colors."

The doctor tilted his head, as though a new idea had occurred to him. "Were you sexually excited?"

"Not before the episode, but during it, yes, I was," and how on earth could you guess that? Leo added in his mind.

Finally, Leo told Dr. Elander nearly everything about his vision, except Angela's specific words to him. The doctor listened making just enough remarks to encourage Leo and put him at his ease. At last he said:

"I want to put an idea to you that you should hold just as a possibility.

"The visions you have described show a gift for eidetic imagery. Now is it possible that the temporary blindness was also, paradoxically, *part of the vision*? You did dial 911, I know, but somnambulists have done as much. But perhaps you were not fully awake until your eyesight began to return, when you reached the hospital."

"I suppose anything is possible . . ."

The doctor continued. "Then consider the idea for a week or two. It doesn't matter whether you accept or reject it, but your attitude will affect how we proceed." He held out his hand. As Leo took it, the question came unwanted into his mind: was it worse to be blind or mad?

# FOURTEEN

While Nigel was at the language school, Orsina was busy arranging for Angela's move to England. Their uncle was reluctant to offer anything beyond economic support. Orsina felt that he did not look forward to Angela leaving home, so she had tactfully looked into the arrangements herself. She spent what seemed like hours a day on the phone with different offices and departments at the University of Bristol, and collecting paperwork from various dusty offices in Venice.

With Nigel's course nearing its end, Orsina decided to reward all concerned by throwing a party. She invited not only his classmates, but the six or seven language teachers and all the other pupils. "The trouble is," she said to him, "there are too many women. We need some men. Young men, preferably." She suddenly grinned. "What if we asked Angela? She has plenty of young men in her villa-hopping crowd."

Nigel expressed mild concern; she should propose it to her sister, but Angela must promise to bring only respectable males, "No drugs, and no Bunga Bunga!" he laughed, trying out the Italian slang for the louche parties of Silvio Berlusconi.

"Would you like me to ask Rupert, too?" Orsina said. Rupert was Nigel's son, the only offspring from his previous marriage, now at an elite business school in Switzerland.

"Go ahead, ask him," Nigel replied.

Typically Italian, the party was arranged at the last minute, in a state of frenzy. The night before the party, Orsina and Nigel worked until very late with Soma, Bhaskar, and specially hired help. Orsina was giving directions in the kitchen when her cell phone rang. And rang. She had left it in the salone and could not hear it. Nigel at last picked it up, and was surprised to find Leo, that unassuming American professor, calling his wife at one in the morning, and from Washington. A few awkward pauses followed; then Leo had a brainwave and said: "I have the information she needed about Angela's university. Could you please let her know I called?"

Leo hung up and punched his fist into the palm of his other hand in anger at his own stupidity. He had been excited about his progress with *The Magical World*, and could not wait for Orsina to know about it. It hadn't crossed his mind that her husband might answer her cell phone.

Later on, at four in the morning, Orsina called him back. She had no time to listen to his decipherment but, in a voice so low he could hardly hear, said: "I'm happy to hear of it, but *please* don't call me again. Nigel doesn't understand these things, and it'd worry him. In fact, he knows very little about the forbidden book, doesn't have a clue. When Uncle gave it to me at our wedding, he thought it was just another family quirk. Anyway, I promise I'll call you regularly, at about this time. Goodnight."

"Oh well, that settles it," Leo said to himself, deeply embarrassed, after he had hung up. "I'll just have to wait."

On the day of the party, a crew came to hang Chinese lanterns on the branches of the great plane tree in the garden, and from the cornices of the ballroom. The guests started to arrive at sundown: the language school contingent by vaporetto; the imported males, many of whom had brought their own partners, by water taxi or in their private gondolas. Angela had talked Orsina into hiring a band well known to the villa-hopping set, three unwashed and half-starved kids from Vermont. They had come on a no-budget tour of Europe, and somehow lucked out with the private summer parties in the north of Italy. The band was already playing from its station in the stairwell. "We can hear them quite well from there," said Nigel. "It's quite enough without having to look at them as well."

Rupert MacPherson had come by train. He had visited the palace only once before, for his father's wedding. The fifteen-year-old Angela had made a deep impression on him when he was seventeen, and he looked forward to seeing what two years had done to her.

Nigel and Orsina greeted him. "Great to see you!" said his father affectionately. "How was the journey? Good. Get yourself a drink. Angela's around somewhere." Rupert felt isolated in a crowd of total strangers. It seemed that everyone was evaluating his Swiss haircut, his glasses, and his conventional tuxedo.

"God, they're a decadent-looking lot," he thought as he passed the long sofas of the portego. "They dress like the models in fashion magazines, and every single one is smoking." The American and Japanese students, ignored by the Italians, formed separate clusters. He comforted himself with the thought, "I bet they wouldn't survive half an hour in Business School Lausanne."

Rupert found Angela in the private salone. She was slouched on a sofa, dressed—barely—in a short strapless dress with a vivid cubist print, chunky modernist jewelry at ears, neck, and wrists. On her left was a young man sporting designer stubble on his macho jaws; on her right, a lanky aesthete in a black silk shirt. She was turning first to one, then to the other, giving them long and passionate kisses. Rupert was appalled. He would have sneaked away, but she noticed him and cried out: "Rupert! Is that you? Wow, you've grown! Come over here and join the party!"

He crossed the room, hesitantly.

"Augusto," she said, turning to the aesthete. "This is Rupert, my sister's husband's son. Gherardo," turning to the other, "Rupert." The young men exchanged an uninterested glance, then lit cigarettes. Rupert noticed how fashionable and sleek they were in their nonchalant way. His outstretched hand lingered for a while, untouched. Every small incident so far had contributed to embarrass him a little more. Angela must have noticed, because she said: "What now? Why are you blushing? Rupert: are you still a virgin?"

Not even at his cruel English boarding school had Rupert been so humiliated. "No, of course I'm not!" he blustered.

Angela burst into laughter, and so did Gherardo and Augusto, while Rupert's face grew as red as a ripe tomato.

"Perhaps he prefers the English vice," said Gherardo in Italian. She ignored the sneer and said: "Come with me, Rupert. Let's see what we can do about that. We may find just the right girl for you. Ciao, you two. Have fun." Without a further glance at her two beaux, she jumped up and led Rupert from the room.

She remembered him as a good-looking older boy, well-mannered but awkward; now his frame had broadened to match his height. She had led him away on a whim, but there was something disarming about his innocence. She felt no urge to mock him as they walked around the great palace, exchanging comments on Venice, the guests, his father, and her sister.

After a while, Angela suggested that they find something to eat. Rupert was so flattered that she had decided to latch onto him, so entranced by her looks, her poise, her perfume, that he mentally forgave her. They filled their plates and went to sit in a quiet corner.

"I hear you're going to Bristol."

"Yes. Some kids have gone there from the English School in Padua—that's where I've been. But I don't know what to expect."

"It's better than Oxford or Cambridge socially, and just as good academically. I went straight from school to the Business School Lausanne, but I know a lot of chaps who went to Bristol. You do speak awfully good English. What are you going to read?"

"Philosophy, Politics, and Economics." She spoke, astonishingly, like a schoolgirl rather than the frivolous young socialite he knew. "Three pretty boring subjects. But my teachers say I'll do all right."

"Of course you will," said Rupert, adding mentally, The men will be all over you.

"I suppose you'll come back to Italy for the holidays?"

"Yes, this is my home. Not so much this place as the Villa Riviera."

"Dad's told me that's a beautiful place. I hope he'll invite me there some time, though I gather it belongs to your uncle."

"What has your dad told you about Uncle Emanuele?"

Rupert hesitated, then said weakly: "That he's a true aristocrat."

"I bet he said more than that. But I won't ask. Emanuele doesn't care whether people like him or not. I like your father, but they don't have much in common."

"That's for sure."

"We've both got odd situations, haven't we? I'm an orphan, and your parents are divorced. Where's your real home?"

"At the moment, it's Lausanne, and when I graduate it'll be wherever I get a job. Probably in the States. My mother's moved to Scotland and remarried. Dad lives in three places at once, as you know."

Angela was silent for a moment. "I wish you were going to be in England. We could see each other."

"Bristol's not far from London. You can come up on weekends and stay at Dad's flat in Kensington. I could fly over for some weekends and meet you there."

"Yes, I'd like that. And maybe I'll stay in England. I'm sick of . . . this life." She paused, then jumped up. "Let me show you the palace. We still need to find you an alcove, you know, for your first experience." She smiled mischievously. "And there's rooms I've never been in."

By now Rupert would have followed her to the ends of the earth. She led him down the service stair to the androne. With a nod to Bhaskar, still on sentry duty, she took a flashlight from a shelf and opened one of the doors. "At high water, this whole place is flooded," she explained, "so the rooms are almost useless. They've mostly been sealed off, but you can go in some of them. This used to be the kitchen."

They entered a vaulted chamber with enormous fireplaces at either end. One of them still held an array of rusty spits, wheels, and complicated ironmongery. A massive oak table stood to one side, its surface deeply concave from centuries of chopping. "They used to roast whole oxen here."

Angela unbolted another door, which led to a complex of storage rooms filled with empty tubs, bins, and barrels. When they reached the last one, Angela pointed the light at the corner, where an enormous barrel stood. "Look at this! A servant once showed me: it's a fake barrel. You can swing these—whatever they're called—open and get inside. The servant wouldn't let me go any further. He said the ceiling might collapse on top of me, or something like that. But there's supposed to be a passage leading to the garden at the back, and a whole lot of rooms."

"I'm game to try it," said Rupert, coming off a bit pompous. "If only he cracked some jokes," Angela thought as he swung the staves outwards, courteously held them open for her, then joined her in the narrow space. They could see that it led to a passage in the thickness of the outside wall. After several yards it turned abruptly to the left and passed a massive iron door; then the brick floor turned to dirt. Angela stopped. "Look," she said, "someone else has been here. There are footprints."

After another turn, she stopped again. "We must be under the garden by now." The passage opened into a broad cellar, vaulted in stone. Broken barrels and other debris cluttered the floor, but that was not what caught their eyes. As Rupert swept the light around, it revealed something horrifying.

Angela squealed, and turned to him clutching his arms. For a few seconds he felt acute terror, till his brain circuits clicked, and he saw not the tentacles of a giant octopus, but the roots of a tremendous tree.

They entered from the ceiling, spread in all directions, and plunged down through the floor like the columns of a grotesque cathedral crypt.

"The roots must come from the big tree behind the palace," said Rupert with awe. "Dad told me it's the oldest tree in Venice." He walked up to it, trying to see what lay beyond.

"Enough!" said Angela, still frightened. "I want to go back." She took Rupert's hand again as he turned back to reenter the passage, but when he reached the studded door, he stopped.

"Look," he said, "it's got a modern Yale lock! That should be no problem so long as it opens inwards. I always get into my flat this way when I forget my keys." He got out a credit card and wiggled it into the crack beside the lock.

"Rupert, I don't want to go any further," said Angela, her voice now urgent.

"O.K.," said Rupert, but curiosity overwhelmed him, as well as the feeling that, in a sense, this was now *his* palace too. He pushed the door a few inches open and peered in, scanning the room with the flashlight.

The room was much neater and more used-looking than the other underground chambers. Perhaps sixteen feet along each side, it had whitewashed walls hung with dim portraits. In the center was a square stone table. Or was it an altar? At its four corners, long-handled axes protruded from bundles of rods. On it were some glass and silver objects which Rupert could not recognize.

"This is creepy," he thought. "What has Dad got himself into?" Angela was pulling on his arm. As he still did not move, she reached past and snatched the flashlight from his other hand, leading him willy-nilly back through the passage, through the barrel, and back to the androne. Without a word they returned to the main floor. Angela was sulking, to the exasperation of Rupert. "I'm sorry, I didn't mean to scare you," he said, hoping for her playful mood to return. He could have added that it hadn't been his idea to go and explore the palace's bowels, but he didn't. Angela slowed down and stopped by a window, open onto the Grand Canal. It was an absurdly romantic view, but the look on her face was a worried one.

"What is it, Angela? What's wrong?"

"It's got nothing to do with you, Rupert. You're a sweet guy, but leave me alone now. Good night."

Rupert did not move; he stayed put, but not as a challenge to her wishes. He looked concerned, and felt bad for her. She must have perceived this, because she said, in a whisper:

"I don't know why I'm like this, Rupert; I really don't. I tire of everything and everyone pretty fast, but then I realize that maybe I'm really tired of myself, and so I sulk. Yes, I know you're thinking I'm a spoiled brat, with nothing to complain about."

Rupert wanted to say that he was not judging her, but she didn't let him. With a tremble in her voice, she went on:

"Sometimes I feel as if I'm losing it all, as if I'm spinning out of control." She paused, then smiled, and added: "But then I figure that I'm just afraid of going away from home. I'm very attached to my family, especially since I've lost my parents."

She paused, and looked away, in the distance. Rupert sensed that she was not finished, but did not rush her. Eventually, she turned back her head, her hair wafting in the nighttime breeze, and looked at him. "It's a very deep bond," she added, "nothing that an outsider could understand." She smiled again, sweetly oblivious of any offense she might have given. "But I do like you," she concluded. "I must go now." Without another word she made straight for her own room.

Rupert lingered by the window, absorbed in thought. He did not know what to make of Angela. At the same time, he felt for her. She was certainly very attractive, and perhaps she wasn't just whining. He reflected on his very small experience of the female universe, and how he must change that. But it was too late for that night. He took a last look at the Grand Canal and went to bed in the little third-floor room assigned to him.

Two hours later, a few guests watched from the gothic windows and balconies as the pearl colors of dawn spread over the sky. Then almost everyone went to sleep. It was midday before the last of the guests surfaced for coffee. Later still, Orsina surveyed the aftermath and wondered what Emanuele would have thought of the night's revelry. Fortunately music leaves no traces—unlike black rubber soles on a polished wooden floor, thought Orsina as she crossed the ballroom. The workmen had already unstrung the Chinese lanterns, but "How stupid: they've left their ladder behind! Bhaskar, please put it away somewhere."

Rupert had to catch the overnight train in order to be back in Lausanne on Monday morning. After Nigel had seen him off at the station, he realized that his son had never mentioned Angela, though they had been together at the party. He was not sorry, because charming as she was, Nigel did not want Rupert drawn into her milieu. Those young people, too rich too soon, would never make anything of themselves for want of a challenge. At best, they might end up like Orsina's eccentric uncle. As these thoughts passed through his mind, Nigel also reflected on his own tendencies. "But I've *earned* the right to enjoy life's pleasures!" he said to himself; "there's a difference."

Angela had left with the villa-hopping crowd. Soon afterwards, Nigel and Orsina loaded up the Ferrari and her Alfa. They were to stay at her uncle's for two more weeks, come back to Venice for the Historic Regatta, then resume their normal life of leisurely commuting between Provence and London.

Nigel was back to the same occupations: driving his Ferrari deep into the vineyards in search of the perfect Amarone, and lately other wines too. Angela often accompanied him, saying that she wanted to speak English like him, not like her teachers. They would return with cases of increasingly rarer vintages. And then, for no apparent reason, Angela would sulk, and speak hardly at all at dinner.

The Baron did not seem to notice. The villa was swarming with his sympathizers. Some were actually camping on the grounds, in a meadow half a mile to the east of the villa. "Out of sight, mercifully," Orsina had thought. This had been a gracious gesture on her uncle's side. He had begun a new cycle of lectures "About the simple statistical truth," as he explained to her when she enquired, "that history does not repeat itself. I touch upon the Holy League and the Battle of Lepanto, *inter alia*. Young minds, I've noticed, always need a bit of color, not so much to substantiate facts, but to fire their imagination."

"Uncle can't help preaching," thought Orsina. But even he, lately, had been quieter. Perhaps he was realizing that being a teacher is hard work; perhaps this would lead him to change his opinion of Leo. But then, Orsina wondered, what did it matter? As far as her uncle knew, he had merely been a fleeting guest, not the man she had loved and with whom she had hoped to slough off the obligations she had been born to. Even now, married, settled down, and the heir apparent to an ancient dynasty, she was always delighted to hear his voice. Still, to her uncle, Leo was a nonentity.

A few days elapsed, and Angela continued to be listless, joyless, and incapable of sustaining a conversation. Nigel said that when they went wine-hunting together she was her normal self. But afterwards she ate little, complained of headaches, and went to bed early. Orsina had never seen her sister in this state, and after dinner went up to Angela's room to try to find out what was wrong with her.

Angela wasn't there. Orsina walked downstairs, and chanced into Marianna. Had she seen her sister? Yes, in the garden.

"In the garden?" wondered Orsina; and then added to herself, "Alone? And where's Nigel?" She hastened toward the garden, saying hello to a number of young strangers, all dressed in black: Uncle's students.

There she was, alone, under the tulip tree. Orsina sat down beside her.

"Angela," she said, delicately, "I've been worried about you lately. Are you sick?"

"No. I just have a headache."

"Is that all?"

No reply.

"Is something bothering you?"

"No."

"Is it Gherardo, or Augusto?"

"Neither."

"How about Rupert? You haven't mentioned him at all since the party. Did something happen?"

"No, other than we had a good time together. I took him down into the cellars, just for fun. I've never dared to go there alone; have you?" Orsina shook her head. "But I got scared and I think it upset Rupert, because he didn't talk to me after that. He just went off to bed."

"Did that upset you?"

"Me? No, good riddance! I don't care for him. He may become interesting twenty-five years from now; he's got a lot of growing to do." Angela turned her face to the side, evidently uncomfortable in her sister's company.

Orsina took a deep breath, and asked the question that had been on her mind for a few weeks: "Is it something about Nigel?"

"Nigel? No!" The vehemence of the reply did not reassure Orsina.

"Are you sure? You can tell me, Angela. Please trust me."

"I told you already: no."

"If it's not that," Orsina continued, relieved, "please tell me what's wrong. Are you anxious about Bristol?"

"Anxious? I can't wait. I may find my own Leo—just as good-looking, maybe a little more . . . manly?" She looked at her sister wickedly. Orsina ignored the comment, and pressed on.

"What is it, then? You're not yourself. Are you sure you're not coming down with the flu?"

"Boring . . ."

Orsina kissed her sister and made to leave. Then Angela spoke: "Orsina: I do have something to tell you."

"Yes?"

"But not now; I'll tell you in the morning."

"Why not now? Why wait?"

"I can't think straight with this headache. I must sleep it off. I'll tell you in the morning; really, I will. I'll feel better then. Good night, Orsina." She stood up, and hugged her sister. Then she left the garden, swaying her hips.

"Headache or not," said Orsina to herself, "that must be the way she walks."

That same day the Pope had spoken from the window in St. Peter's Square, in Rome. Since the bombing of San Petronio, the congregation had been dwindling. The huge square used to fill up with people. Now there were more gaps in the crowd than the Vatican would care to admit. After leading the recitation of the "Hail Mary," the Holy Father said:

"Brothers and sisters, do pray for peace on Earth. Our erring brothers, the Muslims, are beginning to mend their ways. No longer do they take our lives in the house of God. They violate our temples, that is true. But this must be interpreted as their willingness to open up a dialogue with us. Soon, they will no longer engage in sacrilege; soon, they will meet us in the spirit of brotherly love. We must be patient and pray to the God Almighty: may He guide them in this process. The sons of Abraham will soon prosper in peace, united under the same just God. Let us pray."

The Pope had directed his words, and then prayers, heavenward. Had he looked down he would have seen that many, perhaps most of the crowd, were leaving.

# FIFTEEN

In Europe, the tension escalated daily in response to the acts of sacrilege. Mosques were desecrated in return, even set on fire. Skinheads and gangs found a new outlet for violence, and even ordinary people took to the streets in their tens of thousands to wave banners and demand action against the "invaders." Muslim immigrants kept out of sight in fear of their lives, and the jobs they usually did were left undone. This too was blamed on them.

"That's curious," the Baron said at breakfast, taking his cue from an article in the morning paper. "The French demonstrating en masse, and not for fewer working hours! They must be really incensed."

"Why, yes," said Orsina. "But then, complaining in France is a national pastime." "True," the Baron replied. "I must admit in that respect I prefer the British: they are not nearly as excitable."

"I agree," commented Nigel. "And that's why we have moved to Provence."

"Nigel, welcome back to the conversation," said Orsina. "You're no longer sleepy?"

The old housekeeper shuffled in and placed a jar on the table, announcing: "The blueberries are ready, and I've made the Baronessina's favorite jam."

"Thank you, Marianna," said Orsina. "We'll let her open it when she turns up."

"I suppose the jar will remain unopened?" said Nigel. "Shouldn't you wake your sister up, Orsina?"

"The jam can wait. Angela was not well last night," Orsina replied. "She may be getting the flu. If she isn't up by eleven, I think we should call a doctor."

"Eleven o'clock?" Emanuele interposed. "Noon may be more realistic. Your sister is *not* very disciplined. Did you say something about the flu?"

Orsina nodded.

"Well then, she either has the flu, or one of her love affairs has gone awry again," he said. "Who could keep track of them all? Perhaps Bristol's boreal climate will cool her off. Her attending that university may not be such a bad idea after all."

"If Angela's genuinely sick," interposed Nigel, "we should be taking better care of her." Did he have reason to say so? wondered Orsina as she looked at her husband.

The Baron excused himself and Nigel went for a stroll in the garden. Orsina lingered in the breakfast room sipping tea and enjoying the local newspaper with its provincial flavor.

At around noon, Orsina went upstairs. Angela's room was empty; the bed was made. Orsina knocked on the bathroom door No reply. She entered: also empty. As she walked back downstairs, she chanced on Marianna. Had Angela's bed been made already? she asked her. Marianna called for Samanta, who eventually bounced in. No, she had not made the bed because she had found it untouched.

Orsina walked around the house, calling for Angela. In the library she found Emanuele, going over his notes for his evening lecture. "Have you any idea where she could have gone?" she asked him, her voice beginning to show some worry.

"No. Have you looked for her in the garden?"

Orsina searched the rest of the rooms, then the garden. She found Nigel sunning himself and talking finance on the phone. Seeing that she was upset, he quickly ended the call. "Is she still missing?"

"Yes. Could you see if the Vespa is there?"

Nigel returned shortly. "No, the Vespa's gone. I'm sure I saw it last night, beside the cars."

"Could you look all around the courts, and in the coach house?"

"Of course."

He returned within twenty minutes. Orsina was waiting under the tulip tree. "No, the Vespa is not there either."

They tried calling Angela's cell phone.

"*Sì?*"

"Angela, where are you?"

"I'm sorry, *Baronessa*, it's me, Samanta." She had picked up Angela's cell phone, which was left in her bedroom.

Orsina thought for a moment, then decided to speak to her uncle.

"Has Angela gone missing before, Uncle? Is there something about her you have not told me?"

"Are you quite sure she's not around somewhere?"

Orsina described her fruitless search and stood her ground, waiting for an explanation. The Baron folded his papers, took off his reading glasses and said: "Orsina, your sister is rash and unpredictable. There have been a couple of instances in which she left without telling anyone."

"Why?"

"You know, boyfriend problems. We always traced her back to the chalet. She has the keys. No, there's no use in trying to call her there: the other times she unplugged the phone." The family owned a chalet in Ortisei, in the Dolomites, in which they used to celebrate Christmas together.

"You never told me, Uncle. Why?"

"What for? To make you worry? And then pass judgment on your sister? The first time, if you must know, she had gone to the chalet to be on her own after her boyfriend left her abruptly; the second time, she eloped there with another boyfriend."

"You may be right, Uncle," said Orsina. She left the library, not yet ready to raise further alarm bells by mentioning Angela's promise of the night before.

At lunch, no more was said about Angela, but the mood was subdued. Nigel sensed his wife's anxiety, and over coffee said: "Would you like me to go and look for Angela?"

"Please," replied Orsina.

"Where did you say the chalet is? Wait, let me get my GPS."

The itinerary was simple. "I'll phone you the moment I know anything," said Nigel, who had changed his shorts for a loose white linen suit. "And you call me if she turns up here." He roared off.

After about an hour and a half, past Bolzano, the road became curvy, with tunnels, spectacular high bridges, and different gradients in its ascent toward the Brenner Pass.

The tortuous road challenged his driving skills, but it was more a sense of urgency that made him exceed the 130 kilometers per hour speed limit. Shortly before the exit at Ponte Gardena, right after a tunnel, a car from the highway patrol lay in ambush. As the Ferrari 365 GT sped by, they gave chase. Nigel saw them in the rearview mirror and slowed down. Soon he ground to a halt in the emergency lane. The police car stopped immediately behind him.

Three policemen got out and strutted up to him. They were black-haired, swarthy, and looked self-important in their neat uniforms.

"Your papers, please," said one of them, as the other two were busy admiring the Ferrari. Nigel handed him his driver's license and, after a little rummaging in the glove compartment, the registration and proof of insurance. The patrolman scrutinized the papers, then walked back to his car, and loaded the data into the computer.

Meanwhile, the other agents began to ask Nigel questions about the Ferrari. He replied in his best Italian, which so resembled the pronunciation of Laurel and Hardy—"Stanlio & Ollio"—in their Italian-dubbed versions that his wife found it difficult not to laugh. And so did the policemen. They too tried to mask their laughter in broad smiles, or by looking the other way, toward the peaks of the Dolomites surrounding them. Finally, two of them asked Nigel to open the hood, "Just out of curiosity."

Nigel obliged them.

As the two patrolmen ogled at the warm and inviting V-12 engine, the third one left the police car and approached Nigel. He was a new recruit and wanted to impress his chief. Thse papers were in order, he announced. But could he show him the "triangolo" and the orange vest?

"The *triangòlo*?" wondered Nigel aloud. The novice patrolman thwarted a smile, and explained: "Yes, the *trìangolo*. You're supposed to have one on board. It's the law." He was referring to a red triangular reflector which a driver is supposed to place fifteen yards behind his car, should it break down, to signal the following traffic to avoid it. Nigel had no clue that he was supposed to have it, nor did he know if the previous owner had placed one somewhere.

The chief and his partner were enjoying the intricacies of the perfectly restored 1967 engine; so the young recruit decided to be helpful, though it was not his place to suggest to the driver where the reflector might be. "You may wish to look in the trunk," he said. "That's where it usually is."

"Is this really necessary?" asked Nigel.

"If you don't produce it, I'll have to give you a ticket."

"Well, go ahead then, give me a ticket!" Nigel snapped. And added: "I'm in a hurry, so will you get on with it?"

Normally, a policeman would say: "You want a ticket? Fine, suit yourself." But these were not natives, but deep southerners, typically touchy. None of them had appreciated Nigel's curtness; it was an affront. So now, instead of expediting things, they would slow them down.

"What's the problem?" asked the chief.

The recruit explained. In the meantime, the Ferrari's hood remained open, and the various papers in the hands of the young agent.

"*Signor* MacPherson," said the chief, "I really think you should look for the reflector. Will you please open the trunk?"

Nigel frowned. He was not used to being ordered about, and so it seemed to the police, who enjoyed being obeyed all the more for that. Finally, he got out of the car, walked to its back, and opened the trunk.

The agent stared for a moment, then shouted: "Boss, boss, come here quick!"

The other policemen reached the back of the Ferrari, and saw the body of a young woman huddled in the trunk. The chief cursed, and then lowered his forefinger half an inch away from her nostrils, carefully avoiding touching her. He waited, thirty, forty, fifty seconds for a sign of life. There was no exhaling or inhaling.

Angela was dead. Her eyes were closed; her face, composed; her flaxen hair, sheeny.

The three patrolmen turned to Nigel with a feral look in their eyes. Before he could say anything, they had handcuffed him, forced him into the back of their car, and locked him in. They summoned by radio the police, both the criminal investigation department and the forensic unit.

Back-up forces arrived quickly on the scene. Nigel was moved into another police car, belonging to the criminal investigation department, and taken to the police headquarters in Bolzano, the capital of the Alto Adige subregion. The other police units, with the medical examiner and crime lab among them, busied themselves with a meticulous survey of the dead young woman and the car, particularly its trunk, taking photos, looking for fingerprints, hairs, and so on. It was not until late in the evening that the magistrate on duty, who had come to the spot in person, authorized the removal of the body and of the car, which was impounded. Angela was taken directly to the morgue, in Bolzano.

At around 6 p.m. Nigel, still handcuffed in the police headquarters and guarded by two agents, was informed that he was under *fermo di indiziato di delitto*. He was not familiar with Italian legal terms and, while some policemen in the station spoke German, nobody spoke English.

He did understand that the prosecuting attorney was on his way for a preliminary meeting.

By law, Nigel was entitled to a single phone call, and that to his lawyer. His cell phone had been confiscated, and he was asked to provide them with the phone number. Nigel had his lawyer's card in his wallet.

"Chief," said the policeman with the card in his hand, "it's a foreign telephone number, abroad. Shall I still dial?"

Nigel's distress turned to terror. What if they didn't call his lawyer, what then?

"Look at him," said the chief policeman, and then, addressing Nigel: "You're shitting in your pants, aren't you? Don't you worry," he added, "if we can't get in touch with your lawyer, the court will appoint one for your defense. This lawyer of his," to the agent holding the law firm's card, "where is he from?"

"It says 'London' here."

"London, ha?" to Nigel, "Well, England is a member of the European Union. You're entitled to call. Dial up," to the agent.

Mr. Rowes of Rowes, Bloom & McGilles, could hardly recognize his client and friend, stripped of all nonchalance. It was a desperate Nigel MacPherson who was pleading with him on the phone. To make sure that it was indeed Nigel, the lawyer quizzed him about a couple of complex litigations he had handled for him. Amazingly, the answers were correct: that frantic voice on the line must belong to Nigel.

Within a few minutes, Mr. Rowes grasped the situation. Nigel vehemently protested his innocence and his shock at the horrible discovery. He needed a lawyer more than he needed oxygen. "A *criminal* lawyer, now!" Otherwise, he was going to be assigned to some hack, perhaps German-speaking.

Mr. Rowes listened gravely, and then said: "Nigel, pay attention. I'm not a criminal lawyer, but this isn't entirely uncharted territory for me. I don't know the Italian penal code, but I do know that Italy is a civilized country and no one could possibly arrest you, as there too you are innocent until proven guilty. This leads me to believe that you're probably being held provisionally. Do you follow me?"

He did.

"So," Mr. Rowes continued, "an investigation will be under way very soon. You do realize, it *is* rather nasty circumstantial evidence to be caught speeding towards the Austrian border with the dead body of your sister-in-law in your car's trunk. Don't tell me she was beautiful." She was. "Oh dear. And," the lawyer wondered with sudden curiosity, "how old was she?"

As Mr. Rowes heard that she was going to turn eighteen soon, he added, resolutely: "Nigel, I'll arrange everything. Tomorrow morning a top criminal lawyer from Milan will turn up to defend you. Count on it. Now, tell me exactly where you're being held. I need details."

The prosecuting attorney who would be coordinating the investigation and the police Inspector he had chosen for the case arrived at the station shortly after, together. The former, called in Italy the Pubblico Ministero, or PM, came from a rank-and-file background. Tall, slender and graying, with a pair of keen eyes, he had the well-earned reputation of being incorruptible. Both he and the Inspector hardly acknowledged Nigel's presence and went straight to read the statement the police had typed up in verbose officialese. Then the PM addressed Nigel. He introduced himself, and said that his consent was needed for them to inform his relatives. By law they were expected to do so, if he gave consent. Did he?

As long as they did it tactfully, and as long as they informed only Angela's uncle, who was her legal guardian. "Please, do not speak to my wife, the victim's sister. Her uncle will tell her."

In spite of himself, the PM was amused by Nigel's accent. Under strain, it sounded all the more comical. "And what is the name of the victim's uncle?" As he heard, "*Barone* Riviera della Motta," the PM asked the Inspector for a cigarette. A '67 Ferrari on the run; an Englishman as the main suspect speaking Italian like "Stanlio & Ollio"; a Baron—the investigation promised to be a circus.

Nigel watched as the PM himself called the Baron. There were complications. A manservant with an odd accent told the PM that the Baron was engaged. He should wait a minute, and he would pass him on to the Baroness. Before the PM could make the connection, Orsina was on the line.

She was surprised to be hearing from the prosecuting attorney of the criminal court in Bolzano. Was something the matter?

"No," replied the PM, collectedly. "I merely wish to speak to the Baron, if you please."

"The Baron is busy at the moment. Can this wait?"

"No, it can't. I must ask you to put him on the phone."

Orsina, increasingly more worried, complied.

The Baron was greatly annoyed at being interrupted. He did not care who was on the phone. What could a petty prosecutor want from him? From where? Bolzano? What on earth did he want?

He found out, as the PM told him what had happened. "Our condolences, *Signor* Riviera della Motta," he purposefully avoided addressing him by his title of nobility, which the Italian Republic does not recognize. "Mr. MacPherson is being detained; there will be a preliminary interrogation tomorrow at Bolzano's court. Mr. MacPherson here asks that you break the news to his wife."

"Tell her I'm innocent!" Nigel shouted. The PM had already hung up. "See you tomorrow," the latter said. "You're spending the night in custody."

During the phone conversation, the Baron had paled. Then he had been taken ill. Orsina found him on the floor, writhing and gasping for air. She called for Giorgio, who immediately phoned the family doctor, a friend of the Baron's.

"His pulse is weak, and I've injected him with a stimulant," the doctor told Orsina half an hour later. "He should be O.K., but I'll check on him regularly for the next few days. Make sure he gets plenty of rest."

After the doctor had left, the Baron, in a thread of a voice, told Giorgio to ask Orsina to his bedside. Holding her hand, he passed on the PM's news, and saw the expression on her face grow from alarmed to distraught. At first, she could not believe it. It couldn't possibly be a joke, could it? It would be in such terrible taste. But the tragic look in her uncle's eyes spoke volumes. Soon the two of them were weeping in each other's arms.

The tragedy was all the more appalling as it was utterly unexpected, and so horribly compounded by Nigel's involvement. Could he really have anything to do with this? Could he have killed Angela? *Killed* her? No, no, no, he couldn't have! Why? What on earth for? Orsina had tried to ask her uncle these questions, but her sobbing continued uncontrollably, and she only asked them in her mind.

She kept chewing over the questions as she drove straight to Bolzano. She had managed temporarily to swallow her own tears and concentrate on the driving. Ever since their coming to Italy, she had had a sneaking suspicion that Nigel might be having an affair with Angela. But she must be misjudging him; why would he do such a thing? And most of all, that wouldn't prompt him to kill his lover. "Kill his lover"—as this vision materialized in her mind's eye, she nearly lost control of the car, and started crying all over again. The tears in her eyes clouded her vision, and she barely managed to pull over in the emergency lane and stop the car before she gave in to her grief.

At 10 p.m. Orsina finally reached Bolzano, and soon afterwards the police station. Eventually, she was told that her husband was spending the night in prison, and that no visits were allowed. She then mustered her courage and asked about Angela. She was at the morgue and, as her sister, she was allowed to go see her. "In fact," added the duty officer, "we would have called you or another relative to come and identify her. It's routine procedure."

Two policewomen drove her to the morgue, and made her wait in a neon-lit, white-tiled room. Overcome by grief, she shivered as she wept inconsolably.

Shortly after midnight, Orsina was able to see through her tears her sister, lying lifeless on an examination table, a lunar pallor eclipsing her rosy complexion. As she bent down to kiss and hug her, a policewoman was about to stop her, but the nurse said, "It's all right; the autopsy has already been done."

Orsina spent the night in a hotel in downtown Bolzano as Nigel went through all her anguish, and more, in his prison cell.

The next morning, Nigel was transferred from the prison to a room in the court. Awaiting him there was the criminal lawyer Mr. Rowes had been able to secure for him. "Thank God!" Nigel thought. Avvocato Alemanni was perfectly shaven and smiling in his close-fitting Caraceni dark gray suit. "Mr. MacPherson, a pleasure to meet you, although I wish it had been under better circumstances." He shook hands and introduced himself. His English had a strong accent, but was grammatically perfect and very precise, as Nigel listened to a long explanation of how he normally broke down his fees. They were exorbitant, but that was not one of Nigel's worries.

"We have a little time before the interrogation. It's your right to speak privately with your lawyer. Please, tell me all there is to know."

Nigel began by protesting his innocence; related the events of the previous day; and ended by protesting his innocence once more, as well as by expressing his immense shock and sadness at Angela's death, and last but not least his great concern for his wife.

The lawyer listened keenly as he fixed his gray eyes, expressionless as oysters, on Nigel's face. An outstanding and celebrated defense attorney, unbeknownst to Nigel, he was said to be able to judge whether or not a client of his was innocent on the first meeting, simply by listening to the client's version of the facts. Nigel did not know this.

"Now, Mr. MacPherson: Is this what you intend to tell the PM?" he asked after a pause.

"Yes—it's the truth!"

"Is it?"

Nigel controlled himself, and repeated, gravely: "It is the absolute truth. This is all I know. I don't know how Angela's body ended up in my car's boot, and I don't know who put it there. I have no idea if she was dead when she was placed in the boot, or if she died in it. What I do know is that I'm *innocent*."

"Because, you see," continued the lawyer, as if he had not heard Nigel's protestations, "it is fully within your rights *not* to answer a single question during the interrogation; and at present I would advise you not to do so."

"Why? I have nothing to hide. I *want* to protest my innocence."

"Very well, then. But stick to what you told me, exactly."

"As if it were a fabrication? Avvocato, there's nothing to stick to but the truth!"

"Of course. Just adhere to your first version, the one I heard."

The PM had just received the autopsy report from the medical examiners. He read it twice, then called one of the doctors and asked a few questions. Before the interrogation with Nigel, he realized that he urgently needed to talk with the Inspector he himself had selected for the case. He had changed his choice of the day before, and picked one who might be more suitable for this particular investigation. The PM had been informed that Mr. MacPherson's defense attorney would be Alemanni, arguably Italy's most controversial criminal lawyer, a man who thrived on publicity and who, above all, won most of his cases. The afternoon of the previous day he had spoken to a "*Barone*." A manservant had initially answered the phone. These people smelled like money. This was going to be a high-profile case. It appeared lurid enough even if Mr. MacPherson had not been driving a vintage Ferrari with the corpse of his wife's underage sister in the trunk. In fact, the PM had gathered all the information his office could find on Nigel, and realized the extent of his wealth.

The new Inspector was the son of a skiing instructor from Cortina, one of Europe's most exclusive skiing resorts. His father had taught the rich how to ski and he, as a child and then a boy and a young man, had made friends with many rich kids, from Rome, Venice, Milan. Now in his late thirties, tall and handsome, blonde, blue-eyed, and elegantly suited to the limit of his budget, he almost looked like one of them. If nothing else, reasoned the PM, he had been around rich people enough not to harbor resentment against them or, even worse for the sake of the investigation, feel awed. Inspector Ghedina was summoned to court. Unusually, the PM wanted to tell him personally of the autopsy's results.

"The cause of death was cardiac arrest."

"At seventeen?"

"Exactly. Our medical examiners have already managed to get in touch with the family doctor: the victim had no congenital disease of the heart, rheumatic fever, nothing: she was healthy. No, we think she's met with a violent death. That's what the examiners have inferred, and put in their notes. They believe something must have caused her heart attack. What exactly, they're not sure, and leave the conjecturing to us."

"How helpful and how kind," said the Inspector. "Very well: has anything been found on her body?"

"Only a small erythema on her neck. You'll be inspecting the body yourself later. The examiners have noted that, in all likelihood, it is a . . . hickey."

"A hickey? Last time I checked, that didn't cause a heart attack."

"I know, Inspector, I know."

"That's it? No traces of violence on her body?"

"None."

"Then we must be dealing with a very economical murderer," the Inspector remarked. "No fingerprints on her body, right?"

"Right, how did you guess?"

"Again, it fits the profile of an economical murderer. They tend to be careful. Any hairs not her own?"

"No, neither on her, nor in the Ferrari's trunk. Some hairs have been found inside the Ferrari; they will be analyzed and matched. We wouldn't be surprised if they belonged to Mr. MacPherson, but as the car's owner, that would mean nothing."

"Traces of blood, semen, saliva?"

"No."

"Mucus? Fragments of nails? Cuticles?"

"Nothing."

"Anything underneath her nails?"

"No."

"Then, have the medical examiners concluded that the victim has not engaged in sexual activity prior to, or during, her death?"

"They could find no indication of sexual intercourse. But we may presume that there was foreplay."

"Foreplay? Oh yes, the hickey. Any other clue on her? Anything unusual?"

"Maybe, and maybe not: traces of soap have been found all over her body. But the doctors have pointed out that she merely might have taken a bubble bath shortly before her death."

"The soap brand?"

"Not yet known."

"Could you have them reexamine her? They may still be able to determine the brand."

"All right, consider it done. In fact, let me ring them right now." The PM had the cell phone number of one of the experts.

The medical examiner said that he would return to the morgue with a colleague and, together, do their best to determine the soap's chemical composition, though it might be already too late. The traces were faint in the first place. They had only mentioned them because in their experience of post mortem examinations they had never come across a body with so many traces of soap on it. When the PM hung up, the Inspector asked:

"Has the time of death been established?"

"Between 1 and 3 a.m., yesterday."

"Really?" This detail piqued the Inspector's curiosity. "Are the examiners quite certain?"

"They are, and I deliberately chose very skilled experts. They're not local police doctors; they teach at the University of Verona, and have assisted the police many times before. They've earned their reputation in the field."

"In that case, the question arises of its own accord: where was the suspect you're holding at the time of the victim's death?"

"We'll find out soon. Or at least, we'll find out what he has to say about that. I'm due to interrogate him." There was a pause, then the PM resumed. "I think you should drive down to the villa and interrogate relatives, staff, whoever was there yesterday."

"I think that I should have been there already, Sir!" Inspector Ghedina got up.

"Maybe. Well, take your best men and go. I'll call you later and let you know what comes out of the interrogation."

As the PM was meeting with Inspector Ghedina, Orsina had been allowed to meet with Nigel, in the presence of two guards and defense attorney Alemanni.

Nigel was holding her hands; she could hardly hold back her tears, and he hated every atom of his own body: being there was so unjust, it was absurd. He protested his innocence with Orsina, and then tried to comfort her over the loss of her sister. But Orsina was divided in her mind. Something in her could not allow her to trust him completely. During her sleepless night in the hotel room, she had been going over all the times Nigel had gone away with her sister; many times, perhaps too many. Why would he bother taking her along? And she, the flirtatious spoiled brat that she could be, very young and very beautiful, did she get a kick out of playing temptress? But even if that had been the case, why would Nigel kill her? Why? No, he couldn't have. There was no motive, and her husband was not insane.

The PM did not allow Orsina in the interrogation room; only two guards, a clerk, an interpreter, a stenographer, and the defense attorney. At first, he explained to Nigel why he had been, and was being, held: circumstantial evidence pointed strongly at his involvement in the murder of Angela Riviera della Motta. Then he let Nigel relieve his feelings. He repeated to the PM what he had told everybody so far, protesting his innocence all along, and fervently. When he was done, a visibly satisfied Alemanni asked the PM if his client's provisional detention was not too drastic a measure?

"The interrogation has not even begun, Attorney. Let us not be hasty. Now, Mr. MacPherson, Italian is not your mother tongue. If you don't understand my questions, let me know, and we'll ask the interpreter to step in. We have hired her just for you.

"You realize that this is a formal deposition. So, whatever you say, will be used as evidence."

"I know, and there's nothing left for me to add to what I just told you."

"Is that so? I'll be the judge of that. Where did you spend the night between the day before yesterday and yesterday?"

"At Villa Riviera."

"Who was with you?"

"The members of the family."

"Names, please."

"My wife, Orsina; Angela; their uncle, Baron Emanuele."

"Is that all?"

"Yes. Then there was the staff: Dumitru, the butler, and his wife Afina, the cook; Marianna, the old housekeeper; Samanta, the chambermaid. Oh, and Giorgio, the Baron's secretary. And the gardener, Giuseppe. I think he lives in a house on the grounds."

"How did you spend the evening?"

"Doing precious little at the villa; reading magazines, checking my wine guides for more explorations." He explained what he meant.

"And where did you spend the night?"

"In the bedroom that's been assigned to my wife and to me."

"Doing what?"

"Sleeping."

"Alone?"

"No, with my wife."

"At what time did you fall asleep?"

"How would I know? I don't normally look at my watch when that happens."

"Oh really? And we may not look at *our* watches and let you rot in prison for years unless you answer my every question to the best of your abilities!" The PM had spoken quickly and in a raised tone of voice. Nigel asked if the interpreter could translate, and did not like what he heard.

"I can't say exactly when I fell asleep, your honor, but this I can say: both my wife and I were in bed at around midnight."

"Did she fall asleep first?"

"Yes, she did."

"Do you sleep, in the villa I mean, in a double bed?"

"No, we sleep in two separate beds, one next to the other."

The interrogation continued for a couple of hours. Then Nigel was escorted back to prison. The PM explained to the over-eager defense attorney that, as per Article 390 of the Code of Penal Procedure, he would be asking the GIP (the judge for the preliminary investigations, to whom he reported) to validate Mr. MacPherson's provisional detention.

Alemanni objected eloquently, but he too had to await the GIP's decision.

The next day, the GIP, having read the police and the PM's statements, the post mortem report, as well as the transcript of the interrogation, validated the continued provisional detention of Mr. MacPherson.

Soon after the interrogation had ended, at the urging of the PM, Orsina had driven back to the villa, escorted by a police car. She was expected to put herself at the disposal of Inspector Ghedina.

# SIXTEEN

"Please accept my condolences, Baron, on this tragedy in your family," said Inspector Ghedina. "You understand that I have to ask you a number of questions." He felt as welcome as a toothache, but years of professional practice had made him grow accustomed to the feeling, and then indifferent to it. The Baron was distraught. Sitting in an armchair in the drawing room, he looked dwarfed by the imposing surroundings, the image of helplessness. The Inspector cleared his voice and asked:

"Could you tell me where you were the night of the victim's disappearance?"

The Baron cringed as he heard the word "victim." Eventually, he said: "After dinner in the villa, I drove to my studio, about two kilometers south of here. I stayed up until some time past midnight, preparing my lecture for the following day. Once I was done, I left the studio; came back here, to the villa; and went to sleep."

"At what time?"

"I couldn't tell you exactly. Some time before one in the morning, I think."

"Did anybody see you? A member of the family? Of the staff?"

"I don't know; ask them."

"These lectures you mentioned, *Barone*: to whom are they given, and what is their subject?"

Emanuele shot him a fierce glance. "Inspector, I've just spent one of the worst nights in my life. My doctor has ordered me to rest. Could we please speak about my hobbies some other time?"

"I won't tire you out, *Barone*. As for what is relevant or irrelevant, at this stage nothing can be ruled out. So, please, explain, and—let's try to make things a little snappier, shall we?"

Had the Baron been his usual self, he would have made the young man regret his impertinence. But in his present state, he just obeyed. "Over the years," he said, "I have attracted a wide audience of young people. They appreciate my analyses of European history in the light of the *philosophia perennis*."

"Sorry, what was that last word?"

For a moment, the Baron seemed to recover his poise. "*Philosophia perennis*: the ancient philosophy common to all cultures. I assume that it helps them to understand the difficult times in which we live."

"Do the students pay a fee? Are you connected to a university?"

"Nothing of the sort." The answer was brusque.

"Do you have repeat students? Do you know any of them personally?"

"Must you really ask all these questions, at such a time, Inspector?"

"Baron, you must help the investigation all you can. Your niece demands justice. So, I ask you again: Do you know any of these young people personally?"

The Baron was clearly distressed and exasperated, but he made a supreme effort, and tried to reply collectedly. "I avoid cultivating any personal relationship with them. I don't crave the position of the guru, the cult leader, or the father confessor to troubled youth. There's no advertisement for my lectures."

"So, how do they know about them?"

"Through word of mouth. Apparently it reaches most countries of Western Europe."

Ghedina was determined not to be impressed. "Do you even know the names of your listeners?"

"A few have insisted on introducing themselves, but I don't recall their names, and I don't want to."

"Do you know what they do when they're not at your lectures? How they get here? Where they stay, for instance? The Villa Riviera is pretty remote."

"That's their business, not mine." The Baron closed his eyes and took a deep breath, then another. His eyes still closed, he murmured: "Ask my secretary, Giorgio Moser. He lives in Verona."

The Inspector was merciless. "Roughly, could you say how many people were at your latest lecture?"

"About a hundred."

"A hundred?" Ghedina's concern showed on his face, but the Baron had not opened his eyes. "Did your niece Angela ever attend? Baron? Are you all right?" The old man's mouth had dropped open and his head lolled sideways as his chest heaved with short, labored breaths. The Inspector called for help.

Dumitru arrived, and helped the Baron to his feet. "You'd better call the doctor right away," the Inspector said, and walked out of the drawing room. He did not look forward to further dealings with a man who could move so suddenly from pomp to pathos. But he relished the chance to stroll around the villa, so different from the usual squalid scenarios of his professional life.

He reached the kitchen and proceeded to interrogate Afina and Samanta, who looked distressed. Still, he questioned them in depth until one of his policemen interrupted him. "Inspector, we've found something you should see."

"What is it, Colucci?"

"We'll just take you there, by car."

Colucci, a stocky goggle-eyed type consistently passed over for promotion, liked to make a mystery of things, and Ghedina indulged him. They got into the police car, but the Inspector had barely time to fasten his seat belt before they arrived. "What the hell is this?" he asked.

Before them, in a meadow among vineyards, were many tents. Some of their occupants were talking, smoking. "The students!" the Inspector reproached himself, "of course!" He couldn't have imagined that they camped on the grounds, yet he should have! "Colucci, call for back-up forces, immediately. Tell them to *fly* down here. I want twenty more men, with Gallorini among them."

"Inspector, shouldn't I call the headquarters in Verona? They'd get here a lot sooner."

"No, this is *our* investigation. Call our people in Bolzano. *We* will deal with the campers until then. Tell them they must race down here!"

Ghedina got out of the car and walked up to one of the young men. The other ones surrounded him. There were, he estimated, about thirty of them. "This is a police investigation," he said in a loud voice. "I want you all to follow me back to the villa." They looked at him with distrust, even hostility. "Colucci," he called, "come here." The assistant strutted into the circle and looked around as Ghedina addressed the group.

"Now, listen. I've just spoken to the Baron, and he too wants your collaboration. Is that clear? So, follow me back to the villa."

More meekly than he had anticipated, they did. Ghedina led the procession; Colucci, in the car, followed it at a walking pace. Both the Inspector and the policeman had had their Berettas at the ready all along.

They reached the villa, and the other policeman there, with no incidents. Ghedina had the two policemen round up the men in the ballroom. Then he himself stood on the podium, presiding over the Baron's students. "I have a tragedy to announce." There was a murmur as he told them what had happened; then he added: "We'll be asking you a few questions. We hope that you may shed some light on our investigation. That's all."

That wasn't entirely true: the young men standing in front of him were all, technically, suspects. They were on the grounds during the night in which Angela had been killed. That is, *if* she had been killed somewhere within the property. But he had to wait for the back-up forces to arrive, and in the meantime engage in very informal questioning with the students. If he were too intimidating at this stage, they might try to escape.

When the extra policemen finally arrived, the Inspector sighed with relief, and went into the library to use his cell phone. He called headquarters and asked them to put him in touch with a PM from Verona. The PM should call him as soon as possible. It couldn't be more urgent. Then he instructed Colucci: he and his men were to interrogate all the students, get their names, ages, etc. And press them for answers. None was allowed to leave the ballroom. To Gallorini, he said:

"Take a few men and search the grounds: the villa, all the outbuildings. The Baron mentioned his studio—that too. And the garden, the student's camp, the vineyards, the woods. Everything must be searched and inspected."

"Inspector, do we have a search warrant?"

That was Gallorini: meticulous, as one would expect from a graduate in Classics. No, of course they didn't have it yet. Ghedina called Dumitru: "I hope the Baron is feeling better. Please go to his room and ask if I may have permission to search the grounds. Let me know right away."

Dumitru was back within minutes. He put his hands behind his back, like a schoolboy making a prepared speech: "The *Barone* says thank you, he is feeling a little better. He gives you permission to do anything you need for your investigation." Gallorini was informed, and the search was his assignment for the remainder of the day and the next one too. Before he started, Ghedina questioned Dumitru, asking him first of all for his working permit, which he found in order. Then he asked many other questions. When he was done, he told Gallorini to use Dumitru as a guide in his search.

Shortly afterwards, Orsina arrived, escorted by the police car, and saw the Inspector. She was beginning to recover from the initial shock, and now felt tremendous rancor at the authorities for having detained her husband. She had gone through the succession of the events in her mind, and had realized what she had missed in her previous frantic revisitations: she and Nigel had slept together on the fateful night. No, poor Nigel was being suspected unjustly. It was outrageous, how could they do that?

"If you have to ask me something, do it now, Inspector. I'm done with all my tears, and I'm done with all my patience too!"

Ghedina enjoyed the outburst. Since the discovery of the thirty-one students, all possible suspects, he too had begun to wonder how guilty Mr. MacPherson could be. Still, question his wife he must, and did.

"Please accept my condolences, *Baronessa*. Shall I interview you here, standing in a hallway, or is there somewhere less inconvenient for you?"

The Inspector's unexpected good manners brought back the well-bred woman that she was; they adjourned to the drawing room.

Ghedina began questioning Orsina, though he focused more on Nigel than on herself. She claimed to have slept uninterruptedly from midnight until eight o'clock, and that Nigel was with her at the beginning and end of this period. What more could she say?

"No, I've no suspicion that he might have been 'involved' with my sister, if that's what you're hinting at, Inspector." She did suspect something, perhaps a fling, but that could have nothing to do with poor Angela being dead; there was no point in letting the Inspector know. "We are all fond of each other," she continued, "we spend a lot of time together, but we *are* honorable people." Was that true? she asked herself in her mind. All the aristocratic families she knew were, to various degrees, unloving and estranging, and hers was no exception.

"Do you have any idea," the Inspector added, "about who might be responsible for putting your sister's body in Mr. MacPherson's car? As far as you know, does anyone have a grudge against him?"

It was plain to see how much the situation pained Orsina. Still, she found the strength to reply. "No one outside the family even knows Nigel," she said, and when pressed: "Inspector, no member of the family could have done this to Angela. It's simply absurd that on top of suffering such a tragedy, we should have to defend ourselves."

Ghedina enjoyed looking at her, and let her speak. "Why don't you try the crowd that comes to listen to my uncle's lectures?" she continued. "I never speak to them, but I see them all over the place on his lecturing days, and some of them look . . ."

"A bit dubious?" the Inspector prompted.

"Yes," said Orsina, who had checked herself before using Nigel's term: "Fit for the gallows."

"They're being questioned as we speak, *Baronessa*. That doesn't mean that I can arrest them because of their looks."

"Of course not." Orsina paused. The Inspector was not as obnoxious as she had feared. Perhaps he could actually be of help. She certainly wanted justice for her poor sister, so she went on: "I have to tell you that Angela was in a strange mood the evening before." Orsina described their conversation, ending with Angela's promise to tell in the morning.

"Any clue about what she intended to reveal?"

"No, unfortunately. But there's something else."

"Yes?"

"Well, I don't know how to put it. . . . Many of them are the sons and daughters of old friends of the family. We refer to them as the 'villa-hopping' set."

The Inspector looked perplexed.

"Families who still own their ancestral palaces and villas, here, in the Veronese. During the summer, they exchange visits, and hop from villa to villa."

"Lucky them!" thought Ghedina, who said, "I find no harm in this."

"Of course not. But you see, some of these kids are very rich, and very jaded, and that's a dangerous combination. What I mean," continued Orsina, "is that, still in their teens, they've already been exposed to more than their due of fast cars, sex, drugs—you name it."

"Really?" he said, and then thought, "only a hundred and sixty kilometers south of Bolzano, but worlds apart."

"Yes. This isn't to say that my poor sister had any vice. But among her friends there were many bad influences. I was relieved that she was about to go to university in England, away from that crowd."

"I see. Are you suggesting that she might have hopped on her Vespa and gone to one or more of these villas the night of her murder?"

"I don't know," she said with a grimace adding, "please don't use that word. I can't bear it."

"Could you produce a list of some of these friends? I need to question them."

"I'll do that."

"Thank you. Anything else you wish to tell me?"

"Yes: I myself saw Angela walk back to the villa, late in the evening, after our talk in the garden. But it's possible that she might have changed her mind—she *was* fickle—and instead of going to bed, she might have gone out on her Vespa."

"Ah, the Vespa: another piece of the puzzle. If, as you have suggested, she left the villa on it, and met somebody, and then the . . . accident happened, how could she have returned to the villa? Who would have taken her back? And who would have put her in the trunk of your husband's car? The same person, presumably?"

"May I leave now, Inspector? You're asking questions I can't answer, and my uncle is sick."

He bowed slightly and allowed her to go. It was true, he *was* asking her questions that did not pertain to her. But it was a device he had used in the past, sometimes successfully: to encourage a suspect to offer hypotheses as to what might have happened, and then let her contradict herself, or say something revelatory that she did not mean to say. This time, though, he probably just enjoyed speaking to such a beautiful and classy woman. His job seldom brought him such fringe benefits.

Ghedina went to the ballroom to check on the progress. The students were being questioned, and Colucci was overseeing the transfer of all the data to the police headquarters, for their records to be checked. "If there are a few particularly suspicious ones, single them out, and I'll interrogate them myself." For the moment, he preferred ambling in the wonderful villa, looking for clues and inspiration. He chanced on Marianna and started asking her questions, but the old woman wept so much over the loss of the *Baronessina*, she was incoherent.

Finally, he strolled to the garden, and noticed the immense trees and the statues beneath them. He sat on a bench and made a mental report to himself.

"The students are all suspects, all thirty-one of them, if they've spent the night on the grounds, which is likely. The staff are also suspects; I would rule out the women, and Dumitru seems harmless. But again, technically, they all are; never judge by appearances, etcetera, etcetera. The Baron too, and his niece, are suspects, though I tend to think of them as indirect victims more than anything else. I'll also look into the villa-hopping crowd, and that will prove difficult. Finally, the chief suspect, Mr. MacPherson. I'll interrogate him, and for hours on end. I wonder what he might—"

A brainwave interrupted his train of thought. During what he considered his glory days as a young man in Cortina, he had been befriended by a client of his father's, a Scotsman in his forties named, coincidentally, MacPherson. He was a pretty good skier and a judo enthusiast. He even spoke some decent Italian, as he preferred to ski "on the sunny side of the Alps," and had enough money to do so often. Gianluca—the Inspector—taught him some skiing "secrets" on the slopes, so MacPherson repaid him by teaching him some judo. And, as Gianluca was a fast learner, some judo "secrets" as well. He remembered one lesson vividly: it had to do with strangulation.

"The object of strangulation in judo," MacPherson had explained to him, and then only partially illustrated, "is to cause the victim to lose consciousness. There are two ways to go about this. Respiratory strangulation, by pressing on the trachea in front of the neck; this prevents renewal of oxygen in the blood and brings about asphyxia. Then there is a much more sophisticated way: sanguineous strangulation. It consists of compressing the carotid arteries from either side of the neck, under the jawbone. This prevents the blood from irrigating the brain. Loss of consciousness comes rapidly, within fifteen seconds. By the way, if the pressure is not relieved, death occurs within minutes."

But of course! How could he not have thought of it right away? That erythema on the victim's neck, that small area of redness that the medical examiners had interpreted as a hickey, had been something else entirely. He had seen it himself, but had not realized that it was, in fact, an ecchymosis *in the making*, a bruise that had not had time to develop. The young woman's heart attack had been brought about by strangulation! And furthermore, that sort of precise sanguineous strangulation taught by the ancient martial art.

"All right, all right," Ghedina cut himself short, "so what? What does this tell me? The victim was strangled, by a very knowing hand belonging to a cold-blooded murderer." He was shocked that the detail had eluded the experts. It was his own intuition, and a good one too. The media had not written about it, of course, or even alluded to it. Presumably only two people were aware of it: he and the murderer. That gave him an edge—or did it? Of course it did: the murderer knew judo!

"Nonsense!" Ghedina said to himself. But then, on second thought: "I could find out if some of the Baron's sympathizers study judo." Knowledge of ancient martial arts, on the other hand, did not seem to fit the stereotype of the villa-hopping debauchees.

"Excuse me, sir: are you Inspector Ghedina?" The Inspector's musing was interrupted by a strident voice. "*Barone* Riviera della Motta has asked me to make myself available to you. I'm his secretary, Giorgio Moser."

The Inspector summed up the brown suit, the light hair combed to cover creeping baldness, the sharp nose and intelligent eyes. He questioned him at once.

Giorgio, he learned, had seen Angela, her sister, and brother-in-law at the villa, "but although I'm called a secretary, I don't keep regular hours. I get the ballroom ready before the lectures, and I keep track of the listeners. I have a good memory for faces, but none at all for names, and anyway names are never given. It's a very impersonal process; the Baron insists on that." As the Inspector pressed him, he produced, out of his jacket's inner pocket, a ticket for a late night movie.

"The movie ended at, what, midnight?"

"Something like that."

"And what happened next? Where did you go?"

Giorgio blushed. Ghedina pressed him for an answer.

"I . . . I went to a friend's house. It was poker night. The host, I, and two other friends usually start playing at midnight and stop in the wee hours of the morning."

"Oh, I see: a gambling den."

"Not really, Inspector, not at all!" Outside the four state-owned casinos, gambling is illegal in Italy, and Giorgio was well aware of that. "We play for fun, very small sums at best." That was not true: largish sums usually changed hands during those nights, and only solvent players were admitted.

"Right, that's what everybody says," Ghedina replied. "You will provide us with the names and phone numbers of all these gentlemen."

Begrudgingly, Giorgio agreed. Of course, he hoped that this would have no consequences for any of them; it was completely harmless, just a fun way to spend some time among old friends, and—

"Walk me back to the villa," the Inspector cut him short, "and my assistant Colucci will take care of these details. We *will* question your friends." In his mind, he added: "But this particular investigation is only concerned with your alibi, and at present you seem to be the only suspect with one."

As he handed Giorgio over to Colucci, the Inspector finally received the call from the PM in Verona he had been waiting for. From the library, where he had gone in search of privacy, he quickly outlined the unusual circumstances of the crime, and the initial stages of the investigation. Then came his request: he wanted all thirty-one students to be detained provisionally. The PM was taken aback. The Inspector explained. "It's not enough just to arraign them with a writ: some of them aren't even Italians, and they may well disappear before the date set for appearing in court. No, we need to detain them."

"All of them?"

"Yes, all of them."

"You realize, Inspector, that the prisons are overflowing with vandals?" The anti-Islamic demonstrations had given free license to all sorts of hooligans, who had smashed windows, burned cars, destroyed hydrants, vandalized subway stations, and engaged in urban guerrilla warfare against the police all over Europe. Tens of thousands of such hooligans had been arrested.

"So, what do you suggest: that we let the suspects leave, free as birds, and reach them in a month or so with a citation? I'm sure you don't mean to hinder the investigation? Do you realize this is a high-profile case?"

It was arranged: the thirty-one young men would be bussed to the police headquarters in Verona and be held in prison for the 48 hours allowed by law. It would be for the GIP from Verona to decide whether to hold them longer.

It was a busy afternoon for the police, as they set up roadblocks on every approach to the villa, even the footpaths.

Orsina, after having seen to her uncle who was weak but in stable condition, had had a long conversation with Avvocato Alemanni, who called her himself from Milan. He had been pleased to hear about the many campers on their grounds. This made him feel almost positive that her husband could not be detained for much longer. There was, however, the added complication of extradition: Mr. MacPherson was a British subject, and the lawyer was already in touch with a firm from London whose specialty was criminal law. His parting words were of comfort, but also meant to warn her: the case was already in the papers, and they should brace for the onslaught of the media pestering them for weeks. He could refer them to a security firm should they wish to hire bodyguards for protection. Orsina declined, hung up the phone, and wept.

All the students were by now in prison in Verona. Frantic phoning, texting, and web searching was taking place, as Ghedina himself questioned them one by one. Not all of the young men were as polite as the Baron had been, and police records revealed that several of them had been arrested in the past, mostly during student demonstrations that had turned violent. Of the several foreigners, two Swiss were already under suspicion for assaults on drug addicts.

When questioned, the young men corroborated the Baron's evidence in every detail. Yes, the lectures were on history and philosophy. Yes, they did not pay any fee, nor did they enroll in any formal way. Yes, he kept no record of their names. And yes, he avoided personal contact with them. Many of them had hitchhiked to the villa and camped out in a field, where no one had ever bothered them. Others had friends in Verona, stayed in youth hostels, borrowed or shared cars. Some of them had caught a glimpse of Angela, as they happened to cross paths near the villa. But no one knew the slightest thing about the Baron's family or private life.

At the villa, Orsina fell into an exhausted sleep. She woke early, feeling very little rested and still desperate: it was not a nightmare. She got up to prepare for whatever horrors the day might hold. Among other things she packed an overnight bag, to be ready to stay over in Bolzano if necessary. She collected Nigel's passport, checkbook, and other important papers.

Emanuele appeared for breakfast, worn out and pale. "Dear Orsina," he said, "I'm doing everything within my power to help."

"Uncle, how much do you know about those men who come to listen to you?" she asked.

"Almost nothing. Unfortunately for the police, I couldn't name a single one. They just turn up. I can't think what attracts them to an old man's ramblings, but," he spread his hands eloquently, "you see how it is: there's no keeping them away."

"I'm going to Bolzano to see Nigel, and I may be away for the night. Can you take care of . . . the funeral arrangements?" She broke into tears. Her uncle made a supreme effort not to cry himself.

"I will phone Montecuccoli in Venice immediately," he finally said. "Our family has always dealt with that firm. They operated impeccably when they took care of your parents' funeral. I never dreamed we'd be needing their services again." The Baron choked up. Orsina stretched her hand across the table to his and started to sob.

Leo went through the motions of beginning the new academic year, but the events of the summer preyed on his mind: the bombing of San Petronio, and the lost opportunity of Orsina's love, as being her friend and confidant was really a meager consolation. Their sheer weight felt like a physical burden. He could forget them while teaching, but the moment he left his seminar room, they came back. And there was more. His episode of temporary blindness had remained unexplained. It had not returned, but it was impossible not to worry about that, and not to think of it, somehow, in relation to *The Magical World.*

The book, even in its incomplete version, had entered Leo's life to such an extent that he was now consulting it daily. He was definitely making progress with it, yet at the same time resisting the impulse to attempt another meditation. To put it bluntly, he feared lapsing into madness. In the meantime, he had been neglecting his obligations as a Third Order member, failing even to stop by the Dahlgren Chapel, on campus, for the communal morning prayers.

Without fully admitting it to himself, he was beginning to realize that his religious commitment had worked, for years, as a sedative. The outlandish world of mysterious images Orsina had brought into his life through *The Magical World* was proving equally addictive, but also mesmerizing. This new drug did not merely put him to sleep; it was trying, it seemed, to evoke new realities and possibilities to him. He had recently read of how "the hero, without having to expose himself to the cold air, shut up indoors and sitting in his chair, can observe the exact motions and orbits of the planets; and not just watch them, but really touch them." Now, late at night alone in his apartment, he turned back a few pages and reread:

> Sometimes the celestial earth transforms itself into a high hill; then this form is destroyed and replaced by that of broad and spacious fields. This, in turn, is transformed into a limpid lake. Beautiful and alluring islands arise from it, which give birth to other rivers, other springs, and other lakes. These again return to earth and take on the semblance of hard bodies, metallic and mineral, among which one discovers precious gems, emeralds, diamonds, rubies, and the like. Then these turn into green vegetation, varied plant life, and leafy trees. Soon the more perfect forms begin to appear. While all the others vanish, the magical substance transmutes into the appearance of a lively horse, which then takes the outer form of a man or woman. This likewise falls back to earth, and suddenly reappears as a lion.

Leo read the passage once again to memorize the various stages of the apparition. Then he shut his eyes, breathed deeply, and invited them to recompose themselves in his imagination. But stopped abruptly, short of breath, while his eyes snapped open.

He had suddenly felt cold, as if a blast of arctic air had blown into his living room. His heart was racing and he was shivering as he walked to open the window. A warm breeze wafted in. He breathed it deeply, and felt better at once.

After having closed the book and placed it back on the dining room table, he had to resist the temptation to call Orsina. He wished very much to speak to her about the book, but the embarrassment of finding Nigel on the other end was still too fresh in his memory. God knows what he must have thought! Perhaps that was why she had not been calling him for a few days. Or perhaps she had gone to Bristol to help Angela settle in, and had no time for him.

# SEVENTEEN

Three days after the police had begun the investigation at Villa Riviera, Giorgio drove in from Verona. He was to take Marianna to the funeral and bring her straight back again, while Dumitru would follow in the Lancia with Orsina and the Baron. By eleven they were parked on the Tronchetto, then, together, took the launch that was awaiting them to the cemetery island of San Michele.

The exquisite Renaissance church floated like a marble galleon inches above the lagoon. A platoon of media people had lain in ambush since the early morning. It was now a small army. The Baron, Orsina, Marianna, and Giorgio managed to get past journalists, cameramen, and photographers and take their seats in the front row. Some Franciscan friars succeeded in keeping the media from entering too. Inside, many, many people thronged: Rupert, friends, acquaintances, onlookers. A scent of fresh flowers and incense was in the air.

Angela, inside her open coffin, had been placed in the dainty marble-lined Emiliana Chapel. She looked truly angelic in her otherworldly pallor. Candles flickered amid a cascade of white roses. The Archbishop of Venice had given in to the request of a very distraught Baron Riviera della Motta: there would be no Mass, but he would speak a eulogy in praise of Angela.

His platitudes for a girl he had never seen alive were perfect for the occasion. Then, a reduced orchestra with choir and soloists as well as the church's organist, performed Gabriel Fauré's *Messe de Requiem* in its entirety.

At the end, the music floated down to earth, as the lullaby of death dissolved into silence. It gave the mourners the strength to follow Angela to her final resting place, the Riviera tomb.

Two centuries ago, Canova had supplied its design. In a mound of natural rock was an open portal, and beside it a large round stone. Seated on the stone was a life-size angel, with a quizzical expression directed at the viewer. The casual visitors to the cemetery would have recognized the allusion to the resurrection of Jesus, given an approving glance, and moved on to the equally decorative tombs of other Venetian dynasties.

Had they tarried, however, they would have noticed details for which the great sculptor was not responsible, but one of his pupils, instructed by the head of the family.

The arched entrance bore small panels in relief, representing the signs of the zodiac and the twelve labors of Hercules. Peering through the grille that blocked the entrance, he would discern a vaulted chamber with a central pillar like the trunk of a tree, branching into the ribs of the vault, and many sarcophagi lining the walls. And the stone "door" of the tomb bore three Latin inscriptions in the shape of a triangle: *Sideream Amplectitur Lucem*—"It embraces the starry light"; *Sol VLtimus FVlgens Radiis*—"The uttermost sun resplendent with rays"; *MERge CVRate In UStrinam*—"Hide it carefully in the pyre." Only a very few visitors would have recognized there the three principles of alchemy: Salt, Sulfur, and Mercury: in Latin *Sal*, *Sulfur*, and *Mercurius*.

The media were awaiting the funeral procession, and the atmosphere created in the church by Fauré's sublime music was lost.

Orsina had cried all the tears she had; the Baron looked numbed. Old Marianna just could not bear it, and Bhaskar took her to the Palazzo Riviera, to rest.

"*Requiescat in pace*," the Archbishop finally said as Angela's coffin was being lowered into the crypt.

The mourners lingered in the cemetery. Besides, the vaporetti and launches Montecuccoli had hired to ferry them back to Venice were not there yet. The media delighted in having more time to film the distraught family.

Among the crowd was Inspector Ghedina. He had spent nearly five hours the previous day in Bolzano, drilling Mr. MacPherson, and had left with mixed feelings about his innocence, or at least partial guilt. The second autopsy had succeeded in identifying the soap found on Angela's body and, eventually, its brand: Jouvence's *Air du printemps*. The same soap, Gallorini had carefully noted, was found in the villa's every bathroom, even in the staff quarters and the Baron's studio. No progress on that front. So before going back to Verona to interrogate once more all thirty-one of the Baron's students, the Inspector had gone to the funeral, with a purpose that went beyond offering his condolences.

During the service he had been eyeing those who evidently belonged to the villa-hopping set. He now approached them, initially claiming to be a friend of the family. He looked the part too, he was glad to realize. Owing to the circumstances and the Inspector's good acting, the jaded young men and women uncharacteristically opened themselves to him, united in their grieving for Angela.

Ghedina spoke in polite hushed tones, listened, and appraised them one by one. In his mind he began to make a list of those he should question officially. His assistants had already obtained photographs of Gherardo and Augusto, whom Orsina had noted as Angela's latest boyfriends, and he decided that they, at least, must be interrogated. Within twenty minutes or so, he cast away his mask, explained who he was, and asked some young men and a few young women to meet him the next day at the police headquarters in Bolzano.

Colucci popped up to take care of the details—identities, addresses, phone numbers—and the stunned debauchees were obliged to submit one by one to this garlic-smelling cop in his ill-fitting black suit. As he wrote down their details, he told the young people that there would be legal consequences if they failed to appear for questioning. "It's not that we suspect any of you," he lied, reassuringly, "but you may tell us things we don't know and help us find your friend's murderer."

The vaporetti and launches had finally arrived, and most people went back to Venice. "Uncle," said Orsina on their private launch, "I can't believe it's over."

"I know. I'm sorry about the media and the onlookers. I could have had the cemetery swarming with security guards. But the more poor Angela is in the news, the more pressure is on the police to solve the case."

Orsina was about to break into tears again. She looked away from her uncle and said: "I don't think I'll be coming to the palazzo."

"Are you going back to the villa?"

"No, I'll catch a train for Bolzano. My bag's in your car. I want to be close to Nigel."

"Of course. We'll see you to the railway station."

Back in Venice, Giorgio went to the parking lot to collect Orsina's bag and brought it to her at the station. She had found a train leaving shortly for Bolzano.

"And you, Uncle?" she asked as they stood on the platform, "will you be going back to the villa?"

"I think I'll remain in Venice for a few days. Will you be staying at the same hotel in Bolzano?"

"Yes. By the way, Giorgio," he was standing next to the Baron, "could you call them—at the Hotel Greif—and book a room for me?"

"*Comandi, Baronessa*," he replied.

"Please, Orsina, do call me if you need anything," the Baron said; "Giorgio is at your disposal should you need a chauffeur, or whatever."

"Thank you, Uncle. I'll let you know." The train started to move. She blew her uncle a kiss and sat down, alone in her compartment.

For two hours she relived the events of the last few days as if in a trance, cell phone permitting. Normally, she would have turned it off. Talking of serious matters among a crowd of total strangers went against her nature. And yet she could not ignore phone calls. They might be something urgent: the lawyer, the police, the Inspector himself, her uncle.

The phone rang again. She looked at the screen but, like many numbers lately, she did not recognize it. She took a deep breath, and at the fifth ring, answered.

"*Pronto*? Who is it?"

"Orsina? Is that you?"

"*Leo*!"

Leo heard his name pronounced as if charged with the breath of life. Then the line went dead. Had he sent her roses on the sly, proposing a secret lover's meeting, this is how, in his imagination, she would have said his name in response. For the last few days he had been sick with a bad cold, and had canceled his classes. Now, feeling much better and ready to go back to work the next day, he had given in to the temptation to call Orsina and talk about *The Magical World*. But as the silence persisted, his fantasies grew darker. Perhaps Nigel had discovered that she had spent far too much time talking late at night with that American.

That was it, he resolved. He would *not* call her back. Had she lost interest in the book, and in him too? He had had his chance. It was too late now.

His phone rang. "We went through a tunnel, the line went dead."

It was her voice again. She was between Trent and Bolzano, on a crowded train.

"A train? You? How come?" he asked her.

"You don't know?" Orsina stepped out of the compartment, and walked down the corridor, looking for privacy. From the tone in her voice, Leo braced for unpleasant news, but nothing could have prepared him for what he heard.

"Dear God, Orsina! This is so tragic; I'm speechless. Perhaps you don't want to talk about it?"

"Yes I do. I *have* to talk about it; I can't bottle it up."

He could hear her sobbing over the din of the train. "Shall I call you tomorrow?" "No, no: talk to me, talk to me now."

"Oh, Orsina, I am *so* sorry. I can't believe it. And she was so young, so beautiful, and ready to go off to college. How could such a thing happen to her—to your family, after your parents and all? I'm terribly sorry, Orsina, terribly sorry." He was annoyed at the banality of his own words, but that did not matter to her: it was his voice that she needed to hear.

The line went dead again. Leo thought of Angela, and the image that came was the one in his vision: stark naked, lunar, reproachful. Goose bumps crept up his spine as he realized its significance. It had been a portent.

As soon as Orsina's train came out of the tunnel, she called him again.

"I haven't told you everything yet," and she elaborated.

"Nigel in jail? Dear God, this is unbelievable. Of course he would never do such a thing. The police must be crazy. But how did she die? Can you bear to tell me?"

"All we know is that she was found dead in the trunk of Nigel's car."

"Oh, this is *insane*."

"I know it is. But it's what we have to live with." She went on to explain all that had happened since Angela's disappearance, and finished her grim account by saying: "The police have been all over the villa, they've arrested Uncle's students, everyone's under suspicion. I think they're trying, but there's not a single clue yet."

"How's your uncle?"

"He's aged ten years in the past week. He looks like an old man now, but he put on a good face for the funeral. The paparazzi were intolerable, real scum, vampires . . ."

It was good to open her heart to someone she had no misgivings about. "Where have you been?" she caught herself asking in her mind as he replied. The line went dead again.

This time, *he* rang back and she listened to more words of comfort. The situation, she realized, was absurdly romantic: stolen phrases in a train corridor with her would-be lover on the other side of the Atlantic. Why wasn't he there, with her? What was he saying now? That he would spend the night praying for Angela? Ah, sweet fool! Did he really think that would do her any good? Hadn't her sister's guardian angel been sleeping when she needed him the most?

His next words had an urgent tone. They brought her back with a start:

"Orsina, I have to tell you this: do you remember when I called you, and asked you about Angela?"

"Yes, but that was a month ago."

"I know, but I'm afraid I had a premonition. I had the strangest vision of her, and she told me explicitly to *look out for you . . .*"

The train was screeching to a halt so loudly that he could hear it in his receiver. Had she heard his last words?

"Leo, I have to go now. We're at Bolzano. It's been so good just to hear your voice. God, how I miss you! I'll call again soon. Bye, Leo."

"Orsina, please do call me back very soon. Promise me that." She had already hung up.

Nigel was attempting to keep a stiff upper lip. His lawyer had been to see him the day before, and had explained the Italian penal procedure at great length. Seeing that Nigel still protested vehemently that anyone in the free world is innocent until proven guilty, he asked him to write him a check.

"I'll be in touch with you on a daily basis."

"I should hope so."

"Don't worry, Mr. MacPherson. I've got people out of worse cases than this."

Orsina went directly from the railway station to the prison, and arrived just in time to pay her husband a visit, late in the afternoon. Nigel was delighted to see her. While a guard stood studiously looking the other way, she told him about Angela's funeral, and that Rupert would be coming to visit him the next day. As for her, she was willing to stay in Bolzano indefinitely.

"Orsina," said Nigel, "I really can't inflict that on you. It's bad enough I have to stay here! That smooth barrister told me that he and the media will be putting so much pressure on the judge for the preliminary investigations that she'll have to let me go."

When she demurred, he continued, "Orsina, there's nothing you can do. Go home and get some rest. You look devastated."

Orsina smiled at his thoughtfulness, and said: "I don't think so. Tomorrow, for example, I think I'll pay a visit to Inspector Ghedina; he seems a decent man."

"He may be nice to you, but he drilled *me* like a bad tooth!"

"It's his job, Nigel. I'm sure he's already convinced of your innocence. And then, I'd like to meet with the PM, and talk to him too."

"Well, have it your way. I certainly am very appreciative. Thank you, from the heart." They kissed lightly on the lips. The guard escorted her out through the dingy corridors.

Back in the stiflingly Tyrolean city center, Orsina skipped dinner and headed for her room in the hotel. After showering, the thought of another night alone with her grief and her anxiety almost overcame her. But then she remembered: Leo. She had promised to call him.

At first there were some moments of awkwardness, as Orsina updated Leo on the latest developments, which had to do with her husband. Gradually, she began to speak in a more unrestrained way. There must be a limit to grieving and worrying beyond which one is pulled back; perhaps it is one's own body that does so. Survival kicks in. She was surprised at herself: she could talk. But then, it had always been easy for her to talk to Leo.

"There was something you were going to tell me about that call a month ago, when you asked about Angela."

"Yes, I haven't told you about that, but what's happened to you is so much worse."

"Worse than what?"

He told her, much as he had told Dr. Elander, about his meditation on the stars and the earth. "And then there was Angela, standing right there. I found myself floating in space beside her, and she led me to an abyss. It wasn't a comfortable meeting, but her last words were 'Look out for my sister.'"

"Why didn't you tell me about this?"

"I guess because of what happened afterwards." He spoke briefly about his temporary blindness and the tests he had taken since, in vain, as it remained unexplained.

"But are you all right now?"

"My vision returned of itself. It's back to normal, thank God."

"And you didn't want to worry me by telling me about it?"

"No."

"You *should* have told me. I would have worried, but so I should. We're in this together, don't you see?"

She described all she had been doing before the tragedy, Emanuele's visit to the Palazzo and his words to her: "You're more gifted than I." She told him also of her own progress in studying *The Magical World of the Heroes*. In Venice, its metaphors and codes had begun to make some sense, especially after her discovery in the Cave of Mercury. And yet lately, at the villa, she had been resisting it.

"What do you mean, 'resisting'?"

"I realized that it's far more natural for me to study it in Venice than in the countryside. It's as if book and Palazzo went hand in hand. Anyway, I seem to have misplaced the book now, or someone's tidied it away."

"Orsina," Leo said gravely, "I don't know how much of the book is serious, how much is just Cesare's pretentious speculation. But Book Two talks about something he calls 'vaticination,' the old word for prophesying. Again, mine's the incomplete edition, and there's no explanation as to how to go about it, which is very frustrating. Wait, let me go get it."

He was back within seconds. "Here, I've found it. It's called 'First Fruit: Transfiguration of Knowledge and Vaticination'. Here we are:

> 'Let the soul be disposed and prepared by means of the magic Tree of Life; let the senses be purged and made subtle,'

and so forth, I won't read it all.

> 'Let it become, as the ancient Magi say, a firm soul, not a falling one: then, contemptuous of every obstacle no matter how strong, in the free enjoyment of its gifts, *it can see things to come as well as things present and past.*'

"In other words, Orsina: vaticination is not only about prophesying; it's also about seeing things in the present *and* in the past. I still don't know how seriously one should take this book, though I suspect much more than you have so far. But if we could actually obtain what it promises, then we could—"

"See who killed Angela?" She choked up again, as he went on:

"And I do mean *we*. I can't leave you alone in this. I'm coming to Italy to help you. I made a vow to protect you, and after Angela's words, there's no question about it."

"Leo," she now sounded calm, "I have to think about this."

"I can take a daytime flight and be there by late tomorrow."

"Please, give me an hour, and I'll call you back."

"I'll be waiting."

Orsina felt faint, and realized that, appetite or not, she must eat. She ordered some supper from room service. Leo's offer to come and rescue her had touched her heart—but she had no place in her heart for him now, or did she?

"Leo," she told him an hour later, "I'm so grateful to you, and yet we can't do this. Do you understand?"

"No, I don't. What do you mean? That I can't be any help to you? Or comfort?"

"All of that! But the complications. . . . What would I tell Nigel? If they release him in a few days, what would you do then? And the media would pester us worse than ever. They'd want to know who you are, what our relationship is, and what they don't know, they'd make up. The paparazzi would have a feast; our photos would be in all the papers. The family name is compromised enough already. I'm sorry, Leo, but I don't see how it could work."

"I'm sorry too, Orsina. I figured it would be complicated. But if you change your mind, at any time, day or night, know that the offer stands."

"Oh, Leo, I don't know how to thank you. After the funeral, on my way here, I thought I was going insane. I didn't know if I could bear it, but you saw me through that. And I'm sure we'll see each other again—when this is all over."

She hung up and wept as she had never wept before. Had Leo wanted her three years before, she said to herself, she would never have married Nigel, and none of this would have happened.

The next morning, Orsina felt a new determination. No, she was not a maiden in distress in need of a knight. It was for her to do the rescuing.

She called Ghedina. He said that he could see her only briefly but right away.

At the police headquarters, the Inspector greeted her and asked her to his office.

"May I ask you for a favor, *Baronessa*?" He handed over to her a list of names. "These are some of the kids from the villa-hopping set that were not on your own list. I'll be questioning the ones you pointed out shortly. Are there any more you could suggest?"

Orsina looked at the names. She didn't like these youngsters, but she knew their parents and their older siblings, their villas and skiing chalets. "No, the ones I pointed out are those Angela hung around with. But she always goes to their houses. My uncle won't have any partying in Villa Riviera."

"Thank you," said the Inspector. "I have to go now, but don't hesitate to call me if you need anything. You'll be staying in Bolzano?"

"Yes, I'll stay at the Hotel Greif for as long as it takes." They stood up. As they headed toward the door, she added: "Inspector, how long do you think before my husband's release?"

"I wouldn't know. It all depends on the investigation. We may well find something soon."

Something *had* been found. Some twenty kilometers west of Verona, a peasant was working along the Adige river banks. He noticed a strange color in the water, just barely beneath the surface. As he drew by the water's edge, he realized it was a turquoise Vespa. He called the police. One of the first to be informed was Ghedina, whose heart leapt on hearing the news. He ordered a thorough inspection of the scooter.

The Baron had already returned to Villa Riviera. In Venice, the pressure of the paparazzi had been unbearable. Many just turned up at the Palazzo demanding to see him. After Bhaskar turned them away, they would lounge at the cafés nearby, cameras at the ready to take the Baron or any of his visitors by surprise. At Villa Riviera, he had Giorgio hire a small army of private guards, and now all the entrances to the property were barred.

Leo's secretary greeted him as he resumed classes the next morning, "I hope you're feeling better, Professor Kavenaugh," Mrs. Reed said. Then she handed him a copy of the *Corriere*. "Have you read this article, 'The Corpse in the Ferrari'? The victim," she added, "happens to be the sister of Orsina Riviera della Motta. Remember her? She was our intern a few years ago."

Leo pretended to be surprised. "Really? Has the murderer been found?"

"No, but our intern's husband is in a very compromising situation. I hope he had nothing to do with it. We were waiting for you to be back to write to Orsina and offer our sympathy."

"That won't be necessary, Mrs. Reed. I'll do it myself."

The newspapers had initially stuck to the facts. Then they had begun to embroider the story with their own perspectives on the case. *La Repubblica*, a national paper which leans to the left, had already run two editorials. Leo was now reading the second one.

> While the whole of Europe is on the brink of war in what may be described as a tragic attempt to resurrect the Holy League against the Islamic foe, some people still engage in their favorite pastimes. Nigel MacPherson was one of them.
>
> This man seems to thrive on contradiction. Schooled in England's best centers of learning, long ago he rejected culture, and opted instead for a business career. But never trained for it, relying instead on his instincts and his love of traveling and gambling. By trading commodities, from coffee and bananas to palladium and diamonds with everything in between, he has accumulated millions, and now, it seems, billions. He is good friends with Warren Buffett, and like him distrusts financial gurus and prestigious MBA courses.
>
> Still, he proved susceptible to the allure of ancient blood, and married the Baronessa Orsina Riviera della Motta. The Riviera family is also immensely wealthy, as down the centuries they have acquired real estate all over the Veneto region and, what is more, have been able to hold on to it, expand it, and manage its incomes shrewdly.
>
> So far, so good, at least for the characters involved. But evidently Mr. MacPherson was not content with this. He has

the reputation of a Don Giovanni, and his previous marriage failed because of it. With his marriage to the Baronessa he had meant, as the tabloids in England had reported at the time, to mend his ways. For those of you who still have not seen photos of her, the Baronessa is a beautiful woman. The two of them had decided to spend some time in Italy this summer. You are probably all familiar with this. What you could not know is that we have been conducting an investigation of our own on Mr. MacPherson's activities prior to his arrest, though technically we should write his *fermo*, his provisional detention.

Enter Angela, the victim, the Baronessa's sister. We have discovered that the bubbly and stunningly beautiful seventeen-year-old was often seen in Mr. MacPherson's company. A lover of wine, he took Angela along on many a search for the best Amarone in the Veronese countryside. Indeed, we have spoken to several eyewitnesses who could have sworn that the two of them were lovers simply by how they behaved together. And the couple never failed to make an impression, as they arrived at the various wineries in the Ferrari 365 GT.

What went wrong between Mr. MacPherson and Angela is a matter of speculation. But there is something suspect, lurid, and ultimately tragic about the situation. For the sake of justice, it is hoped that the truth will surface. Yet one cannot help but wonder: if historical minorities such as Mr. MacPherson and the young Baroness had vanished once and for all from the face of the Earth, wouldn't it be better for us all?

If based on genuine information, this editorial from *La Repubblica* had dealt a minor blow to the investigation in Italy, but a major one to Inspector Ghedina's self-esteem. How could a reporter from a newspaper dig up such potentially incriminating background information about the chief suspect, and not he? But then, during the long hours of his interrogation Mr. MacPherson had omitted to say anything of his wine-searching jaunts *with* the victim. Was this a deliberate omission? Or had he just not mentioned anything because he thought it innocent, as perhaps it was? The Inspector scheduled another interrogation: he would get to the bottom of this. Meanwhile, he instructed Gallorini to do exactly what the reporter had done: question every Amarone producer in the Veronese.

The GIP in Verona, the judge in charge of the preliminary investigation, after some arm-wrestling with the PM from the same city, had persuaded him to release the Baron's students from provisional detention. Days of interrogation and checking had produced no evidence against them. The PM, acting as a mouthpiece for Ghedina, pleaded with the GIP: some students should continue to be detained. "Which ones?" asked the GIP. Those involved with martial arts: karate, kung fu, tae kwon do, judo, and so on.

The request had seemed absurd to the GIP, so Ghedina was obliged to explain both to him and to the PM about the "sanguineous strangulation," in his view the cause of the victim's death. As a result, seven young men continued to be detained, and interrogated about their hobbies.

The media and the public clamored to know the reason for the continued detention. Both the PM and GIP responded with "no comment." The *segreto istruttorio* states that it is the duty of a judge to keep all facts pertaining to an inquest secret. Yet somehow the reason leaked, and the public's morbid curiosity reached a new high.

For all the recent advances in dactyloscopy, no fingerprints had been detected on the Vespa except for Angela's. The scooter was undamaged, not even dented. The second gear was engaged, suggesting that it had been driven by somebody into the river, whether willfully or accidentally. However, no bodies had been found, and if there had been footprints on the banks, the recent rainstorms had washed them away.

The villa-hopping youth provided no new leads either: most of them had good alibis for that night. Augusto and one other did not, and would continue to be questioned. The *registro degli indagati*, in which the name and details of every suspect is filed, continued to grow. Yet Inspector Ghedina had to admit to himself that, for all his dogged work, he was clueless.

# EIGHTEEN

The manager of Hotel Greif had been honored to enlist the Baronessa Riviera della Motta among his guests. Even under normal circumstances she would have been quite an addition to the roster; now, she was nothing short of a celebrity, with her photo in every newspaper. The hotel had been recently renovated, combining quaintly Tyrolean touches with German technology. It could use some publicity, and the Baronessa had seemed a godsend. But the manager's mood had gone from elated to worried. He decided that he would wait until eleven in the morning. Then until noon. When the bells from the nearby cathedral announced that it was midday, he took a deep breath, picked up the phone and dialed the police. Having followed the investigation in the press, he knew who to ask for, and when Ghedina came on the line, the manager told him what was worrying him.

As soon as he hung up, the manager called a friend of his, an editor at the *Dolomiten - Tagblatt der Südtiroler*, Bolzano's main newspaper, in German. Herr Silbernagl and Inspector Ghedina arrived almost simultaneously at the hotel. The manager told them: for the last two days, the Baronessa had not returned. Yet her clothes, her cosmetics were in her room. She had left no message or instructions to the staff. Ghedina asked to be taken to her room, while he rang Bolzano's prison, and asked if she had come to visit her husband. The clerk checked the register and eventually answered: "Not for the last day and a half." Ghedina knitted his eyebrows and entered the room.

The manager was anxious to explain: "The bed has been made because the maid tidied the room after the Baronessa left it, two days ago. Since then, nothing has been touched."

Orsina's fragrance was still in the air, all the more so when the Inspector opened the closet and took a look at her few clothes. On the dressing table were her cosmetics and a couple of perfumes. On her night table, a box of tissues and what seemed to be her cell phone.

"Is it possible that someone from the staff has left their cell phone here?"

"I don't think so, Inspector. I'll find out at once, but that may be the Baronessa's."

Ghedina quickly appraised the situation as Herr Silbernagl took notes. His investigation needed this development like a hole in the head. It was not enough to be investigating a nearly clueless murder case involving an underage heiress; now her sister had vanished. Was that a fact, or was he jumping to conclusions? His findings were telling: not so much the presence of her clothes and cosmetics, but her cell phone. She might have forgotten it, but would have already come back to get it; or, would have called for somebody to forward it to her wherever she might be. In her current predicament, being reachable at all times was simply too important. No, the Baronessa had probably gone missing.

Silbernagl had reached the same conclusions; both men were writing them down, Ghedina in the police report, the journalist in the sketch of an article for the next day.

For a provincial paper, the Baronessa's vanishing was a scoop, and the other Italian newspapers were quick in cannibalizing it. But, as it transpired privately, it was more than a vanishing.

The Baron, already back at the villa, had received a phone call. A stranger's voice had told him: "Prepare to pay dearly if you don't want to find your niece in another car trunk." The man had hung up before the Baron could say anything. Gasping for air, the Baron had managed to call Inspector Ghedina straightaway, and tell him the horrible news: his niece had been kidnapped, for ransom.

The Inspector pretended to be surprised. He knew about the phone call anyway, as he had been tapping the Baron's phone since the beginning of the investigation. It seemed logical to him to say: "Baron, let's not lose heart. We're already investigating this case too, and we shall leave no stone unturned."

"And a fat lot of good it'll do us!" Emanuele snapped. "You still don't have a clue about my poor niece, and now the other one is kidnapped. You're an incompetent idiot!"

There was more despair than anger in his voice. Ghedina did not comment, but said: "Your phone will be tapped from now on, *Barone*. The kidnappers will call you back to give you details. Try to keep them on the line as long as possible. Oh, and another thing," he added as an afterthought, "it's standard procedure: your assets will be frozen. Gallorini will be at the villa within an hour or so. Please, make sure that your secretary puts at his disposal the exact information concerning all your bank accounts, holdings, stocks, bonds, etcetera. It's in your best interest to cooperate."

"Go to hell!" The Baron hung up.

"Right on the money," thought Ghedina, "the standard reaction to the standard procedure." He had already taken care of Mr. MacPherson, in case the kidnappers tried to contact him about the ransom for his wife. No calls were allowed in to him in prison, except from his lawyer. And those calls were monitored and recorded.

The whole Italian Department at Georgetown had read the Italian newspapers by the time Professor Kavenaugh reached his office at ten in the morning. Mrs. Reed handed over the papers to him, but thought it indelicate to let him find out on his own. Perhaps she should sweeten the pill. She had worked at the department for twenty years, and for almost a dozen of them she had been his assistant. Professor Kavenaugh had always behaved in an exemplary way to her, the other staff, his colleagues, and the students. She owed him, she thought, a little tact, as she realized that he was an unusually sensitive man.

So, she herself told him of Orsina's kidnapping. Leo looked nonplussed. Finally he said, as he looked at the papers, "This would not be sensationalistic speculation, would it?"

"I wouldn't know, Professor, but I don't think so, unfortunately. Poor family, all these tragedies."

"It's not another tragedy yet," Leo shouted, but only in his mind, "you bird of ill omen!"

The class he was to teach was about Foscolo's epistolary novel, *Last Letters of Jacopo Ortis*, in which the poet bears his soul by mirroring, letter after letter, his restlessness in both love and politics. Normally, the Professor would put down Foscolo's nearly demented fervor to the excesses of Romanticism; that day, his students were treated to such an impassioned rendition of some excerpts from the novel, that for the first time it came alive.

Was this Professor Kavenaugh? they wondered as they watched him quote passage after passage from memory. "I knew not how to comfort her, how to reply to her, how to advise her," he was quoting Foscolo.

". . . Oh, angel! Yes, yes! Would that I could forever weep, and thus dry up your tears! This miserable life of mine is yours, utterly; I consecrate it to you; and I consecrate it to your happiness!" All but one among the young women welcomed the change—he looked so handsome when he recited those lines; the young men wondered, in their minds: "What the hell is he getting so worked up for?"

For the next class he had to teach, Leo's romantic fervor was replaced by a trancelike state. As soon as he could, he took refuge in his apartment. The news of Orsina's kidnapping had made him sick. In the bathroom, he retched until he succeeded in vomiting, mainly bile, as he had skipped breakfast and lunch. What had happened? What was going so terribly wrong? Why?

He took a long unsparing look at himself in the mirror, then moved to the living room overwhelmed by books, hating every one of them and above all himself. Galileo and Garibaldi had been happy to see him home early, yet never had they been so ignored.

"What am I?" he was thinking. "A perfect idiot. What have I made of my life? What have I accomplished? I've ruined the life of a woman, and terminated that of her unborn child, *our* child. Then I've lived as a diligent automaton for many years. I was a promising young man, too promising and too self-confident." What had he made of all that promise, and of his brilliant mind? Nothing but a couple of books and a sheaf of articles that no one wanted to read. And the one time he had had the opportunity to redeem himself, with Orsina, he had thrown it away. He had been such a fool, and such a coward too, he could not stand himself.

Jumping out the window offered itself as a suitable end to a life less than mediocre. But with his luck, he probably wouldn't die; instead, he'd land on his landlady's thickly mulched rose garden and be paralyzed as a consequence; great—more misery in store. Orsina's confession in Italy had made him realize his enormous stupidity. To cope with it, and above all with the loss, he had sworn to become her protector. He had made a vow, then offered to rush to her side, but had done *nothing*. And now she had been kidnapped, and her life might well be at risk.

He had read and reread the Italian press. The Inspector in charge of Angela's murder so far had proved ineffective. All he had was Nigel as the chief suspect. Much as Leo was jealous of him, he could not bring himself to believe that he had anything to do with Angela's death. And now, the same Inspector was also in charge of Orsina's investigation. What would he do next? Apprehend the manager of the Hotel Greif because he might have been the last one to see her?

No paper had mentioned the finding of Orsina's cell phone in her hotel room. The only journalist aware of that all-important detail was Silbernagl, who had the good sense to omit it from his article in the *Dolomiten*. He did hope that it would lead Inspector Ghedina to a fast solution of the case. As South Tyrol depends heavily on tourism, he dreaded the consequences of two back-to-back tragedies, both in the province of Bolzano.

Leo could not know that Inspector Ghedina had checked all the calls Orsina had received and made, all the way back to her coming to Italy with her husband. Leo's number in Washington had come up many, many times, and stuck out. It was the only number in the US she had dialed, and with what frequency! For several weeks she had dialed that number, and always late at night, Italian time. Sometimes very late. She had stayed on the phone for a long time, half an hour usually, sometimes more. Then, shortly before her vanishing, she had called this person many times, short calls each. Finally, when she was already in Bolzano, a very long phone call and two shorter ones, late at night.

On to something at last, Ghedina had stopped himself from dialing that number at once. It would have been clumsy to let the person know he was on to him, or her. No, he had the police trace the number.

Leo picked up the receiver and dialed. He did not have the phone number for the palazzo in Venice, so he was calling the villa. Dumitru answered. Leo introduced himself, and the butler recognized him. Could he speak to the Baron? It was urgent. Much as he dreaded it, he must speak to him. Was there something he could do to help? Were the police making any progress? Should he come to Italy and try to help them?

The Baron gave him an earful. "How could you intrude when one tragedy is heaped on another? Have you no shame, you American bastard? And who do you think you are? Never call again and get lost. Go to hell!" More than hanging up, the Baron had probably smashed the phone, judging from the "thud" Leo heard.

His pride was not involved; in some perverse way he had enjoyed being insulted, as he had spent hours insulting himself. He rushed back to the bathroom for another bout of vomiting. He wiped his face, returned to the living room and let some time go by. Then he called back the Baron.

This time, Marianna answered. She recognized him, although she was beside herself with grief. In a very emotional way, she mumbled one thing too many for Leo to grasp fully, as she spoke half in Italian and half in dialect. He did understand that she refused to pass him on to the Baron. It would have been no use, and then: "*La polisia l'è ciula.*" The police are dumb. Only he could help *la Baronessina*. "*El Baron l'è furbo come 'na volpe, e te sì orbo come 'na talpa e sordo come 'na campana.*" The Baron is as sly as a fox, and you're as blind as a mole and as deaf as a post. Leo listened gravely without saying a word. Marianna concluded: "*Mai sveiàr el can che dorme*," let sleeping dogs lie.

She then broke into tears and was no longer capable of speaking.

What did he have? A freaking bestiary! He jotted it down for clarity's sake: a fox, a mole, and dogs. He had never cared for the peasant wisdom of proverbs, but this was no time to be a snob. What was Marianna trying to tell him? That he had been as blind as a mole and as deaf as a post. What had he failed to see and hear? And she had also warned him: the Baron was as sly as a fox, and he should let sleeping dogs lie. What did she know? For a moment, he felt that she might have guessed much more than the Inspector and his minions had. Or were these merely the rantings of a desperate octogenarian whose Italian he could scarcely understand?

Leo debated within himself for the rest of the day. He tried to pray, but for the first time since his reconversion found it impossible to turn his mind in that direction. He was at his wits' end when he lay down on his bed. Perhaps he fell asleep, perhaps he was delirious. But eventually he awoke. His mind was made up.

Mrs. Maria Reed, gray-haired, gray suited, and indispensable to the Italian Department, checked into her office precisely at nine in the morning and switched on the answering machine. The first message was from Leo, who had left it at 5:47 a.m. In a voice that sounded already distant, he said that he was going to Italy on an urgent matter, and that his classes were canceled indefinitely.

"Indefinitely? What?" wondered Mrs. Reed. She listened to the message again, to make sure that she had heard it correctly. She had, and yet it was so atypical of Professor Kavenaugh. What could be so urgent? The other messages were claiming her attention. Three of them, increasingly more insistent, were from one Inspector Ghedina, from the *questura* of Bolzano. He was practically ordering her to call him back. It was a police investigation.

Mrs. Reed had married an American, but her parents had come from Italy and she spoke Italian fluently. As she dialed the phone number in Bolzano, she remembered having read the Inspector's name in the newspapers.

"Mrs. Reed?" asked Inspector Ghedina.

"Speaking."

"Thank you for calling back. We were about to call you again. Now, we don't have much time, so I'll be brief. I am investigating the death of Angela Riviera della Motta and the kidnapping of her sister, Orsina Riviera della Motta. I hope you won't mind my asking you a few questions. They concern Professor Leonard Kavenaugh."

"I don't mind," Mrs. Reed said somewhat anxiously.

"And you don't mind if we record them? Good. Now, as far as you know, is there any sort of relation between Professor Kavenaugh and Orsina Riviera della Motta?"

"She worked here, as an intern, a few years ago." She gave him all the details.

"I see," said the Inspector. He sounded disappointed. Why, was he expecting some gossip? Apparently he was, since he next asked: "Is there anything that would lead you to believe that there might be more than a professional relationship between them?"

"Not at all!" Mrs. Reed snapped. "Professor Kavenaugh is a man of impeccable ethical and professional standards. I'm even surprised that you would ask."

"Oh no," thought Ghedina, "she's a fan." Aloud: "Is there anything else you can tell me about the professor?"

Should she tell him? she asked herself.

"*Pronto*? Mrs. Reed? Are you there?"

She was. With some misgivings, she finally told the Inspector that the professor had left, bound for Italy on a very urgent matter.

"Really? And when?"

"A few hours ago, I should think."

The Inspector thanked Mrs. Reed, and said that he might call her again. "And don't hesitate to call me should you have anything to add." He hung up, turned to Colucci and said: "*Si viene a cacciare nei pasticci da solo*?" He's coming to get himself into a tight corner?

Ghedina instructed both Colucci and Gallorini to send a circular, by e-mail, to all points of entry as well as to all police headquarters in Italy: should the name "Leonard Kavenaugh," US passport number so and so, turn up, it should be reported immediately to them in Bolzano. "Immediately" was repeated twice. This was a double filter. Even if Leo should somehow manage to slip by unnoticed at an airport, in Italy any sort of hotel, even the humblest pensione, is expected by law to ask the guest for his passport, which is photocopied. The copies are then faxed to the local police headquarters.

"Colucci and Gallorini: get a clerk, somebody we can trust, and instruct him to resend the same circular every other hour until we catch the *professore. Capito*?"

A few minutes later a young, bespectacled man knocked on Ghedina's door, and entered the office saying: "May I have a word with you, Inspector?"

"Who are you, exactly?" The face looked familiar.

"I'm the clerk who's going to be e-mailing your warning on Leonard Kavenaugh round the clock."

"And what do you want?"

"To caution you, if I may."

"To caution *me*?" Ghedina was already put off.

"Yes. I've been following the Riviera investigation, and with all due respect I must point out that Kavenaugh is *not* wanted for murder, kidnapping, or even any known crime. He is merely a suspect. So, our warning will receive very low priority, especially by the local police headquarters, should he manage to get through passport control at an airport or another point of entry."

Ghedina was fuming, but said nothing. The young clerk mistook his silence as a cue for him to elaborate. "As you know, hotels routinely fax the passport details to the police headquarters, where a few bored clerks shuffle them from one pile to another; eventually, they take the time to punch the data into a computer. I think—"

"That you should get the hell out of my office, and do exactly as you are told! Is that clear?" Ghedina had roared his rebuttal, and the clerk was already hurrying back to his computer. "That young prick," he thought, "what nerve! Of course, he haxs a point, but what else can I do?"

The only female student who had not enjoyed Professor Kavenaugh's fiery rendition of Foscolo's words of longing was Claire Staines. Now a graduate student, she had been a sophomore when Orsina had been an intern at Georgetown. Even as a freshman she had had a crush on the professor. The year after, she had chosen her major—Italian—and taken all the classes he offered at her level. She often visited him in his office, after class, and he patiently indulged her. She *was* a good student. Pretty too, in a cropped, boyish way, though that did not matter to him; what did matter was that she would willingly take on extra-curricular projects such as the Italian Club and Italian Movie Month. She had not welcomed the arrival of Orsina, who often took over the Professor's duties as his teaching assistant. Not that she wasn't a capable teacher, that was not the point: Claire considered her a rival.

Leo had no clue that he aroused such interest. One day, Claire had gone to his office to discuss a paper with him, but had found it empty. She sat down, having decided to wait for him. On his desk, on top of a pile of papers and junk mail marked "M.R.—Please shred," lay a sealed envelope. "Professor Kavenaugh" was written on it in a calligraphy she recognized: Orsina's. The letter had been hand-delivered. She picked it up and smelled it. A faint fragrance of roses hit her nostrils. She thought about it for a moment, and then slipped it inside her backpack and left the office.

Claire walked briskly to her dorm room, resisting the impulse to read the letter on the way. In her room, she ripped it open with her fingers. Paper cuts made them bleed as rose petals poured out of the envelope, but she did not care. She read the letter once, then reread it. She became flushed as tears streaked down her cheeks. When her fingers stopped bleeding, she folded it carefully, tucked it back inside the envelope, and swept the rose petals away.

Now, years later, first she had witnessed the Professor's strange behavior in class, and associated it with the news about Orsina's kidnapping. Then she had read the notice Mrs. Reed had posted on the lecture hall: "Professor Kavenaugh has gone to Italy on urgent business. All his classes are canceled." Mrs. Reed had judiciously omitted "indefinitely." "Please check with your adviser for alternate classes." Claire had left at once, heading not for the counselor, but for her room off campus. She took Orsina's letter from her locked files, made a photocopy of it, and walked back to the university.

When Claire reached the office of the Dean of Georgetown College, the receptionist warned her that it was almost impossible to see Dean Throckmorton on a walk-in basis. "I'll wait here, all the same," said Claire, and sat down in the anteroom. Finally, she was admitted and took a seat, facing the Dean.

"Dean Throckmorton, I have something to confide."

The Dean was taken aback; she said nothing, but showed that she was intrigued.

"What I'm here to tell you may be of vital importance. That said, my . . . disclosure may jeopardize my status here. So, before we proceed any further, I have to ask you for a note in writing in which you promise that this will *not* be the case."

"What?" The Dean looked carefully for the words. "This is not a joke, is it?" The young woman looked too serious for it to be a joke. "Well, Ms. Staines, in my many years I've never come across such a request. Don't you think this is a bit unorthodox?"

"It is, Dean Throckmorton. But I have an outstanding academic record, and I'm close to getting my M.A. I can't risk it."

"I understand, but I'm afraid I can't promise what you are requesting."

"Please! It may be a matter of life and death!" Claire had raised her voice and now dropped it as she leaned forward over the desk. "It has to do with Professor Kavenaugh," she added.

The Dean yielded to the student's request and scribbled down a note on her own stationery. Claire read it over and asked the Dean to date it. She did.

Finally, Claire explained the whole incident of the letter Orsina had written for Professor Kavenaugh and personally delivered to him. The Dean was aware of Orsina's kidnapping, and of her sister's death. She also knew that the young aristocrat had been an intern at the Italian Department, and that Professor Kavenaugh had just left, very suddenly, for Italy. And Mrs. Reed had had a quiet word with her about an Inspector from the Italian police who had questioned her on the phone about the professor in relation to Orsina. This was no time to reprimand the student for her action. Could she see the letter? Claire handed over the photocopy of it and left the office with the promissory note.

The Dean put on her reading glasses.

My dearest Leo,

I got an extra glimpse of the truth, this morning, staring at my breakfast; I thought I heard it say: "What's the point, Orsina? What's the point in pretending?"

Here's the scenario for a match made in heaven: the sun and the moon finally meet, and there is instant recognition; so much so, that the first time they look into each other's eye, planets change course and collide. But then, oddly, they engage in hide and seek.

How many art house movies have we seen together? And the concerts! Do you think I didn't notice that you only picked harpsichord recitals and contrapuntal music from the most Teutonic of composers? So many times I felt that those pieces may actually improve if played *backwards*. God forbid if we should listen to Schubert or Chopin. But it didn't matter at all. What mattered was being together, in our proper place in the firmament.

The other day I was at the cherry blossom festival. Spectacular to say the least; and you, silly one, why didn't you come? Promise me at least that we will go together to the Valle del Jerte in Extremadura, in Spain. I've seen cherry blossoms in Japan, now here in Washington, but the ones in Extremadura are heavenly. I was little more than a child when I went there with my parents, and I remember running from tree to tree on a carpet of petals, euphoric, inebriated. Shall we get the plane tickets, Leo?

Why am I not addressing you as "Professor"? Do I still need to explain? It was absurd even on our first meeting. By the way, you've never drunk wine in my presence. Were you afraid of what you might reveal? But then, afraid? How could a "Leo," a lion, be afraid of wine? You aren't a Protestant, for God's sake! The Sufis did nothing else, though Islam prohibits it—and good for them!

When I was a child I used to help out during the *vendemmia*, for fun. We have a villa in the Veronese with acres and acres of vineyards. I was given shears and a pail and was set loose, on my own. How many bunches of grapes would I collect? Not many. I loved to wander from vineyard to vineyard, eating grapes here and there. Then, when the grapes were gathered in one of the many tuns, I and other children would wash our feet with detergent, jump in and squish the juice out of the grapes by stomping on them. Then we would drink much, so much of it, even if we were told not to. And at night we would be sick.

Our houses then were full of old servants. Many of them have died since, but one survives: Marianna, the villa's housekeeper. I had been assigned an English nanny, a spinster who would have preferred to be in charge of a boy. She was so cold, I often wondered if it was all an act? It seemed impossible to me that one could be so unfeeling. Anyway, Marianna was all the opposite, so whenever we were in the countryside, I spent time with her. She always washed her hair with vinegar, and sometimes mine too, not with vinegar, of course. She spoke to me in her dialect. At first I didn't understand, but I wanted to, so I learned it. Of the many things she said, one I remember in particular: *la Baronessina l'è dotata, angioleto.* I, the "little angel," was gifted.

Then, one day, Marianna suffered a stroke. She was taken to the hospital, and the diagnosis was hopeless. Not that anybody let me know, but I overheard my parents say so. I felt very sad. I wanted so much to help her, but wasn't even allowed to go visit her at the hospital. So, I began to *want* her to get well. I did not pray; I simply wished her well with all my heart and with all my mind.

To make a long story short, a few weeks later Marianna was back at the villa, healed. Her recovery had made no sense to the doctors, and the word "miracle" had been the only explanation.

I was overjoyed, but not surprised. Somehow it made sense that I could help her where doctors could not. Remember,

I was a child. There were other episodes in which I was able to influence events at a distance. I won't go into them now, but I want you to know that I have never told any of this to anyone.

As I grew up and began to reason the way I was taught at school, I distanced myself from all this. It no longer made sense to me, on the contrary: it scared me. So, I decided to neglect my "gifts" altogether.

From time to time there was some strange talk in our house, particularly from my uncle, Hermeticism and the like. He needed a lot of words to grasp what was obvious to me with no training whatever. Moreover, I would look at him, and see that he was not really "there," try as he might, always gloating on a mass of ill-digested esoteric erudition. My father was more like me, I think, but for some odd family tradition he was not supposed to delve into his brother's field of studies, and never did. Whatever: I was a free spirit, and found most places in Europe stuffy. That's why I came to America: to go riding with the buffaloes—but instead I stumbled on you!

And even in Rome, you were already beaming your message, though you didn't realize it, and perhaps still don't, but I doubt that very much.

That flicker of recognition when our eyes met, it wasn't "just" lovers' recognition, though that would be magical in itself. You must have read Ficino's *De amore*. There. You are as gifted as I am, Leo, but even more in denial. Don't ask me why you're gifted, I don't know. I do know that we are not just like each other. It's more than reciprocity; we *are* each other.

We haven't even kissed yet, you fool, and I'm proposing, what? Marriage? And a lot more. I'm proposing our *hierosgamos*. Even if you don't know it rationally, you must sense that through our sexual union we can participate in the condition of divinity. This truth has found its way even among the official teachings of Christianity: think of Mary as the Bride of Christ.

But maybe I'm saying too much. Let's fly to Extremadura; let's go see the cherry blossoms together, shall we?

Soon my year in Georgetown will be up. Will you let me go? That would be against nature; I can't think of any other way of putting it.

I have written to you from the heart. Your intellectual deconditioning has been very thorough, I know. But it's beyond human power to resist what is divine in us. Remember, we're not only in each other: we are each other.

Yours forever,

Orsina

# NINETEEN

There were long lines at immigration in Rome's airport. Leo, who had come through it so many times, had never seen it like this. It was overrun with policemen and even soldiers brandishing machine guns, as if the country were under martial law. Because of the acts of terrorism and desecration, the reprisals and riots, security had become the first priority in Italy.

Finally, Leo stepped up to the booth and handed over his passport. The policeman, a man in his twenties of dark complexion, looked at it and then at him. Watchfully.

Once more, he checked the photo in the passport, and then tried to match it to Leo's face. "Is this an old picture?"

"Seven or eight years old, I think. I don't remember exactly," Leo replied.

"And the passport was issued by the Italian Embassy in Washington. Why?"

"I live there, and I have dual citizenship. My mother is Italian."

"Oh yeah? What's the other citizenship?" he asked with a mistrustful tone.

"US."

"American, ha? And why do you use the Italian passport?"

"To avoid long lines when I come into Europe, though not this time, I guess."

The policeman did not seem convinced. He dialed a number on the phone, and spoke in an undertone for some time. Leo could not hear what he was saying and was getting nervous. Was something the matter?

Eventually, the policeman hung up the phone and said: "Make sure you renew your passport, and use a current picture. Next in line."

Leo went through security screening all over again, got on another plane, and flew directly to Venice. Near the railway station, also heavily patrolled, this time by *carabinieri*, he checked into a cheap hotel. He wanted to be as inconspicuous as possible, and close to an escape route.

The concierge asked for his passport and he handed it over. After some compliments on his Italian, he realized that he must have given him his US passport. But of course: it was blue, not burgundy. "No matter," he thought.

He was shown to a tawdry room with rickety furniture and light gray industrial carpeting. The bathroom was just adequate; the sheets were clean. He dived into bed and slept for twelve hours.

It was four o'clock in the morning, Venice time, when Leo woke up, numb from the effects of the two flights and the long sleep. He was very hungry, but even more in need of fresh air and exercise. Why not walk around the magical city until the cafés opened? Many previous stays in Venice had thoroughly familiarized him with the city. He dressed and set off along the Strada Nova, then changed his mind. He would probably find breakfast sooner off the tourist circuit, in a workmen's café, so he turned back and crossed the Grand Canal, heading southwest into the drab regions of parking lots, delivery docks, and decrepit warehouses.

Leo went cautiously down the dark alleys, and felt more comfortable on the canalside *fondamenta*, better lit and more open to the sky. As it was, the only signs of life were some *pantegane* looking every bit as vicious as their reputation—teeth-gnashing rats the size of plump cats. Leo kept well away from them, and his mind was soon turned inward.

His crazy decision to come and save Orsina armed only with a seventeenth-century book on alchemy had put him beyond the pale of normality, if his vow to be her savior had not already done so. He must take the consequences. Obviously the normal world was impotent in the face of recent events. But would he fare any better? In *The Magical World of the Heroes* Cesare della Riviera had built a masterly labyrinth to lure the Hermetic wayfarer, only to bog him down in deliberate ambiguities; the threads of his quicksilver discourse constantly dispersed and then regrouped in the most inscrutable ways.

Leo had reread the entire book during the flight from Washington, ending it with the usual feeling of bafflement and exasperation. He had stared for quite some time at the cover of his edition. It seemed to show the Seven Sleepers of Ephesus about to be rudely awakened by an Islamic bomb. He thought of San Petronio, Santiago, Chartres, the other churches in France, and, lately, the rococo Wieskirche in Bavaria and St. Stephen's Cathedral in Vienna; of the continuing assaults on mosques; of the demonstrations and riots in the streets of so many cities in Europe. A sleeping continent had woken up to the consequences of an alien presence, with no love for Western culture and no respect for the separation between reason and religion. But how was Leo to connect this with the book that he had just finished?

His heart called him back to Orsina. Because he had linked his destiny with her and her ancient family, he had felt compelled to plunge into the abnormal world of their forbidden book. He had tried to understand it, decipher it, make sense of it. But that, he finally conceded, had proved impossible. He desperately needed elucidations, and to obtain them he must get hold of the *real* book, the family's own manual of transcendence.

He tried to call to memory every hint about the forbidden book. It passed down a single line, apparently, being given to only the eldest son or daughter of each generation. The rest of the family knew about it, because they witnessed the traditional presentation on the marriage eve, but it didn't seem that they were much interested. He couldn't know that Angela had been reading parts of it, despite her uncle's prohibition. Did each possessor hand on his own copy, or was there a stock of them from which each received his or her own? Presumably the latter, for Leo recalled the unopened copy that he had handled in the villa library, "privately printed for the Riviera family in 1757." It was doubtless presented in just this form, so that admiring relatives would gain nothing from looking at it. Aristocratic reserve and respect for tradition would do the rest—the sort of thing, in the Baron's words, that must be "incomprehensible to an American."

As for copies in circulation, Orsina had one, and Emanuele must have another. In 250 years, probably no more than a dozen generations had elapsed, so there was almost certainly a cache somewhere, and the family secret must include knowledge of its whereabouts. It must be sufficiently hidden to prevent unqualified persons from blundering into it, but then what would happen if one of the heirs died before his eldest child was married and initiated? There must be a fail-safe system that would enable the heir, and only the heir, to find it for himself.

Anyone could read the incomplete 20th-century edition that Leo now had in his pocket. Maybe that had been released as part of the system, containing the necessary clues if only one knew how to apply them. But only a family member would know that there was anything relevant there.

If the stock were hidden somewhere at Villa Riviera, Leo's case was hopeless: there was no way he could enter and search under the eyes of the Baron, the servants, secretary, and probably the police. But, "it's as if book and palazzo went hand in hand." Those had been Orsina's words, almost her last words to him. The recollection came with pain and urgency, both intense—*almost her last words to him.* He had lost his train of thought, but managed to recover it, and with an intuition. Of course, this must be the Cave of Mercury which she had discovered, and would have explored in good time, if only. . . . He must take up her quest at the point where she had been forced to drop it, in the heart of the Palazzo Riviera.

By now Leo's meanderings had taken him through the maze of Santa Marta's working-class alleys to the Giudecca Canal. A café was open, and Leo slipped in to pee and have breakfast.

As he stepped out and walked along the fondamenta under the first rays of dawn, he tried to recall everything he had heard about the Palazzo Riviera and its inhabitants. It was understaffed, he knew that, with only an Indian couple as the permanent guardians. Orsina had described them during one of her nighttime conversations: "Like a pair of devoted dogs, who'll do anything for the person who feeds them. All they care about is to make enough money to bring their children from India. Nigel spotted that right away and bought their loyalty. They must be deadly bored in Venice, though. The house is empty for months on end, and I've no idea what they do with themselves."

With the Baron away at the villa, they probably didn't get up early, Leo thought, and this might be a good time to survey the site. He hastened his step along the Giudecca, then struck inland beside one of the minor canals.

A few people were now going to work, and near San Barnaba's neoclassic façade a boat full of fruits and vegetables was setting up as a floating greengrocery. A priest in a black cassock crossed the square and unlocked the main door of the church. Then Leo noticed two rather conspicuous shoppers: surely there weren't that many Indians living in this quarter? Perhaps the palace guardians were early birds after all.

Leo immediately sat down at a café table that commanded a view of the market boat and its customers. The Indian man made a few purchases while the woman looked on; perhaps she couldn't speak enough Italian. Then he handed her the shopping bag and preceded her along the quay to what Leo realized must be the back door of the Palazzo Riviera. It was a small green-painted door in a wall, over which were visible the branches of a giant plane tree. Leo could see that the man opened the door without using a key. He must have thought that there would be little risk in leaving it unlocked for such a short time, at this hour of the morning—unless an intruder were waiting for just that window of opportunity.

That was enough for the time being. Above all, Leo thought, he must not become a conspicuous or familiar figure. As no one had yet come to serve him, he left his table and headed for the nearest vaporetto stop.

Leo spent the day alternately dozing and planning his break-in.

At 6:45 the next morning, he arrived at the vaporetto stop again, a small backpack on his back, and this time waited in the shadows of the church, nearer to the green door. Sure enough, it opened, but this time it was only the Indian man who came out, shopping bag in hand, and walked straight toward the market boat. "His wife probably doesn't stand by the door waiting for him to return," thought Leo. Within ten seconds he had crossed the little canal, turned the handle of the service door, and was inside.

He was in a dark corridor, but off to the right a gleam showed through a frosted glass door. Surely, with only two servants in the vast building, he could lurk and avoid discovery; and as for the Cave of Mercury, to judge from Orsina's description, it might as well be on another planet. With a quick backward glance, he opened the door and closed it quietly behind him.

As his eyes accustomed themselves to the darkness, Leo saw that he had come straight into the androne. The morning light, percolating through the pierced canal entrance, revealed a magnificent staircase, two gondolas resting on trestles, like a pair of coffins, and an ancient fire pump. He quickly moved away from the service door and stood in the deep shadow behind the apparatus. Moments later the Indian came through the garden door, groceries in hand, crossed the androne, and disappeared up another staircase at the canal end. As his footsteps died away, the silence was broken only by the drip of a wall-fountain. Biding his time, Leo stared at the floor, which was inlaid at regular intervals with the family's emblem: the Tree of Life with a stylized river (for the Riviera) flowing from its roots. Right at the start of anyone's route through the palace, was it a propitious signal?

Among the many outlandish books Leo had consulted at the library in Washington after reading too much C.G. Jung, he had come across a thin volume by one Victor Émile Michelet. In it, the author explained that a proper coat of arms was built upon astrological calculations, and represented the directions indicated to the lineage by their ascendant. Both the secret and the destiny of a patrician family pulsated within the coat of arms. Down the centuries, the Tree of Life of the Riviera lineage had grown tall and strong, as if perpetually watered by the river. Lately, however, several tragedies had occurred to the family. The tree must be suffering, as if the river had dried up during a severe drought. Leo was overwhelmed by a foreboding of doom. With no water to irrigate it, the tree was destined to wither and die. It was ironic that the palazzo should be built above seawater, which does not sustain the life of either trees or humans.

Leo realized that he had been caught up in a reverie: it was cold, he had not slept enough, but it was the last thing he could afford to do at the moment. He snapped out of it and concentrated on what to do next. From what he knew of Venetian palaces, the servants would not spend their time on the *piano nobile*, the main floor, unless serving the family there. They would have their own quarters on an upper story; that was why the Indian had not gone up the principal staircase, which he could well have done, with no one to object.

Leo, therefore, would take the ceremonial way. Immediately he noticed the sculpted figures on the banisters. Their attributes mimicked the garden sculptures of the Villa Riviera and, from what he could remember, they had the same inscriptions, but they were all *putti*, cheerful toddlers aping the gestures of their elders. Was this a way of saying that the Great Work was nothing but child's play? As a trespasser in a palace, with an indefinable or even compromising relationship to the kidnapped woman, he felt horribly responsible and not at all playful.

The ballroom was still gloomy, with its windows facing every direction but east. Leo felt sure that he was not going to find the "windowless storage room" there. If only Orsina had told him more about the place during their conversations; but the architecture hadn't seemed important then. The visual impressions he had formed during the whole telephone episode that ended with her fall were of some unfrequented wing, or floor, of the palace; though everything he thought he knew about it, he was beginning to realize, was his own fantasy. He'd better make a circuit of the main floor, anyway, while no one was about. It hit him then that his actions were marked by a calm self-control, a distinct coolness that, according to Cesare della Riviera himself, belongs to the hero. He had expected trepidation, as never before had he broken into a house. But then, a hero?

All the doors stood wide open for the air to circulate, and Leo wished he could have been an inquisitive tourist free to roam; but the parquet floor creaked ever so loudly, or so it seemed to him as he explored each room on tiptoes. He recognized them all too poignantly from their furnishings as Nigel and Orsina's grand bedroom, Orsina's room from before her parents died, Angela's room, and the comfortable salone fronting the Grand Canal. He paced them meticulously and as quietly as he could, comparing their lengths with that of the portego, its frescoes now gloriously lit by the morning sun; but there was no space for a concealed chamber on that side. He was about to explore the opposite range of rooms when from an open doorway came the sound of voices—rough, female voices in some Slavic-sounding language—and moments later the noise of a vacuum cleaner. Feeling horribly exposed, Leo ran up the staircase and did not stop until he reached the top.

But here the door to the fourth floor was locked, and before Leo could gather his wits, he heard Indian voices on the stair beneath, footsteps running up, and the slamming of a door on the third floor. He could not have made a worse choice for a hiding place. The staff would be going up and down it unpredictably, and to open any door off it would risk bumping into one of them. The androne level was unsafe, because that was where everyone entered; the main floor now belonged to the cleaning maids; the third floor was presumably where the Indians lived; and the fourth floor, which Orsina had said was Emanuele's domain, was locked. All he could do was to hide out until things calmed down. As a precaution, he got some of his equipment out of his backpack: a ski mask and a toy gun he had bought in town, a 1/1 scale replica of a Beretta. If there were a showdown, he would act the burglar, threaten the staff with the gun, and hopefully get away.

There were constant comings and goings on the stair beneath his hideout. Every time they approached, his whole body tensed, and he prepared for the worst: he would kick someone downstairs if he had to. The acoustics of the empty palace amplified everything: voices, both

Indian and Slavic, vacuum cleaning, the clatter of crockery, nameless errands. Whenever it subsided for ten minutes and Leo began cautiously to creep downstairs, a door below flew open again and footsteps approached, stopping just short of the uppermost flight.

Leo felt the urge to pray, but seemed blocked from access to his habitual phrases and invocations. He turned his mind inwards, hoping to find there the familiar words and moods of the Rosary, but his soul, too, was like a block of ice. It was as though he had left his Christian world behind him when he determined to follow the ancient pagan symbols of *The Magical World*. Other gods and goddesses than Christ and the Virgin were active in this place, and if he wanted help, perhaps he must call on them.

But how absurd: he could not and would not pray to Apollo or Artemis! Yet what were these pagan gods? According to the teachings of the book, they were the sun and moon within man: the sun of his higher intelligence, the moon of his natural energies. Between them, as figured in that sculpture in the villa garden, they generated the Philosophical Child, the newborn Hero. Was this what he was becoming, against all his training, beliefs, and self-image?

There was no one to pray to, then, but himself: to that serene and frozen self that seemed to stretch above him like a protecting roof. *Est deus in nobis*: there is a god within us, as some pagan poet wrote. He was his own guardian angel. With an effort of will, all the harder since it felt like the defiance of a taboo, Leo addressed it. The words that came were, unexpectedly, the so-familiar phrases of the *Veni, Sancte Spiritus*, Come, Holy Spirit, and "Water what is parched, straighten what is crooked, bend what is rigid . . . " Turn everything into its opposite, even his faith in powers greater than himself. To the Hero, none such existed. He was god and man in one, like Hercules, taking the place of Atlas with the weight of a frozen sky on his shoulders.

Perched on the top step and perfectly still, Leo waited like a stealthy predator. After two hours or so, the body asserted its rights and demanded food and drink. He had neglected to pack any, but then he had not expected to spend so much time in the palazzo. An hour later, Leo no longer had any choice: good burglars just don't wet their pants.

The cleaners had been silent for some time, and the only sound now was from a television—no, more like some Bollywood video—coming from the floor beneath. He slunk down the stair to the *piano nobile* and went straight into Angela's bathroom, only just checking the automatic habit of flushing. Then he drank from the tap, avidly. Feeling ready for anything, and wishing that he'd been this bold hours before, he entered the north range and passed through the dining room and kitchen. His heart leapt as he came to a corridor, with a door leading inwards. Perhaps it was child's play, after all, he thought as he entered the dark room.

Orsina had mentioned a stepladder on wheels, from which she was unable to reach the key in Mercury's hand. Then she had lost her balance, but slithered down a pile of folding chairs and tables. There they all were, as Leo's flashlight now revealed. And there was something else that couldn't have been there before: a tall, metal extension ladder, folded up but still reaching almost to the ceiling. And of course there was an electric light. From a windowless room, who would see it? He switched it on, still shuddering at the "click."

Nothing stirred. He slid some old rags beneath the feet of the cumbersome ladder and started moving it around the room, an inch at a time, until it rested by the ascending Mercury figure. He felt that he was almost levitating as he climbed to the vaulted ceiling and took the iron key out of the plaster hand. He laughed a little crazily when he saw that it was shaped like the Mercury symbol. In order to open the cave door, he had to descend the ladder and move it a little further.

Finally, at three o'clock by his watch, he was ready. He shouldered his backpack, turned out the light, turned on his flashlight, and, ten feet above the floor, fitted the key to the lock.

To his surprise, the door opened inwards of itself, and a loud musical sound, like the twanging of an out-of-tune banjo, shattered the silence of the room. But there was no going back. Leo bridged the short gap between ladder and doorway and swung himself inside. Turning around, he pushed the door back into place and locked it with the key. Behind the door, he saw the cause of the sound: a device of springs and wire strings that were plucked when the door was opened. The lyre that Mercury gave to Apollo! Of course, the God of Thieves *would* equip his cave with a doorbell, or a burglar alarm.

The space in which he now stood was just a landing, from which an extremely narrow spiral staircase went up and down. As far as he remembered his orientation, these stairs must be contained in the thickness of the wall between the Cave of Mercury and the ballroom. He could hear the television more clearly than before, which was reassuring. Even if the servants had heard that twang, they would have no idea of what it was, or at least so he hoped. They probably didn't even know that this stair existed. As for him, he had had enough of the upper regions, and this time he was going down. "*Coli umbras inaccessas*," the book had said: revere the inaccessible shades.

Leo counted the steps in order to keep his sense of where he was in the palace, but the tight spiraling caused a momentary vertigo. When at the fortieth step the stairs ended and a narrow corridor opened before him, he guessed that he was at the canal level of the androne but had no idea of the direction. The corridor led directly to an oak door, which opened easily and, as soon as Leo was past, closed behind him with a discreet click. Suddenly nervous, he tried the handle: it had a modern lock, and had locked itself.

For the first time, Leo came close to panic. Had he been fool enough to get imprisoned in an inaccessible and soundproof cellar? He could feel his heart pumping as he shone his beam around.

No, there was another door in the opposite wall, standing a few inches open, so there must be another way out. The relief caused a lightheadedness, as he explored the room with his flashlight.

Leo realized immediately that this was a kind of alchemical family shrine. There were portraits in dull golden frames, presumably of ancestors, and in the center of the room a solid stone altar the size of an average dining table. The only other pieces of furniture in the room were an iron-bound chest and a baronial chair, almost a throne, with a fat red cushion. There were bronze rings let into the corners of the altar, and slotted into these were four fasces, also apparently of bronze, standing about six feet high, with their ax-heads pointing outwards. The table held four candles in baroque silver sticks, and beside each candle, placed with meticulous symmetry, a glass decanter or alembic containing dark, cloudy liquid. Around the base of each, a complicated geometrical figure was engraved into the stone. The center of the table was occupied by the Riviera arms, and laid upon this was a silver casket.

Leo did not waste time admiring the interior decorations or the way the room was evidently waterproofed and climatized. He cautiously opened the casket—might that entail another surprise by Mercury?

No; he was staring at what he had hoped to find: a book, magnificently bound, secured with metal clasps.

On closer inspection, he read the title on the spine: *Il mondo magico de gli heroi*. Here it was at last: the forbidden book! It seemed as if his heart stopped beating, and an immediate rush of dizziness followed. Gasping, he managed to stir back to consciousness, as he involuntarily hyperventilated. Then, he plucked up courage, and stowed the heavy tome in his backpack.

He made for the other door, forcing it far enough to squeeze himself through and leaving it open. There was no longer any point in disguising his tracks—which he now saw himself to be adding to other footprints in the muddy corridor.

From the increasing dampness, Leo guessed that he was now outside the palace walls, and this was confirmed when he arrived at a long vaulted cellar.

Here and there, the ceiling was dripping, and there were puddles on the floor. Most remarkably, the roots of a tree were growing down through the ceiling, then penetrating the floor. Or had the cellar been excavated around tree roots already there? Their size was so great that Leo realized they could only belong to the giant plane tree he had seen in the garden. Among them was another stone altar. What rites had gone on here in the family's glory days?

More urgent than answering that question was finding a way of escape. Leo could see only two possibilities: trying to find another way back, or taking the dark passageway at the far end of the vault. Without hesitation he took the latter; if he was already under the garden, it made little sense to go back into the palace.

The passage was short, ending with an iron door so decayed that to Leo's horror its upper hinge broke loose at his first tug. He had passed through the garden wall, and the water of the side canal was lapping his feet.

Opposite Leo, the vegetable boat was doing a roaring pre-dinner trade, and the Campo San Barnaba was thronged with tourists. Some of them noticed the black-clad man standing blinking in the water-gate and waved. He had the presence of mind to wave back. But the entrance was made for people to enter straight from their boats. To get out, he could swim, but that was out of the question with the precious book in his backpack; or thumb a lift from a passing gondola; or try to swing himself up and onto the garden wall. Any of these would make a spectacle of him. But this sure escape route was a thousand times better than getting himself entangled in the palace again.

Leo checked the door busily a few times, trying to look like a workman rather than a burglar, then carefully closed it and returned to the vault to wait. He relieved himself against the roots of the tree, smiling at his former thoughts about its need for watering.

As the hours passed, he hovered between dream and waking, haunted by images of a frozen sky that was also himself, the incalculable weight of the giant tree, the palace, the water-soaked earth pressing on the vault. Above all, the weight of his vow to Orsina.

It was hours later when Leo felt that it would be safe to exit. The day had been a physical trial of cold and discomfort, but the satisfaction of having burgled the palace and successfully abducted the book sent thrills up and down his spine.

At the stroke of eleven he levered the iron door open once more, closed it, standing on the narrow canalside step, and jumped up to grasp the top of the garden wall. After a few agonizing edgings from arm to arm, he was able to drop down onto the fondamenta and scuttle across the little bridge. Moments later, a crowd began to emerge from Ca' Rezzonico, the baroque palace next door, and he blended into it as it moved towards the vaporetto stop.

Venice goes to bed early on weekdays. Ravenously hungry, Leo resorted to the only place open near his hotel: the railway station buffet. Back in his quarters, he had a hot bath. Finally, he took the tome out of the backpack and laid it delicately on the small table. He sat down, switched on the old lamp with its greasy parchment shade, and unlatched the book's tarnished silver clasps.

# TWENTY

Everyone was surprised when Felipe walked into Madrid's police headquarters to confess a crime. The Commissioner began to pay close attention as the anxious, shortish and skinny young man explained how he had blown up the statue of Santiago Matamoros, Saint James the Moor-Slayer. He expressed deep sorrow for the damage and the human suffering he had caused, and insisted that *he* was responsible for it, no one else.

A few hours later, Felipe was being interrogated by the Inspector in charge of the Santiago investigation, who had flown in from Galicia the moment he was notified. All sorts of details emerged that only the perpetrator could be aware of. There was no doubt: Felipe was the culprit, and had acted of his own volition.

*El Pais*, *El Mundo*, *La Vanguardia*—all the Spanish newspapers were quick to report the development, echoed by the TV and radio. Traveling rapidly, it bounced around the newsrooms of Europe and the rest of the world. No Islamic militant faction had had anything to do with the bombing of Santiago: it was the work of a lone Catholic fanatic!

In the meantime, Inspector Ghedina was following a new lead. In Verona's old center, once the forum of the Roman city, he was in the car beside Colucci, both dressed in plain clothes. Four other plain clothes agents, on loan from the local police force, were ready to close in on the suspect. The phone call had arrived a few days before. A gruff male voice with a Roman accent had asked the Baron for a million Euros in cash if he wanted to see Orsina alive again. A specific time for the drop-off of the money had been given as well as an address, in Milan. The Baron had managed to keep the extortionist on the line long enough for the police to trace the number. It came from a cell phone, registered to one Rossella Bortolan. She lived in Verona, in Piazza delle Erbe. At exactly 18:00 the four policemen, as well as Ghedina and Colucci, were to knock on her apartment's door.

The Inspector checked his watch: 17:56. He got out of the car. With his assistant and the four agents, he climbed to the third floor. The agents brandished their Beretta PM 12S submachine guns. At 18:00 on the dot Ghedina banged on the door.

There was a distinct aroma of *polenta* coming from the apartment. A middle-aged woman wearing an apron opened the door. The Inspector showed his credentials and said: "I have reason to believe that Rossella Bortolan lives here."

The woman was terrified at the sight of the guns and started to cry. "Of course she does; she's my daughter. What has she done? Oh, what has she done?" she managed to ask through her tears.

"We're here to find out," Ghedina replied, collectedly. These were the things he hated about his job. Assuming this was not a crafty front, here was a housewife cooking and he had to threaten her with the artillery.

Two agents had found Rossella in her room, poring over a schoolbook. They escorted her to the Inspector at gunpoint. The plan had been to take her to the nearby station for questioning. The threatening call to the Baron had come from her cell phone; there was no doubt about that. But was it possible?

Ghedina was looking at a frightened fifteen-year-old with glasses and freckles. "*Signora* Bortolan," he said to the mother, "do you mind if we ask your daughter some questions?"

"What have you done, Rossella? What have you done, *figlia mia*?"

"Mama's a drama queen," thought Ghedina. Aloud to Rossella: "Listen, you don't need to be afraid; just answer my questions, and don't lie. We're here to help." To the agents: "Lower your guns, will you?"

Rossella did not look reassured at all. What was he going to ask her? If she had made an extortionary call to Baron Riviera della Motta about a ransom payment in a gruff male voice with a distinct Roman accent? He took the roundabout approach. Where did she go to school? what grade? did she like the teachers? and the classmates? Finally, he came to her cell phone: could he take a look at it?

"No."

"No? And why not?"

"Because it's been stolen."

"What?"

Rossella repeated her reply word by word, but sotto voce, as it had annoyed the Inspector.

"When? When was it stolen?"

"About a week ago."

"A week?" and, in his mind: "Shit!" Aloud: "You don't know who stole it, right?"

Rossella, however intimidated, gave him a commiserating look.

"*Touché*," he thought. Too much fast food, too little sleeping, too many false leads: he was fed up. Anyway, he asked: "Where was it stolen, would you know that?"

"I think at the tearoom, downstairs. I was having a hot chocolate, on my way back from school. I'm pretty sure I'd laid it on the table. When I left, it wasn't there, and I couldn't find it anywhere. Have *you* found it? Can I have it back?"

The Inspector told the girl and her mother that everything was fine, and not to worry. He could not wait to get out of the apartment, and away from the four agents, who were now eyeing him with something less than respect. He had quite a reputation, already. Not only was he in charge of Italy's two most talked-about investigations about which he seemed not to have a clue, but he was also the one who insisted on detaining a group of penniless students because they practiced martial arts, as if that were a crime.

"To hell with it," thought Ghedina, "nobody said it was going to be easy."

The book that lay before Leo was bound in dark green vellum, gold-stamped with the heraldic achievement of the Riviera: the Tree of Life and the spring issuing from its roots. The leather was stretched over wooden boards, to which the elaborately fashioned clasps were firmly anchored. The book's size had already raised his suspicion that it was not the same as the private edition of 1757 that he had encountered in the library of Villa Riviera. In fact, it was not even a printed book, but a manuscript. The title page read: *Il mondo magico de gli heroi. Opera dell'illustrissimo Barone Cesare della Riviera. Manu proprio, Anno MDLXXXIII*: the work of the illustrious author himself, written in his own hand in 1583!

The cover was rubbed, but the pages inside were scarcely marked by the fingers that had turned them—not many, Leo supposed, in over four hundred years. How had it survived in such fine condition? Perhaps it was never opened, but kept in its velvet-lined casket like the bones of a saint in a reliquary—and on an altar, too. Moreover, the pages were not paper, but fine parchment, on which the handsome script of Cesare della Riviera stood out in dark brown ink.

Leo was exhausted, but this unhoped-for discovery revived him. He leafed through the book to get a sense of the whole presentation. The familiar text, written in large Roman letters, occupied the center of each page. Framing it was a commentary, written in smaller italics.

Now Leo turned back to the first page and began skimming the main text. It was noticeably shorter than the version he was used to, missing all the references to biblical passages, Catholic doctrines, writings of the saints, and the activity of demons. This streamlined text confirmed his intuition of earlier in the day: that those had been the icing on the cake offered to sweeten the Church's censors when the book was printed, twenty years later. How young had Cesare been when he wrote it? He must have been a prodigy of esoteric learning, thought Leo as he started on the commentaries.

If the book was to yield any useful secrets, this is where he would find them, or so he hoped. But as he returned to the reality of the situation, exhaustion overwhelmed him at last. If he tried to read on in his present state, he could miss subtleties and hints, perhaps even codes, that might be there. Reluctantly, Leo fastened the book shut, put it in his suitcase, and went to bed.

Early the next morning he got up, dressed, breakfasted, and returned to his room for a session of serious study.

By the standards of the 21st century, the commentaries were wordy, but they soon made it plain that the alchemy in question had nothing to do with turning lead into gold. The "laboratory" was nothing more or less than the human mind, and the equipment was the will and the imagination:

> Pay no heed to the puffers, to those who at immense expense build furnaces with mighty bellows and purchase curiously formed, fire-resistant vessels into which they pour I know not what dross and ordure, thinking that through its cooking and the foul stench it emits they are bringing the First Matter to the state of nigredo, then, adding dew gathered with difficulty and

> great labor at dawn, they consider that their precious matter is nourished and purified thereby. Not so, for they are ignorant mountebanks and great deceivers of humanity. Yet the common crowd loves to be deceived by the promise of great riches, little heeding that in pursuit of these, what little gold they already possess is quickly spent, and that they are left poorer than before. The fire-resistant alembic of the true alchemist is his imagination, when his eyelids are closed, his ears covered, and all distractions put far from him. He should enter his secret chamber, to which none other possesses the key or even knows the entrance, and there he should sit conveniently in a chair, his feet planted firmly on the floor and his hands laid in an orderly way upon his knees. Let him be cautious and moderate in his practice, and not strive too soon for too high a goal. The initial practice should not exceed the time that others, in their childlike ignorance and superstition, dedicate to the vain repetition of the Rosary. Now, the fire of the alchemist is nothing other than the great desire he has for the conquest of the Second Tree of Life. Without this secret fire, all his efforts are in vain, for he does not care sufficiently whether he achieves it or not. Only the Hero, for whom the conquest of the Tree is more desirable than food or drink, more alluring than a beautiful virgin's bed, more precious than life itself, can light this fire and, with the bellows of the breath, fan it into ever more ardent flame. Then, when the fire is raised to its highest degree of ardent aspiration and contempt for the lowly condition of common mankind, let him begin the separation.

Cesare della Riviera went on to detail how this separation was to be imagined, and what imagery would be helpful in the process. It involved a kind of self-analysis, in which the various parts of one's being were methodically scrutinized. One tried to perceive the procession of visual and verbal thoughts as if one were a detached spectator, letting them rise and fall. Likewise, one watched one's emotions, especially as aroused by emotion-laden images or memories, which would be different for every person. In this way, one came to know what prejudices, habits, knee-jerk reactions, and obsessions made up one's personality.

Leo thought that he recognized what the author was driving at: in his recent studies in Washington he had repeatedly come across an aphorism by Hermes Trismegistus: "He who knows himself, knows the All." But as he continued to read, he realized that that was not it. Conventional reasoning, he should know by now, rarely applied in things esoteric. In fact, there was no question of changing the traits of one's personality; this Leo found the most novel and disturbing element in the work. The alchemical path that the author was describing had nothing to do with moral improvement or curing one's faults, once they were seen for what they were. The author wrote about this:

> Take no heed for your sins, for all men are sinners and will ever be so, and their sins are like the innumerable heads of the Hydra, which grow again as soon as they are cut off. If you fast, you will acquire a sin; and if you pray, you will be condemned; and if you give alms, you will do evil unto your spirits. Let the Hero pass on to his further labors, else he will never conquer the Nemean Lion, lift Antaeus from his parent Earth, or take the Apples from the Tree of the Hesperides.

The more he read, the more Leo felt distanced from the world of the senses. Gradually the author unfolded a series of meditations intended to reverse the normal attitude to reality. Instead of imagining the physical universe as the container for the individual body, and the body as the container for life and consciousness, one was to turn the whole thing inside-out. The outermost container was one's own individual consciousness, before it contained any object. Inside that came the thoughts and desires of one's inmost self. These, in turn, created the illusion that we know as the physical body; and this imaginary body, with its five senses, then exteriorized the final illusion of a physical world, in fact the whole universe as we know it.

Leo had studied enough philosophy to recognize the theory that "I" am the only reality, with all its dangerous consequences for "you." But this was about taking the heavens by storm and going far, far beyond the human condition. In the more cryptic language of the commentary:

> The body does not possess life, as the soul possesses life, for life is not a product of the body, but the body is a product of life. Let the Hero transfer the center of himself into this profound life, removing the limit that makes of it a finite quantity; let him strengthen it with the spirit and make its flame ever greater and higher, till he surpasses all those

> conditions and supports that come to him from without, of which he has need only so long as he is external to his own being, confined to the elementary order and active therein. When he is no longer separate from his own being, when his life is completely integrated, so as to be identical to the life of its life, there occurs the renovation and the restoration of the Hero. His body is in effect no longer a body, but is now in the state of a power that he fully possesses, hence it is free from all that which may affect its sensible manifestation; and this is the incorruptible, celestial, and radiant body.

There came a knock on the door. In fact, Leo thought that he had heard knocks, on and off, for a while. It felt as if he were being called back to the world. It was the maid, asking to tidy up the room.

"Just a moment," he replied. He quietly closed the book and placed it in his backpack. Then he opened the door and let her in. Shouldering his pack, reluctant to take any risk with the precious book, he walked to a nearby bar, enjoying the tepid air of a sunny autumn day, as he had felt somewhat cold in the hotel. He ate a panino, drank a cappuccino, then a glass of mineral water, then another one. Finally, he headed back to the hotel.

The concierge—a little old man with a hare-lip—gave him an inquisitive look. The last thing Leo wanted was to be conspicuous, so he improvised. "I'm still trying to get over my jet lag. I guess there's no better remedy than sleeping it off, wouldn't you say?" The concierge nodded in silence as Leo was already climbing the stairs.

In his room, he laid the manuscript carefully on the table, and plunged back in.

The text had a lot to say about the Labors of Hercules, all twelve of them, and the importance of the number 12 in the esoteric traditions, but the commentary explained that they were all just varieties of the alchemical principle of *solve et coagula*, dissolve and coagulate.

The method involved consisted largely of making some supreme physical or mental effort, then releasing it and entering a thought-free state that bordered on the higher consciousness. Gradually the gap and difference between the two states would increase. When the Hero had learned to enter the higher consciousness at will, he could perform actions in that state that resonated down through the lower levels of being, having their final effects in the physical world, where they seemed to others—the uninitiated—to be magic.

The book was teaching attitudes and techniques that would take years to master, and then only if one were especially gifted. Leo's heart sank, until he realized to his surprise that he had already done a lot of the meditative exercises, though in different modes and with very different intentions. He was familiar with the inner world of images, at first from practicing the Spiritual Exercises of Ignatius Loyola, and more recently in his devastating encounter with Angela and the abyss.

Ever since he had begun to read the manuscript, Leo had felt cold, though not enough to stop reading. But as he was not getting any warmer, he finished the first part and paused. He checked the radiator in his room: it was quite warm. And the window: it was not ajar. He opened his suitcase and reached for a sweater.

The second part of the book described the twelve fruits of the Tree of Life. In today's world, Leo considered, some of these would be dismissed, or at best explained away as "paranormal." They included clairvoyance (seeing things beyond the reach of the eye, as well as beyond the reach of telescope and microscope alike), precognition (seeing things to come), telepathy (the transference of thoughts from one mind to another), and psychokinesis (the power of the mind to move objects).

In another category was the power to heal oneself "without the assistance of those ignorant butchers, the barber-surgeons, or of those blown-up pig's bladders of self-importance, the physicians who squeeze the pulse and scrutinize the colors of urine, hoping to extract the last possible ducat before their victim dies." In place of this, Cesare recommended what he called the "Herculean regimen" of early sleeping, brisk walks or horseback rides, a diet rich in "peasant bread and weeds," and the strict avoidance of brothels.

Leo felt impatient at the wordy delivery of this platitudinous advice. Was he on to anything? Orsina was missing, she was probably in great danger, and there he was, studying the centuries-old scribblings of a very strange mind in a drafty hotel room. He was getting colder, as if wearing an extra layer had had no effect on his body temperature. Yet he was compelled to read on, as if the manuscript itself called him back.

Cesare's commentary now moved on to the subject of control over the mineral, vegetable, and animal kingdoms. The Hero supposedly developed a "magic touch" in which he conveyed some sort of energy through his hands. This energy was then wielded in specific gestures that Cesare likened to those of a swordsman, and cast, or flung, at their intended recipients. Using obscure fencing terms, he described how the magic touch was to be used for energizing plants, and for controlling hounds, horses, and wild game. Then the same principles were extended to the control of men, and here Cesare certainly meant males, for he stated that "the secret of controlling women is something that I will not write down here, lest it be abused by the concupiscent, to the great danger and disgrace of the weaker sex."

Finally, he addressed the achievement of the "firm, not falling soul," which supposedly put the Hero's soul beyond the reach of death. At this point, Leo felt his concentration waning. In any case, he thought, most of the fruits of the Tree of Life were things he could well do without. There was only one that he wanted right now, and that was what Cesare called "vaticination," after the Latin word for prophecy. Leo himself had spoken about it to Orsina during their last conversation. He remembered it only too painfully. And he had come to Italy on the tenuous hope that, once having the forbidden book in hand, he could read what secrets the author had not unveiled in the regular edition. For by "vaticination " Cesare meant the ability to see, beyond the boundaries of time and space. In his own words:

> The possibility of vaticination follows immediately from the premise that beyond the sensible or elementary order, the magical world of the Hero also contains the possibility of a knowledge that is no longer bounded by the scythe of Chronos, the all-devouring god of Time. This first fruit of the Tree of Life was possessed by the ancient vates, to whom past, present, and future were laid open like a book, and which the Hero can read both forward and back.

Leo did not care to see into the future; he could leave that to God. He desperately needed to see into the present, to discover what had become of Orsina.

It did not seem much to ask, just a bite at the first fruit of the Tree of Life. Of course Cesare's instructions for enjoying those fruits assumed that one had already graduated with first-class honors as a Hero. Would they work for someone who had not? Leo could only try.

He left the book open on the table and hung the "Do Not Disturb" notice on the outside of his door. There was probably no need for that: it was eight in the evening and already dark. He went back to the manuscript and repositioned the reading lamp so as to brighten the pages as much as possible. The room was as silent as the grave, and now colder. Steam, he noticed, came out of his mouth. He thought fleetingly that he should have gone to a better hotel, and began to read the instructions on how to vaticinate.

The Baron was to drive personally to his doctor's office in Verona. Since the first tragedy, his health had left much to be desired; the doctor, his old trusted friend, was to accompany him to a private clinic, for a checkup. The phone call in which he had set up the appointment with his doctor had been recorded and listened to by the police, without arousing suspicion. But instead of heading toward Verona, the Baron had taken the highway. He had business to attend to in Milan.

As soon as his assets had been frozen, the Baron had begun to receive visits from friends and acquaintances. These were supposed to be old-fashioned condolence calls, but some financial details were also being discussed. Most visitors left with unwritten but firmly agreed-upon bills of exchange. They would pay another visit very shortly to the Baron and bring him a certain amount of money in cash. Their discretion was essential. Within a year, he would pay them back with a 50% interest on the principal. Emanuele's wealth hinged chiefly on real estate, and not only in Italy. The creditors knew that he could and would meet his every financial obligation. And so, under the nose of the police (two agents still patrolled the villa), the Baron had succeeded in raising the money for the ransom, in cash. It was now stuffed inside a briefcase, waiting to exchange hands in the center of Milan.

The appointment was at 6 p.m., in Piazza Cavour, precisely between Via Palestro and Via Manin, at the entrance of the Public Gardens. After negotiating rain along the highway and intense traffic in the city, the Baron was parked by the entrance of the gardens a little less than half an hour ahead of time.

"You'll see a kiosk there," he had been told on the phone by the kidnapper. "At 18:00 sharp you'll take the money right there. Somebody will be expecting you. Now, tell our friends the police who are listening in that if they show up with you, you'll get a piece of your niece in the mail; shall we say, a finger? An ear? Both? Be there with the money, alone."

The Baron looked at his watch. He got out of the car and walked to the kiosk. It was dark, cold, and the gardens had closed an hour earlier. He was now standing beneath the tin roof, as it had started to rain, holding on to his briefcase. Some people passed by, but did not approach him.

He must have spent twenty or thirty minutes in the same place. It continued to rain. There was a man across the street who seemed to be staring at him, but it was hard to say in the dark with sheets of rain pouring down. Now the same man was lighting a cigarette, under his umbrella.

Suddenly, the Baron was grabbed from behind. Two men held him by the arms and lifted him. Moments later, he was inside a van. His briefcase had already been snatched from him. Two more men were inside the van.

"*Acchiappato, con la grana; adesso cosa*?" Caught, with the dough; now what? one of the men said in a small microphone; the reply came into his earphone. The Baron could not hear it.

The van's door slid open, and another dripping man hopped in. "Good evening, Baron."

"Ghedina! You, here!"

"May we take a look at your briefcase?" One of the agents passed it on to him. "Let's see, what do we have here? Let me guess: one million Euros, in 500 Euro bills, all two thousand of them?"

The Inspector gave the briefcase to one of his men: "Count the bills," he said, and added, turning to the Baron, "what am I to do with you? You've broken the law; you're obstructing justice; you've done business with illegal money-lenders. And the list could go on."

"You have used me," said the Baron. "You made me wait for half an hour before closing in on me. The kidnappers must have noticed you and called off the pick-up. My poor niece will now be maimed. It's all your fault. I despise you, you stupid good-for-nothing, and I wish eternal ill on you and all your loved ones."

Something in the way the Baron had uttered these words, with a solemn yet sinisterly calm menacing tone, made the agents shudder.

Ghedina parried the affront, and the curse. "You've also offended a public official. If you shut your mouth now," he continued, barely controlling himself, "I'll make nothing of it. You realize that I could arrest you right now. But watch it: my patience has a limit.

"We're as concerned about your niece's safety as you are, but you're not going to help her any by giving in to the demands of the kidnappers. Your money is confiscated. One of my men will drive you back to the villa in your car. You'll sit in the back, with another of my men." The two agents the Inspector had chosen to drive the Baron back were getting out of the van, in the rain.

"Before you step out," Ghedina added, "know that I'll have to keep closer watch over you from now on. You'll keep us informed on your whereabouts and your movements. I didn't like your stratagem of the doctor's appointment. I mean, I'd hoped more would come of it, and so I let it go. But from now on, you'd better not lie anymore."

As Ghedina was being driven back to Bolzano late in the night, he could not help mulling over the day's events. He had hoped that the kidnappers would show up. They did not, or perhaps they did, but spotted the police. Obviously he was not dealing with amateurs. Was the Baroness really in more danger now? The law that freezes the assets of the family made sense in principle. But it had probably been drawn up by little people like himself, who would never live through the experience of a loved one being kidnapped. The feeling of utter impotence must be terrible. He would have felt sorry for the Baron, but not after that reptilian curse. The man had broken a few laws, but arresting and putting him away would serve no purpose: the investigation needed him as a decoy for the kidnappers. As for the Baroness, he did sympathize with her, and worried about her safety. He knew from experience that she was in a very dangerous situation. What a pity they hadn't kidnapped her uncle instead!

The Inspector had arranged for an officer from the *polizia tributaria* to come to the police headquarters in Bolzano to impound the money the Baron had raised for the ransom. Then there was a new report to write. An exhausted Inspector Ghedina finally checked into his apartment in the outskirts of the city after 3 a.m. He looked forward to a few hours of sleep, and crashed to bed.

At 6:37 in the morning, as he was about to enter the REM phase of sleep, the phone rang, and rang again.

"*Pronto*," Ghedina answered in a hollow voice.

"That passport number you were looking for."

"Yes?"

"It's turned up."

"Where?" Ghedina was suddenly awake, groping for the lamp switch.

"In Venice."

# TWENTY-ONE

> According to the rabbinic *targum* on the Book of Genesis, the ancient Hebrews obtained this fruit by stealth, in the following manner. They cut off the head of a firstborn child, preserved it with salt and spices, and mounted it upon a wall. Beneath its tongue, they placed a leaf of gold inscribed with mystical letters. The head, which they called *theraphim*, would then answer questions that were put to it concerning past and future things.

Leo felt a strong revulsion, both at the notion itself and at Cesare's giving credit to what must be, he hoped, a legend. He read on:

> There are also those, even in our own day, who, being underprivileged aspirants, perform vaticination through the art of necromancy, not slaying their own firstborn but obtaining the cadavers of those recently slain, whether in battle or through the power of the secular arm, and emulating the ancient science of *haruspicy* or divination through the entrails. Such uncouth methods may suit those as bloodthirsty as tigers and as vile as toads, but the Hero will have no traffic with them; for our Tree of Life is not to be sought among the dead, but among the living, and by those who are more than living.

The author was irked by the crudeness of these necromantic practices. Once more Leo was alarmed by Cesare's lack of moral concerns: divination through entrails was not loathsome because it required a human body, but rather owing to its "uncouthness." In addition, Cesare went on to explain, he was dubious of the results of any magic performed with material means. Such methods may create without the operator's knowledge a crack or fissure through which "chaotic and sub-personal" forces can enter. "These are a great peril to his soul, for they can lead to its disintegration and loss, which the superstitious call eternal damnation," whereas all his efforts should aim for an integration of himself in a superior form, a "more than living" state.

Any magical working is hazardous, Cesare noted in an underlined sentence, the first Leo had encountered so far in the manuscript. Even when successful, it may cause "eruptions and fluxes." He named several herbs useful in treating these, *agrimonia*, *lysimachia*, *potentilla*, *verbascum*. As a general protection, he urged the Hero to preface any magical work with an *oratio*, for the purposes of banishing "unnecessary spirits," and an *invocatio* for attracting "necessary" ones. These spirits, he added, are not "demons and angels such as the Church believes in," nor are they to be called respectively "evil" and "good"; they are simply spirits at large in nature that can either help the Hero or hinder him.

Since the mind has difficulty in imagining impersonal forces, Cesare allowed the use of time-honored formulae of invocation and banishment, complete with names and the traditional gesture of the flaming pentagram.

> He should turn to the corners of the earth and invoke them by the names of their four winds, which are well known to all, saying: "O Boreas (or the other names), I command you to keep wrapped within your bosom all detrimental and deceiving influences." So doing, he should make the sign of the pentacle with the index finger of his right hand extended, reaching first to his left foot, then to the place above his right shoulder, then the place above his left shoulder, then his right foot, then the place directly above his head, back to his left foot, and finally point to his heart, making in his imagination the symbol of the fiery five-pointed star. And thus he should do with the other winds.
>
> Then, having once settled himself, the Hero discards his Sulphur and his Salt, and enters the Cave of Mercury.

Leo knew that these last instructions referred to the state of inner concentration favorable to the play of images. He began the breathing routine that was prescribed in the commentary: "breathe in for the count of four beats or steps of a moderate pavane, hold the breath for two beats, and expel it in the time it takes to make six such steps." This sequence was to be repeated twelve times, inducing a mild hyperventilated state.

Following the instructions, he then visualized the wall of the cave as covered by a black curtain embroidered with stars. Beside it, one was supposed to imagine the figure of Mercury himself, and at the appropriate time, when one's concentration was perfect, ask the god to draw the curtain back.

The first time Leo tried it, his unconscious mind played a trick on him. What appeared behind the curtain was the very room in which he lay, the banal hotel furnishings all seen as through a camera obscura.

The second time, the curtain revealed his own face, as he saw it every morning in the shaving mirror. It was as though the effort to send out his energy had backfired and bounced back upon the sender.

He tried it several more times with similar results, each attempt preceded by a good ten minutes' breathing and concentration, then got up and paced around the room in frustration. Despite the intense breathing and the furious pacing, he was even colder now. After drinking a glass of water wishing that it were hot tea instead, he returned to the book and reread the section of the commentary that gave instructions for achieving vaticination. It contained in passing the phrase "having enclosed the greater world within the lesser one," which he had overlooked as typical Hermetic jargon. Now, on a more careful reading, he recognized it as a reference to the instructions contained in the first part: the lessons in reversing the normal relationship of self to world.

This was the trouble, thought Leo the Italian teacher, with trying to use the subjunctive before one had learned the present tense. It was sheer arrogance to think that he could skip half the exercises and expect instant fluency in the magical language of heroes. But then, did he not possess the "secret fire" of desire, raised to fever heat? His residual Catholic superego added as a palliative "and my intentions are pure."

Leo looked away from the book, his head in his hands. He thought about the reversal of worlds, and of the diagram in which Cesare had shown the head of the Hero containing the concentric circles of the elements, planets, and stars. His imagination expanded to interstellar spaces, deepest blue, with the floating planets crisscrossing in their orbits. In the background was a multitude of stars: red, violet, green points of intense brightness. These too formed into galaxies, spun in their spirals, condensed into clouds, and shot a burst of white foam across the sky that Leo, in some inarticulate part of his mind, knew to be the Milky Way. Then, practicing the *solve et coagula*, he returned to the physical reality of his head, resting on his hands. He felt the tongue in his mouth, the eyes swiveling in their sockets, the wrinkling of his nose, and the slight rustling as he flexed the tiny muscles in his ears. Then he reentered the cavernous spaces of his brain. Here was the stellar world again, more vivid than before. The planets were dormant, and the stars more constant, forming themselves into constellations like those on celestial globes, the shapes of Bears, Orion, Scorpio, and so on, visible beyond their component stars.

Leo's consciousness returned to his head, and again expanded to the cosmic vision, in slow rhythmical sequence. As he did so, the question occurred to him: "Who is controlling this?" Could there be something outside both microcosm and macrocosm deliberately timing their alternation, like the puppeteer pulling the strings? The answer came instantly and without articulation of the word: it is the Will. As Cesare's commentary had said, "in the magical world, the Hero's will has precedence over knowledge, and in his liberty he despises the Goddess Necessity."

The exercise had already put Leo into a state of semi-trance, in which the inner events were more real than either his physical environment or his mental activity. The introduction of the concept of an overarching Will seemed to expand his field of inner vision, as though he were a great balloon that had suddenly been inflated. With it came a sensation of intense cold, far beyond the mundane chilliness that Leo had felt at the beginning of his exercise. This was a cold against which clothing and even fire were no protection. It was the absolute coldness of interstellar space.

He had been there before, he recognized, during his vision of Angela, but then he had been the servant or victim of events. Now he felt that he was their master, a god looking down at his creation. Uttering a command in a language beyond words, he summoned Mercury and ordered him to draw away the curtain of the sky.

What was revealed behind the curtain might have taken Leo by surprise, but he was now as objective as a camera, impassive as a force of nature, beyond any personal emotion or reaction. It was the back view of Baron Emanuele, clearly recognizable from his slicked-down gray hair. He was dressed in a silk brocade bathrobe, and in the act of opening the door to let someone in. A person entered, a woman. It was Angela. She did not speak, smile, or greet her uncle, but crossed the unfamiliar room, which now came into the view of Leo's all-seeing eye. It was a large, square sitting room, its walls painted from floor to ceiling and hung with antlers and other trophies. The windows were shuttered against the night, and modern standard lamps cast a few pools of golden light on sofas and oriental rugs.

Angela entered a small, lighted chamber off the main room, kicked off her slip-on sandals, and lay down on a bed. Emanuele followed her.

From this point, Leo's perception was not limited to the visible spectrum, but seemed to take in the mental states of both uncle and niece. Angela's was that of someone suspended between sleeping and waking, and her bodily movements were as automatic as those of a sleeper who turns over in bed. Emanuele, on the other hand, was a red-hot fire of will and desire. It was not the simple sexual desire for a beautiful seventeen-year-old, though there was an element of that in it. It was all-devouring desire for power. Leo knew, without discursive thought, that the Baron was consciously aiming at a state similar to that in which Leo now found himself: an autonomous will beyond the restrictions of time and space, which had only to utter the Fiat! and what it willed would be done. But he was using a different technique from that of pure meditation and imagination. It belonged to an order of events that Leo would never have conceived of in his normal existence, but which he now registered without surprise and without emotion. Emanuele was trying to unite his mind with Angela's, and use the latter as a vehicle for projecting his will. To what end, was not presently given.

Emanuele lay down on the bed beside Angela and passed one hand under her neck. The other hand he raised to his own neck, as though cupping his ear. Leo had never heard of the technique, used in certain Tibetan cults, of momentarily stopping the flow of blood to the brain in order to induce a trance state. If he had, he would have dismissed it as a very reckless thing to do, risking permanent brain damage or worse. Now the same wordless intuition told him that Emanuele and Angela had practiced this before.

As Emanuele pressed gently on Angela's neck, she remembered Orsina. She had promised to tell something to her sister. What was it? It was important. She began to struggle against growing oblivion.

Emanuele squeezed harder. He took his hand away from his own neck and half rose, bending over Angela whose eyes were now open with a questioning, confused look. He pressed his lips down on her protesting mouth, as though to suck out her soul. Angela had now forgotten what she was going to tell her sister. She had forgotten that she had a sister. As her brain missed its accustomed supply of blood, emergency signals started to fire in her autonomous nervous system. Her heart fluttered. The abyss gaped.

The Baron pressed his thumb into his own carotid artery and felt the familiar tightening of the skull. He closed his eyes and, in his imagination, entered Angela's empty mind.

As though passing through the doorway into another world, for the first time in his life Emanuele succeeded in entering a state of full-blown magical ecstasy. He beheld the god whom, in his previous exercises, he had often tried to visualize: Mithras, coming to meet him in the guise of a golden youth. The joyous and radiant figure wore a Persian cap and a star-spangled cape, and held the short sword favored by his military devotees, the Roman legionaries. With all the twisted logic of a dream, Emanuele knew that he was a bull, and bowed himself in adoration. Mithras mounted his neck and plunged his sword deep into the throat of the beast.

Back in the physical world, the Baron's muscles contracted with the force of a *rigor mortis*. His fingers and thumb pressed deeper into Angela's unresisting neck. The baroreceptors in the carotid area began to send panic signals to the heart, urging it to slow down and reduce the blood pressure. After ten minutes or so, it had stopped, but Emanuele was oblivious, suspended in a timeless paroxysm.

Then he came to himself. Angela was still in his arms, breathing no longer; dead.

Although Leo had no sense of himself during this vision, the feeling of intense cold now returned: yet he sensed that this was not only his own state, but the Baron's too.

For an indeterminate time after his eyes opened, Emanuele did not move. Then he rose from the bed, pulled his dressing gown tightly around himself, and let himself out of the front door. Leo now saw that he had been in a small hunting lodge, fronted by a walled courtyard. The Baron went to his Lancia, opened the driver's door, and rummaged around the dashboard. He walked back to the lodge wearing his driving gloves, returned to Angela's body, and removed its few clothes: t-shirt, skirt, and underpants.

The Baron was not tall, but he was strongly built, and had little difficulty in maneuvering the limp body in a fireman's lift and lowering it into the bathtub. Still wearing gloves, he took soap and a sponge and scrubbed every inch of the unresisting flesh. He washed her hair too, and blow-dried it with great care. Then he took three large towels from a cupboard in the bathroom, spread two of them on the bathroom floor, dried the body with the other, and put its skimpy garments back on, down to the sandals.

With absolute self-collection and economy of movement, Emanuele now wrung the driving gloves over the sink to the last drip. He methodically put them back on, and opened the front door of the hunting lodge. By the Lancia, parked in the courtyard, he opened the trunk. Going back inside, he hoisted the body once more and carried it to the car, shutting the trunk lid over it. Then he returned to the inner rooms and gathered up the bedclothes and towels, took off his bathrobe, and put them all into a washing machine that occupied a tiny room of its own. He added detergent and started the washing cycle, then left the lodge in his shirt, trousers, and damp gloves, locking the front door behind him.

The night was still, moonless, and warm. Using his sidelights only, Emanuele drove the first of the two kilometers towards the villa; then, where the road rose over a knoll, he stopped, turned the car around. He was driving back to the lodge.

Leo could read his intentions: he had to deal not only with Angela's body, but with her Vespa. He opened the trunk again and, with some difficulty, extracted the stiffening body from it. This he now placed in the front passenger seat, propping it up with the seat belt. Then he lifted the Vespa into the trunk, which did not shut completely, and drove away once again. Emanuele's mind, disciplined and focused, now carried the intention of bypassing the villa, driving for an hour or more on roads which, at this hour of 2:30 a.m., were deserted, then dumping the body and the scooter to simulate an accident.

But as the little road to the hunting lodge passed through the villa's back courtyard, Emanuele had another idea. He switched off the lights altogether, put the engine in neutral, and turned it off. By inertia, the car slowly and very quietly reached Nigel's Ferrari. With a glance up at the windows, all of them now black as the starlit night, he got out of his car. With his gloved hands, he turned the handle of the Ferrari's trunk and resisted its spring so as to open it silently. Then he came around to the Lancia's passenger door, opened it with similar care, and lifted out Angela's body. A few footsteps, and he settled her crouched limbs into the Ferrari's trunk. He closed it with the softest click, returned to his Lancia, started the engine and, with the least possible pressure on the accelerator, glided away.

As soon as he was out of sight of the villa he switched on his headlights and drove at normal speed along the river Adige. Some thirty kilometers from the villa he stopped by the water's edge, and hauled out the Vespa. He did not start its engine, but was careful not to leave it in neutral; instead, he put it in second gear, squeezed the clutch, and walked it into the river with scarcely a splash. Then he shut the trunk firmly and drove home. By 3:30 he was surreptitiously letting himself into the back door of the villa. Half an hour later, he was asleep in his own bedroom.

As the Baron's consciousness, onto which Leo's intuitive vision had been locked for the past hour, faded into oblivion, Leo's own consciousness began to return. He had fallen on the floor, and seemed to be sprawled in a pool of cold sweat, his teeth chattering uncontrollably. As he started to move his stiffened limbs, his fingers and toes felt as though they had been flayed and were now being scraped with shards of ice. "Can't I just die?" he groaned as he half rose and tried to open his eyes. But he could not. The thought flashed across his mind that this unspeakable vision had struck him blind, permanently this time. Would this be his punishment for storming the gates of perception and beholding things that he was never meant to see, things whose memory would torment him for the rest of his life? He felt so weak that he had to concentrate just to keep breathing. Prostrated, he lingered in the dark, shivering in his own cold sweat, so enfeebled that he could hardly move or think.

Shortly after eleven in the morning, Ghedina entered the hotel, escorted by Colucci and five policemen. Their Alfa Romeos had devoured the 170 miles from Bolzano. Except for the Inspector, they were all in uniform. There was no need to show their credentials to the dumbfounded concierge.

"Do you have a *Signor* Kavenaugh among your guests?" the Inspector asked.

"Why, yes, but—"

"Where's his room?"

The concierge, an even older colleague of the one with the hare-lip, hesitated.

"Tell me now, will you?" the Inspector urged him, as the policemen drew their guns.

"It's room 331, but—"The police were already running up the stairs.

Ghedina knocked, then banged on the door. "Open the door; it's the police!"

No reply.

"We know you're in there. Open the door—now!"

Perfect silence replied to the command. Ghedina turned to his men. "Force it open."

The heaviest policeman hurled himself against it just as the concierge was arriving with the key. The flimsy door yielded at the first attempt. The policeman stepped back.

"Watch it, boss," said Colucci to Ghedina, "he may be armed."

But Ghedina, the first one to glance inside, stopped himself short. "Stay back!" he said, barring the door. "Colucci, get me Venice's *prefetto* on the phone, right now."

Leaning forward with his arm, but still not stepping inside, the Inspector switched on the light. There was blood everywhere. The bathroom door had been left open, and he could see blood on its floor, too. The room's gray industrial carpet was blood-soaked, and there was blood on the table, on the bed, everywhere. No body was in sight.

"The *prefetto* is on the line, boss," said Colucci, his eyes bulging with curiosity. Ghedina grabbed the phone and explained the situation to the chief of police. He asked for the immediate dispatch of the crime lab. "Make sure it includes a serologist, it's of the utmost importance."

The concierge was sneakily walking along the corridor toward the stairs. Ghedina called him back. "Come here." He did, meekly. "Now, tell me: have you seen *Signor* Kavenaugh today?"

"Yes, sir."

"When? Why didn't you tell me already?"

"I tried, but you cut me short. He checked out this morning."

"Did he? When?"

"At around ten."

"God damn it! Did he mention where he was going?"

"No." The concierge paused, then corrected himself: "Actually, he did ask me for something."

"What?"

"The nearest bookshop."

"A bookshop? What the hell?" wondered Ghedina in his mind. "Tell me, did he look normal to you? Did he seem agitated?"

"Oh, he looked . . . awful, sir. I did notice that."

"Awful? How do you mean?"

"Feeble. Weak. As pale as a corpse." The concierge could almost have been describing himself.

"And with all that he still asked for a freaking bookshop?" Ghedina asked in his mind. Then, aloud: "Can't you remember anything else?"

"No, I don't think so."

"Did he leave with his luggage?"

"Oh, yes. He had a suitcase and, I think, a backpack."

"Is that all?"

"Yes."

"All right, go downstairs, and remain at our disposal."

When the old man had gone, Ghedina said to Colucci: "Go down too, with a man. Keep watch on the concierge, any phone call he may make or receive. In fact, any phone call that comes through to the hotel. And wait for the crime lab. When they arrive, send them up immediately."

Still not entering the room, Ghedina tried to imagine what might have happened, and jotted down a series of conjectures in his notebook. They all seemed far-fetched. Something was certain, though: Professor Leonard Kavenaugh was up to no good. He might have a firm alibi: Ghedina had checked, with the collaboration of Interpol, and established that Kavenaugh had been in Washington when Angela was murdered and also when Orsina was kidnapped. But what did that prove? The professor could have been the mastermind behind either crime, or both.

Ghedina noticed how he was calling the aristocratic sisters by name. They had become very familiar to him. Uncharacteristically, he had begun to feel sorry for them, and for their whole family, and all the more now that Kavenaugh had slipped away. Ghedina knew only too well that the moment he had learned that the American was in Venice, he should have informed the local police, asking them at least to keep him under surveillance until Ghedina could get there. He had deliberately not done so; for his career, it was a risk worth running. The dual investigation was his pet project, and this was going to be his first masterstroke after all the derision he had been suffering at the hands of the media. Besides, all he had meant to do with Kavenaugh was question him. There had been no sufficient reason to apprehend him, perhaps not even to suspect him of anything other than adultery, which is not a crime. Nothing could have prepared him for this blood bath.

"Inspector Ghedina?" A burly man was addressing him. "I'm Inspector Giannelli; at your service," he said somewhat begrudgingly. Giannelli was followed by several technicians, comprising the crime lab, and some more policemen.

"Thank you," said Ghedina. "We're up to our necks in a bloody mess."

"Yes, I can see that," said Giannelli, peering inside the room.

"Who's the serologist?"

"I am." An anemic-looking, lanky man had replied.

"All right. Now, *you* go in, only you for the moment. Try not to step in the blood."

"Easier said than done . . ." replied the serologist as he entered the room.

An hour later, the scene of the potential crime—"potential" for no body had been found—had been thoroughly inspected. The photographer had taken hundreds of photos, while the forensic chemist and serologist had been busy; the former, looking for hairs, body fluids other than blood, nail fragments, fibers, and relevant chemicals and particles; the latter, concentrating on the abnormal amount of blood. The serologist had collected countless samples. Ghedina consulted him.

"I find the scene unreal, Inspector," he said. "I don't want to jump to any conclusions before doing the lab work."

"But . . ."

"Well, usually, when the reason for bloodletting is a wound, let's say inflicted by either one or multiple bullets or by a blade of various sorts, there's a single or multiple gushes from the victim's body. The victim falls to the floor and some of the blood spatterings on it are more intense the closer they are to the wounds on the body. But in *this* case, the victim, that is, if we are dealing with a human being—"

"What do you mean?"

"As far as we can tell at this stage, unlikely though it may seem, an animal, say, a goat, might have been slaughtered in here."

What on earth was Kavenaugh up to?

"Anyway," the serologist resumed, "*if* it is a *single* person's blood—which we will soon find out by matching all the samples—he or she seems to have *oozed* blood from the *whole* body. I can't detect any area of higher intensity on the floor. That is very unusual."

"Any alternative idea?"

"Maybe, but a very remote one."

"And that would be?"

"Lectospirosis, which the victim may have contracted by drinking water contaminated by the urine of rats."

"Did you say *lectospirosis*?"

"Yes, rat fever. Many things happen to the person infected: vomit, diarrhea, fever, headaches. In the acute state, he can bleed through the skin, even die."

"But how likely is this to happen?"

"In Venice? With our thousands of resident *pantegane*? Very likely, as long as one drinks canal water. That is what's most unlikely. Of course, a person could be *forced* to do that, but that's for you to determine. I stick to scientific facts. We'll soon know more about this man by analyzing his blood, assuming, of course, that it is his."

Ghedina went downstairs. Once more, he spoke with Venice's chief of police. Not on the phone this time, though—he had come in person after hearing an early report from Inspector Giannelli.

"Sir," said Ghedina looking him straight in the eye, "I have strong reasons to believe that Leonard Kavenaugh is a dangerous individual. As he is believed to be currently on Italian soil, I urge you to alert all police headquarters in the country, and all points of entry too, airports, ports, and the customs along the borders with France, Switzerland, Austria, and Slovenia. I myself will shortly be calling the police headquarters in Bolzano to give them the same instructions.

"Leonard Kavenaugh poses a grave threat to society. How exactly, we are still determining. But he may well be a murderer. To avoid further tragedies, he is to be found and apprehended. My office is e-mailing to yours his photo and passport number, both US and Italian. He must *not* leave the country."

The chief looked nonplussed. Ghedina took him aside, and had a very quiet word with him. He suspected that the American might be linked with the tragedies that had recently befallen the Riviera della Motta family, and explained how. This confidential intelligence won Ghedina the chief's full collaboration. All measures would be taken nationwide so as to find and arrest Leonard Kavenaugh. The hotel was by now mobbed by policemen, and *carabinieri* to boot. They had overflowed the modest lobby and spilled into the street.

A reporter from *Il Gazzettino di Venezia*, noticing the tumult, realized something was up, and ventured inside the hotel, squeezing through the crowd. On the fly, he obtained an interview with the chief himself; then, with Inspector Giannelli, as Ghedina huffily declined to comment. Gianelli told him what had been found in room 331 and, without realizing that it was still classified information, what the chief had just told him: that Kavenaugh might well be linked to the kidnapping of the Baronessa. The reporter dashed to the newsroom to put his scoop to use.

# TWENTY-TWO

"Could you wait here?" The taxi driver nodded, and Leo got out in the rain. As he stood up, he had to lean on the car so as not to collapse. In a daze, he managed to reach the massive doors, the only breach in the walls. It was very dark, and it took him some time to find the doorbell. It was a chain; he pulled on it. A bell tolled at some distance from the doors as the rain kept pelting down.

After what seemed an interminable wait, he rang again. It was now raining torrentially and, on the exposed top of the hill, the gusts of wind forced him to lean against the wall. He rang again, more feebly, and waited for another age.

Then he concentrated on mustering enough strength to walk back to the taxi. He had no idea where to ask the driver to take him, but it was no use staying there.

He was halfway to the car when the door creaked open and a monk thrust his head outside. "Who's there?"

"I'm a lay brother," Leo answered in a voice drowned by the rain, and started back towards the door.

"Speak up; what did you say?"

"A lay brother, I'm a Third Order brother." With this exertion, he staggered and nearly fainted.

"Are you drunk? How dare you interrupt our prayers?"

In an unbidden flash, the twelve labors of Hercules came to Leo's mind. Cesare's magical hero was supposed to emulate them; but he, poor fool, could hardly manage to beg for hospitality! He commanded his own body to snap out of it, just for a few seconds, and said, as convincingly as he could: "*Padre*, I'm a brother of the Third Order of Franciscans. I have come here seeking a time of solitude and peace. And of prayer. Could you host me, please?" Rain was streaking down his face as he said so.

Father Teresio looked at him appraisingly from under his hood, though he could see little in the gathering darkness. "Have you got any luggage?" he asked at length.

"In the taxi."

"Get it and follow me."

"Thank you, Father, thank you." Leo remained by the wall, leaning against it, and beckoned the driver. But the latter merely rolled down his window by a couple of inches. "Please, help me with my luggage. I'll give you a big tip."

Father Teresio showed them the way to a cell. A bed was in it, a closet, a writing table, a stool. A bare bulb hanging from the ceiling provided the illumination.

Leo stumbled into the cell and sat down on the bed. He paid the driver and succeeded in keeping his eyes open as he listened to the instructions the monk was pouring out.

"All the Hours of the Divine Office are said in common in the hermitage church. We rise at half an hour after midnight for Matins, Lauds, and Meditation; these last for an hour and a half. Then we rest till sunrise, when we go again to the church for the Office of Prime, and then return to our oratories to celebrate Mass. A slight collation is then taken, and the time between that and Tierce is spent in spiritual reading. We sing Tierce at nine, and follow it with the conventual Mass. The remainder of the morning till the Office of None, at eleven, is passed in study and manual labor.

"Will you be up at one in the morning for Matins? I will tell you then of the other Offices. Our lay guests are not expected to observe our schedule in its entirety, but this is a place of prayer."

Leo had exhausted his strength. He could only sit on the bed and stare at the monk speechlessly. "You seem very tired, brother. Rest well, and Heaven bless you." Father Teresio left him alone. As Leo laid himself down on the bed, he passed out.

He woke late in the morning, still in his damp clothes, realizing that he had skipped many of the prescribed prayers. He must get well, as quickly as possible. He got up from the bed, and fell to the stone floor, passing out again.

Discovering him before too long, the monks understood that their brother was sick, and tended to him as they tend to their vegetable gardens.

Within a few days, they witnessed his recovery. Father Teresio had judged that their guest was not really ill, but worn out. He was not the first to reach the monastery in such a state. Stress was a demon capable of vanquishing even the strongest in the mundane world. All they knew about him was his name: Leonardo, he had said. That seemed to suffice, along with his unspoken but evident gratitude.

Back on his feet, Leo had begun to attend Mass and some of the Offices, to give the impression that he was there to seek spiritual healing, not to hide from his pursuers. For he must be a wanted man by now. He had left his hotel room looking like a slaughterhouse. They had his name, his passport details. Surely the manager had called the police, and they were looking for him.

When Leo had finally been able to reach the light switch in his dark hotel room, he had lifted his hands to his eyes and rubbed them. They felt sticky, both hands and face, but his eyes opened. He blinked, and to his immense relief, he could see. The first thing he made out was a pair of bloody hands. Next, he saw a pool of blood on the table before him. He looked around, moving his neck cautiously, as though it might break, or else in terror of what he might see next. There was a pool of blood on the gray carpet, too. Blood was dripping from around his fingernails. He could feel it squishing in his shoes. To his horror, he saw blood oozing through the pores of his skin. As he lay on the floor, outspent, motionless, he recalled the interview with Dr. Elander, and wondered whether this was reality, or a new phase of his vision.

After some time, he concluded that this was reality, and he was still alive. He slowly and painfully raised himself to his feet and staggered to the bathroom. The mirror showed him his face: blood smeared on his cheeks, still oozing from the corners of his eyes, and dripping from his nose. He turned on the shower. Unable to stand up, he squatted in a corner, and let the water cleanse him. His breathing was irregular and labored. He vomited repeatedly, observing the bile gather with the red water by the drain hole.

As the shower washed his blood away, the pain gradually diminished. His fingers and toes had stopped bleeding and felt only raw, while his face and the skin all over his body felt no worse than after a bad sunburn.

So this was not death yet, but what happened when you "vaticinated" as an uninitiate. He managed to crawl out of the shower. Sitting on the floor in the bathroom, leaning his back on the wall, he looked across the room at the blood-soaked carpet. Some light was beginning to creep in from the window. He could only move in slow motion, and had to concentrate on his every action. He wanted desperately to fall into bed and sleep, but he knew he must not do that. From the closet he took out the plastic laundry bag, and put his bloodied clothes and shoes in it. Then he slowly dressed. His watch told him that it was eight in the morning.

Leo was lying on the bed in his cell, going back over all these details in his mind, when a young monk knocked and entered, carrying a tray. "*Pasta e fasoi*, Brother Leonardo! That should put some strength into you. And there's plenty of rye bread and butter. I hope we'll see you in chapel soon."

As Leo gratefully ate the beans and pasta, he continued his reminiscing, deliberately retracing every detail. He felt that his quest now hung by a hair, and that his every action from now on must be disciplined and calculated.

With a series of supreme efforts, he had packed his suitcase, sticking the laundry bag in it; put the ancient manuscript in his backpack; dragged his feet downstairs; settled the bill; gone to the nearest bar and drunk a quart of milk with many espressos in between. Then, at a snail's pace, he had walked to the bookshop the concierge had told him was nearby, and found what he needed: a book for tourists on a tight budget called *Lodging in Italy's Monasteries*. Yet he had not bought it.

He smiled at the recollection. Had the police questioned the bookseller, she could have shown them from the register exactly what books had been bought early in the morning. That would have given them a clue, however vague, that he couldn't afford, as he didn't know how long he would feel so terribly weak and unable to survive on the run. So he had copied a single suitable address. He had then managed to reach the railway station and get on the first train to Padua.

Once there, he had dragged his feet to a café in a daze, barely able to keep his eyes open. Much as he wanted to leave immediately, he just did not have enough strength even to push himself up from the table. He sat there for hours, drinking *caffelatte*, coffee with milk, three cups of it. Eventually he gathered enough energy to find a taxi to take him to the Camaldolese hermitage in the Euganean Hills. He had hoped that in a monastery he would not be asked for identification and, mercifully, had not been.

"So, here I am," he thought as he took his empty soup bowl back to the kitchen, caressing his fast-growing beard. "What can I do next?

Where is Orsina? How can I save her?" He felt ominously that she needed him, and that only he could save her. For all his success in stealing the forbidden book and then taking a bite at one of the fruits from the Second Tree of Life, the vaticination had failed: he had learned about Angela's fate, but nothing about Orsina's. He had burst the barriers of time and space, but only in regard to the past. Unlike a dream, he found that he had total recall of the experience, but how could he be certain that he had seen what really happened? Could his dislike of the Baron and his own fantasy have scripted a completely fictitious scenario? Had he hallucinated?

No, he said to himself. That was as real as his blood. The forbidden book was unspeakably powerful, and dangerous, especially in the Baron's hands. And it left him no choice: he must return to the exercise, and force it to reveal what he needed to know, no matter what the cost to his own health and sanity. But what if he died this time?

Leo asked himself the question again as he walked back to his cell. He was past caring for his own life: if necessary he would open the book at the same page, and go through the whole agonizing process again. Yet he realized that he mustn't do this. If he died, Orsina would be left to herself, to her kidnappers, and, assuming she was released, to whatever her uncle had in mind for her. Leo had read in the papers of his despair over the death of his niece, had seen the photographs of his weeping at the funeral—yet *he* had killed her, he, her uncle and guardian. Nigel, financial genius though he might be, would be no match for that brilliant, arrogant, twisted monster if it came to a battle for Orsina's soul.

Should he call the police? No. They might give him a hard time explaining the blood bath, but far worse, they might detain him, thus neutralizing Orsina's only potential rescuer, while the Baron could continue in his pursuits, whatever they might be. Who would believe Leo? What proof did he have? He had seen Angela's death at the Baron's hands in a vaticination. The police would laugh in his face, and at best have a hack psychiatrist assess his sanity.

Why had the Baron acted so ruthlessly? What was he trying to achieve through poor Angela, apart from magical ecstasy? And why did he need her for that? Wasn't he a Della Riviera? Leo did wonder how he himself had been able to achieve vaticination at all. Cesare della Riviera had clearly stated that "underprivileged aspirants perform vaticination through the art of necromancy," and he certainly had done nothing of the sort. Was he to infer that, although a beginner, he was *not* an underprivileged aspirant? How could that be?

Another knock on the door interrupted his train of thought. It was Father Giacinto, who lived in the cell next door.

"Brother Leonardo," he said, "I'll be working in the garden. Some fresh air would do you good. Would you like to join me?"

"Gladly."

Outdoors, Father Giacinto said: "Winter is approaching. I'm only looking after artichokes here in the open. Could you help me weed around the edges?"

After about half an hour's work, Father Giacinto invited "Leonardo" to take a walk in the garden, all contained inside the monastery's cloistered walls.

"Look at this tree," Father Giacinto said. They were now standing a few paces away from an age-old matriarch of a yew tree. Her crown was irregular, with many dried twigs and branchlets, while her higher boughs were a cascade of foliage—thick and luxuriant—dark green when seen from the sky and of a pale lemon color from beneath. Bright red berries punctuated it to the joy of many visiting birds. Sizeable burls and knots had grown over the scars from many storms. The massive trunk, of a reddish-purple hue, was hollow. And inviting. *Padre* said: "Shall we step inside?"

They did.

"Isn't this a beautiful little house? The yew is known as *l'albero della morte*, the tree of death, because all his parts except the flesh of the berries are poisonous, and because it is often found in cemeteries, especially in the north. But I call it the tree of life." His words were echoed by the cavernous trunk. "We have some time between prayers and manual work, here. So I've studied botany. Well, it appears that the yew is technically immortal."

Leo looked baffled.

"Yes," the monk continued, "if no external agent intervened, no overwhelming windstorm and above all no chainsaw, it seems that a yew would go on living forever. It simply refuses to die. In time, after centuries of life, if left to itself it sends some branches down to the ground, and from it they sprout up again, as new trees.

“I’ve also learned that this tree was growing on Earth long before the dinosaurs. Fossils have been exhumed and dated. Could the Creator, in His infinite wisdom, have placed it on Earth as a reminder to us? As the second tree of life?”

Leo was listening keenly. Father Giacinto elaborated. “Yes, we were sent off from the Garden of Eden; yet the Creator left us with trees and fruits and vegetables and herbs to remember it by. If we ignored them, if we ignored His gifts to us, wouldn’t that be sin?” He smiled, then said: “Follow me; some more fresh air will do you good.” They ambled to the monastery’s kitchen garden. A section of it was inside a hothouse. They entered it, and Leo instinctively unbuttoned his jacket.

“You see,” the monk said, “we grow all sorts of herbs here. The elixir you’ve been drinking since you arrived has been made with some of them for centuries. The same old recipe. Doesn’t it work like magic? I can’t tell you the recipe—you know, it’s one of those secrets that if I told you I’d have to kill you.” He winked, smiling. “These are God’s gifts, brother, and we should cherish them. The prophet Ezekiel says that after our fall from grace we were catapulted into the world of reality. It is true, but in it there are vestiges of what the Garden of Earthly Delights used to be like, and it is our duty to try and recapture it.”

It was almost sunset, time for the monks to go and sing Vespers. Leo excused himself.

On the way back to his cell Leo chanced on another guest. They were the only two guests, he was told. Rafael—who looked uncannily like Christ in a famous painting by Mantegna—spoke briefly. He was just out of rehab, he said straightforwardly, not trusting himself to reenter the real world just yet. “And you?” he asked quietly, “are you also out of rehab?”

Leo, very thin and emaciated, realized that he looked the part, but said, “No, I was under a lot of stress, couldn’t cope anymore. I’m here to recover.”

The only link Rafael kept with the outside world—the monks had not objected—consisted of a few newspapers. Every morning the owner of a newsstand from nearby Abano Terme delivered to him *Il Sole 24 Ore*, Italy’s leading financial daily, *Il Corriere delle Sera*, *La Repubblica,* and *Il Gazzettino di Venezia*. “Never gave a damn about the real world, so I thought I might try to read about it, for a start. I have a whole stack of newspapers, the last ten days' worth. You're welcome to look at them."

Leo spent the evening going through the newspapers, starting from the earliest date. He learned that there had been quite a development in Nigel's predicament.

As a probatory device, Avvocato Alemanni had requested the PM urgently to subpoena the chambermaid employed at Villa Riviera. Apparently Mr. MacPherson himself, on hearing the news of his wife's kidnapping, had insisted with his lawyer that he take this step. The PM had yielded, for the *assunzione di testimonianza* could not be denied, as per article 194 of the Code of Penal Procedure. Both the PM and the GIP, the judge in charge of the preliminary investigation, had wondered about this tardy request: why hadn't Mr. MacPherson asked for her testimony weeks before, as soon, in fact, as he had been detained?

The answer came in court, to the delight of the media, which gloated over every detail. A somewhat garishly dressed Samanta was being questioned both by the PM and Inspector Ghedina. With candor, she confessed to a relationship with *Signor* MacPherson. When pressed by the PM, she admitted to having had sex repeatedly with the guest of the family, the husband of her employer's niece.

"Did you have intercourse with him during the night of the 4th to the 5th of August?" asked the PM.

"Yes."

"Why didn't you tell us when you were questioned at the villa? Watch what you say, because now you're in trouble, as an accessory after the fact."

"I . . . I didn't want to compromise *Signor* MacPherson."

"Really? Yet you don't care about compromising him now, do you?"

Ghedina took over the questioning. "What made you change your mind?"

Samanta, the articles related, had stuck to her version and had reported to the media waiting outside the court all that she had confessed during the interrogation. No embellishment was needed. *Signor* MacPherson was a generous lover, she declared. The last night they had sex, he had waited for his wife to fall asleep, then had slipped out of his bed, and out of their room. He had stolen away toward the staff's sleeping quarters and had been with her almost until dawn. She remembered that distinctly, as she had urged him repeatedly to go back to his wife, or he might be caught. But *Signor* MacPherson was so horny . . .

As a result of Samanta's confession, Nigel finally had an alibi. It strengthened Leo's belief that his vaticination had not been a hallucinatory delusion: he too knew that Nigel had *not* killed Angela. Nigel's release, therefore, seemed imminent. How could he be detained any longer?

Another unforeseen event was in store, Leo learned as he read the more recent newspapers. Nigel had been interrogated once more, this time jointly by Inspector Ghedina and the PM, as the GIP herself presided over the proceedings. In the end, the GIP had granted the PM's request: Mr. MacPherson was to remain detained.

An outraged Alemanni rushed to sue the PM, the GIP, the Court of Bolzano, and even the Minister as well as the Ministry of Justice for the protracted and in his view illegal and unconstitutional detention of Mr. MacPherson in the investigation of the death of Angela Riviera della Motta.

A celebrated editorialist from the *Corriere* obtained an interview with the PM himself. The reason for Mr. MacPherson's continued provisional detention was simple: during the preliminary investigation, he had lied repeatedly and was therefore not to be trusted. He had omitted to speak about his many jaunts in wine country in the company of the victim; he had lied about his activities during the night in which the murder had taken place; now, he wanted the world to believe in the belated confession of the chambermaid. Had he arranged for her to be paid handsomely for her lies? He could afford the type of money that changes a person's life and might well induce her to lie on command. Avvocato Alemanni could have quietly conveyed the offer to her and reached an unwritten agreement. His career read as a long list of court victories, but more than once he had shown that his approach to the law was Machiavellian. The chambermaid's belated confession, which contradicted her earlier one, was an instance of inculpatory evidence: evidence that without a specific and/or particular fact cannot be proved. Reasonable doubt did persist. Neither Ghedina, the PM, nor the GIP was even remotely satisfied by the latest alleged evidence as conclusive proof of Mr. MacPherson's innocence.

More pressing but less useful news concerned Orsina. Her uncle's pathetic attempt to pay the ransom despite the explicit ban to do so and the freezing of his assets had won him the sympathy of the public. Letters and e-mails continued to reach the newspapers: couldn't the police have turned a blind eye and allowed the wretched man to pay the ransom? Since the aborted attempt to pay the kidnappers, no news had been heard of Orsina. But at least, Leo was relieved to read, no part of her body had arrived by mail so as to induce the Baron to pay up, no matter what.

On a more international level, more repentant desecrators of Christian holy sites continued to turn themselves in. Self-incriminating confessions were raining in from all sides. Young militants from the ultra-right admitted to the recent desecrations of Europe's most hallowed places of pilgrimage. They said that their intent had been to blame such sacrileges on the Muslims, so as to escalate the tension and usher in the creation of a modern Holy League, whose goal was to kick the invaders out of Europe.

Leo wondered at this strange phenomenon, but was nevertheless relieved by the news. The good tidings somehow had filtered through to the monks, who were giving thanks to God and the Blessed Virgin, patroness of their monastery, for having instilled wisdom in their lost sheep. It wouldn't be long, thought Leo, before the Pope seized the moment and capitalized on the very Christian penchant for forgiveness.

A few more days went by at the monastery. Rafael, feeling more confident, told Father Teresio that he would be staying only another week. September had turned nippy and crisp as the chestnut trees of the Euganean Hills were beginning to shed their leaves. One night, unable to sleep, Leo left his cell and walked outdoors, into the garden. It was cold, cloudless, moonless. But the stars shone keenly.

His mother had taught him stargazing. "Look for Polaris, the North Star, and think of it as your guiding light. A long time ago, sailors would be lost without it." This was the first thing he had learned; and the North Star was found within the constellation of the Little Bear—in Italian, Orsina. It's as if one of his fondest memories had prepared him since childhood for her. He suppressed a sigh; this was not the time for regrets but for action.

Back inside his cell, Leo wondered what his next move might be. By association, another constellation had come to mind: Leo. He remembered suddenly that Hercules, in one of his labors, had been asked by the goddess Juno to kill the Nemean lion—leo in Latin. Hercules had strangled it to death and then placed it in the sky, as the constellation Leo. He shuddered: what if *The Magical World of the Heroes* was not asking him to be a hero by emulating the labors of Hercules, but rather one of his victims?

Both this belated insight and his experience of vaticination made him reluctant to reopen the forbidden book, now smeared here and there with his own blood. Of one thing he was certain: he was not going to try any more of its magical exercises. The last one had nearly killed him. But his fate was now inexorably tied to the book, and Cesare della Riviera, for all his inhuman qualities, seemed to be the only person capable of guiding him in rescuing Orsina.

The next day, after trying in vain for hours to come up with a plan, Leo retrieved the book from his backpack. For all its beauty and erudition, he felt a physical revulsion for it, and knew that he could no longer study it as he had done before. Orsina was still missing; time was too short. The tools of scholarship seemed feeble in comparison with the door that it had opened to other levels of being. He remembered the ancient divinatory practice of the *Sortes Virgilianae*, in which one opened Virgil's *Aeneid* at random and took as counsel the first line that appeared. Why not give it a try with the forbidden book, and see what it had to say? "It's a start," he said to himself, half-believing in it. "It's already a giant step for me to be able to reopen the book."

The volume fell open near the end. Here, in the penultimate chapter, called "The Powers of the Cave of Mercury," was the sentence:

> Not only will the Hero enjoy the fruits of immortality, but his happy influence will forever rain down on his descendants, if only his four witnesses stand in his stead.

Leo had paid little heed to these four witnesses, but Cesare's commentary now riveted his attention:

> Know that the four witnesses are the four bodily humors: the sanguine, being blood; the choleric, being yellow bile; the phlegmatic, being phlegm; and the melancholic, being black bile. The Hero shall extract them in moderate quantity from

> his own body and hermetically seal them in four vessels. These shall be placed on the *ara gentis* in a convenient location where none but the firstborn shall enter, protected by sigils of the four elements and by the ancestral *fasces* of the Riviera.

So that was the meaning of the shrine in the Palazzo Riviera, with its axes and four vials. *Ara gentis* meant "altar of the family." Like an Egyptian pharaoh's tomb, it preserved the physical relics of the Hero, in the belief that his influence was thereby captured in some occult way. What exactly these humors were, and above all how Cesare had extracted them, were matters that Leo did not care to think about. He read on:

> Let the firstborn seek the *descensum arduum Averni*, to whose gate Mercury jealously holds the key, having first learned the *pharmacopoeia* of the Art. Let him tend the *ara gentis* and ensure that no harm come to the four witnesses. This shall be the place of his most solemn resort, for the practice of our mysteries. Thereafter he shall enter and leave at will through the broader path, seeing to it that no swine force their way thither, to snuffle up our precious pearls; nay, not even Hebe, the companion of his bed, shall know of this. But our Tree shall send its roots into the magical earth, and guard it from all harm.

The references to the Palazzo Riviera could not be clearer. Leo did not want to know what "mysteries" Emanuele had been practicing there, with or without his niece. The Commentary had already stated outright that "as Jupiter chose as wife his sister Juno, so a kinship of blood is favorable to the practices of the weaker kind. For though they cannot contain their alembic within themselves, let it be a work shared with a *soror mystica*." A mystical sister? Leo shuddered: having lost one companion of his blood, might the old monster be hoping to pursue his magic with Orsina? Ironically, her having been kidnapped could be seen as a blessing in disguise. But what was he thinking?

This little act of divination had brought Leo no closer to discovering her; yet it had pointed him straight to the palazzo on the Grand Canal, which, in Orsina's words, seemed to be interconnected with the book. He would try it once more, with the clearly formulated question: "Where is she?"

This time, the book fell open at an earlier page, with one of those familiar cryptograms: MENSTRUUM, derived from the phrase *MENsura STRUcturae Verae Magiae*—"Measure of the structure of true magic," or equally, "Measure of the true magic of the structure."

Leo had already "measured the structure," pacing off the rooms in search of some chamber hidden among them, yet the chamber he had found was not thus concealed: the Cave of Mercury was a regular room, with a door that people passed by every day. And as for the primary meaning of the word, he thought wryly, had he not himself bled? He turned to the commentary, in which Cesare concluded the chapter with a typical piece of mystery-mongering:

> As the menstruum is hidden securely in the womb, prepared by Nature for the nourishment of the fetus, so the Hero, at need, will find a secure and secret place through due measure. *Coli umbras inaccessas.*

That phrase, with its multiple meanings of "worship/frequent/cultivate/inhabit the inaccessible shades/shadows," sounded promising in the context, but had yielded only the meaningless COLUMBINA, from *COLi UMBras INAccessas*: "dove-like" or "dove-colored." It did not seem to get him any further.

# TWENTY-THREE

"I never know with what name you sages call him who too willingly obeys his heart: for he certainly is no hero; but is he perhaps a coward for this?" Leo knew many passages from Foscolo's *Last Letters of Jacopo Ortis* by heart, and this one seemed appropriate. The world, however, considered him neither a hero nor a coward but, in one word, a criminal. The reporter from the *Gazzettino di Venezia* had published the strange circumstances in which room 331 of the Hotel Luna had been found. *Professore* Kavenaugh had already been wanted by the police for questioning in relation to the kidnapping of Orsina Riviera della Motta; now, he might well be wanted for murder.

The next day, Leo read echoes of the article in both the *Corriere* and the *Repubblica*, adding some embroidery to it as well as his photo, downloaded from the Georgetown University website. It was in black and white, about five years old, and reproduced in low definition. Leo caressed his thickening beard and hoped it would be enough to disguise his identity. The monks did not read the papers; Rafael had read them, and not made the connection. Or had he? He had been looking at him in a funny way, lately. Leo took a deep breath: maybe he was just being paranoid.

Among others, there was an article in the *Repubblica* entitled "Deeds and Misdeeds of Ispettore Ghedina." Much of the Inspector's conduct in the dual investigation was being criticized, including his abuse of *custodia cautelare*, provisional detention, though for that he had found good accomplices in the PM and the GIP, both in Bolzano and in Verona. The accusation of breaching the civil rights of ordinary citizens was not meant to break a lance for the chief suspect, Mr. MacPherson, but rather to call attention to the Baron's seven students; they were still being held.

But the next day, Leo learned that the PM in Verona had revoked the provisional detention of the students and set them free. Being himself unjustly suspected of various crimes, Leo sympathized with the students, whose only fault, probably, was being near the villa when the murder was committed. That was assuming it had taken place there, which, according to Inspector Ghedina's investigation, was far from certain. The papers reported no news about Orsina, other than that she was still missing. Leo was thinking about her day and night, and was prepared more than ever to do anything that might help her. Perhaps revisiting the events he was aware of might be useful.

"If the Baron killed Angela," Leo began to ponder, "*he* could be the one who's kidnapped Orsina, or at any rate staged her kidnapping. It sounds so improbable, what with borrowing to pay the ransom, and even going personally to the drop-off place, only to be humiliated by the police. . . . Still, why would he have kidnapped Orsina?"

Leo checked himself. Just because he had disliked the Baron, and now found him monstrous, he must not allow his emotions to interfere. Could Orsina have found out about her sister's murder? But how, when professional detectives were at their wits' end trying to solve it? During their last phone conversation, she hadn't mentioned anything about suspecting someone, hadn't even alluded to that. Someone else, however, had been suspicious all along. What had Marianna, the old housekeeper, told him, exactly? "The Baron is as sly as a fox." But she'd also called Leo "as blind as a mole and as deaf as a post."

Of course! How did *he* find out about it? Through the Book! The Baron knew that Orsina had the book; why, he had personally and solemnly given it to her; had been urging her to study it; he knew that she is "gifted." He must have been terrified that *she* would gain the fruits of the Tree of Life, practice vaticination, and *see what he, Leo, had seen*.

No, that was not it. The Baron didn't need to kidnap Orsina to prevent her from vaticinating. All he had to do was make her copy of the forbidden book disappear—and it had! Orsina herself had told him on the phone that she couldn't find it. This once more confirmed the Baron as Angela's murderer, but cleared him, in Leo's mind, of suspicion as Orsina's kidnapper. But then, had the book really been stolen by him, or had it just been misplaced by, say, Samanta? Once more, Leo was groping in the dark and wasting precious time. What was he doing, hiding away and mumbling prayers along with a group of peace-loving men who had renounced the world? Foscolo's words did *not* apply: he was not a hero, granted, but he *was* a coward.

The next morning brought unexpected news about Nigel. In very orderly chronological fashion, *Il Sole 24 Ore* explained the surprising decision concerning the English billionaire. The very day after Angela

Riviera della Motta's death, Inspector Ghedina had gone to Villa Riviera to question her relatives, namely her uncle and sister. Within a few hours, Agent Gallorini had joined his boss and proceeded to search the villa. The police did not have a search warrant yet, but it was the Baron himself who exhorted them to do all they could to find clues leading to the murderer of his niece. This all sounded like privileged information, thought Leo. Perhaps the *Sole 24 Ore* had an informer within the police? Anyway, Gallorini had confiscated many items from the villa: the Baron's computers; boxes and boxes crammed with letters he exchanged with scholars all over the world; essays he had written for his lectures; documents from the Romanian staff, even the chambermaid's diary, only because an agent had found it in a peculiar place: under her mattress.

Most of the time since had been spent in going through the Baron's formidable writings, a task for which Gallorini's academic training, before he gave up hope for a classicist's career, served him well. The letters and documents showed colossal erudition but no unlawful plot of any sort. Only after Samanta's deposition had it occurred to Gallorini to read her diary. And there it was, in her own round and childlike calligraphy: the itemized chronicle of her affair with the Englishman. Gallorini had shown her diary to both Ghedina and the PM. One by one, the incriminated entries dated and minutely detailed her encounters with *Signor* MacPherson, as she continued to refer to him, down to the various sexual positions they tried and indulged in. On that last fateful night, the couple had been experimenting with a variety of them, with long pauses in between. Samanta had written the last entry as soon as Mr. MacPherson had returned to his room. She was still shaking with excitement. The sex, the secrecy, *Signor* MacPherson's very generous tips: all this kept her from sleeping and compelled her to write down her feelings. The diary had been confiscated a day and a half after she had penned that entry, and as no one had touched it since, this evidence, which had been in the investigators' hands all along, conclusively exculpated Mr. MacPherson from the charge of having murdered Angela Riviera della Motta. When she had met with her death, he had been otherwise engaged.

The PM, with the GIP's assent, was not only forced to revoke the order of provisional detention but, pressed by Alemanni, to issue a formal apology on behalf of the Court of Bolzano. The next day, however, the readers were told that Mr. MacPherson, once released, had asked his lawyer to drop all legal actions against the various judges, the court, and the Minister and Ministry of Justice. He was deeply ashamed of his own conduct, and hoped for his name to disappear from papers and tabloids. He said that he would put all his energy and means toward the search for his wife.

Although the *registro degli indagati*, in which the name and details of every suspect is filed, by now numbered many pages, Ghedina's investigation no longer had a single plausible suspect. Leo smiled in spite of himself: the Baron was indeed a sly fox. As for Orsina's kidnapping, *Leo* was the chief suspect! The irony of the notion sickened him, but he read on.

During the last week, the papers had much to say about the "repentant desecrators." It turned out that they had many things in common. All were young Caucasian men, most of them from a working class background, and all leaning to a vaguely traditional ultra-right wing. They all stated that they had not realized that a simple act of vandalism could produce the results it had, when multiplied by many similar acts happening all over Europe. But even as they were desecrating the holy site of their choice, they did not necessarily do so of their own volition, but as if they were possessed. They recollected acting as if under the influence, not of alcohol or drugs, but an inner influence guiding them and their acts. Now that it had faded, they had begun to think clearly and to put things in perspective.

It seemed a specious argument, possibly invented to reduce their sentence. Europe was on the brink of civil war; indeed the war could have escalated and become a full-blown clash of civilizations, involving two or more continents with millions of casualties. The young men realized that they had been the catalysts of events far greater than they could have envisioned. Now that they could think clearly once more, they had felt an urge to go to the local authorities and confess. As soon as Felipe had confessed the most serious crime, the bombing of Santiago Cathedral, they had mustered the courage to do as much, their acts being not terrorism but merely sacrilege.

It was time for Vespers again. Leo thought it wise to join the monks, but even as he sang, and then ate alone in his cell, his mind could not stop worrying.

What had the Baron made of Angela? How long had he been abusing her? Why had she allowed it? Leo had no answer to these questions, but did remember from his vaticination, and vividly, her entrance into the Baron's studio: she looked like a zombie. Did Emanuele have some hypnotic power over her, possibly the 'power over women' that Cesare was too much of a gentleman to reveal? And then, what was he doing with this magic? Was he trying to attain a state of mystical exaltation? Trying to make himself a god? When he was lecturing those young men about transcendence, he was obviously hinting at some strange practices.

"Those young men . . . " Leo wondered, "wasn't there a zombified look about them, too? There'd have to be, for them to sit for hours listening to the Baron's sermons!"

Discouraged by his lack of progress, frustrated, angry even at himself, and feeling that he might have not done justice to the hints furnished by his divination a few days before, Leo returned to the forbidden book. Since logical deduction had yielded no results, he still had nothing better to pin his hopes on for finding Orsina.

Opening the book he searched for a certain passage. Here it was: the one on how "the Hero, at need, will find a secure and secret place," with its cryptogram about "inaccessible shades." Who needed to find a secure and secret place? The Baron? Orsina? Himself? All three? This was too close to ignore. He looked at the ends of the other chapters which Cesare concluded with Latin tags. There was one that Orsina herself had mentioned, the very first time they had discussed the cryptograms, in Villa Riviera's garden: *Pulsa cineres, elige lacunam*. "Pulsa" had many meanings, too: strike, beat, urge, disturb, and so on. What did one do to ashes? One swept them away. Then what? "Choose the hole/pit"—to put them in? All Cesare said before offering this ambiguous advice was:

> Aeneas in his great need descended to the Underworld through the Cave of the Sibyl. The Hero, however, needs no Sibylline guidance, but only this: *Pulsa cineres, elige lacunam*.

"My God," Leo suddenly exclaimed, "what sort of joke is this?" Failing to elicit any Latin or Italian word from the motto, from *PULsa CINeres, ELige LAcunam* he had hit on the name PULCINELLA. And what had the last one been? COLUMBINA. They were both characters in the *Commedia dell'arte*, the popular street theater of Italy, and the originals of the Venetian carnival masks. Before long, he had found two more such passages. In one of them, the commentary concluded as follows:

> Should the Hero be pursued by all the Furies, he shall vanish from their sight if he only knows this: *Arcanorum lectio chimæra nostra.*

The Latin tag had the highly appropriate meaning: "Reading secret things is our chimera," and, from *ARcanorum LECtio CHImera NOstra*, yielded the name of ARLECCHINO, Harlequin. The other passage read: "Let the Hero, beset with cares, take refuge in the hollows of trees, with satyrs and fauns for company, for *Panisci talia onera*," meaning something like "Such are the burdens of Pan," and, from *PANisci TALia ONEra*, condensing to PANTALONE, Pantaloon.

What the hell was this? A comic subtext hidden in the haystack of alchemical learning? And invariably coupled with references to dire need and concealment? The incongruity was too much for Leo: he shut the book and shook with hysterical laughter.

A short while later, Rafael handed Leo the newspapers of the previous day. The *Gazzettino* had a photo of the Baron in San Michele, laying flowers on the family tomb, in memory of Angela. So the Baron was in Venice? Grieving at the cemetery and in his palazzo, the public was led to believe. Leo was so outraged that he joined the monks at prayer, to numb the feeling through repetition of familiar Latin phrases.

At night, when his mind had cleared, Leo could not stop thinking about the Baron. He reviewed mentally all that he knew about the Palazzo Riviera and its secret hiding places. Mindful of the book's advice concerning the "true measure of the structure," he thought of how hiding places could be concealed in such a massive building. Perhaps he should view the *palazzo* from the outside and sketch every window-opening; then, once inside, he would identify them. If there were incongruity, it would point to the "measure of the structure" that had been compromised or fudged, just as in the secret staircase, to form a hidden chamber or hideout. Oh, wasn't he clever? No, he was a poor fool! What did Pulcinella & Co. have to do with anything? What on earth?

It was late, it was cold in the cell and, as ever, he was in the dark. He fell asleep, and dreamed that there was something growing on his cheeks, not beard, but lichens; mosses were growing out of his nostrils and ears. He woke up in a cold sweat. What was happening to him? By living in concealment, was he becoming a living dead?

Leo got off the bed and groped for the light switch. He saw that steam was coming out of his mouth—this time, though, because there was no heating in the monastery. Of course, that was it! Angela had looked like an automaton, a zombie. Although she was a flirt, she could not have wanted to violate all taboos with her uncle and guardian. No, no: that empty stare in her eyes spoke volumes. The Baron's students had looked like zombies, too. Then, the young men who had turned themselves in, presumably also his students, had spoken of "acting as if under the influence, not of alcohol or drugs, but an inner influence" guiding them and their acts. But when such an influence had faded out, they had begun to think clearly. Why had it faded out? Had somebody talked them out of their convictions? No article in the papers had reported anything of the sort.

It was then that a terrible suspicion finally dawned on Leo, as through it the whole scheme seemed to make sense. Leo recalled his last conversation with Orsina: the Baron had told her that she could profit from *The Magical World* much more than he could. Surprised, she had asked why, and her uncle had stated: "It's simple: you are more gifted than I am."

Leo opened the book and looked feverishly for a passage that he vaguely remembered reading when still in Venice, in which Cesare had written a charitable word for those who were *not* gifted. He found it:

> Some who would achieve the Fruits of the Tree of Life did not strangle serpents in their cradles, that is to say, they are not born with the powers of demigods as Hercules was, and will never achieve these Labors unaided. However, if they cultivate the love and friendly cooperation of a Hebe, then through suitable intercourse with her they may be led to accomplish no lesser marvels.

In an appendix, Cesare described the practices of sexual alchemy that such underprivileged aspirants could resort to. Leo found them appalling, but was forced to conclude that that was it. Emanuele, having realized that he had not "strangled serpents" in his cradle, that he was not gifted by birthright, had had to settle for another sort of strangulation. He had cultivated Angela's "love and friendly cooperation" and used her for his weird, life-threatening rituals. Leo could hardly believe that the old man had been doing some of the more explicitly sexual things with his own niece, but at this point nothing seemed impossible.

How long had this been going on, to reduce her to that state of mindless subjugation? Leo had seen that same empty stare on the faces of the Baron's students. They too were under his thumb. By using poor Angela as a medium, the Baron had been able to exert his influence over them, which would explain his constant lecturing over the summer. Hence the blossoming of sacrilegious acts all over Europe, all carried out, according to the papers, by young ultra-right men of similar background. But then, as if the spell had been broken, the compulsion to desecrate the holy sites had faded out, and they had come to their senses. When? Shortly after Angela had been found dead!

Of course! The Baron, as Leo had seen in the vaticination, had overdone it, and in his rapture had killed Angela. Left to his own devices, he had not been able to continue his practices, and had lost control over the disciples. *That was why* he—*who else*?—*had had Orsina kidnapped: for her to take Angela's place; to influence many more disciples to carry out sacrilegious or outright terrorist acts to blame on the Muslims; and finally achieve his goal: to unleash a war between Christian Europe and the Islamic invaders.*

Was Leo losing his mind? Or had he finally grasped the grand design? The commentary said it with brutal clarity:

> A kinship of blood is favorable to the practices of the weaker kind.

That was why the Baron had resorted to Angela first, and now. . . . The Baron was in Venice. Since his failed attempt to pay off the ransom, the police must be keeping a close watch over him. Wherever he went, the paparazzi lay in ambush. If indeed he had kidnapped Orsina for his magical purposes, she must be where he had privacy, where he could be at ease with himself and her, unwatched, unguarded—only in the palazzo.

But *where* in the palazzo?

Leo hated himself for not having reached these conclusions earlier. Unable to sleep, he waited for dawn. Then he said goodbye to Father Teresio and the other monks, and gave them a donation, much smaller than he would have liked because he had to conserve his cash. Rafael was still sleeping, and anyway it was best to slip away without giving him a chance to ask any questions. Padre Teresio called a taxi.

Leo knew that it is difficult to buy a weapon in Italy; not even a hunting rifle is sold without a firearms license. It was all the more impossible for a fugitive, walking casually into a gun dealer's shop. On the way to Padua, a rhyming slogan kept echoing in his tormented mind: *Usag trentasei / fascista, dove sei?* He had once taught a class about Italy in the Seventies, and the terrorism of the Red Brigades. "*Usag trentasei*" was the trade-name of an outsize monkey wrench; *fascista, dove sei?* meant "Fascist, where are you?" Kids belonging to the ultra-left back then used to buy that wrench and go hunting "fascists."

In Padua, Leo told the taxi driver to drop him off by a hardware store. As he waited for it to open, he restlessly walked around till he found a dumpster. He threw his suitcase in it, by now useless ballast. With the forbidden book and a few other things in his backpack, he went to a bar and drank a *cappuccino*, then two *espressos*. He walked back to the store. As soon as it opened, he entered.

# TWENTY-FOUR

When Leo saw the proud mass of Palazzo Riviera and thought of Orsina imprisoned inside, his first impulse was to storm it then and there. But if he were caught and overpowered, that could be the ruin of them both. He sat down on a marble bench outside the church of San Barnaba and took several deep breaths. Then he took out a sketch pad and began to draw the visible part of the palazzo, hoping that he would pass as an artistic tourist.

He carefully recorded every window, using his pencil and thumb to measure the distances between them. When he had finished, he walked around to the passage that ran by the north side of the palace and drew the upper portion of it. Then he went to a café and waited for the afternoon light to fade. In the meantime, he tried to turn his distorted sketch of the north side into a full-face view, then reconstructed the floor plan as far as he could remember it from his previous break-in.

When it was almost dark, Leo returned to the south side, where the little canal ran by the garden wall. No one was in view, so he swung himself along the garden wall and dropped down onto the threshold of the canal door. He knew this door well, having fussed over its broken hinge to entertain the tourists, and then spent three hours sitting behind it. This time, as he tried to lever it open, the lower hinge gave way and the whole door collapsed in front of him with a metallic crash. Electrified by a massive jolt of adrenaline, Leo grasped the Usag 36 and made his way down the steps.

The last time he had been here, in the vault of the tree roots, he had entered from the family shrine. This time he went on past the shrine door, still ajar as he had left it, and noticed that there were footprints facing toward him. He followed them until the dirt-floored passageway ended in a small round chamber, lined with curved walls of dirty wood. Two of the slender wall panels seemed to be flapping loose, and indeed as he pushed, they opened and he exited from the false barrel. He found himself in a series of cluttered storage rooms, then in a large disused kitchen, and this, to his relief, opened directly into the androne.

Now he was on familiar ground. He knew the main staircase, leading to the ballroom, and also the service stair up to the fourth floor. He also had a good idea of how the main floor was arranged, and that there were probably no further secrets to be discovered at that level.

Minutes after Leo had entered the canal door, Bhaskar returned from shopping. As he crossed the Campo San Barnaba, he noticed a black void where there had always been a door. Once in his third-floor quarters, he took off his coat and put away his purchases, then climbed to the fourth floor and knocked on the Baron's sitting room.

"Excuse the interruption, *Signor Barone*, but I am worried. The canal door in the garden wall is open. I noticed it when returning from my errands. It seems to have fallen in. I thought you should be informed."

"I will be down directly," boomed the Baron. "Meet me in the androne, and bring a flashlight."

"As you say, *Signor Barone*. I am very sorry to disturb you like this, and . . ." Unforgiven, Bhaskar backed away.

Leo was about to climb up the service stair when he heard footsteps coming down it. He just had time to duck behind a pillar by the entrance, noticing the presence of a wheelchair before Bhaskar emerged. The Indian was behaving oddly, holding a powerful flashlight in one hand which he shone into the darkness at the far end of the androne, and a kitchen knife in the other, with which he made sudden stabs at the air. Leo felt that if it came to the worst the monkey wrench would be the superior weapon.

After two minutes, Emanuele came down the stair, with another flashlight and, amazingly, a sword. Here Leo hoped to avoid a confrontation, being certain that superior swordsmanship would be among the Baron's accomplishments. Run through with a long blade, he would be of very little use to Orsina. The pair headed for the door from which Leo had come. Emanuele turned back to the servant. "This door should not be open," he said curtly. "Do you know where it leads?"

"No, *Signor Barone*. I'm not allowed in this part of the palace; I never go—"

"Enough; you're going there now. Follow me." The two of them entered, and their voices grew dim. Leo crept into the disused kitchen, from which he could again hear the Baron's angry voice and Bhaskar's meek replies. When their sound had faded completely, he retraced his steps through the storage rooms, as far as the false barrel.

The trapdoor had been left flapping open. Leo carefully closed it, then, as quietly as he could, maneuvered a real barrel against it. Among the debris he found a long iron bar, probably a spit, which he wedged between the door and the wall. Within two minutes he was out of the cellars and climbing the service stair.

Bhaskar was following very closely behind the Baron when the latter suddenly stopped. He had noticed that the door to the shrine was gaping open. "Stop!" he snarled. "Now go in, very slowly, and switch on the light to the left of the doorway."

Bhaskar entered the family shrine, where none but the Baron had been for the past twenty-five years, then he screamed. Two giant rats were on the altar, preening their whiskers amid a mess of shattered glass and brown slime. A nauseating smell filled the room. The *pantegane* took one look at the intruders and leapt off the altar, straight at them. The two men instinctively jumped back, and the rats scuttled between their feet and out through the passage. Bhaskar was gibbering with fright, but the Baron pushed him aside. He went up to the altar and opened the silver chest.

Leo passed the *piano nobile* and left the service stair at the third floor. This, like the second floor, was centered on a long hall looking onto the Grand Canal. He opened the doors, finding sparsely furnished rooms behind them. Each time he checked them against his sketch of the windows, to make sure that they were all accounted for.

As he started on the north side, he had a shock. The first door he opened revealed a lighted room, but there was no sound. Leo peered around the door: it was a small living room with tatty furniture, a television, and a strong smell of curry. There was no sign of Soma, and Leo was just shutting the door again quietly, not wanting to confront her at this stage of his search, when he heard the distant but distinct sound of Indian music.

Emanuele, fuming with rage, checked the door leading to the secret stair, which was locked, then left the shrine, slamming the door behind him.

"Turn left!" he said to the trembling Bhaskar. They passed through the vault of the tree roots. "Now into that doorway; on you go!" Soon they were at the canal entrance.

"*Signor Barone*, you see that I told the truth. The door has fallen in."

"I can see that, you fool, and a lot more besides. No, don't try to prop it up. Now, back to the palace, the same way we came, and be quick!"

Bhaskar scampered along the passage and into the barrel-entrance. "*Signor Barone*!" he called back, "The trapdoor is shut!"

"Then open it, you brainless monkey!"

Bhaskar pushed, to no avail. The Baron tried, too, but the false door was strong, and the iron bar stronger still. In a futile gesture, Bhaskar stuck his kitchen knife into the slit, and the blade broke off. Emanuele was speechless with rage. After several futile attempts, he said: "Follow me." But when they reached the shrine, the Baron realized that, while he had taken the trouble to select the ideal sword for a duel, he had not brought his keys. He had slammed the shrine door shut, and, unlike young Rupert, was unaware of how easily some Yale locks can be persuaded to open.

Panting from their exertion, the two returned to the broken canal door. "*Signor Barone*, how are we to get to the palace from here?"

"Can you swim?"

"No, no, *Signor Barone*, I've never learned to swim; oh please, have pity!"

"You useless mongrel. You'll have to lift me up onto the wall. Stand here, and make a stirrup of your hands."

"Excuse me, *Signor Barone*: what is a stirrup?"

"Oh God, you idiot, hold them like *this*, and I put my foot in them." Bhaskar obeyed. The Baron grabbed the door jamb with one hand, Bhaskar's shoulder with the other, and levered himself up. "Now, lift me up higher."

Bhaskar's hands hurt from the crisp leather soles of Emanuele's shoes. He could not lift him any higher, but Emanuele was already scrabbling for a handhold on the wall above. Bhaskar shifted his weight, and his foot turned on the uneven stones. As his ankle twisted, he let out a cry and swayed sideways. The two men parted company, the Baron hanging on to the wall, his legs kicking in thin air, and Bhaskar falling into the inky waters of the canal.

Leo crept silently from one spare bedroom to another, pausing to catch the faint strains of the music. He checked his sketches again, but found that he had lost count of the windows. Now he heard footsteps, too, and a distinct clink of dishes. The sounds were coming from overhead, in the direction of the ballroom. He needed to go up higher.

As he dangled from the garden wall, the Baron thought how this must be the most idiotic situation he'd ever found himself in. He painfully worked his way along to the canalside, dropped down, and rested for a while, his fingers bleeding. Not since his time in the army had he been in physical straits of any kind, and the strain told on him. He was vaguely aware of splashings in the canal, and regretted that his sword had fallen in. He got up and limped to the principal door of the palace. It was locked, and so was the adjacent service entrance. The Grand Canal entrance, even if it were open, was accessible only from the water. He rang the bell again and again, hoping to arouse Soma. But Soma would not come to the door. He was locked out of his own palace, with his servant God knows where, perhaps drowned.

Bhaskar would indeed have drowned then and there, in a canal six feet deep and narrow enough to jump over, had a waiter from the café not heard the splash and hurried over to see what had happened. He saw a brown face appear once above the water, utter a gurgling scream, and then vanish again. Without noticing the other man suspended above the doorway, he kicked off his shoes and jumped in. He had worked all summer on the Lido and was a good swimmer. He rescued Bhaskar, subduing his violent flounderings with a blow to the chin.

The Indian had been brought inside the café, shivering and not very coherent. The waiter and the proprietor could get little sense out of him. He kept saying "Palazzo Riviera," and pointing to it, evidently anxious to return. After a while the waiter decided that he had done his duty, and went to the back of the café to change into his leisure clothes. Bhaskar, dripping from head to toe, crossed the bridge to the canalside, where the Baron was ringing the bell again. "*Signor Barone, Signor Barone*: I'm all right now. Can't you enter?"

"No, I can *not*. Every door is locked, and I suppose you don't have your outdoor keys either, do you?" Without waiting to hear what words came out of Bhaskar's open mouth, he continued, "No, don't bother with excuses. Let's go find a phone."

Leo climbed the stair, past the place where he had been trapped on his previous visit, and this time found the door open to the Baron's apartments on the fourth floor. The lights were on, but no voices were to be heard. It seemed likely that the Baron and his servant were still downstairs. The southern enfilade revealed a sitting room, more intimate than the one below on account of its low ceiling but equally unwelcoming with its museum-quality furniture. Next there came a bedroom, a study, and what looked like an alchemist's laboratory, with gas tubes, glass vessels, and large majolica jars of mysterious substances.

The doors on the north side were all closed, and the rooms behind them in stark contrast to the Baron's exquisite apartments. They were dusty and almost empty, lit with bare bulbs which Leo now had no hesitation in switching on and leaving on. But they must once have been cherished, as they were all painted from floor to ceiling. The room fronting the Grand Canal was set up as a puppet theater, and its walls showed Arlecchino and Columbina flirting and embracing in a woodland setting. The next room contained the puppets, a sad crew of broken bodies and torn garments strung up on pegs. Here was the quack *Dottore*, shown attending Columbina's bedside. On one wall he was squinting at a urinary flask, on the other threatening her with a clyster.

The third room was devoted to Pantalone, the grotesque old man who is always trying to woo a young maiden. Here he was leading Columbina by the hand before an equally grotesque notary, while Arlecchino lurked in the background, winking at her. Lastly came a room painted entirely with figures of humpbacked Pulcinella in his ill-fitting white suit, cone-shaped hat, and long-nosed mask. He was shown courting, riding a donkey, getting drunk, and playing with children who looked just like himself.

All this Leo took in beneath the threshold of consciousness, straining his ears to catch the music. He thought he could hear the phone ring somewhere in the distance. Now that he was in the topsy-turvy world of the *Commedia dell'arte*, the enigmas of the book seemed to hover on the brink of solution. He recalled the Latin tags of the masked figures, ending with Pulcinella's *Pulsate cineres, elige lacunam*: Sweep the ashes, find the hole. Where does one find ashes? In the hearth; but not in this one, for the stone flags of the fireplace were remarkably clean, and partially covered by a Turkish prayer rug. Leo pushed it aside, to reveal a pair of iron rings sunk into the stone.

He expected a struggle, but the hearthstone was made to pivot, and opened easily. Underneath it he recognized the brickwork of the spiral staircase. This was evidently one of its terminals, as the shrine, four floors below, was the other. He started down it, and soon came to a cramped landing, like the one leading from the Cave of Mercury. Leo could hear the whining music clearly now, together with indistinct muttering; a woman's voice; the chink of a glass. In darkness, he paused and allowed his pupils to dilate. A yellow beam of light showed beneath the door, dimly. He took a firm grip of the wrench and threw open the door.

He stood on the threshold of a small, low-ceilinged room. There was a cot, clothes in disarray, towels flung over a chair. On a serving table was a stack of used dishes, diapers, a chamber pot. As though in mockery of the squalor, the whole room was painted with fauns and satyrs. But Leo's attention was on the open doorway to the next room: from it he heard "Bhaskar?" and something in a foreign language. "Bhaskar?"

In semidarkness, Soma was kneeling beside a mattress on the floor. When she saw Leo, she screamed, but he was on her in a moment, his hand over her mouth.

"Shut up!" he hissed, and brandished the wrench in her face. "On the floor, face downwards. Do as I say, now!" She did. "Put your hands behind your back." She obeyed. Leo had anticipated some such encounter, and took out of his backpack a hank of rope and a roll of duct tape, his eyes never leaving the terrified woman. He tied her hands to one another, and then to the radiator; next, he wound the tape tightly around her mouth.

On the mattress lay a woman, blindfolded, motionless. Was she dead? Was *Orsina* dead? Had they killed her?

As Leo screamed Orsina's name, and she did not reply, did not stir at all, rage seized him. His first impulse was to turn around and kill her jailer; then, a stronger urge overwhelmed him: to run downstairs and find the Baron—oh, to squeeze his neck, to sink his fingers inside it, to watch him writhe and turn cyanotic. Leo could see himself throw him on the ground half dead; he could see himself raise his arm and bring the wrench crushing down on the Baron's head—one, two, three, four, five, six, seven blows, till he must stop to catch his breath, and to stare at the wreckage of Emanuele's skull mixed with his brains and blood.

Leo was dashing out of the room to do just that when he heard a moan: Orsina? Had *she* moaned? Was he hearing things? He turned on his heels and the next instant he was by her.

She was wearing a nightdress and an adult diaper. What had they reduced her to? He called her name, repeatedly; she did not stir. He knelt by her, put his ear on her chest, grabbing her hand. The hand was *not* cold; there *was* a heartbeat. As a spate of emotions threatened to paralyze him, Leo forced himself to think, to be rational and efficient. "Heaven bless you, Orsina, Heaven bless you," he kept repeating in his mind as his intellect gave orders: look for her clothes, for example. He found them, folded on a chair. With trembling hands, he dressed her. There were two bottles of pills on a tray by the mattress, hypodermic syringes and needles, some ampoules. He pocketed them all, picked Orsina up, and carried her out of the room, kicking the door shut behind him.

The phone in the *palazzo* had rung and rung, but Soma had not answered. In frustration, the Baron handed the cell phone back to the bar owner, then joined Bhaskar outside, where he had left him. "There's no way to get in until the maids arrive in the morning," he said with disgust. "You'll have to spend the night in a hotel. Come with me: they'd never take you in looking like a drowned rat."

Emanuele led the way to a pensione across the Campo. The owner knew who he was and greeted him effusively, then halted as he saw the Baron's shivering and sneezing companion. "My servant has locked us out of my palace, and on top of it, he has fallen into the canal. Give him a room for the night, and wake him up at seven o'clock."

"And yourself, *Signor Barone*?"

"I shall be at the Gritti."

With Orsina in his arms, Leo maneuvered her carefully up the stairs and through the fireplace entrance, then readjusted his lift as he carried her to the main staircase and right down to the androne. The significance of the wheelchair behind the pillar was now clear: she must have arrived in it. He eased her into the seat. She moaned and half opened her eyes. Even under extreme duress, emaciated and unconscious, she was beautiful, and he kissed her on the forehead as he tucked a blanket around her. He wheeled her out of the service door and along the canalside, crossing the little bridge into the Campo San Barnaba. He stopped and looked around in the darkness, taking in the cold air. There was no trace of the Baron or of Bhaskar. Once more, he hid the Usag 36 under his shirt, as the *carabinieri* had already searched his backpack on the vaporetto on his way from the railway station.

The few passengers at the vaporetto stop helped him to lift Orsina in her wheelchair onto the ferry, and, a few stops later, to carry her back onto dry land.

Pushing the wheelchair gingerly with his left hand through the crowd and the patrolling *carabinieri* at the railway station, and using his right hand to keep Orsina from falling forward, Leo headed for the ticket office. He bought two tickets for Trieste, the city on the border with Slovenia, and paid for the first time with a credit card. Then he studied the Departures board and headed for another platform, where a train was about to leave. He carefully picked up Orsina and climbed aboard. A passenger kindly carried up the wheelchair. Leo unfolded it, and eased Orsina back into it. She was still only half awake.

The ticket collector came around shortly after leaving Venice. Leo bought two tickets for Padua, paying cash. Perhaps the false lead to Trieste was a bit too obvious; perhaps he was being paranoid. The collector, thinking the young woman asleep, and noticing the folded wheelchair, leaned forward and said: "Such a beautiful woman, on a wheelchair—what a pity!"

Leo nodded with a hopeful expression and was relieved to see him move on. Lack of privacy, he realized, was going to be a concern. The long carriage was crowded, and people were already staring. Certainly, the two of them made for an odd couple. She was very beautiful, but alarmingly gaunt, not to mention fast asleep. He—fully bearded, unkempt, and wild-eyed—looked more like a captor than a rescuer. Moreover, Orsina's photos had recently been in the news, from TV to newspapers and magazines. Might someone recognize her as the kidnapped aristocrat? And him, as her alleged kidnapper? His own photo had been in some publications, and in relation to her. Did the carriage have to be so brightly lit?

Leo helped Orsina out of the wheelchair and onto the seat next to his; she leaned on his shoulder, curled up beside him like a fern in spring. Feeling her breathe was enough for Leo to forget the circumstances, and the possibility that the Baron, Inspector Ghedina, or God knows who else might pounce on them. Fugitives have no time for emotions, yet Orsina's calm breathing beside him reminded him of the breath of life, and of the stunning reality of having given it back to her.

Padua came and went; Orsina was still half-insensible. Leo had not formulated a plan yet, but he realized that she must be awake before they could get off the train. When would the sedatives wear off? he wondered as he bought another two tickets, this time to Vicenza. Luckily, it was a different ticket collector. But the passengers, most of them, were the same ones who had boarded the train in Venice. They noticed this second purchase, and stared at the couple—wondering?

The train approached Vicenza, slowed down, screeched to a halt. Leo was growing very worried. Orsina had no ID card on her, so no hotel would take her in. He did have his passports with him, but using either one would cause the police to show up in short order. With the Baron at large, he couldn't leave Orsina in some police station. Besides, they would take him in, at least for questioning, and then who would protect Orsina? No, there must be a better solution.

A little man was pushing a cart down the isle crammed with soft drinks and snacks, advertising his goods in a strong southern accent. Leo bought a bottle of mineral water and some cookies. Orsina might be thirsty, and perhaps even hungry, when she awoke. He would not even begin to consider the other possibility: that, by the time the train terminated in Milan, she would still be only half-awake.

Once more Leo bought another two tickets, this time all the way to Milan, so as not to repeat the suspicious process in Verona, and then Brescia, and Bergamo. His cash was dwindling.

Verona came and went; Orsina was still dozing. His right arm was resting on her shoulder. How more obvious could it be, he wondered, finally staring back at one woman who did not seem able to take her eyes off them? Orsina was everything to him.

Between Verona and Brescia, Orsina stirred. She opened her eyes and whispered: "Leo . . . You've saved me." She smiled as tears streaked down her cheeks, still leaning on his shoulder.

Feeling anything but calm, Leo whispered in Orsina's ear: "Everything's fine. It's all right. You're safe now. I'm here with you. Don't cry. We mustn't look conspicuous. Be happy, Orsina, it's all right." He kissed her lightly, on her hair, then on her cheek: something to keep the pain away. He offered her some water. Was she hungry too? She devoured the cookies, eventually asking, "Will you see me through this, Leo?"

"I will, Orsina, I will. It's all I live for."

By the time the train reached Brescia, Leo had accompanied Orsina to the bathroom, and helped her in, as she was still unsteady on her legs. As he wheeled her back to her seat, he noticed the woman who had been staring at them. He smiled at her; she smiled back.

Leo updated Orsina. "Your husband has been released from prison, acquitted of a crime he never committed." How he was so sure of his innocence, Leo did not mention. But a solution was presenting itself, however tentatively. Nigel might well still be in Italy, "deeply ashamed of his own conduct," as he had read in *Il Sole 24 Ore*, and eager to rescue his wife.

"Orsina," Leo said.

"Yes?"

"There's something you must know."

"Tell me, Leo."

He would whisper it in her ear. "I love you, Orsina. I love you, and I always have. I always will; it's nothing that could ever stop."

"I know," she said, closing her eyes. "I love you too," she added. She brought his hand to her lips and kissed it.

Leo wished that this moment could last, but he had to get to the matter at hand. He asked: "Would you . . . would you happen to remember Nigel's cell phone number?"

"What?" her eyes snapped open.

"Please, Orsina, we need to get in touch with him. Try to remember." She tried, and did remember it. Leo got up and walked directly to the "staring lady," a few seats down the aisle.

"Forgive me for being so upfront," he said, looking her in the eye, "but may we borrow your cell phone for a moment? It's a local phone call, and my battery's run out." The woman looked surprised, but consented.

Leo briefly explained to Orsina that *she* must ring her husband and tell him to meet her at 1:13 a.m. exactly at Milan's central railway station. It was a wild guess: for all he knew, Nigel could be anywhere else in Italy, or in Provence, or in London.

Nigel answered, and could not believe he was hearing his wife's voice. Overwhelmed by emotion, he could only listen. But she asked where he was. In Milan. That seemed to please her very much, so he elaborated. As soon as he had been released, he had gone there to hire some of Italy's best private detectives. He had spent the whole day interviewing them. She cut him short, and told him where and when to meet her.

Milan's central station was shrouded in fog. Leo carried Orsina down to the platform, eased her back into the wheelchair, and looked around. Nigel was there. As soon as he spotted Orsina, he hurried toward her. But Leo intercepted him, and Nigel nearly screamed for help, thinking he was being attacked by a bum.

"It's Leo Kavenaugh, you fool! Don't you remember me? For God's sake, *don't make a scene!* Act as if this were a routine pick-up of a relative of yours."

Nigel was baffled but complied, and bent to kiss his wife on the cheek. "Listen to Leo," she murmured in his ear, "he saved me."

Leo resumed. "Now, listen carefully. Orsina's been kept under heavy sedation, I presume since she was kidnapped. Before you go to the police, take her to a private clinic for a checkup. I hope she's O.K., but you must make sure she is.

"If she's fine, *then* you let the police know. You realize that they'll question her for hours on end; you mustn't put her through that at present. Now, about her protection. Hire bodyguards, surround Orsina with them. Never let her out of your sight. There must be *no contact whatsoever* with her uncle. None at all—is that clear? Not with him or with any of his staff. The man is incredibly dangerous and he's totally out of control."

Perhaps *Leo* was out of control, Nigel thought, but his wife was there, safe; nothing else mattered at the moment. He asked, incredulous: "Is he the one who had Orsina kidnapped?"

"You'll find out." He looked at Orsina, who had not let go of his hand since they had gotten off the train. "She'll explain it to you herself,"

Leo added. "Follow my instructions, and she'll be fine. Then get out of Italy with her, but never lower your guard. Adopt the same security precautions. And don't tell a soul that you've seen me. Orsina was on that train *alone.* Is that clear?" Then, turning to Orsina, in Italian: "I must go now. If I stayed with you, the police would make a mess of things. They couldn't prove a thing against your uncle, so they'd go after me. I don't care if I rot in prison forever, if that helped you. But it wouldn't. Your uncle would be free, and soon enough he'd be after you again. He's working at a grand scheme, and you're just a pawn in it, like Angela was before you. I have to leave now."

"*Ti credo,*" she said—I believe you—her eyes full of tears.

"Leo," interposed Nigel, "how can I ever repay you?"

The mere word "repay" made Leo's blood boil. Before he replied, Orsina spoke for him, quietly but with intensity: "You can help him get out of Italy safely."

Nigel had kept up with the news. He knew that Leo was wanted by the police as the suspected kidnapper of his wife.

"Don't worry about me, Orsina."

"Nonsense," she said, with a flicker of her normal energy. "Nigel: find a way to get him out of Italy, will you?"

"Yes, yes, I'm thinking."

The passengers from the train had all left, and the three of them were alone on the platform. The usual platoon of *carabinieri,* plus some loiterers and prostitutes were eyeing them from not too far off. It was time to move away from the station. Nigel said: "Here's what you'll do." He took out a pen and a pad, and scribbled something. "Ten days, no, make it two weeks: exactly two weeks from today, at 1 p.m. sharp, dial this number, with country code and all, as it's written. It's the custodian's mobile phone, the custodian of our place in Provence. Our house phone there may be tapped, but I doubt his mobile phone is. There'll be instructions on how to get out of Italy safely. Consider it done."

Orsina looked at Leo. "Promise me that you will call, Leo," she said. He looked at her intently, and promised.

Leo escorted Orsina and Nigel downstairs to the taxis. "May I see your cell phone, Nigel?" Leo asked. He weighed it in his hands for a moment, then flung it against the station wall, stomped on it, carefully collected all the fragments, and handed them to Nigel. "No cell phone for a few days; throw the pieces out later; don't get a new one." Nigel said nothing. "Now," Leo continued, "go inside, find a pay phone, wake up your lawyer, and ask him to recommend a private clinic in Milan, and to meet you there in half an hour. Make sure he tells no one of this."

As Nigel strode off, Orsina grabbed Leo's hand once more; "I wish you could stay."

"I'd only be in the way, and make things more complicated. Also, there is something I must do, alone."

"I know. Take good care of yourself, Leo. I'll be waiting for you." He leaned down and kissed her.

Upon his return, Nigel reported that he'd spoken to Avvocato Alemanni, who had been extremely helpful, despite being awakened at this ungodly hour. His recommendation was to go to the Casa di Cura Privata Capitanio: first-rate medical attention and good privacy, too. Alemanni would meet them there.

"Good," said Leo. "I'm sure your cell phone was tapped; and that Orsina's call was recorded. You don't want the Inspector breathing down your neck first thing in the morning, do you? Your wife's in no state for that yet. Now you're no longer traceable." Leo let his words sink in and then added: "Cheer up, the worst is over."

Nigel stretched his hand to shake Leo's, but was handed instead bottles of pills, needles, ampoules. "That's how Orsina was kept sedated, I assume. But do not show them to anyone, least of all the clinic's doctors: they'd ask too many questions, maybe alert the police. You'd better go. Taxi!"

After easing Orsina into the car, while Nigel was putting the folded wheelchair in the trunk, Leo gave her one last embrace. She hugged him back, and whispered: "Promise that you'll call, Leo, two weeks from now. Promise me that." Leo, choked up, nodded, and smiled for the first time in weeks. Then, with the forbidden book still in his backpack, he vanished into the foggy vastness of Piazza Duca d'Aosta.

Emanuele spent an uneasy night in the luxurious Gritti Palace Hotel. By eight o'clock he was crossing the Grand Canal by the Accademia

Bridge, and soon after, he was ringing the doorbell of his own home. Bhaskar opened the door, and his face told the Baron all that he needed to know. When the women from the cleaning service let him in, he had gone straight up to the fourth floor and down the spiral stair to the secret apartments. He had found Soma tied to a radiator in a state of collapse, and Orsina gone. Bhaskar had managed to carry his wife down to the couple's own quarters, where she was now resting in bed. "I think we should call a doctor," he added.

"No, we shouldn't, you idiot," said Emanuele. "I'll pay one of the maids to stay and look after your monkey-wife. We don't want anyone nosing around. Meet me here in fifteen minutes, and bring cleaning things—lots of towels and plastic bags—but not the maids."

Emanuele went upstairs to change his clothes and collect his keys. When he came down again, he and Bhaskar entered the disused kitchen for the second time and passed through the storage rooms. They saw how the unknown intruder had blocked the door in the false barrel and, removing the obstacles, entered it and turned the corner to the door of the shrine. Unlocking the door and switching on the light, Emanuele surveyed the wreckage while Bhaskar hurried to clean it up. The glass vials upset and broken, the foul smell of their syrupy contents; this much the rats might have done. But who had left the door open? And the disappearance of the book could not be blamed on the *pantegane*. No, there was conspiracy here. Emanuele checked the Yale locks on both doors: they worked perfectly. He brusquely dismissed Bhaskar and sat down in the red-upholstered chair.

The Baron's ancestors seemed to utter reproach from their portraits. Cesare della Riviera was painted at full-length, robed in black with the white cross of the Sovereign Order of Malta on his shoulder, one hand on the pommel of his sword, the other, gloved, resting on a book. A tree was barely discernible in the background. Cesare's look was ambiguous, the eyes hooded and serious, the lips on the brink of a smile. It was the fluids of his own body, preserved through alchemical coction for four centuries, that had been mopped up from the altar he had set up and consecrated. It was that book written in his own hand that had never left the shrine.

How could such a sacrilege befall the dynasty? Would the fortunes of the Riviera survive this? the Baron wondered. He had no doubt that the magic behind Cesare's shrine was real, and that the geometrically placed relics had radiated an occult influence for the protection of the family, like the Lares, the ancient Roman household gods, yet more potent. During long hours of meditation in this chamber, Emanuele had often felt a stern but benevolent presence. Now it was just as palpably absent. He tried to recall some carelessness that might have led to its dissolution, but his own conduct, unlike his nieces', seemed to him to have been impeccable.

After his melancholy reflections, the Baron climbed the long spiral stair back to his own apartments, feeling every one of his sixty-four years. He crawled out of the fireplace under the sardonic stare of Pulcinella. Emanuele had always tolerated the *Commedia dell'arte* figures out of a conviction that Arlecchino was an allegory of Sulphur, Columbina of Mercury, Pulcinella of Salt, and so on through the other alchemical subjects. Now they seemed vapid and leering, the stupid comedians that they were. Were they laughing at his expense? Why, after all his elaborate scheming, Orsina had vanished into thin air now that he needed her most!

His clean clothes were already dirty, and Emanuele felt soiled. He took a warm shower and changed into pajamas and dressing gown, then rang for Bhaskar. "Sit down," he said in English, "and tell me exactly what has happened—if you want your children back in that sewer of your country to remain alive."

Bhaskar, already terrified, started to sob.

"Shut up, you useless Shudra," screeched the Baron. "Tell me, is it possible that my niece got up of her own accord, tied up your wife, and left? Haven't you been keeping her under sedation?"

"Oh we have, *Signor Barone*, we have," replied Bhaskar, his eyes shot with tears. Soma has regularly made the injections; she was a nurse-trainee in Delhi, as you know. Day and night she has spent with the patient, and never left the secret rooms. I have fetched and carried everything, in and out."

"Could you get any sense out of her yourself?"

"She says that a man came into the room, a tall man with a beard, threatened her with a hammer, tied her up, and gagged her. That's all she can tell me."

"Enough already. Now," changing tone, "I made a promise that if you and your wife carried out my commands without question and without fail, I would pay to bring your children to Italy. You have now failed, and my promise is void. But my power is not. Do you know how much it costs to have vermin like your little monkeys killed in India? Less than a meal at a restaurant here."

Bhaskar could only stutter in response. The interrogation went on for another half hour, but after he had kicked the servant away in fury, questions still thronged the Baron's mind.

Who could have known that Orsina was in the palace? How could someone have known how to enter it and find the concealed rooms? Emanuele went through the list of possible suspects. Nigel? Could he have carried out such a daring plan? He might have a mind for business, but that was that: in the Baron's view, he was little more than a lucky gambler. Ghedina? That was an unwelcome thought: that the Inspector in charge of finding Orsina should somehow have actually found her. But he would have surrounded the palace with policemen and searched it from top to bottom, and even then most probably missed her. No, someone knew about the underground chambers and the secret stair, and was cunning enough to block the trapdoor in the cellar, once he and Bhaskar were through it. Had Orsina herself ever discovered them? Had Angela? Emanuele knew for a fact that the girls' parents, the dullest of people, had never entered the "palace within the palace." It was Orsina's grandfather, Publio della Riviera, who after initiating the twenty-nine-year-old Emanuele into the family mysteries, had given him the rooms on the top floor as his own apartment, and from that day to this, none but illiterate cleaning maids had set foot there. Well, that was not quite correct. Early in their marriage, his ex-wife had been there on and off, but the Commedia figures, she said, gave her bad dreams, nor could she put up with the stink of Emanuele's little "laboratory."

Of all these people, Angela was the most likely to have discovered the secret layout for herself. But the idea of any of her feckless friends executing this abduction was unthinkable. Who, then, who had been so knowing and so daring?

# TWENTY-FIVE

The Baron had a light lunch and, over coffee, opened the last few days' newspapers. Disgusted by the media's gossip and slanders about his family, he had deliberately not been reading them for some days, but now he found that he'd better catch up. *La Repubblica* had an editorial on Nigel, or rather a tirade against him. The sordid circumstances of adultery in his own villa sickened the Baron. He would fire Samanta. Embittered, he switched papers, and his eyes fell on an article in the local *Gazzettino.* Leo Kavenaugh was now being sought by the police "to help them with their enquiries" into the Della Riviera affair. Not only that, but the man had vanished, leaving a Venetian hotel room "daubed with human blood from floor to ceiling."

Here was one suspect that Emanuele had not thought of: that good-looking American with his earnest professorial ways. The Baron remembered inviting him to attend his lecture on transcendence and seeing him yawn before slipping out with Orsina. And, furthermore, that Orsina had asked him to the villa to help her study *The Magical World of the Heroes*, though he himself had put a stop to that. Could the American have been having a secret affair with her? It did not seem to fit his character either to be passionate or to carry out a commando-like raid. But the facts were unpleasantly there: Orsina had been abducted, the Baron humiliated and, worst of all, the shrine vandalized and robbed of its most precious relic. Then there was the blood. Surely the pseudo-Jesuit wasn't doing *that* sort of magic?

If Kavenaugh had stolen both book and Orsina, where were they now, and what were they going to do? Elope? Return her to Nigel? Either way, Emanuele's plans to use her as a magical companion were now wrecked, unless she decided to divorce MacPherson and return to live in her Italian homes. Even then, it would be impossible to subdue her, as he had done so easily with Angela, who had been under his spell since she was a child. And then, Orsina might decide to adventure on vaticination herself, and see into the past. The accusation of having murdered her sister would follow. Of course, no court of law could accept a vision conjured up by magic. But still, what a disagreeable prospect! Might Orsina hire a mercenary or two to dispose of him? He doubted it, but women, he knew from occasional experiences, do have irrational traits.

Emanuele turned to the *Corriere della Sera* and read another version of the Della Riviera saga. When he saw the article on the confessions of the young men, his confused and depressed mood turned to outrage. Was it for this that he had labored? What was becoming of his crusade, the Reconquest of Europe from the Islamic hordes, in which he had cast himself as a Charles Martel or Godfrey of Bouillon reborn? So long as there was breath in his body, he had no intention of stopping halfway.

Finally, the Baron reached that morning's edition of the *Corriere*, and read an article with unhoped-for and growing delight. It dealt with the sacrilege at the Cathedral of Chartres. For once, the desecrators had *not* turned themselves in. The French police had conducted a brilliant investigation and arrested seven young men. They were not ultra-right fanatics; they were, in fact, Moroccans, financed by a Saudi Arabian fundamentalist group with alleged ties to the country's royalty. They had first admitted their action, with pride, then stated in various interviews that "the infidels in the West are the Muslims' inveterate enemies"; that Muslims are to "arrest them, besiege them and lie in ambush everywhere" for them; that they are to "fight them until Islam reigns supreme"; and, to end with a bang, that they are to "cut off their heads, and mutilate their members," for "If a Muslim does not go to war, Allah will kill him." The French media had pointed out that the young fanatics had quoted passages from the Koran. The article ended by reporting that massive anti-Islamic rallies were being planned in Paris, Lyon, and even Marseilles.

France had done this, wondered the Baron? This was a major *coup*, and a strong message to the rest of Europe and the world. He felt an unaccustomed surge of euphoria, but suppressed it. It was not too late. He must act immediately.

The first call the Baron made was to Giorgio. "My new cycle of lectures at the Villa Riviera will proceed as planned, starting on Friday afternoon. It is of the utmost importance that the work not be interrupted. But remind the young men that there is to be absolutely no camping on my property, and no strolling around the villa grounds either."

"*Barone*, I'll contact the usual leaders immediately, and they'll alert the network."

On Friday, Giorgio came to the villa an hour before the lecture and found the Baron in the library. "Have they begun to arrive yet?" he asked, looking up from his notes.

"I haven't seen any," said Giorgio, "but I made it plain that they weren't to wander around the grounds as they used to. They'll probably fall in the door just before the lecture."

At ten to two, Giorgio knocked again at the library door. "*Barone*, I'm afraid that no one has arrived yet."

"Are you sure that you gave them the right day and time?"

"Yes, *Barone*, and I confirmed it too."

"Whatever has become of them? It's time for me to go in, anyway."

Emanuele and Giorgio entered the ballroom from the door behind the lectern. Their steps were loud in the echoing hall.

"This is very strange, Giorgio. What's your explanation of the matter?"

"*Barone*, I cannot understand it." Giorgio was visibly embarrassed. "I left e-mails and phone messages with the usual people, as I always do. After your phone call from Venice, I contacted them all over again, to confirm the date and time of the lecture. Each one passes it on to ten or a dozen others. It's informal, but very efficient, and it's never failed before."

"I asked for an explanation, not an excuse."

Giorgio hesitated. "*Barone*, I didn't know how to tell you this, but one of the leaders, a Swiss I call Raoul, told me that he wasn't going to attend the lectures any more."

"What did this Raoul say to you?"

"He just wasn't going to attend, but he'd pass the message on."

"Is that all he said?" Giorgio hesitated. The Baron raised his voice. "What did he really say?"

Giorgio took a deep breath. "He said he wasn't fool enough to spend another night in an Italian jail."

"And the others?"

"A couple of them said something similar."

"It seems as though your network is all too efficient, doesn't it?" snarled the Baron. "You are dismissed for the day, Giorgio," he said, in a calmer tone. "I want to be left alone."

Half an hour later, the Baron was in his studio again, at the heart of his magical kingdom. It was here that for years he had performed the rites with his magical companions: first with hired women, but without much success; then, far more potently, with Angela. Having realized only too painfully that he was not "gifted," the Baron had finally followed the commentary's injunction:

> As Jupiter chose as wife his sister Juno, so a kinship of blood is favorable to the practices of the weaker kind. For though they cannot contain their alembic within themselves, let it be a work shared with a *soror mystica*.

No doubt about it, the magical work had been effective: against all odds he had succeeded in attracting a band of some hundred disciples who had made considerable sacrifices to attend his lectures. And in recent months, he had gained the ability that the greatest of the Riviera had possessed: that of causing men to act in his interests, rather than in their own. That small seed, that semen sown in a magical spirit, had grown into a mighty tree. The unsuspecting masses had been prodded into action by the violation of their sanctuaries; the ploy had been discovered as his influence had ceased and the impressionable young men had given in to fear or, worst of all, to that most despicable of feelings: repentance. But genuine Islamic fundamentalists had unexpectedly come to the Baron's aid by desecrating the Cathedral of Chartres. The masses were aroused once more and, if further prodded, they would not let up until the alien presence was banished from Europe.

This was true politics! Not the popular mandate of democracy, the aberrant notion that the low can govern the high; not the wranglings of parliaments or the farce of plebiscites, but the skillful manipulation of human beings for purposes which only high initiates could comprehend. It was their calling to change the world, as the noblest of the Riviera had always done. Emanuele would not take second place to any of his exalted ancestors. He was political through and through, and his ambitions stretched far beyond this initial phase of arousing the sleeping masses. Once the Muslim threat was dealt with, he would work towards his grander vision of a Europe cleansed of Judeo-Christianity and restored, at long last, to pagan imperialism.

As Emanuele came down from his musings, he faced the reality of his situation. Through a regrettable lapse of self-awareness, he had lost his ideal magical companion. Through no fault of his own, he had lost his band of shock troops, without which his political plans were seriously hampered. Through some malicious enemy, the occult support of the Riviera family spirit had been compromised, if not irrevocably destroyed.

Had he also lost Orsina? When she recovered from her long sedation, whoever had abducted her would tell her where she had been. She would realize that her uncle, and none other, had been her kidnapper. Might she recall that unfortunate episode too, he wondered? Would she then contact the police? Her husband—now probably a contrite libertine, the worst kind—would surely urge her to do so; besides, the police would interrogate her anyway, and with the curiosity of one unanswered question too many. Even if her kidnapping were past history, its proximity to an unsolved murder would strike even Ghedina, and he would follow up any leads arising out of her testimony. What she would have to tell the police would reflect suspiciously, to say the least, on himself. He might well be arrested and charged with the crime of kidnapping, for which the penalties were severe. From there, the steps to suspecting him of covering up Angela's murder would be small indeed.

At what point, Emanuele wondered, could he intervene in this potentially catastrophic sequence of events? The only accessible link was Orsina herself. He must find her and neutralize her, by whatever means were necessary. And since he could not do so at this moment on the physical plane, not knowing where she was, he must invoke the aid of high magic.

A battery of tests had found Orsina slightly anemic, but overall in decent health. A course of vitamins and minerals coupled with a period of rest would complete her recovery. "As for post-traumatic stress," the clinic's doctors had agreed, speaking confidentially to her husband, "that is another matter entirely." And her trials were not over. Upon leaving the private clinic, Orsina felt that it was her duty to inform Inspector Ghedina of her release, and agreed to his demand to question her. She gave him an appointment at the hotel she and Nigel had temporarily moved to in Milan.

Inspector Ghedina had to scold Colucci as they were escorted through the Hotel Principe di Savoia to the MacPhersons' suite: "Just act naturally and stop gawping!" Nigel was there with some brawny men in dark suits and Avvocato Alemanni in his usual Caraceni outfit. The Baroness was sitting in an armchair, her legs aslant, looking gaunt and shaken but still very beautiful. Ghedina greeted her formally and asked permission to record the interview. The bodyguards stepped out and Colucci turned on the recorder.

"*Baronessa*, please tell me all that happened."

After a long pause, she said: "I'm afraid there isn't much to tell, Inspector. I'm sure you'll be reading the test reports from the clinic. I'm told that traces of an anesthetic were found in my blood. The fact is, I was sedated from the very beginning."

"By whom?"

"I don't know."

Ghedina was both baffled and frustrated. "Please explain yourself, *Baronessa*. What happened?"

"The last thing I remember is being in a café in Bolzano. Giorgio," the Inspector looked at her keenly, "yes, Giorgio Moser, my uncle's secretary, had taken me there."

"What was *Signor* Moser doing in Bolzano?"

"After my sister's funeral, my uncle had put him at my disposal as a chauffeur. He'd just dropped me off close to my hotel, as I'd asked him to do. I expect that after that he drove back to Verona. Anyway, I walked to a café nearby and drank an espresso. The next thing I remember is waking up, very weak and with a splitting headache, on a train bound to Milan. Eventually, I asked a woman to lend me her cell phone and called my husband. He came to pick me up at the station in Milan and took me directly to the clinic."

"Is that all?" The Inspector did not try to conceal his disappointment. "Are you quite sure, *Baronessa*?"

"Yes, Inspector, I *am* quite sure." In fact, she did remember other things. Giorgio had *accompanied* her into that café, and had ordered an espresso for her while she had gone to the toilet. Then she remembered drinking it as he drank one too. Then, a jumble of bad dreams and total blanks.

Most of the time, she was unconscious. Occasionally she would awaken in the dark, or perhaps she was blindfolded, long enough to eat and drink. Somebody fed her. Then she would feel a vague pinch on her arm, and plunge into deep sleep. One episode, however, stuck out, and there was nothing she could do to forget it. But she would reveal none of this to Ghedina. She had made up her mind as soon as Leo had left her at the railway station in Milan. No, the police were hopeless, and her uncle needed to be dealt with. And then there was the unbearable shame. It was best to wait for Leo, who had already proven to be Emanuele's only capable opponent. Ghedina would remain clueless—it would be nothing new for him.

The Inspector was still sitting expectantly. Was he hoping for some spontaneous confession? More details? Or merely enjoying what he was seeing? "One more thing," he added slyly, almost as an afterthought. "What can you tell me of Professor Leonard Kavenaugh?"

"Professor Kavenaugh?"

"Yes."

"I wouldn't know what to tell you. I expect he's at Georgetown University, in Washington, teaching classes."

"No, he is not." Ghedina explained the strange and sinister circumstances surrounding Leo's latest stay in Italy. "I'm asking you about him, *Baronessa*. I know you were in daily contact with him by phone during the weeks before your sister's murder. You even called him many times from the train on your way to Bolzano from Venice, after your sister's funeral. What could be so urgent? Finally, you called him again very late at night, twice, the day before you were kidnapped."

"What are you suggesting, Inspector? Leonard and I are *friends*; I was his assistant at Georgetown University. Before the tragedy, I was studying some ancient books, in Latin, as a pastime, and I took advantage of his expertise. Is there really no news about him?"

Hearing about the room daubed with human blood seemed to have shocked Orsina. It pained Ghedina, but he pressed on. "Are you sure you're not omitting something, *Baronessa*? Remember, I'm not only investigating your kidnapping, but also your sister's murder. I have become very suspicious of this professor. I suspect foul play on his part."

"I'm sorry to hear that. I don't think he could hurt a fly. On the contrary, I do hope no harm has come to him."

Ghedina leaned forward and almost whispered, so that only she could hear: "A letter you wrote him some years ago has come to my attention."

Orsina was taken aback, this time visibly. How could that be, she wondered in her mind as she made an effort to keep still? Hadn't Leo himself told her that he had had his secretary shred it along with the junk mail? Was *that* the letter the Inspector was referring to? She must not jump to conclusions.

But it was. Dean Throckmorton, immediately after having read Orsina's letter, had called Mrs. Reed, from the Italian Department; together, they had phoned Inspector Ghedina, with the secretary acting as interpreter. The letter had then been faxed over to him.

"I have read that letter, *Baronessa*. We had it translated. So you can see why, when you say 'we're *friends*' about you and Kavenaugh, I simply cannot believe you. And of course, I don't like this: what other lies are you telling me? What else are you omitting?"

"Very well, Inspector. You seem to enjoy sticking your nose where it doesn't belong. I will admit that, when I was at Georgetown, years ago, I . . . I fell in love with him." Orsina too was now whispering. "But, how can I put it? My love was unrequited. Since then, I returned to Europe, met Mr. MacPherson, and got married. Professor Kavenaugh and I, I repeat, are just friends."

Ghedina's curiosity was not satisfied. "*Baronessa*," he said, "do you remember the call you made from the train to your husband?"

"Yes."

"You just told me that you made it from a borrowed cell phone, did you not?"

"Yes, that's what I said."

"You see, *Baronessa*, your husband's cell phone was tapped. So, we *heard* your call," unfortunately for Ghedina, only the next morning, but that he did not need to reveal. "We traced the other cell phone too, the one you borrowed, to its registered owner."

Orsina did not bat an eyelid; Ghedina pressed on. "The woman said you were with a tall, thin man all along; that *he* asked her if he could borrow her cell phone. So we showed her the photo of Kavenaugh . . . " Ghedina paused artfully. Orsina waited, then said: "Inspector, I'm sure you take your job very seriously, and I thank you for it. But, if you don't mind, I'm very weak, so, if you have a point, could you please get to it?"

"The point is, *Baronessa* . . . " the point was that he did *not* have a positive identification from the woman in the train. She said that the man with Orsina was a lot slimmer, bearded; he seemed older, different in many ways, maybe taller; she was not at all sure that he was the man in the photo.

"Yes, Inspector, the point is?"

"Was Kavenaugh with you on that train? Did he have you kidnapped, and then change his mind? Or did your uncle or your husband pay the ransom to him, and he was dropping you off?"

"Inspector, you're not only insulting me by implying that I've lied to you; you're insulting a good friend of the family. I told you already: I woke up in that train alone, by which I mean next to no one I know. Yes, a bearded man was sitting close by, so I asked him if he had a cell phone to lend me. He didn't, but asked the woman for me. Then he helped me off the train until my husband arrived. That's all."

"That's all," repeated Ghedina in his mind, unconvinced, while he gestured to Colucci to turn off the recorder.

On his way out, Ghedina said to Nigel: "You know where to find me if your wife suddenly remembers anything." They looked at each other with strong mutual dislike.

"Before you leave, Inspector," said Nigel, "have a word with my lawyer."

"Inspector," said Alemanni quietly, "you should know that my clients will be leaving tomorrow, and do not intend to return to Italy any time soon. They want to avoid the assault of the media, of course, and the *Baronessa* needs to recover. Should you need to contact them again, you are advised to let *me* know. They will not reply to any of your calls unless you've contacted me first. Is that understood?"

# TWENTY-SIX

The next day, Inspector Ghedina was in Verona, on the third-floor landing of an oldish building in the central part of town. Colucci and Gallorini were with him, as well as four policemen in assault gear. The porter, downstairs, had told them that the man they were looking for was at home.

"Break down the door," Ghedina said to the four agents.

Gallorini wondered if they shouldn't have knocked first, but it was too late: the door had already been smashed in.

Giorgio was in the living room, surprised and alarmed; he had been working on his laptop. "What the hell? What's going on?" he asked.

"Giorgio Moser: you are under arrest," said the Inspector. "Officers, handcuff him."

"Under arrest? What for? On what charge? Hey, wait a minute!"

"Resisting arrest would be very unwise in your situation," Ghedina explained; "it'd be like adding insult to injury."

Giorgio allowed the policemen to handcuff him, then repeated his questions: "Will you explain, please? Why am I being arrested? On what charge?"

"You want the whole list?" Ghedina smiled sardonically, then said: "Perjury; lying to the authorities; obstruction of justice; tampering with the evidence; kidnapping; concealment of individuals; sex offense; and, last but not least, murder. You are a principal to the crimes in the first degree, and an accessory before and after the facts. You're looking at a life sentence with no pardon. Any other questions?"

Dumbfounded, Giorgio fell back on a chair.

"Good," commented Ghedina, "sit there and let it all sink in. Gentlemen, let's search the place." They began the search, leaving Gallorini to watch him.

The apartment was large and surprisingly well-appointed. Evidently the Baron paid his secretary well. Ghedina and his men went through drawers, books, correspondence, and confiscated documents, two computers, and so on. In the meantime, Giorgio had time to consider his own predicament. Of all the charges, that of murder was outrageous.

He had never killed anyone. Some of the other ones were unwarranted too, and a few, in a sense, unfair. But the Baron had warned him when he gave him the task of abducting Orsina.

"Giorgio," he had said, "the essence of an initiatic trial is that you ask no questions, not even in your mind. What you are asked to do may seem absurd, even immoral, by the world's standards, but you cannot yet see the deeper meaning of events. For example, the Knights Templar were required to spit and tread on a crucifix, then thrust their tongues into the anus of a goat. Would you do that?"

Giorgio's nose wrinkled as he replied: "If it were a true initiation, I would."

"Times have changed, and so have the trials of initiation. But the intention remains the same. By your unquestioning obedience and faithful execution, you awaken the impersonal Self within you. And do not forget, Giorgio: you also awaken the blood of the warrior caste that flows in your veins."

The abduction had been easy enough: sneaking a sedative into a cup of coffee, helping a staggering Orsina into his car, and handing her over to Bhaskar and Soma at a quiet dock in Fusina, near Venice. Making the ransom demands on the phone in a Roman accent had been almost a joke, though that too had taken nerve. But now the real test was beginning.

Giorgio resurfaced from his recollections. Gallorini was still watching him; he was still sitting, handcuffed, in his own living room. Ghedina would be back soon, and then they would take him to the police headquarters. But would the Inspector succeed in persuading a PM, and the latter, in turn, a GIP, to hold him provisionally so as to put him on trial? On what evidence? There wasn't any, not even circumstantial. After the embarrassment caused by MacPherson's detention, no judge would realistically hold him, especially not on a related case. The Court of Bolzano had been humiliated by the media and become a laughing stock in the juridical world; no other court of law in Italy would wish to go through a similar ordeal.

The crucial question was whether Ghedina had some evidence up his sleeve, and that hinged on what the *Baronessa* might have told him after her release. But she would almost certainly not have mentioned her uncle. She knew what she was up against and would have no confidence in the police. She might have to be dealt with later, unfortunately, but that was the Baron's business.

Giorgio was a consummate poker player. He knew when and how to bluff, and won more often than he lost. Ghedina, he surmised, must have been bluffing all along. Like all amateurs he had overdone it. Smashing down the door; handcuffing him; all those accusations—it was exaggerated and unnecessary. No, Giorgio concluded, it looked like a desperate bluff.

Ghedina was back. They had collected many things to confiscate, and it was time to leave. But Giorgio kept his seat.

"Why don't you spare yourself more unpleasantness?" asked Ghedina. "You don't mean us to carry you out, do you?"

Giorgio looked Ghedina in the eye and asked, calmly: "Inspector, may I see your arrest warrant?"

"What's the hurry? You'll see it later if you must."

"I'm afraid that won't do, Inspector. I've done nothing wrong. You're the one who's broken the law. You've burst into my apartment without a search warrant or an arrest warrant. Isn't that so?"

Gallorini looked at his boss with a questioning glance; Ghedina looked away. Giorgio noticed, and elaborated. "You have no right to be here harassing me with slanderous accusations, and least of all do you have any right to arrest me. Too bad for you, but Italy's not a fascist police state, and hasn't been for the last sixty years or so. Now," Giorgio continued, very collectedly, "take these handcuffs off and allow me to call my lawyer."

A long, silent pause ensued. All policemen were looking at their boss, awaiting instructions. Ghedina was looking at the floor, fuming. "Remove his handcuffs," he said.

Giorgio massaged his wrists, and added: "Of course, you have no search warrant either, and the least you can do is put everything you were going to confiscate back where you found it. Isn't that so, Inspector?"

Ghedina was obliged to nod.

"And, you'll have to pay for the broken door, hinges, and jambs and God knows what else. My lawyer will take you to the cleaners." The counterbluff must be thorough, he felt, if it was to work. He dialed his lawyer's number and made sure that Ghedina's men could hear every word.

As the policemen left the apartment, Giorgio relaxed; his icy calm turned to triumph and his voice followed them: "I'm suing you, Ghedina. You're in deep shit. Start looking for another job, you fascist bastard!"

At Villa Riviera, the Baron rang for Dumitru. "I'm going to spend some time in my studio," he told the butler. "On no account should I be disturbed." He went up to his dressing room and put on full court dress: white bow tie and waistcoat, black tail coat, knee breeches, silk stockings, and shoes with rhinestone-spangled buckles. From a leather box he took his military and civil decorations, which he pinned onto the lapel, and the heraldic insignia of the Order of Saints Maurice and Lazarus. Over all, he threw the cloak of the Order of Malta; then he took his dress sword with its belt and scabbard, and descended the stairs.

To climb into a car seemed so inappropriate that Emanuele decided to walk the two kilometers to the hunting lodge, as his ancestors, in absence of a horse, would undoubtedly have done. He walked slowly, emulating the famous "royal gait" of the Sun King, Louis XIV. Not the slightest sign of the modern world was visible as he trod the avenue between the great horse chestnuts, his imagination gradually sinking into the mood of the past.

Emanuele locked the door, covered the windows, and lit candles in the tall silver candelabra. He took his sword from its sheath, and set it between his knees as he sat in an upright chair, resting his gloved hands on the pommel, breathing deeply. In a state of feverish exaltation, he felt that at last he had come of age: he was no longer to be counted as one of those weaker brethren who required the assistance of a female companion. No, with Angela he had at last achieved full-blown magical ecstasy. From an initiatic perspective, her demise had been no accident, but a successful rite of passage, and a glorious milestone too: it symbolized his being empowered as a magus.

He had had Orsina at his disposal in the palazzo, and could have pursued his sexual alchemy with her as he had intended to do. But he had never had any control over her, least of all now; his attempts had been a fiasco, and he had been forced to keep her under heavy sedation. And now she had been abducted: good riddance!

Finally the proud heir of a long line of magical heroes, as a full-fledged magus he could take the straighter path to transcendence, and achieve the magical working alone. And if on the way he should meet Mithras, he would not repeat his error: this time he would not become the bull, but the God. Then there was no limit to what he could achieve. He would be the first of his line to storm the gates of immortality: to regenerate the physical body, as described in *The Magical World*, and transform it into "another incorruptible and celestial body, that is none other than the celestial Mercury."

# TWENTY-SEVEN

Often, since the investigation had begun, Inspector Ghedina had felt very close to unraveling either the murder of Angela or Orsina's kidnapping. Like a hound, he had gotten a whiff of a trail leading straight to the fox. But then it would grow cold; the fox would once more outsmart him. He would arrive late at the scene of a crime; or at the wrong scene; or, worse yet, not arrive at all when he was most desperately needed. He felt sure that Orsina had left much out of her testimony. That was why he had paid that surprise visit to Giorgio, hoping that the secretary, under pressure, might confess something. Instead of a confession, he had gotten a lawsuit.

There was little Ghedina could think of at this point. But he felt that it was his duty to return to the Baron, pay him a visit to comment on Orsina's release, and congratulate him on it. He told Gallorini to get ready to drive him down to Verona. The pensive agent, a book always in his pocket, would go down better in the Baron's salone than the crass Colucci.

They reached Villa Riviera a couple of hours later. The security guards told him that they had orders to let him through at all times.

"The Baron's not such a disagreeable type, Gallorini, do you think?" said the Inspector as they swept down the drive.

"He's been through a lot," said the sergeant non-committally.

"He humiliated himself by breaking the law to pay his niece's ransom. I have to say, I respect him for that."

"True. But I think he knows a lot that no one's told us."

"I've got no hard feelings toward him. He should be in a better mood now. Let's get him talking, and he may let something slip."

Dumitru opened the door. No, he said, the Baron was not at home. Ghedina pressed him. Dumitru would only give vague answers. The old instinct of the hound resurfaced; Ghedina stiffened.

"That's his Lancia, isn't it? If he's not at home, where's he gone to?"

"He went to his studio," the butler conceded at last, "but he told me that on no account was he to be disturbed."

"How long ago was this?"

"The day before yesterday. That was the last time I saw him."

"Does he usually stay there so long?"

"Not usually, but I always obey his orders."

"Of course you do. Does he have a phone there?"

"No. If he takes his cell phone, he always turns it off."

"Then we must go and rouse him," said Ghedina.

The blinds were drawn at the hunting lodge, and there was no answer to the Inspector's knock. He tried the door. "This is no time for pussyfooting around," he said to Gallorini. "Open the door."

The sergeant hesitated.

"No, don't smash it. It's not right to spoil antique woodwork."

Ghedina returned to the police car and fetched his briefcase.

The simple old lock yielded easily to a skeleton key.

As Ghedina's eyes became accustomed to the dim light, he saw a hunched figure on the floor of the bathroom. "Turn the lights on, Gallorini."

The figure stirred as Ghedina stooped over it. The Baron's tongue protruded from its mouth, and he panted in what the Inspector recognized as the symptoms of thirst.

"Quick, get him some water." He helped Emanuele to drink, but it was not easy. The Baron's right side seemed to be inert. "*Barone, Barone*: do you hear me?" There was no flicker of recognition in the Baron's eye. "I think he's paralyzed. He must have had a stroke. Call an ambulance, *presto*!"

Ghedina was not surprised at an elderly man, already under much stress, suffering a stroke. What did surprise him was the Baron's garb, in full evening dress with decorations, and silk stockings, for goodness' sake. Had he come home from a reception, a lodge meeting, or what? The Inspector discreetly removed the Order of Saints Maurice and Lazarus on its ribbon and unpinned the decorations, putting them into a desk drawer. "Gallorini: get up to the villa and tell that butler what's happened. Then come back here."

Half an hour later, Ghedina watched as the medical orderlies gently loaded the Baron into an ambulance. The two policemen were left alone with Dumitru. Ghedina told him to hurry back to the villa and get in touch with the Baron's lawyer.

"Gallorini: open up those blinds now. And you can open some windows, too. This place stinks of sickness. We're going to search every cranny."

The lodge seemed to have few secrets. In one corner, covered by a jacquard throw, was a large easel and a painter's equipment: canvases, expensive brushes, turpentine and linseed oil, tubes of oil paint. The brushes were uncleaned, and the paint was crusted on the palettes. "It looks as though he gave up painting all of a sudden. But where are the results?" The only decorations in the room were the grotesque paintings on the walls.

"Do you think he did these? They're really weird."

"No," said Gallorini. "They're old; as old as the lodge, I'd guess."

Ghedina was going through the drawers of the tiny kitchen. "Go look around the back, and see if there's a shed or cellar entrance."

Gallorini returned.

"There's nothing but a big garden incinerator."

"There's nothing more suspicious, you mean! Let's take a look."

The two men sifted through the few inches of ashes. "See here, Inspector: staples and nails. They're like the ones on the backs of those canvases."

"That's right. So he paints, but then he burns his work. Very aristocratic, I guess," said Ghedina, doubtfully.

The search of the lodge continued. They came to the bedroom. "Help me turn this mattress over, Gallorini," he said. The double bed all but filled the room, and it was awkward to manipulate it in the narrow space. "Here's a spot that doesn't get cleaned," Gallorini remarked, peering at the dust balls beneath the bed. "And here's something else."

The sergeant was reaching down into the crack between the headboard and the wall. He extracted a sketchbook and handed it to Ghedina, who blew the dust off and opened it. It was a standard artist's book, filled with sketches in ink and pencil. They were amateurish in their lack of proportion and their inexpert shading, but highly detailed, like medieval work. Every one of them showed a nude girl, seemingly eleven or twelve years old, and then increasingly more grown up into her teens, in a variety of poses.

"Kiddie porn," remarked the Inspector. "No wonder he burned his paintings."

Leo sat on a bollard, looking over the harbor. "Be at the yacht dock at 15:30 hours on Thursday. There are two harbors; the one you must be at is called Porto Sole. Look for a boat called *Lusimus*." That had been the message conveyed by Nigel's custodian. The smell of iodine, the salt seawater, the blinding sun flickering and dancing on the calm waves, the screeching of seagulls—all this Leo was taking in as he watched the yachts come and go.

An hour later, Leo was wondering if there might have been a mix-up. Had he misunderstood the custodian's broken English? Was he too tired to think properly? It certainly had been a couple of rough weeks since he had left Orsina at Milan's central railway station, and then two more uncomfortable days to reach San Remo, a touristy village on the Italian Riviera, close to the border with France. He wondered if he shouldn't try to ring the custodian again. There was little sense in sitting on a bollard indefinitely. He took out his wallet, and counted the coins: 3 Euros and 28 cents, all the money he had. He got up, and started to walk back to the village to look for a public phone booth.

"Dr. Kavenaugh, I presume," came a braying English voice. He turned and saw a shortish man of his own age, dressed in a suit of salmon-colored linen that flapped open on a naked, hairy torso. It wasn't exactly warm, but certainly less cold than in continental Italy, on the other side of the Apennines, where Leo had been until the morning.

"Yes, I'm Leonard Kavenaugh."

"Nigel was quite right! He said to look for an American hippie don, and here you are. We're docked over there."

Leo followed the man, who called himself Teddy, to an old-fashioned motor yacht, all teak and understatement. They crossed the plank bridge, which Teddy immediately drew up, shouting, "I've got him!" Within minutes he was steering the yacht out of the harbor, and Leo was sitting at a table below, the object of curiosity for three other men and two beautiful women.

A tall young man made the introductions. "I'm Nicky; this is Nico, don't confuse us; his wife Sophie; Marcus; and his wife Pauline. The wives prefer to speak French, but I'm sure that won't bother you."

The beautiful and elegant Frenchwomen, some fifteen years younger than their husbands, smiled uncertainly at Leo. Having been told next to nothing about him, they perceived him not as a "hippie don," but rather as an out-and-out tramp.

"We're playing 'Fuck the Frontiers,'" explained Nicky. "We and three other boats. The idea is to dock in as many places as possible without being stopped by the customs or registering with the police."

Leo grasped the idea, which did not make him feel confident. Was this Nigel's brilliant plan for his escape from Italy? Then a suspicion crept up on him. He remembered how incompetently Nigel had behaved at the railway station in Milan, always one step behind every development, constantly asking for explanations. Was this the world class financier and shrewd speculator? How could he have been so clueless? Or had it been all an act? But what for? The answer, now, was apparent: *to make him walk willingly into a trap*! Were these dandies also acting? Had Nigel hired them to deliver him straight to the police? What a perfect way to get rid of a rival! "What do you do if you're caught?" Leo asked gruffly.

"Plead ignorance, refuse to speak anything but English and, if need be, pay up. But then you lose points. Currently we're winning by two ports. Do you care to know what's the prize?"

"No."

"Of course you do: the losing crews have to walk the plank," said the bluff, bearded Nico, and the company dissolved in helpless laughter. "Have a drink?" he added. "Or a pee, or perhaps a shower?"

"All three," said Leo. He would play along, keep his wits about him, and improvise if needed. He must not allow suspicion to cloud his reasoning.

He returned from the well-appointed bathroom wearing a robe he had found in it. He had no extra clothes, and the ones he had been wearing for over two weeks stank.

"Well, how about a Dolce & Gabbana outfit?" asked Marcus, an aquiline fiftyish type.

Leo looked away, annoyed.

"Yes, yes, you have to blend in when we arrive at Antibes. All the more so if the coastguard nabs us before that. We've come prepared." Pauline handed over the clothes.

Leo resurfaced from the bathroom dressed in rust-colored four-wale corduroys and a pink shirt, a fawn cashmere pullover hanging around his neck, his feet in handmade suede moccasins. The men looked him over matter-of-factly: his makeover was just part of the game. Their wives, on the other hand, looked at him appraisingly, and smiled.

"Now you're fit for the Captain's table; let's have a drink," said Nico.

The blend of Pimms, vodka, Cointreau, and God knows what else went down everybody's throat. Leo drank the entire highball out of thirst, indifferent to the punch it packed, and then asked for a glass of water. He had survived on a sandwich a day for the last two weeks, and skipped even that lately. He had slept very little and had been cold all along. But it had been worth it.

The yacht was following the coast, heading toward the border between Italy and France. It was not the only one. The sea was not as crowded as in summer, but the sunny day had brought out many fellow boatmen.

Pauline spoke to Leo for the first time. "Your beard," she mentioned with a disapproving glance. His beard was a mess, and his moustache, overgrown, covering his lips. "Would you mind?" she said.

"What now?" he thought. "Leave me alone, will you?" But said nothing and turned his back to her.

"Perhaps he's seasick, or just an oddball." Marcus whispered.

"Nigel did mention that he was a bit paranoid," Nico added.

Undaunted, Pauline came back with razor and scissors, handing both over to Leo. He could not be bothered.

"If you like . . ." she began, then exchanged a glance with Sophie.

"To hell with it," Leo thought, and relented.

A turquoise towel wrapped around his neck, Sophie first cut Leo's beard and mustaches with the scissors as closely to the skin as she could. The yacht rocked a little, so there were a few close calls, followed by an "oops!" Both women were atwitter, chirping and giggling as they groomed him. Just then, the coastguards were looking through their binoculars at the many yachts and boats plying the waters, deciding which to pick for an inspection. Leo caught sight of them in the distance, but there was nothing he could do.

Oblivious to the spying eyes, Pauline claimed the honor of performing the "surgery." Sophie lathered Leo's cheeks and part of his neck for what seemed to him an eternity. He smelled distinctly of lavender, the soap he had used, and sandalwood, the lather. Pauline bowed and began to shave him.

The coastguards kept observing them. The Englishmen were enjoying every second of it.

The high-powered boat began to move their way, picking up speed.

"Here they come, look out!" said Marcus.

Leo looked at it with the corner of his eye, and his heart sank. As the boat got nearer, he said to himself, "Fuck it, I'll go to jail; I don't care."

Pauline kept shaving him, oblivious to it all.

The coastguards' boat suddenly decreased its speed. Leo looked at it directly, no longer afraid or even worried. It began to turn, in the direction of a rickety fishing boat.

"Who knows?" thought Leo, who could not believe his eyes, "maybe by zooming in on two beautiful women shaving a colorfully dressed dandy, the coastguards have dismissed the rich and idle, and focused instead on some potential smugglers."

"We did it!" Marcus said twenty minutes later, triumphantly. "Look over there, that's Cap d'Ail; we're in French territorial waters."

"Like that," thought Leo, "no customs, no immigration, no passports checked. Child's play."

Pauline was giving her last touches to Leo's shave. She was so close to him that he could have counted her every freckle. He stared into her big brown eyes, and smelled not only her perfume, but her breath too. The situation presented such a contrast with what he had gone through during the last several weeks that he finally closed his eyes. Pauline took it as a cue. "*Voilà*, handsome!" she exclaimed, and leaned forward to kiss him lightly on the lips.

He did not stir; as soon as she moved away from him, he got up.

"Is there something to eat?" Leo asked. "Bread would do."

"We'll be grabbing a bite soon," Nicky replied, feeling uncomfortable in the presence of this sullen stranger. Something about him reminded Nicky of an intractable, untamed beast.

"You must forgive us; Englishmen always remain schoolboys," explained Teddy after they had anchored for a snack—fresh French bread, cheese, and olives. "They're always trying to outwit the masters."

Leo did not comment; he was devouring the bread, barely registering what they were saying. He felt so tired that he had to struggle to keep his eyes open, yet he was anxious to see Orsina. He had been anticipating this moment for fourteen days and nights, and he knew that it was now close.

Shortly after eight in the evening, Antibes witnessed the arrival of *Lusimus*, and the putting ashore of Leo. He kept his old leather jacket and battered backpack.

"A plastic bag would be better than that thing," sniffed Nico. "What do you want it for? Wow, it's heavy. There must be—let me feel—I'd guess a family bible and a two-foot spanner inside it. And I thought that hippies traveled light."

"I'll dump the wrench," said Leo, extracting the oversize tool without explanation and tossing it overboard, "but I'll keep the family bible. I promised my old mother it would never leave my side."

"Oh," said Nico, not quite sure if this was a joke. Sophie smiled on as Pauline giggled.

Orsina, he was told, had asked to be phoned as soon as the *Lusimus* was an hour from Antibes. Leo was standing in the bows and saw her from afar: an unmistakable figure under a lamppost—or was it her aura that he sensed, before he even caught sight of her?

# TWENTY-EIGHT

Leo thanked the maid and closed the door of the guest room assigned to him. Like everything in Nigel's Provençal farmhouse, it was impeccably furnished with well-buffed antiques and every modern comfort. Farmhouse it may have been once upon a time, with its peasants working the vineyards and olive groves as far as the distant forests to the north, but "château" would not have been an overstatement.

Leo looked longingly at the bed, on which he could happily have flopped and slept for a night and a day. But it was not to be. Nigel had contrived to combine the perfect haven for an exhausted guest with the most unwelcome treat: a party. Leo reluctantly opened the towering armoire to drop off his precious backpack, and found hanging there a blue suit, shirt, socks, black shoes, tie—even underwear, with a card pinned to the lapel of the jacket. "Look your best tonight. O."

He took off the outfit that Marcus had given him on the boat and put on the more understated garb. As he checked the result in the mirror, he wondered whether, when he got home, he shouldn't dump his worn professorial wardrobe and make a habit of elegance. Then he thought of his students sniggering behind his back if he started showing up in Dolce & Gabbana, and laughed at his own conceit.

Downstairs the guests were thronging the entrance hall, talking at the tops of their voices. He could see Nigel chatting with Teddy, Marcus, Nico, and their wives in a cluster around the champagne buffet. Then he saw Orsina, conspicuous in a short black dress.

As their eyes met, he knew that she was an internal exile in her own home, wanting nothing so much as to be rid of this forced jollity. She crossed the hall to join him.

"I missed you, Leo."

"I missed you too, Orsina. You're looking well."

"I've put you next to me at the table. I think we'll survive it."

"I actually look forward to the food."

"We've both lost a lot of weight."

"True. This beautiful suit has a little room for growth; and thank you for thinking of it." He wanted to end the sentence with *amore mio*, my love. It came so naturally to him, but he restrained himself.

"I've been thinking about little else for two weeks." She turned away, on the brink of tears, then bravely added: "I don't mean the suit, that was an impulse-buy, yesterday afternoon in Nice."

"You even knew my shoe size. How do you do it?"

"Women notice things. I think . . . it's time to go in to dinner."

The table was set for twenty-four, and the dinner was a gourmand's feast of *fruits de mer.* Huge platters of crushed ice punctuated the table, each supporting a mountain of crabs, crayfish, prawns, oysters, whelks, mussels, and whole *coquilles Saint-Jacques* with their brilliant orange roe. The champagne continued to flow, until the diners sat back in their chairs contemplating the empty and shattered shells like victors of some undersea battle. Nigel chose the moment to say a few words.

"Dear friends, it's been my pleasure to host the annual 'Fuck the Frontiers' feast. As you all know by now, this year's winners are the crew of the good ship *Lusimus.* So here's to my dear friends Teddy, Nicky, Nico, Marcus, not forgetting their wives Sophie and Pauline, who I'm sure did most of the hard work."

The French wives looked at each other and smiled.

"But there is much more to celebrate," Nigel went on. "Since we were last together, Orsina and I have been through hell and back." He paused for a moment, the mood of the room becoming suddenly somber. "I'm sure you've read the newspapers. You may or may not believe what you've read there. Some of it's true, some is just journalism of the worst sort. The one thing you won't have read about is the part that Leo Kavenaugh has played in all this. Leo, come here!"

Leo wasn't expecting this; he reluctantly came to Nigel's side.

Nigel held out his hand, then awkwardly embraced him. There was uncertain applause. "Leo, I want to thank you for saving Orsina's life; nothing matters more. And then, for saving me from a lifetime of remorse, should something—" his voice breaking with emotion, "have happened to Orsina. That's all."

The conversation was muted for a while, and by the time the party spirit had revived, Leo had already crept away.

Returning from the toilet, he took a wrong turn and entered a small library with an irresistible sofa. He sat down on it, then lay down, and fell instantly asleep.

Orsina left the party soon after, stepped into her study, and found Leo there. She pulled a blanket over him, kissed him on his forehead, and there he slept untroubled.

Leo woke around ten, and felt embarrassed when he remembered where he had spent the night. He hurried up to his own room, and first of all checked that the forbidden book was still where he had put it. It was. He then showered and put on the informal outfit topped with his old leather jacket.

In his guest room he found a small refrigerator with all he needed for a simple breakfast. After the last two weeks, every little luxury seemed like heaven. Looking out of the window, he did seem to have come home to Paradise. Two gardeners were at work on the laurel hedges. Beyond these stretched a long field dotted with a flock of black sheep. Orsina, he thought, where was she?

Leo went downstairs, through the echoing hall, and down into the graveled courtyard before the house. On the north side was a long, low block, in the same brick and stone style as the main building, with squat slate-roofed towers at each end. The wide doorways indicated that this was a stable or coach-house. Peering through the windows, he saw Nigel's famous collection of vintage sports cars.

Rounding the corner, he wove his way between the laurel hedges and looked back at the perfect building. While this place bore the stamp of Nigel, it also carried the perfume of Orsina's presence; surely it was she who had planned the gardens.

As this thought occurred to him, he saw a ground-floor window push open, and there she was, waving to him. She looked gorgeous in her simple floral dress. He hurried back to the house and looked up at the window.

"Good morning," she said, and smiled.

"I'm sorry I fell asleep in your study; you should have woken me up," he began.

"It's a comfortable place," she replied. "I've often read myself to sleep on that sofa. Do you feel better now?"

"I feel reborn," he said. Then, after a pause, "This place is so beautiful. Are the black sheep yours?"

"No, they belong to a farmer. He uses our grounds."

"Are the other guests staying in the house?"

"No, they've all left. Nigel's still sleeping it off."

"Orsina, there's something very important I've got for you. Do you mind if I go and get it?"

"Of course not. I can't think what it could be—you arrived with almost nothing; but come down here, to my morning room."

As he mounted the stairs two at a time, Leo thought of all the things he might have said better, just now and also the night before.

Orsina's morning room had a single window facing east over the park. She sat on a sofa to one side of the mantelpiece; Leo in a chintz-covered wingchair opposite her. Without a word he opened his backpack and handed her the forbidden book. Then, as she appeared too stunned to speak, he started to tell her all that he had done since returning to Venice.

There was no tactful way of revealing how Angela had died, but he felt that her sister must know. He told Orsina what he had seen in his vaticination. At this, she began to weep uncontrollably. Leo left his chair to join her on the sofa, embracing her tenderly. When she had calmed down, he went on:

"After I left you at the train station, knowing that the police were looking for me, I wasn't able to move around freely. I knew that eventually I'd have to get out of Italy, God knows how. But I had two weeks for my mission: to make sure that your uncle was neutralized. I'd seen what he had done, and I'd learned about his powers over people. I knew that with Angela gone, he'd soon be after you. Yes. His sort of magic required a companion of the same blood. Incest, in fact."

Orsina's memories of her captivity came back to her, and she suppressed a shudder.

"No human justice," Leo resumed, "would ever understand what your uncle was about, and it looked as though they'd never even suspect him. He'd literally got away with murder. But I'd taken an oath to protect you, and as long as he was at large, you were in mortal danger."

She said nothing, and eventually gestured to continue.

"Your uncle couldn't trust you anymore because of the book. He knew that you're gifted in a way that he isn't, and he himself urged you to study it. Before all this happened, he'd given you the clue to the Cave of Mercury, knowing that it would eventually lead you to the secret shrine. Obviously he had you marked out as his occult successor, but after Angela's death all that went wrong for him.

"The more gifted you were, the more likely you were to discover the first fruit of the Tree of Life, vaticination. And then the past would be opened up to you. He couldn't let that happen, so first he stole your book. But he couldn't be sure that you hadn't already internalized it. He must've been consumed by worrying about that. And he also needed you desperately to aid him in his magic."

By now, Orsina had settled herself with her head on Leo's lap, her eyes closed. "What did you do?" she asked, without opening them.

He held her closely, and answered: "From Milan, I took the bus to Verona and hiked out to the forest, the one around the hunting lodge. I stayed in the woods in an abandoned woodshed for two days and a night, watching for him to come or go. I went back to the city once a day to eat and check the newspapers.

"*L'Arena* carried the story that the Baron had suffered a stroke in his own home. Ironically, I'd missed this completely—that day I was roaming the grounds looking for a way around the security guards. The next day, all the major papers reported the story in detail. Inspector Ghedina, pursuing a lead on the Riviera murder case, had discovered him in his hunting lodge, just in time to save his life. They said he'd been hospitalized in Verona's main hospital, in critical condition."

"I know. And then?"

"By this time I mistrusted everything. A man who can stage a kidnapping as he did might equally stage a stroke. He'd already put on a whole repertory of suitable reactions to Angela's death, hadn't he?

"So I went to the hospital. I was looking pretty seedy by that time, but I introduced myself with an appropriate accent as the under-gardener at the Villa Riviera. I went on about how the Baron had been like a father to me, and a nurse brought me in to see him.

"He was conscious, and for all the nurse could tell, he recognized his devoted gardener, because he tried to raise one hand. Half of his face was paralyzed, and he couldn't get out anything but grunts. I could tell that it made him furiously angry, but the nurse said 'that's all he can say to anyone now.'

"They were feeding him intravenously, and while she was fussing with the apparatus I chatted her up, told her how good he'd been to my mother, and so on. Then I asked if there was any hope for his recovery. She shouldn't have, but she told me confidentially that the doctors had examined his test results that morning, and that his heart was in poor shape. 'But one never knows: there's always hope for a miracle, and I've seen a number of them in my life,' she said. Somebody called her then from the hallway: some sort of emergency with another patient.

"I couldn't believe I was standing there, alone, with the monster. As I bent over him, it came to me how easy it would be to kill him right then and there, using his own method against him. He looked as though he knew what I was thinking. Then I said clearly into his ear: 'I have seen you meet the god Mithras, and I have seen you kill Angela.'" Leo paused.

"And then what happened?"

"Eventually, I heard footsteps in the hallway. The nurse was coming back. I bowed down as if to kiss him, then got up. 'He's fallen asleep,' I said, and the nurse replied, 'Good, he needs all the rest he can get.' I thanked her and left. That was all."

"They tell me that he died peacefully that afternoon."

Leo looked away for a moment, then added: "Finally, thanks to your husband, I got here safely."

Orsina let it all sink in. At length, she pulled his arms more tightly around her.

How was she coping with what she had gone through? He did not dare ask.

"I know what you're thinking," she put in. "What can I say? I'm happy to be alive." She breathed deeply, and rephrased. "I must be happy to be alive. I must stop thinking that he could have taken my life instead of Angela's, and maybe should have. I should have known what was going on. I had the means to do so. I should have met him on his own magical ground. If I'd been studying *The Magical World* since my wedding, I could have destroyed him. Instead, I was playing the chatelaine.

"I still can't believe that monster could violate Angela, God knows for how long. And then me, too." She looked him in the eye: "Yes, Leo, he tried to . . ." She was on the brink of tears, again. Must she really do this to herself, wondered Leo? What for?

She regained control of herself, and explained. "I was kept sedated most of the time, and always in the dark. Once, I was only half conscious,

I heard Uncle's voice. He was whispering absurdly sweet words in my ear. Then he began to touch me, to fondle me. I could hear him panting, and feel his weight over my body. I could smell his breath, feel his sweat on my face. His hands were under my nightdress, Leo."

She sat up and continued. "In desperation, I mustered whatever strength I had left and kicked out. He tried to calm me, still stroking me with his warm hands. One of my kicks must have hit him. I heard a shout, then a curse. Next, I was slapped violently on the face; soon after that I felt that odiously familiar pinch on my arm, and passed out."

"I'm sorry, Orsina, I'm so terribly sorry. But," he hastened to add, "that must have been the only time. It's very possible that he hasn't violated you at all."

"How do you know?" It was the most painful of conversations, but she obviously needed to get it off her chest, and he wanted to ease her pain.

"I've read the secret edition of *The Magical World* many times during the last two weeks. There's a passage in it that I've learned by heart, because the more I worried about you and what you had endured, the more it gave me hope. When Cesare writes about ungifted practitioners of magic, like your uncle, he notes that 'if they cultivate the love and friendly cooperation of a Hebe, then through suitable intercourse with her they may be led to accomplish no lesser marvels.' Elsewhere in the text, he stresses that a condition for this friendly cooperation to work is love. The twisted bastard had managed to influence Angela in such a way, I saw her in my vision looking like a zombie, defenseless and even affectionate in his arms. But he never had any control over you, so—"

"That's enough, Leo, that's enough. I'll learn to live with it." She buried her face in her hands, and cried. But soon, she was willing herself to snap out of it, and did.

"Forgive me, Orsina. I'll never mention the past again. I promise. But what of the future?"

She opened her eyes; it was her turn to explain. Facing Leo, she said: "Thank you, Leo; thank you for everything you've done. I'll never be able to thank you enough."

Leo felt that *he* was grateful to her for allowing him to be of help, but he didn't say it out loud. There'd been enough show of soul for the day; she was still weak. He simply smiled. She resumed.

"My life has become very complicated. As soon as Uncle died, the family lawyer contacted me. I have inherited his whole estate. I don't yet know what that includes, but there's property scattered all over the place, and not just in Italy.

"My lawyer says that the million-Euro ransom that Uncle pretended to pay must have been raised from friends, on the security of his properties, and that they'll certainly let me know in a discreet way when it's due for repayment. He thinks that the police may be persuaded to give back the money they confiscated. And Uncle's assets are no longer frozen. I won't tell the lawyer that it was Uncle who kidnapped me; I have decided never to tell anyone. It's our secret, Leo."

"You're forgetting Bhaskar and Soma."

"No, I'm not, nor am I forgetting Giorgio."

"Giorgio?"

"Yes, he's the one who abducted me. But he must have been brainwashed by Uncle as much as poor Angela. I can't realistically say that he acted of his own will when he became his accomplice. As for the Indian servants, they were blackmailed.

"The three of them know only a small part of the truth. It's in their best interest to keep quiet forever. Of course, I've fired them all; it's the first thing I did. But I don't feel revengeful. What matters is that the monster is dead."

Leo felt that it was time to change the subject. "Nigel seemed happy last night," he put in.

"Happy for me, yes, and relieved to be off the hook himself. He'd prefer to forget about the whole thing, obviously. As for Inspector Ghedina, he's been so useless, I don't owe him a solution to anything. So, all things considered, I agree with Nigel: forgetting would be just fine. But what's left is immense. There are the two properties you know about, the Villa and the Palazzo. I feel an enormous responsibility to the Riviera family. That's why I can't simply get rid of them, as Nigel could get rid of this house if Provence started to bore him. I feel absolutely burdened with *things*, with *places*, with *wealth*, and I feel all this responsibility landing on me when I'm weaker than I've ever been.

"By the way," she added in a different tone, "Nigel and I sleep in separate bedrooms now. We've agreed that our marriage hasn't worked out, and never will. When all the publicity's died down, we're going to get a very quiet divorce." She forced a smile as Nigel was heard outside.

Two days later, the chauffeur was driving the impeccably restored Citroën DS toward the airport in Nice. Orsina was sitting in the back with Leo, holding hands.

"After what you told me," Orsina said at length, in English, "I've decided to have the hunting lodge demolished. I love Villa Riviera too much; I'd never sell it. But the lodge must go."

Leo continued to hold her hand and said nothing.

"As for the Palazzo," she added, "it's too important for the dynasty, but I know that I could never sleep in it again. Not after what happened."

"You don't have to tell me anything, Orsina. I'm sure you'll make all the right decisions. Just give yourself some time."

She looked him in the eye and smiled.

The moment they both dreaded had arrived. Leo was going back to the States, and was about to go through security at the airport. His plane was leaving in half an hour. Orsina had brought along a sizable bag from the local *chocolatier*. "Here, Leo," she said, handing the bag to him. "Here's something to remember me by."

Leo thanked her and peeked inside, expecting a big box of chocolates. Instead, there it was: the forbidden book. He looked at her. Was she sure about this?

"Yes, Leo. You keep it for now. You must have finally realized that you yourself are gifted. How else do you think you would have come through vaticination alive?"

"Yes, I've been thinking about that. It's both humbling and scary."

"No, no need to be afraid. The two of us will work on the book, together, soon." The boarding of his flight was announced one more time.

"Orsina, I know that this is not the place, nor the time, but I meant to ask you if—"

"Not now, Leo, not yet. *Soon*. We need just a little more time. Keep the book in a safe place, promise me."

"Yes, of course." Mechanically, he took out his passport and boarding card. "It's really time I went, Orsina; unless, of course—"

She kissed him. He could feel her tears on his face. She hugged him tightly. It was dizzying and blissful. Leo was more than prepared to miss his flight. What was he leaving for? He closed her embrace, but she broke away from him. "Go, go," she said, "you've got things to straighten out in Washington."

"Orsina . . ."

"Go, now, go. We'll be together soon, very soon, and then nothing will set us apart again, nothing." She choked up, but then added, "Have a good flight, *amore mio.*" As he hesitated, she turned on her heels and made for the exit.

The security clerk said: "*Monsieur*, do you still want to catch your plane? Your passport and boarding card, please."

Leo handed them over, and shortly after went through.

# AFTERWORD

## Plots to blow up the fresco in San Petronio, Bologna

The fresco by Giovanni da Modena in the Basilica of San Petronio, Bologna—inspired by a scene from Dante's *Inferno* in which the Prophet Mohammed displays his own entrails—exists in reality. On two distinct occasions, Islamist groups directly linked to Al Qaeda threatened to blow up the church. In 2002, a plot was discovered, orchestrated by a key figure known as 'Amsa the Libyan,' who was arrested in Britain for possessing false papers, and suspected of having passed orders from Al Qaeda leaders in Afghanistan and Iran to terrorist cells in Europe. Four more suspects were arrested by the Italian police. In 2006, six terrorists were arrested, three of whom were later deported from Italy, two detained and one placed under observation, while a seventh man was still sought.

## Saint James the Moor-Slayer

The statue of Spain's patron saint, Santiago Matamoros (Saint James the Moor-Slayer), exists in reality inside the Cathedral of Santiago de Compostela, one of Europe's supreme pilgrimage sites. The Compostela statue is an 18th-century work by Jose Gambino depicting St. James on a white horse hacking off the heads of Moors, symbolizing the *Reconquista* (reconquest) of the Iberian Peninsula. In 2004, in the wake of the Madrid train bombings, it was decided that the statue be removed to avoid provocation to Muslims. After strong public objection, however, church officials were forced to overturn their decision.

## Anti-Islamic Activism

Anti-Islamic activism in the European radical right, or ultra-right, is a reality, and there are many groups and individuals acting independently of the political forum whose common features are, apart from strong anti-Islamic sentiment, nationalism, racism, xenophobia, anti-democracy, and the push for a strong and encompassing state.

## Villa Riviera

The Baron's country residence is based on Villa Costafredda, in the town of Colognola ai Colli, between Verona and Vicenza. Formerly a convent, it is a rare example, for the region, of rococo style, and has belonged for centuries to one of Verona's most illustrious noble families, the Maffei-Faccioli.

## Palazzo Riviera

The Riviera palace in Venice is closely based on the real palace called Ca' Rezzonico, now the Museum of the Venetian Eighteenth Century. It is the work of Baldassarre Longhena and one of the first baroque palaces on the Grand Canal. Palazzo Riviera is situated as though inserted between that building and the adjoining Campo San Barnaba.

### *Il mondo magico de gli heroi*

The "forbidden book" is an authentic alchemico-magical text by Cesare della Riviera (Milan: Pietro Martire Locarni, 1605). A landmark in the final, triumphant flowering of Renaissance Hermeticism, Della Riviera's treatise draws on John Dee's "hieroglyphic monad" and launches a particularly Italian stream of spiritual alchemy, which persists to this day. There is at present no English translation of the book, but two modern editions: (1) with text in modernized Italian, Introduction and Notes by Julius Evola, Carmagnola: Edizioni Arktos, 1982; (2) original text in modern characters with Introduction by Piero Fenili, Rome: Edizioni Mediterranee, 1986. Most of the quotations in *The Forbidden Book* are authentic, translated by the authors. There follows a reproduction of the frontispiece of the first edition.

IL

# MONDO MAGICO DE GLI HEROI

DEL SIG. CESARE DELLA RIVIERA:

Nel quale con inusitata chiarezza si tratta qual sia la vera MAGIA NATVRALE:

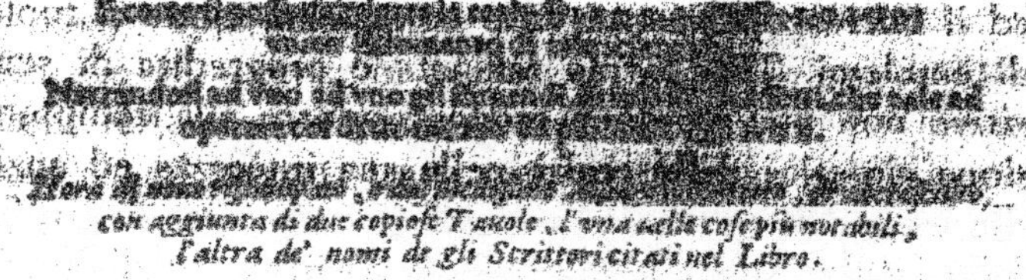

*con aggiunta di due copiose Tavole, l'una delle cose più notabili, l'altra de' nomi de gli Scrittori citati nel Libro.*

CON PRIVILEGIO.

IN MILANO, Per Pietro Martire Locarni. 1605.

*Con licenza de' Superiori.*

## The Baron's lecture on transcendence and the castes

This closely follows the principles of Traditionalist or "Perennialist" philosophers and social critics such as Ananda Coomaraswamy, René Guénon, Julius Evola, and Frithjof Schuon. See the latter's *Castes and Races* (Bedfont: Perennial Books, 1982).

## Police and judicial procedures

The entire police investigation and the criminal/judiciary procedure are carried out exactly as currently contemplated by Italian law. The authors have consulted Italian lawyers for all pertinent details of both civil and penal Italian legal procedures. In particular, the police asking for the *triangolo* is a classic stratagem of the Italian Highway Patrol, so as to fine even the most virtuous of drivers (very few are aware that by law every car is supposed to have one on board).

## Magical practices

In describing magical practices the authors' principle is to exclude anything they have learned directly from modern-day alchemists and magi. With one notable exception, as mentioned below, their descriptions are of practices that have been published, in whatever language and however remotely.

The general philosophy of magic "as science of the Self" is based on the writings of the Gruppo di Ur. See Gruppo di Ur, *Introduzione alla magia quale scienza dell'Io* (3 vols., Genoa: Fratelli Melitta, 1987). The first volume only has been translated by Guido Stucco as *Introduction to Magic* (Rochester, Vt.: Inner Traditions, 2001).

Correspondence of elements and humors. This is part of the system of fourfold correspondences (including the compass points, the winds, the Evangelists, and much else) described in the classic texts of Western ritual magic, beginning with Cornelius Agrippa's *Three Books of Occult Philosophy* (Cologne, 1533).

Breathing exercise. Although certainly practiced in the West, the science of breathing is best described in texts from the Indian yogic tradition. It is mentioned in Patanjali's *Yoga Sutras* and elaborated upon in the *Hatha Yoga Pradipika*.

Alleged use of decapitated head for divination. From Athanasius Kircher, reporting on rabbinic commentators, in *Oedipus Aegyptiacus*, vol. 1 (Rome, 1652).

Apparition of Mithras. The vision is based on the Mithraic Ritual of the "Great Magical Papyrus of Paris," published in *Introduction to Magic* (see above).

Hematidrosis, or bleeding through the pores. Reported by a deceased Greek publisher and high-ranking initiate of various rites, known to one of the authors. He resorted to it at great personal risk for the purpose of healing the gravely ill.

Pressure on the arteries. This means of attaining an altered state of consciousness is known in Tibetan yoga (see W.Y. Evans-Wentz, *Tibetan Yoga and Secret Doctrines*, Oxford University Press, 1958). Oral tradition holds that the representation of the Tibetan adept Milarepa with his hand to his ear is actually practicing it. However, it is never suggested as something to be used on another person, and any experimentation with self or others would be foolhardy and potentially fatal.

Phantasm of the living. The literature of psychical research records many instances in which a living person has appeared where a body is demonstrably not present, often to utter a warning or shortly before death. The classic study is *Phantasms of the Living* (London, 1886) by Edmund Gurney, F.W.H. Myers, and Frank Podmore. The question of the ontological reality of such apparitions, i.e., whether it *is* the person, is still unresolved.

The Baron's sexual alchemy. Derived from reports of such practices in the Italian esoteric tradition and in branches of the Ordo Templi Orientis. See Giuliano Kremmerz, *Istruzioni riservate. Da un manoscritto segreto dell'Ordine Osirideo Egizio*, with an essay [in Italian] by Peter-R. König and notes by V. Fincati. Published unpaginated, without place or date, by Associazione Culturale "Il Filo di Arianna"; Peter R. König, *Der O.T.O. Phänomen Reload*, Munich: A.R.W., 2011, vol. 3.

# Architectural Plans of Palazzo Riviera in Venice

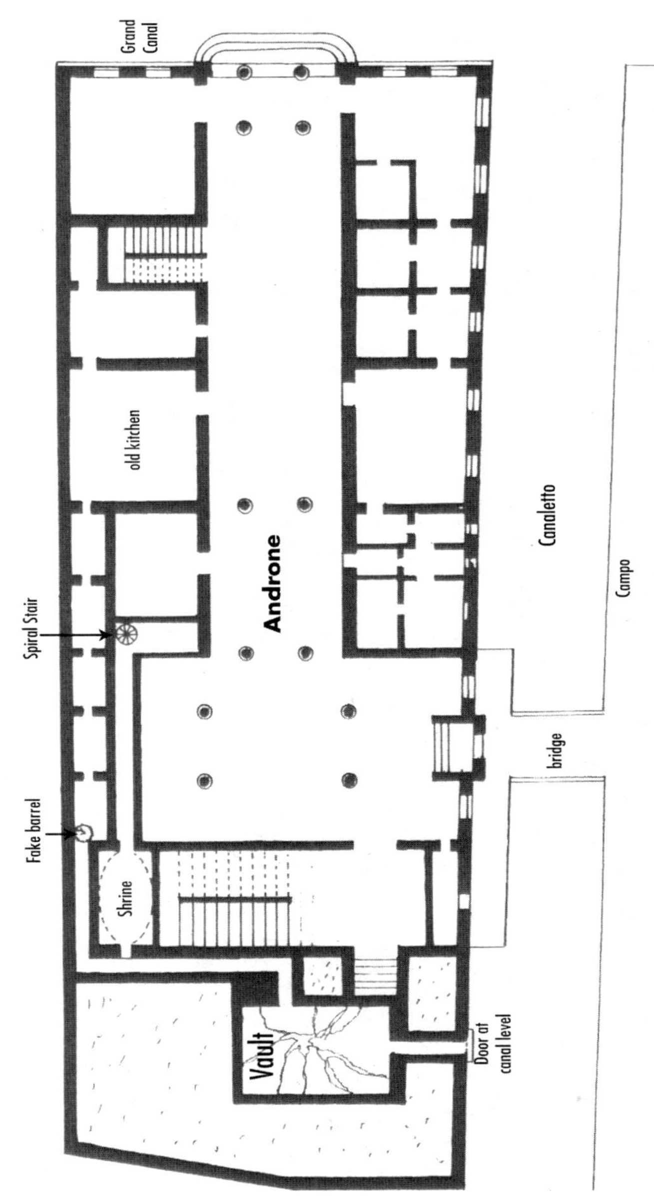

## Floor 2 (piano nobile)

Landing
up from floor 1
Tree
Nymphaeum
Ballroom
Cave of Mercury
Library
Small Salone
Music Room
Dining Room
Portego
Master bedroom
Orsina's room
Angela's room
Salone

## Floor 3

Hidden Chambers
in roof of Ballroom
Musicans
Gallery
Upper Ballroom
Servants Quarters
Portego
Spare bedrooms

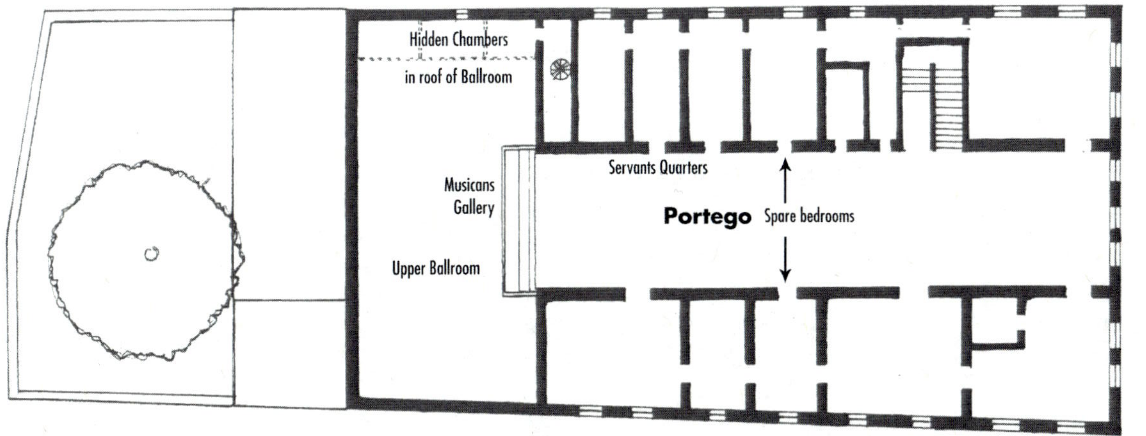

## Floor 4

Room of Arlecchino (Puppet Theater)
Room of Dottore
Room of Pantalone
Room of Pulcinella
Trapdoor in Fireplace
Portego
Emanuele's Apartments
Salone
Bedroom
Pharmacy
Study

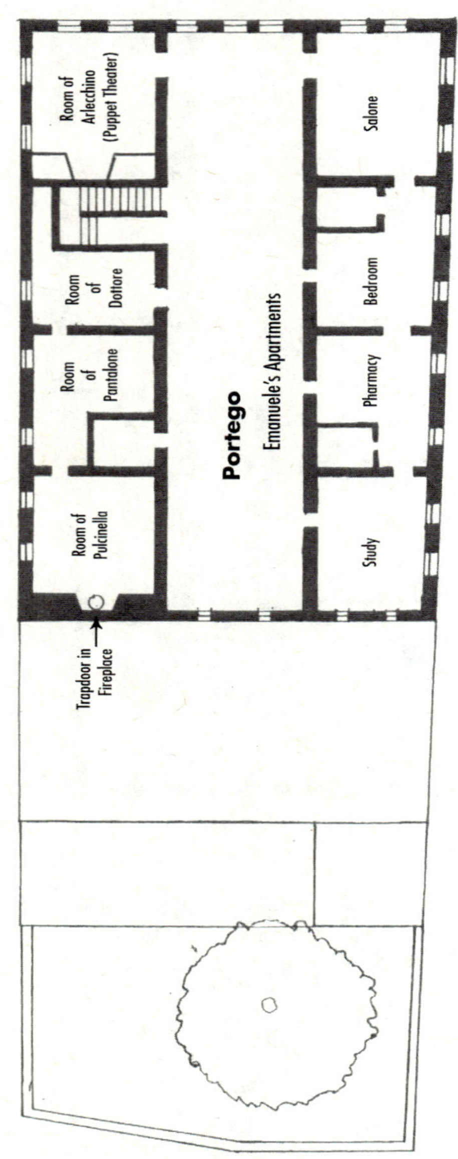

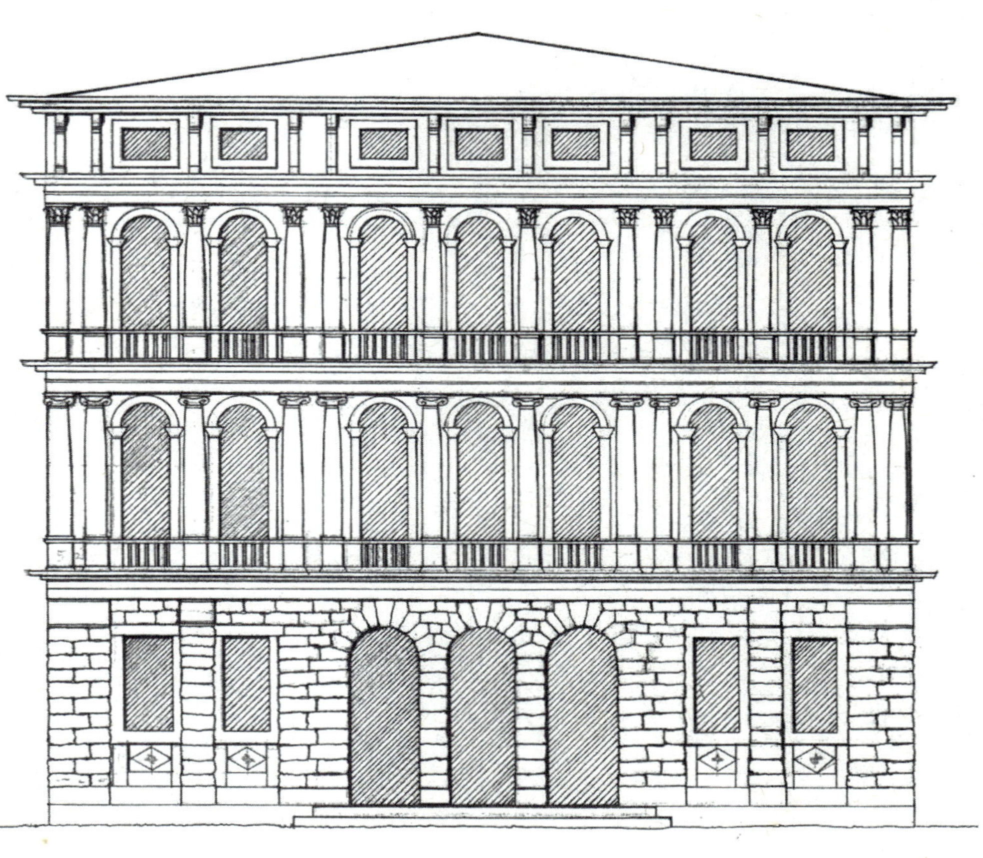

Grand Canal façade of the Palazzo Riviera,
drawn by Hannah McClennen, M. Arch.

# ACKNOWLEDGMENTS

Our gratitude to:

Our wives, for everything.

The contessina Giovanna Penco Salvi for her indispensable sympathetic magic and much more besides.

Hannah McClennen, for drawing the architectural plans of Palazzo Riviera.

Giovanni Quintavalle, attorney at law, for his advice on all legal details pertaining to Italian law, both penal and civil.

Juan Pedro Aguilar, M.D., for his ophthalmological advice.

Humberto G. Junco, M.D., for his medical advice.

Gianfranco de Turris, for providing us with one of the editions of *Il mondo magico de gli heroi*.

Christopher Sinclair-Stevenson, for his "rosé principle." Marco Salvi and Gardner Monks for a lifetime of support. Paola Juilland, so kind, thoughtful, and ever willing to help.

# About the Authors

Joscelyn Godwin was born in England and lives in Hamilton, New York, where he is professor of music at Colgate University. He is a composer, musicologist, and translator, known for his work on ancient music, paganism, and music in the occult.

Guido Mina di Sospiro is an award-winning, internationally published novelist born in Argentina, raised in Italy, and educated in the United States. A graduate of the University of Southern California, he lives in the Washington, DC, area with his wife and their three sons.

# A Note about the Cover

The cover's background is the "oculo" from the "Camera degli Sposi," the bridal chamber, a room frescoed with illusionistic paintings by Andrea Mantegna, in the Ducal Palace in Mantua, Italy. The falling signet ring bears the supposed Riviera heraldic shield, which in fact appears on the title page of the 1605 edition of Il mondo magico de gli heroi (*The Magical World of the Heroes*) by Cesare della Riviera (in actuality, such a colophon, or printer's mark/device, was used by the publisher/ printer Pietro Martire Locarno on the title page of his books). It shows the Tree of Life, along with two other trees. On the 1605 colophon the motto "*CRESCIT OCCVLTO*" (it grows in secret) appears on a banner across the three trees and the word on the trunk of the middle tree is "*VELUT*," continuing the quotation from Horace, Ode I, 12: "*Crescit occulto velut arbor aevo fama Marcelli*." This refers to Marcellus, deceased nephew of Augustus: "In the secrecy of time like a tree grows the fame of Marcellus."